DANCE *of* COURT & THEATER

DANCE *of*
COURT & THEATER

The French Noble Style
1690-1725

WENDY HILTON

Edited by Caroline Gaynor
Labanotation by Mireille Backer

PRINCETON BOOK COMPANY, *Publishers*

To my teacher
Belinda Quirey
and
in memory of the late
Cyril W. Beaumont
and
Robert M. MacGregor
with my gratitude for their spiritual
encouragement and practical support

Illustrations:

From the New York Public Library by courtesy of the curator, Genevieve Oswald; from the British Museum, courtesy of The British Library Board; from the Musée de Versailles: Cliché de musées Nationaux—Paris.

The illustrations from *The Art of Dancing* by Kellom Tomlinson, are from the British Library; those from Essex's translation of Rameau's *Le Maitre à danser*, from copies in The Sibley Library, Rochester, New York.

Copyright © 1981 by Princeton Book Company, Publishers
All rights reserved
Library of Congress Catalog Card Number 78-70248
ISBN 0-916622-09-6
Printed in the United States of America
Designed by Russell Rollins
Page Layout by Diane Backes
Typography by Backes Graphics

Preface

Louis XIV of France was an enthusiastic dancer and under his influence the art of dancing reached a high level artistically, technically, and scientifically. During his lifetime (1638-1715), dancing in the serious or noble style was developed for the first time along sound theoretical principles which, combined with a symbolic system of notation, made it more readily transmittable in print. The purpose of my book is to analyze the style, technique, and notation of court and theatrical dances in the serious style, preserved in print by Louis's dancing masters in the early eighteenth century.

Misconceptions about eighteenth-century dance

With so much significant material available, it seems surprising that until now only a handful of researchers have been motivated to explore it. Perhaps the greatest problem has been the misconception that nineteenth-century dances were the same as those of the eighteenth century because they retained the same names. Nineteenth-century dancing masters composed quite lovely gavottes, menuets, and sarabandes in the style and technique of their own time. Believing these to be dances of the eighteenth century, present-day choreographers have added their own touches and the result is a misrepresentative pastiche of styles. Many discouraging compositions of this type have been seen in so-called eigtheenth-century productions on stage, film, and television.

First investigations

I was one of those thoroughly discouraged by such dances, and am deeply indebted to Belinda Quirey who guided a rather skeptical student through the first steps of eighteenth-century dance. The early lessons proved to be exasperating because of the difficult coordinations involved in even the most basic steps. But enormous pleasure lay ahead in the style of motion, and the rhythmic similarities and contrasts between steps and music. My enjoyment grew as the richness of the dance and its musical and theatrical implications were revealed. Belinda Quirey possesses a certain genius which may best be described as kinesthetic historical perception. Through this gift she is able to illuminate style, which is the essence of research into any lost performing art.

When I became interested enough in eighteenth-century dance to wish to study it intensively, I found that no comprehensive modern analytical texts were available. It is true that the theory of the notation could be learned quite well from the existing eighteenth-century publications, but it originally had been intended for those who knew the dance steps it symbolized. The notation was a shorthand system that showed, to some extent, what to do but not how to do it. The modern scholar must glean the "how" primarily from verbal descriptions by eighteenth-century dancing masters and pictoral evidence. The abstract symbols of the notation are then invaluable in confirming or clarifying the masters' texts.

Since 1961, I have concentrated exclusively on eighteenth-century dance, my theoretical work always being confirmed, modified, or expanded through performing, choreographing, and teaching dancers and those without dance experience. In recent years, the number of students of eighteenth-century dance has increased, and the need for an instructional text has become urgent. Before publishing my present conclusions, I reached a point of conviction about them, at the same time retaining an open mind toward new avenues of thought. No scholar can ever be in a position to know how accurately the style of motion of an earlier age has been restored.

Approach

My book is directed to diverse disciplines. In the field of dance, it is for those who wish to perform and choreograph, as well as for those who are interested in the basis of nineteenth-century ballet. Social historians, drama students, teachers, and producers will find information on procedure, carriage, and bows and courtesies. For musicians and musicologists, there is both specific and general information about the relationship of the dances to their music, music which was composed during the seventeenth as well as the early eighteenth century.

The analysis contained in Part Two of this book is based upon the work of the two foremost French writers on dance, the dancing masters: Raoul Auger Feuillet, who published the dance notation system in 1700; and P[ierre] Rameau, the most explicit of the French theorists, who published in 1725. Selections from one other writer have been incorporated, Kellom Tomlinson, a master who lived in London. Tomlinson's work, which covers much the same material as Rameau's, was completed in 1724 but not published until 1735. I have restricted the inclusion of comparative material from other writers on the principle that minutia of comparison will not facilitate the establishement of basic theory in a hitherto almost totally unexplored field of research.

The instructional text is given in a definite manner. When alternatives are offered, they are presented concisely, and subjective comments are designated as such in sections headed Author's Notes. In the technical sections, theory and practice, technique and style are presented in conjunction as often as possible so that the theory does not obscure the art. The text can be read for information and theory only, or applied by students who wish to dance (hereafter described as performing students). At certain places a different route is indicated for performing students, directing them to special exercises, and sequences notated for practice. The bibliography gives primary dance materials and selected modern works concerned with the arts, life, and times of Louis XIV.

Part One, the introductory chapters, is intended to give only very general background information. Readers may be surprised at the omission of so-called familiar "facts," the sources for many of which are in need of scholarly verification. I have gone to perhaps extreme lengths to avoid reiterating misinformation of long standing. For instance, it was established in 1967 that the Christian name of the famous seventeenth-century dancing master, Beauchamp, was Pierre and not, as had previously been thought, Charles-Louis. (The Encyclopedia Britannica gives both Pierre and Charles-Louis, presenting not one, but two distinct personalities.)

Performing
students
from all
disciplines

Before eighteenth-century dances can be revived and conclusions about performance practice reached, it is necessary to master the dance notation, and be able to perform with style and technical expertise the steps it symbolizes. Complete mastery includes the ability to perform the steps in different meters and speeds. Every student must realize the importance of mastering the arm motions. In their execution lies a whole dimension of experience relating to style, articulation, phrasing, and nuance.

Professional dancers used to performing in other specialized areas, such as nineteenth-century ballet or a contemporary dance style, are asked to pay particular attention to the greater degree of relaxation required in the noble style of the eighteenth century. The relaxation, however, is physical and not mental.

All readers

To aid the reader, I have incorporated two terms not yet in use in the period under discussion: choreographer, denoting a composer of dances; and choreography, denoting a dance composition. With an audience from several disciplines in mind I have avoided the use of certain specialized terms. I ask the understanding of those who find such a lack frustrating. I should perhaps also request the indulgence of a gentlemen educated at Oxford who remarked:

I do HOPE you will write your book in academic terms so that an educated person such as myself can understand it.

Acknowledgments

Readers of this book should join me in an expression of heartfelt gratitude to Mireille Backer, Caroline Gaynor, and Anne Witherell.

Mireille Backer donated her knowledge, time, and energy to the Labanotation analysis, and appraised and criticized the manuscript during the early stages of writing.

Caroline Gaynor undertook to become the book's first "performing" student as part of her work as editor. Her outstanding ability for clear, analytical thinking made her the ideal person for the task, and the process proved invaluable. Ambiguous explanations were reconsidered, and the *Short Study Guide for Performing Students* was incorporated as a result of her work.

Anne Witherell donated many extra hours to the seemingly endless task of drawing the hundreds of examples in eighteenth-century dance notation.

Many thanks to the numerous colleagues who were kind enough to give advice on specialized sections of the text, most especially: Michael Collins, Ann Hutchinson, Meredith Little, Carol Marsh Rowan, and Erich Schwandt.

Finally, my thanks to the Arts Council of Great Britain for its generous research grant, and to the Ingram Merrill Foundation New York, for funding some of the prepublication costs. Also to the following generous benefactors, my deepest appreciation: William Bales, Dean Emeritus, Dance, SUNY at Purchase; Ingrid Brainard, Dir., Cambridge Court Dancers, Boston; Nancy Burtchby, Music, Douglass Coll., N.J.; Constantine Cassolas, Ass. prof., Voice, City Coll., N.Y.; Frank van Cleef, Hartford, Ct.; Joy van Cleef, Hartford, Ct.; Albert Cohen, Chairman, Music, Stanford U., Ca.; Miriam R. Cooper, Prof. Emeritus, Dance, Douglass Coll., N.J.; Douglass Coll. Alumnae; Peggy Egan, photographer; Robert W. Gutman, Dean, F.I.T., N.Y.; Martha Hill, Dir., Dance, The Juilliard School, N.Y.; George Houle, Prof., Music, Stanford U., Ca.; Arnold Kuam, Prof. Emeritus, Music, Douglass Coll., N.J.; Gordana Lazarewich, Ass. Prof., Music, U. of Victoria, B.C.; Robert Lincoln, Prof., Chairman, Music, Douglass Coll. N.J.; Mary Ella Montague, Chairperson, Dance, Sam Houston State U., Tx.; Alan H. Pressman, Dr. of Chiropractic, N.Y.; Elizabeth H. Rebman, Music Librarian, Stanford U., Ca.; Kenneth A. Rebman, Prof., Math, Cal. State U., Hayward; Frederick Renz, Early Music Foundation, N.Y.; Carol Marsh Rowan, Ass. Prof., Music, U. of North Carolina at Greensboro; Christena L. Schlundt, Prof., Dance, U.C. at Riverside; Erich Schwandt, Prof., Music, U. of Victoria, B.C.; Julia Sutton, Musicology, New England Conservatory, Boston; Virginia Suttenfield, Stamford, Ct.; James Wilson, Prof., Music, Douglass Coll., N.J.;

W.H.

Contents

PART ONE

The Noble Style of Dance
in the Age of Louis XIV
General background of Court and Theater

King Louis XIV of France, 1638-1715.
Portrait by Rigaud. Musée de Versailles.

CHAPTER ONE

Dance at the French Court, 1650–1715

Style:
The ideal

In seventeenth- and eighteenth-century France nobility of mind and spirit was the ideal cultivated by the highest social classes: the nobility, the aristocracy, and the gentry. With the King as their epitome, the aristocracy were supposed to set an example to the rest of society as a personal obligation incurred by having more time and money than most people to devote to self-perfection.

The ideal models for the nobleman were drawn from classical Greece. The Greek gods and goddesses, all slightly larger than life but not possessing unfortunate extremes of exalted spirituality, made perfect sense to seventeenth-century French esprit. To emulate the ancient Greeks one must be serene, have breadth of vision, a commitment to harmony and order, personal courage, and a distaste for passionate excess. Wit, a lively sense of irony, and a capacity for fun were all important attributes, both in the lexicon of Greek mythology and in the French interpretation. The dances created to reflect these ideals were not expressive of the passions. Each created a particular atmosphere ranging through serenity, majestic grandeur, tenderness, and gaiety; the grandeur never becoming pomposity, the tenderness a yearning sentimentality, nor the gaiety, inelegance.

Personal
presence

Of the majesty of Louis XIV a court commentator wrote, "that terrifying Majesty so natural to the King." A noble carriage and air was an inherent part of its possessor's way of being. Essentially, a nobleman cultivated a personal presence at once alert and poised, open and relaxed, and, through these qualities, impressive. Lessons in dancing, deportment, and the complexities of social etiquette were begun in early childhood, and it was part of a dancing master's work to instruct his pupils in all these refinements.

Occasions
for
dancing

Dance in the serious or noble style had two aspects for the French courtiers. They performed social dances in the ballroom, where it was usual for only one couple to dance at a time, and theatrical dances in court entertainments. In the latter the content of the dances approximated those composed for the ballroom, but the costumes were elaborate and symbolic of the dancers' roles.

Ballet des Arts, 1663.
Costume design for the role of Beauty. Bibliothèque Nationale, Paris.

*Ballets
de cour*

The ballets de cour were lavish spectacles given in theaters constructed within the royal residences. The King, courtiers, and professional performers participated, and members of the public were admitted as spectators. A mythological or heroic plot or theme usually linked the scenes, which included verses, lavish symbolic costuming, stage machinery, music, and dance. Comic dances and mimed episodes were interspersed with the serious ones, and troupes of acrobats were often employed. The whole culminated in a grand ballet in the serious style. Superiority of talent rather than of social rank usually governed the casting. In the noble entrées, dancing masters might dance alongside the nobility, while a nobleman often elected to take a comic role.

Portrait of Louis XIV painted when he was about six years old. Musée de Versailles.

An account of the King dancing at the age of eight:

The King wore a coat of black satin with gold and silver embroidery of which the black showed only enough to set off to advantage the embroidery. Carnation-coloured plumes and ribbons completed his adornment, but the beautiful features of his face, the gentleness of his eyes joined to their gravity, the whiteness and brilliancy of his skin, together with his hair, then very blond, adorned him much more than his clothes. He danced perfectly, and though he was then only eight years old, one could say of him that he was one of the company who had the best air and, assuredly, the most beauty.[1]

Louis XIV as a child. Musée de Versailles.

Louis XIV as Apollo. Bibliothèque Nationale, Paris.

In a seventeenth-century court ballet, Louis XIV was usually the central figure of the performance, his roles reflecting his deification; the King's most famous identification was with the Greek sun-god Apollo, a role he danced many times. (From this royal heritage comes the "premier danseur noble" whose dances, and those of the ballerina, are the focus of nineteenth-century ballet.)

Following the death of his father, Louis XIII, in 1643, Louis XIV, at the age of five, ascended the throne under the regency of his mother, Anne of Austria. She appointed as prime minister Jules Mazarin, in whose hands the effective power to govern lay until his death. The young Louis devoted considerable time to dancing (an enthusiasm inherited from his father) and in 1651 danced his first role in his first ballet de cour, *Le Ballet de Cassandre*.

A serious aspect was added to the young Louis's participation in court ballet following the disturbances of the Fronde, a revolt by a group of dissident nobles intent upon curbing the power of the monarchy. The troubles of the Fronde continued with brief intervals of calm from 1640 to 1653. Although the activities of the Frondeurs were eventually unsuccessful, they caused the court considerable embarrassment and succeeded in weakening the popular faith in the monarchy. When peace reigned once more in Paris, Mazarin sought ways to reestablish confidence in his government and in the person of the King, who was then fourteen years old, beautiful to behold, and talented as a dancer. In the ballet de cour, Mazarin found an ideal vehicle for the achievement of this latter purpose.

In February 1653, Mazarin caused an unusually magnificent and lengthy spectacle to be mounted, *Le Ballet de la Nuit*. The stage machinery was by Giacomo Torelli, the verses by the poet Isaac de Benserade, and some of the music by Jean de Cambefort. The choreographer(s) are still unknown. The ballet consisted of forty-five entrées of considerable diversity, resolving in the grand ballet which depicted the glorious rising of the sun following the events of the night. The rising symbolized the rising of the King, le Roi Soleil, who was surrounded by dancers representing Honor, Grace, Love, Courage, Victory, Favor, Renown, and Peace. The ballet was very successful and was repeated six times in the ensuing weeks. Louis's love of dancing and display continued and a new ballet de cour was staged each year, usually as part of the Carnaval celebrations.[2]

Louis XIV in 1667 with his son, the Dauphin, born in 1661.
Testelin. Musée de Versailles.

Louis as monarch

On March 9, 1661, Mazarin died. Louis XIV, barely twenty-three, assumed absolute power. His decision not to have a first minister but to be directly responsible for all government policy was influenced by the uncertain political climate of his youth. The agitations of the Frondeurs had left a deep impression on the young King. Louis appointed his ministers from the bourgeoisie, determined that his nobles be ornaments, not rivals, to the throne. The emphasis he placed upon balls and theatrical entertainments was as much for the diversion and occupation of those taking part as for the creation of a picture of magnificence with which to impress the rest of Europe. It should not be thought that the courtiers, deprived of serious governmental and political responsibilities, had time on their hands. For those not engaged in one of the frequent wars, every moment of the day in the enclosed world of the French court was highly organized around rituals, from the King's levée at eight o'clock in the morning to the grand coucher late at night.

Académies

In 1661, Louis expressed his interest and concern for the art of dancing by founding the Académie Royale de Danse to improve the level of amateur and professional dancing, and to establish scientific principles for the art. In 1669, when in his early thirties, Louis made his last stage appearance in the *Ballet de Flore,* although he continued to dance socially. In 1672, he established the Académie Royale de Musique (previously founded in 1669 as the Académie d'Opéra, and later to become the Paris Opéra). For some years nobles and professionals continued to dance side by side, but a resident ballet company of purely professional dancers was being built. The dance of serious aesthetic purport continued to be that of the noble dance of the court. So similar did this aspect of dance at court and theater remain that in the early eighteenth century a couple dance might be performed first by professionals in the theater, and then adopted as a ballroom dance; this did not mean that theatrical dance was simple, but that social dance was complex.

French
influence

Throughout his long reign, Louis was determined that the French court be the most brilliant and influential in Europe. He increased the political and military strength of France, and his fortunes rode high until 1686 when a group of European leaders, alarmed by the overgrowth of French power, formed an alliance against him. The wealth and strength of France began a slow decline, but the brilliance of the court shone undiminished, and French fashion and taste continued to predominate in Europe.

Dance
notation

The French social dances were danced at the most fashionable courts of Europe, where French dancing masters were usually employed. The transmission of new dances, and the preservation of old favorites, was made easier and more reliable when a system of dance notation was evolved during the last decades of the seventeenth century. The first collections of ballroom and theatrical dances to be published in notation appeared in 1700. It is therefore from this date that the study of eighteenth-century choreography can begin.

The palace and gardens illuminated. La Pautre, 1679. Bibliothèque Nationale, Paris.

The Palace of Versailles in the late seventeenth century. Patee. Musée de Versailles.

Social dancing

Danses à deux

Ballroom procedure at its most formal followed the long-established pattern of a hierarchical society, a pattern Louis XIV exploited to its utmost: those of highest social rank danced first, followed by others in strict order of social precedence.

The most important dances were the danses à deux, which were performed in order of precedence by one couple at a time while the rest of the company watched. Because the ballroom floor was not crowded with many dancers, the beautiful and usually symmetrical spatial patterns could be seen to advantage by all. Equally visible to the audience was the quality of the dancers. To be an accomplished ballroom dancer required not only grace and elegance, but also a keen intellect. Two to four new ballroom dances had to be learned each year and the old favorites from previous years retained. At Louis's court, a courtier probably had to keep some twelve dances at the ready, a considerable feat of memory in view of their diversity and complexity—a complexity which proves that the average level of social dancing at the French court must have been high.

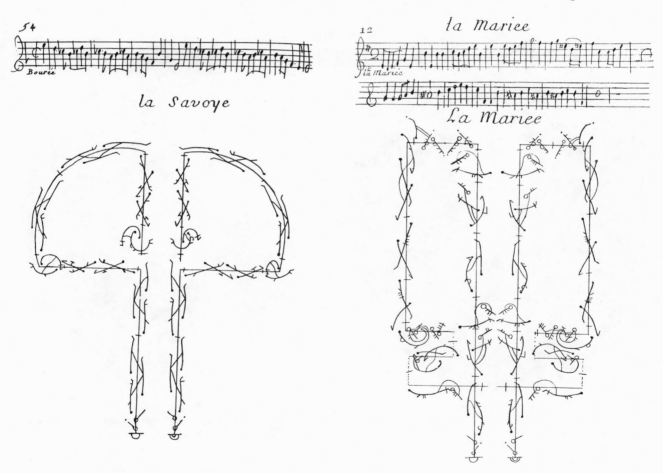

The first figures of two popular danses à deux, "La Savoye" and "La Mariée." *Recueil de dances composées par M. Pécour.* Feuillet, Paris, 1700.

The danses à deux were composed for the court by eminent Parisian masters. Each dance was choreographed to a particular tune, usually a favorite from a theatrical entertainment. Of the many popular types of ballroom dances—the menuet, passepied, gigue, forlane, bourrée, gavotte, sarabande, and loure—only some of the menuets and passepieds, relatively uncomplex choreographically, could be danced to any air of the dancers' or musicians' choosing. The other dances were very varied in their step content, and intricately related to their music. A dance usually took between two and three minutes to perform, and only occasionally would a step-sequence be repeated in the choreography.

Court life

Within the structure of court life, dancing alone with a partner before a crowd of spectators must have seemed quite unexceptional. The formal life of children began at an early age. When in company, children, dressed like adults, were expected to behave in the manner of adults. Thus, through a disciplined social upbringing, young children were able to endure lengthy formal encounters such as that experienced by the little Princesse de Savoy.

Le Duc de Bourgogne.
Bibliothèque Nationale, Paris.

La Duchesse de Bourgogne.
From the engraving after Nicolas de Largillieres.
Bibliothèque Nationale, Paris.

Princesse de Savoy

The Princesse de Savoy, at the age of ten, was brought to court by Louis to marry his grandson, the Duc de Bourgogne. The composure and stamina demanded of the child upon her arrival at court followed hours of travel preceded by Mass. Her arrival at Fontainebleau on November 5, 1696, is described by the courtier and avid diarist, M. le duc de Saint-Simon:

Dance at the French Court, 1650-1715

The entire Court was assembled waiting to receive them on the horseshoe staircase, with the crowd standing below, a magnificent sight. The King led in the little princess, who seemed to be emerging from his pocket, walked slowly along the terrace and then to the Queen-Mother's apartments, which had been allotted to her, where Madame and her ladies were waiting. He himself presented the first of the Princes and Princesses of the Blood, asked Monseigneur to name the others and to be sure to see that she was greeted by all who had that right, and then went to rest . . . Monseigneur was thus left with the princess, both standing. He presented to her all those, men and women, who had come to kiss the hem of her dress, and told her whom she should kiss, that is to say, Princes and Princesses of the Blood, dukes and duchesses, and other tabourets [persons whose rank permitted them to sit upon armless stools called tabourets] and Marshals of France and their wives. This ceremony lasted a good two hours.[3]

Grand bal

The Duc de Bourgogne and the Princesse de Savoy were married the following year, 1697. (Later they bore Louis's eventual successor to the throne, Louis XV.) Saint-Simon describes the festivities:

On the Wednesday there was a grand ball in the gallery, superbly ornamented for the occasion. There was such a crowd, and such disorder, that even the King was inconvenienced, and Monsieur was pushed and knocked about in the crush. How other people fared may be imagined. No place was kept—strength or chance decided everything—people squeezed in where they could. This spoiled all the fête. About nine o'clock refreshments were handed round, and at half-past ten supper was served. Only the Princesses of the Blood and the royal family were admitted to it. On the following Sunday there was another ball, but this time matters were so arranged that no crowding or inconvenience occurred. The ball commenced at seven o'clock and was admirable; everybody appeared in dresses that had not previously been seen. The King found that of Madame de Saint-Simon much to his taste, and gave it the palm over all the others. Madame de Maintenon did not appear at these balls, at least only for half an hour at each. On the following Tuesday all the Court went at four o'clock in the afternoon to Trianon, where all gambled until the arrival of the King and Queen of England. The King took them into the theatre, where Destouches's opera of *Issé* was very well performed. The opera being finished, everybody went his way, ·and thus these marriage-fêtes were brought to an end.[4]

The Order of the Dances at a Court Ball: the branles, danses à deux, and contredanses.

Un Branle au Louvre, Israel Silvestre, seconde moitié du XVII siecle.

The branles, with which all formal balls opened, were dances performed in a linked line, the couples joining up in order of rank. The order in which couples would perform the danses à deux which followed was thereby clearly established in advance.   Balls would end with contredanses, the communal, less formal and complex dances introduced from England in the 1680s. The contredanses became increasingly popular as the eighteenth century progressed.

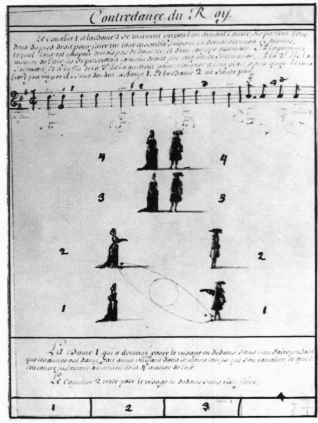

Figure from *Livre de contredanse du Roi*.   Lorin. 1688. Ms. Bibliothèque Nationale, Paris.

Another wedding which offered Saint-Simon ample opportunity for social commentary was that of the Duc de Chartres (son of Louis's brother Monsieur, le Duc d'Orléans, and Madame Elizabeth Charlotte ["Liselotte"] of Bavaria, Monsieur's second wife) to Mlle. de Blois, one of Louis's illegitimate daughters. The first ball of the wedding celebrations followed the settlement of a handsome dowry. Saint-Simon observes:

That day the immense dowry was declared; and on Sunday there was a grand ball, that is, a ball opened by a branle, which settled the order of the dancing throughout the evening . . . the Duc de Bourgogne danced on this occasion for the first time and led off the branle with Mademoiselle. I danced also for the first time at Court. My partner was Mademoiselle de Sourches, daughter of the Grand Prévôt; she danced excellently.[5]

The Duc de Chartres and his bride were married the following day, and the next day, Shrove Tuesday, another grand ball was held:

On Shrove Tuesday, there was a grand toilette of the Duchesse de Chartres, to which the King and all the Court came; and in the evening a grand ball, similar to that which had just taken place, except that the new Duchesse de Chartres was led out by the Duc de Bourgogne. Every one wore the same dress, and had the same partner as before. I cannot pass over in silence a very ridiculous adventure which occurred at both of these balls. A son of Montbron, no more made to dance at Court than his father was to be chevalier of the order (to which, however, he was promoted in 1688), was among the company. He had been asked if he danced well; and he had replied with a confidence which made every one hope that the contrary was the case. Every one was satisfied. From the first bow, he became confused, and he lost step at once. He tried to divert attention from his mistake by affected attitudes, and carrying his arms high; but this made him only more ridiculous, and excited bursts of laughter, which, in despite of the respect due to the person of the King (who likewise had great difficulty to hinder himself from laughing), degenerated at length into regular hooting. On the morrow, instead of flying the Court or holding his tongue, he excused himself by saying that the presence of the King had disconcerted him, and promised marvels for the ball which was to follow. He was one of my friends, and I felt for him. I should even have warned him against a second attempt, if the very different success I had met with not made me fear that my advice would be taken in ill part. As soon as he began to dance at the second ball, those who were near stood up, those who were far off climbed wherever they could to get a sight; and the shouts of laughter were mingled with clapping of hands. Every one, even the King himself, laughed heartily, and most of us quite loud, so that I do not think any one was ever treated so before. Montbron disappeared immediately afterwards, and did not show himself again for a long time. It was a pity he exposed himself to this defeat, for he was an honourable and brave man.[6]

Appartement

Grand formal balls, such as those described above, were not the only occasions for dancing. Fancy dress masquerades were often held, especially at Marly, the King's favorite country house where greater relaxation and informality of manners were permitted. Dancing also had its place in the appartement, a social gathering of the court which took place at Versailles three times a week in the winter. At an appartement, formal etiquette and procedure were also somewhat relaxed and a choice of activities was available. One of these was dancing. In December 1682 Liselotte wrote:

Every Monday, Wednesday, and Friday is *jour d'appartement.* All the gentlemen of the Court assemble in the King's ante-chamber, and the women meet in the Queen's rooms at 6 o'clock. Then everyone goes in procession to the drawing-room. Next to it there is a large room, where fiddles play for those who want to dance. Then comes the King's throne-room, with every kind of music, both played and sung. Next door in the bed-chamber there are three card tables, one for the King, one for the Queen, and one for Monsieur. Next comes a large room—it could be called a hall—with more than twenty tables covered in green velvet with golden fringes, where all sorts of games can be played. Then there is the great ante chamber where the King's billiard table stands, and then a room with four long tables with refreshments, all kinds of things—fruit-tarts, sweet-meats, it looks just like the Christmas spread at home. Four more tables, just as long, are set out in the adjoining room, laden with decanters and glasses and every kind of wine and liqueur. People stand while they are eating and drinking in the last two rooms, and then go to the rooms with the tables and disperse to play . . . If the King or Queen comes into the room, nobody has to rise. Those who don't play, like myself and many others, wander from room to room, now to the music, now to the gamblers—you are allowed to go wherever you like. This goes on from six to ten, and is what is called *jour d'appartement.*[7]

In Liselotte's voluminous correspondence, there are numerous references to dancing which indicate that it suffered a temporary decline later in the 1680s and early 1690s. This was doubtless due to the altered atmosphere which prevailed at court following the death of Queen Marie-Thérèse in 1683. Louis became closely associated with Madame de Maintenon, former governess to some of his illegitimate children. Their marriage, if one took place, was a closely guarded secret, but Madame de Maintenon nevertheless held a powerful puritanical influence over Louis. Dancing remained important for grand balls, but its decline as a popular pastime becomes apparent from the following letter Liselotte wrote in 1695 to the Duchess of Hanover:

As far as I can see, your young people of Hanover do as ours do. Here no one dances these days but everyone is learning music. It is the height of fashion these days, and the fashion is followed by all young people of quality, men as well as women.[8]

Liselotte's son became very interested in music and was soon "looking out all the old ballets to discover how music used to sound."

In 1697, Liselotte predicted that dancing might become popular again because "the Duchesse de Bourgogne dances to perfection." The prediction was fulfilled. The young Duchesse enlivened the King's later life, and through her personality, talent, and influence at court the popularity of dancing among young people was restored. Louis constantly gave, and urged others to give, balls and masquerades for the pleasure of his overindulged grand-daughter-in-law.

Liselotte describes one masquerade given in 1699:

Bal masqué

I must tell you about the masked ball at Marly. On Thursday the King and all the rest of us had supper at nine o'clock, and afterwards we went to the ball, which began at ten o'clock. At eleven o'clock the masks arrived. We saw a lady as tall and broad as a tower enter the ballroom. It was the Duc de Valentinois, son of Monsieur de Monaco, who is very tall. This lady had a cloak which fell right to her feet. When she reached the middle of the room, she opened her mantle and out sprang figures from Italian comedies. Harlequin, Scaramouche, Polichinello, the Doctor, Brighella, and a peasant, who all began to dance very well. Monsieur de Brionne was Harlequin, the Comte d'Ayen, Scaramouche, my son, Polichinello, the Duc de Bourgogne was the Doctor, La Vallière was Brighella, and Prince Camille was the peasant . . .
The Dauphin arrived with another party, all very quaintly dressed, and they changed their costumes three or four times. This band consisted of the Princesse de Conti, Mademoiselle de Lislebonne, Madame de Chatillon, and the Duc de Villeroy. The Duc d'Anjou and the Duc de Berri and their households composed the third group of masks; the Duchesse de Bourgogne and her ladies the fourth; and Madame de Chartres, Madame la Duchesse, Mademoiselle d' Armagnac, the Duchesse de Villeroy, Mademoiselle de

Tourbes, who is a daughter of the Maréchal d'Estrées, and Mademoiselle de Melun, the fifth. The ball lasted until a quarter to two o'clock . . . On Friday all the ladies were elegantly attired in dressing-gowns. The Duchesse de Bourgogne wore a beautiful fancy costume, being gaily dressed up in Spanish fashion with a little cap . . . Madame de Mongon was dressed in ancient fashion, Madame d'Ayen in a costume such as goddesses wear in plays. The Comtesse d'Estrées was dressed in ancient French style and Madame Dangeau in ancient German style. At half-past seven or eight o'clock masks came and danced the opening scene of an opera with guitars. These were my son, the Comte d' Ayen, Prince Camille, and La Vallière in ridiculous men's clothes; the Dauphin, Monsieur d'Antin, and Monsieur de Brionne as ladies, with dressing gowns, head-dresses, shawls, and towers of yellow hair much higher than are usually worn. These three gentlemen are almost as tall as each other. They wore quite small black and red masks with patches, and they danced with high kicking steps. D'Antin exerted himself so violently that he bumped into Monsieur de Brionne, who fell on his behind at the Queen of England's feet. You can imagine what a shout of laughter there was. Shortly afterwards my favourite, the Duc de Berri, went to disguise himself as "Baron de la Crasse" and came back and performed a very comical dance by himself.[9]

Masquerades sometimes took place in rather bizarre circumstances, about which Saint-Simon naturally wrote with enjoyment: "Madame du Maine gave several in her chamber, always keeping her bed because she was in the family-way; which made rather a singular spectacle."[10]

The balls
continue

The latter years of Louis's reign were beset by financial difficulties because foreign wars had drained the country's resources. Nevertheless, Saint-Simon recalls that Louis increased the number of balls as a display of bravado. The court appeared gayer than ever.[11] Accounts for the year 1708[12] list ten balls within a six-week period:

5 January	Bal du Roy à Versailles
16 January	Bal du Roy à Versailles
21 January	Bal du Roy à Marly
23 January	Bal du Roy à Marly
25 January	Bal du Roy à Marly
3 February	Bal du Roy à Versailles
12 February	Bal de Madame la Duchesse de Bourgogne à Versailles
15 February	Bal de Monseigneur à Versailles
17 February	Bal du Roy à Marly
19 February	Bal du Roy à Marly

The King's desire to maintain an impression of status quo, combined with the Duchesse de Bourgogne's enthusiasm for dancing and fancy dress, certainly served to perpetuate the succession of balls. Saint-Simon remarks how, on one occasion, the King "made people dance who had long passed the age for doing so." On another, Saint-Simon and his wife collapsed thankfully after a three-week period of continuous court entertainment:

I passed the last three weeks . . . without ever seeing the day. Certain dancers were only allowed to leave off dancing at the same time as the Duchesse de Bourgogne. One morning, at Marly, wishing to escape too early, the Duchesse caused me to be forbidden to pass the doors of the salon; several of us had the same fate. I was delighted when Ash Wednesday arrived; and I remained a day or two dead beat, and Madame de Saint-Simon could not get over Shrove Tuesday.[13]

Several ballroom dances were dedicated to the Duchesse de Bourgogne. In 1704, Feuillet published a new dance of his own composition expressing joy at the birth of her first son, the Duc de Bretagne. The joy was short-lived because the infant died unchristened in 1705.

The first figure of Feuillet's dance, "La Bretagne," dedicated in 1704 to the Duchesse de Bourgogne in celebration of the birth of her son, the Duc de Bretagne.

The Duchesse bore a healthy son in 1707, but the following year had a miscarriage. It is evident that Louis was quite anxious about the question of his succession from the manner in which he received the news:

M. de la Rochefoucauld protested out loud that it was a thousand pities, since she had miscarried before and might well have no other children. "And if that should happen," interrupted the King furiously, "what do I care? She has one son already, has she not? And if he dies, is not the Duc de Berry of age to marry and have children? Why should I mind who succeeds me; are they not all grandchildren of mine?"[14]

And, as it happened, the fears which he hid with an angry bravado became a dire reality with time. The final years of Louis's life were beset with personal tragedy. In 1711, his son died suddenly and the following year he witnessed the deaths of his beloved Duc and Duchesse de Bourgogne and their second son. The Duc de Berry, Louis's only remaining grandson, died in 1714.

Louis himself died on September 1, 1715, a few days before his seventy-seventh birthday. The heir was his six-year-old great-grandson Louis, third and last son of the Duc and Duchesse de Bourgogne.

Louis XIV in his later years. From an engraving by A. Trouvain. Bibliothèque Nationale, Paris.

Louis XV. Portrait by Rigaud. Musée de Versailles.

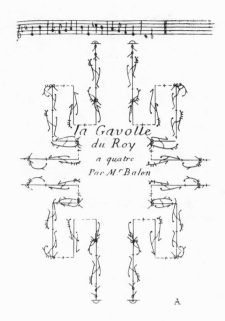

A

The first figure of "La Gavotte du Roy," a dance probably designed for the seven-year-old Louis XV to dance with three others. Its choreographer was Jean Ballon, famous star of the Paris Opéra, and first dancing master to Louis XV. *Recueil de danses pour l'année 1716.* Dezais, Paris.

FOOTNOTES

1. Mme. de Motteville's description of Louis dancing at a ball as a child is from Charles A. Sainte-Beuve, *Portraits of the Seventeenth Century*, trans. Katherine P. Wormsley, 2 vols. (New York: Frederick Ungar Publishing Co., 1964), vol. I, pp. 413-414.
2. For information about the ballets de cour see Marie-Françoise Christout, "The Court Ballet in France: 1615-1641," *Dance Perspectives* (New York), 1964; also *Le Ballet de cour de Louis XIV 1643-1672* (Paris: Editions A. & J. Picard, 1967); and Margaret McGowan, *L'Art du ballet de cour en France 1581-1643* (Paris: Centre Nationale de la Recherche Scientifique, 1963).
3. Lucy Norton, ed. and trans., *Saint-Simon at Versailles* (New York: Harper and Brothers, 1958), p. 33.
4. M. le duc de Saint-Simon, *Memoirs of Louis XIV and the Regency*, trans. Bayle St. John, 3 vols. (London: George Allen and Unwin Ltd., last ed. 1926), I, pp. 108-109.
5. Saint-Simon, *Memoirs*, I, p. 16.
6. Saint-Simon, *Memoirs*, I, pp. 19-20.
7. Maria Kroll, ed. and trans., *Letters from Liselotte* (London: Victor Gollancz, Ltd., 1970), p. 40.
8. Gertrude S. Stevenson, ed. and trans., *Letters of Madame* (New York: O. Appleton and Company, 1924), p. 117.
9. Stevenson, *Letters of Madame*, pp. 175-176.
10. Saint-Simon, *Memoirs*, I, p. 232.
11. Saint-Simon, *Memoirs*, I, p. 330.
12. Marcelle Benoit, ed., *Musiques de cour* (Paris: Editions A. & J. Picard, 1971), see the year 1708.
13. Saint-Simon, *Memoirs*, I, p. 157.
14. Norton, *Saint-Simon*, p. 140.

Some Contemporary Creative Artists Influential in France & England*

	France	England
Writers	Pierre Corneille 1606-1684	John Milton 1608-1674
	Issac de Benserade 1613-1691	John Dryden 1631-1700
	Molière 1622-1673	William Wycherley 1640-1716
	Philippe Quinault 1635-1688	Elkanah Settle 1648-1724
	Jean Racine 1639-1699	William Congreve 1670-1729
	Antoine de la Motte 1672-1731	George Farquhar 1678-1707
	François Voltaire 1694-1778	John Gay 1685-1732
Composers	**Jean-Baptiste Lully 1632-1687**	Christopher Gibbons
	Marc-Antoine Charpentier	1615-1676
	1634-1704	Matthew Locke c1630-1677
	Pietro Francesco Cavalli	John Blow 1649-1708
	1602-1676	Henry Purcell 1659-1695
	André Campra 1660-1744	George Frederick Handel
	François Couperin 1668-1733	1685-1759
	Jean Philippe Rameau	
	1683-1754	
Dancing masters	Henri Prévost d.c. 1662	Josias Priest
	Pierre Beauchamp 1631-c1719	Mr. Isaac d.c. 1715?
	d'Olivet	John Weaver 1673-1760
	Louis Pécour 1653-1729	John Essex
	R. A. Feuillet c1650-c1709	Kellom Tomlinson
	P. [Pierre] Rameau	Anthony L'Abbée c1680-1737
	Jean Ballon 1676-1739	
Artists	Gaspare Vigarani 1586-1663	Inigo Jones 1573-1650
	Giacomo Torelli 1608-1678	Christopher Wren 1632-1723
	Charles le Brun 1619-1690	William Hogarth 1697-1764
	Jean Bérain 1637-1711	
	Ferdinando Bibiena 1657-1743	
	Antoine Watteau 1684-1721	
	Giuseppe Bibiena 1696-1756	

*Artists discussed in this Chapter are in bold type.

CHAPTER TWO

Five Theatrical Personalities, 1632–1729
Lully, Molière, and Beauchamp; Pècour and Campra

Jean-Baptiste
Lully

The young Louis's enjoyment of dancing in a court entertainment must have been greatly enlivened by the presence of an Italian a few years his senior, a composer, dancer, and gifted comic, Giovanni Battista Lulli. Later, as a naturalized French citizen, Lulli became Jean-Baptiste Lully. Born in Florence in 1632, Lully was brought to the French court in 1646 at the age of fourteen to be valet de chambre and teacher of Italian to Mlle. de Montpensier, the Grande Mademoiselle. Also a violinist, Lully became a member of her string band.

Jean-Baptiste Lully, 1632-1687.

Lully's talent for composition did not go unnoticed by Louis, and he was soon writing dance music for the court. In 1654, an important ballet de cour with verses by Isaac de Benserade and music by Lully, *Le Ballet de la Galanterie du Temps,* presented for the first time Lully's own orchestra, the Petits Violons du Roi (or the Petite Bande). Lully's group of twenty-four musicians should not be confused with the long-established Grande Bande, or twenty-four Violons du Roi. Lully had previously expressed his dissatisfaction with the Grande Bande to Louis, who granted him his own orchestra, later to be famous throughout Europe. Of Lully's diverse talents, not the least was his extraordinary ability to ingratiate himself with the King.[1]

Molière

An indisputably great creative talent belonged to the dramatist and actor who adopted the stage name, Molière. Born in 1622 and baptized Jean-Baptiste Poquelin, he was apprenticed to his father, valet of upholstery to Louis XIII. But the theater held Jean-Baptiste's heart. Encouraged by his grandfather, he persuaded his father to let him pursue academic studies for five years at Clermont, a Jesuit school. There he made the acquaintance of the influential Prince de Conti, a meeting which was to develop into a lifelong friendship. Upon leaving school, Jean-Baptiste had no choice but to assume his father's post, an unsympathetic position he soon abandoned in order to haunt the Harlequin Théâtre of Paris. Before long he succeeded in founding his own troupe of strolling players, the Illustre Théâtre, and adopted the name Molière.

Molière with his company, a rough and ready egalitarian group, spent years touring the provinces and was always assured a warm reception by Conti as well as by Monsieur, le Duc d'Orléans, brother of Louis XIV. In 1658, Orléans secured Molière an audience to perform for the King. After presenting a standard tragi-comedy, Molière entreated the King to "allow him to give one of those little farces by which he had acquired a certain reputation in the provinces."[2] The piece, one of his timeless comedies, *Le Docteur Amoureux,* so pleased the King that he allowed Molière's troupe to be housed in the Petit Bourbon in Paris. Its future success was assured.

Pierre Beauchamp

The dancing master reputed to have played the major role in dance development as the seventeenth century progressed was Pierre Beauchamp, who was born in 1631.[3] Considered an outstanding performer and choreographer by his contemporaries, Beauchamp was born into his profession. Both his grandfather and father were violinists, the latter a member of the King's orchestra, the twenty-four Violons du Roi.[4]

Seventeenth- and eighteenth-century dancing masters, were masters of every aspect of their art. They were expected to teach dancing, dance in a variety of styles, play the violin, and sometimes compose dance music. The title maître à danser, or maître de danse, covered all these activities. A master's training began at eight years of age, took six years, and culminated in stringent examinations instituted and supervised by the musicians guild, the Corporation des Ménêtriers, to which dancing masters had belonged since the fifteenth century.[5] Beauchamp passed his examinations and was taking part in court ballets by 1648. During the next decade he established himself as a performer, dancing both in the noble style and in character parts, or so contemporary livrets (libretti) indicate. Beauchamp also composed music for some of the ballets de cour.

L'Académie Royale de Danse

Tensions had developed in the Corporation de Ménêtriers so that by 1661, when Louis XIV came to power, the dancing masters requested an establishment of their own. The King reacted favorably to their petition and appointed thirteen senior masters as academicians. Their major functions were to improve and perfect the performance and teaching of the art of dancing, the level of which had declined during the recent periods of war.

In 1661 or 1662, the King's dancing master, Henri Prévost, died, and it was perhaps then that Beauchamp attained this post. According to Rameau, the King took a lesson from Beauchamp every day for twenty-two years. Soon Beauchamp rose to the honored position of *Compositeur des Ballets du Roi.*

Comédie-ballet

The year 1661 also saw the production of Molière's first comédie-ballet, *Les Fâcheux*, with Beauchamp as choreographer, dancer, and composer of at least some of the music. Molière would ultimately write twelve comédies-ballets. He explains that the format of the comédie-ballet, in which the dances were interpolated into the action of the play, came about for practical reasons. Only a few good dancers were available to perform a variety of dances and time was needed for costume changes. Dances were therefore not, as was customary, presented in groups as separate entities outside the action of the play, but inserted into it from time to time, the dances complementing the drama and thereby making "comédie and ballet one."[6]

Molière, seated on the right, dining with Louis XIV. From a painting by Jerome.

The first figure of a character dance en-
titled, "mamaouchi"—grand panjandrum—
the grotesque Turkish title bestowed upon
M. Jourdain in Molière's comédie-ballet *Le
Bourgeois Gentilhomme.* The role of M.
Jourdain was played by Molière himself.
This dance has survived in an anonymous,
undated ms. in the Bibliothèque de l'Opéra
in Paris. The dance perhaps composed for
the first production of *Le Bourgeois
Gentilhomme,* for a revival, or an independent purpose.

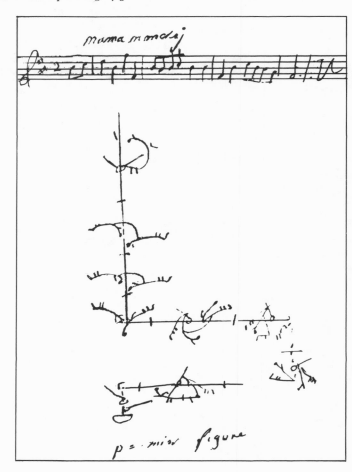

In his enthusiasm over the first comédies-ballets, Louis XIV offered Molière the services of Lully. They collaborated on eight comédies-ballets from *Le Mariage Forcé* in 1664 to *Le Bourgeois Gentilhomme* in 1670. Lully had one of his greatest personal successes with the comédie-ballet, *George Dandin*, given in 1668. This work concluded with a grand finale involving more than one hundred persons playing, singing, and dancing.[7] In 1670, Molière and Lully collaborated for the last time. The work was *Le Divertissement Royal; Les Amants Magnifiques* in which Louis XIV intended to appear, but changed his mind at the last minute.

Molière's final and perhaps best known work, *Le Malade Imaginaire*, was written in 1673 in collaboration with the composer Marc-Antoine Charpentier. Molière played the leading role. Unfortunately, there was nothing imaginary about the poor state of his own health. He collapsed in his dressing room at the end of a performance and died soon after.

L'Académie Royale de Musique

In 1672, the King granted Lully the direction of the Académie Royale de Musique. This was in fact a new name for the Académie d'Opéra which had been founded under the direction of another composer, Pierre Perrin, in 1669. Beauchamp, who in the meantime had become director of the Académie Royale de Danse, had been appointed maître à danser for the Académie d'Opéra in 1671. He continued in this post under Lully's direction.

Lully's ascendency

With the prestige of his new position and a full awareness of his influence over the King, Lully manifested his desire for power and was indulged. To the patent giving Lully directorship of the Académie a stipulation was added forbidding any other theater to produce a work that was sung in its entirety without Lully's written permission. Between 1672 and 1684, this suppression was reenforced with new decrees. The penalties for nonobservance were extremely severe. In 1673, the number of musicians (including two singers) who could appear in productions at theaters other than the Académie Royale de Musique was restricted to a meagre ensemble of eight. Even Lully's close collaborator, Molière, had found himself in the exasperating position of being unable to perform some of his own works without Lully's permission. It was no doubt fortunate for many when Lully died in 1687 from complications following a minor wound, accidentally self-inflicted when he struck his foot with his conductor's staff.

The ultimate size of Lully's renowned orchestra is uncertain but it was probably quite large. In the ballets de cour Lully had augmented his Petits Violons du Roi with brass and wind players from the Grand Ecurie (the King's stable), and sometimes with other instruments. After 1661, Lully also combined the Petits Violons du Roi and the previously despised twenty-four Violons du Roi in certain performances.

Design by Vigarani for Lully's *Atys*, first given at the Paris Opéra in 1676.
Nationalmuseum, Stockholm.

After 1672, Lully composed an average of one tragédie-lyrique each year to commissioned livrets by the poet Philippe Quinault. A tragédie-lyrique contained a prologue and five acts dealing with a serious or heroic subject.[8] It is also interesting to learn that Lully may have taken a hand in choreography. Abbé Dubos wrote:

Lully gave a lot of attention to pantomime and drew upon the talents of Louis Hilaire d'Olivet, a "maître de danse particulier" for this purpose, using Des Brosses and Beauchamp to compose the "ballets ordinaires."[9]

Beauchamp's later career

Soon after Lully's death, Beauchamp left his post as maître à danser at the Académie Royale de Musique but continued his other duties. Included in the Versailles accounts for the *Ballet de Flore* in 1688 is a note of payment to "Pierre Beauchamp, directeur de L'Académie Royale de Danse et compositeur des ballets du Roi."[10] In the late 1670s, Beauchamp began to devise the system of dance notation which came to be used in the eighteenth century.

It has been thought that Beauchamp died in 1705, but a later date is suggested by the announcement in the *Mercure*, March 1719, that Jean Ballon replaced Beauchamp as Composer of His Majesty's Ballets. Only one dance certainly by Beauchamp exists in notation, an elaborate theatrical solo for a man. No portrait of Beauchamp has been identified, only his signature remains.[11]

Beauchamp's signature.

The first figure of "Sarabande de Mr de Beauchamp." The music is anonymous.

Of Beauchamp's work the dancing master Rameau writes:

I cannot bestow too much Praise on the just Reputation he acquired: His first Essays were Master-strokes, and he always equally shared the Suffrages the Musician daily gained. He was learned and curious in his Compositions, and stood in need of Persons capable of executing what he had invented. Happy was it for him that there were at Paris, and at Court these most able Dancers, viz. St. Andre, Favier the Elder, Favre, Boutteville, Dumiraille, and Germain: But how excellent soever their Talents were, the Palm, by their own Concession, was reserved for Pécour and L'Estang.[12]

Louis
Pécour

It was Pécour who inherited the achievements of Lully and Beauchamp at the Opéra. He was, in fact, Beauchamp's successor at the Académie Royale de Musique. Pécour made his debut as a dancer at the Académie in 1673, performing in Lully's first tragédie-lyrique, *Cadmus*. He proved an outstanding and versatile performer and Rameau was later moved to describe his qualities with enthusiasm:

Pécour appeared in all Characters with a Grace, Justness and Activity; and both [Pécour and L'Estang were] so agreeable in their Conversations, that the greatest Lords took a Pleasure to have them in their Companies.

And as a choreographer:

He stood in need of all his Qualifications to succeed worthily the former Master, which he compleated by the infinite Variety and new Charms with which he set off those same Ballets which Beauchamp had before performed.[13]

Louis Guillaume Pécour (t),
1653-1729.

André
Campra

Pécour assumed his appointment, the most prestigious in the dancing profession, in 1687 at the age of thirty-four. Rameau says that Pécour had previously proven his worth as a choreographer at court. The Versailles accounts show his appointment as "maître de danse des pages du Chambre"[14] in 1680 and note his resignation in 1692. He retired from the stage in 1703 but was still maître à danser at the Opéra when he wrote an approbation for Rameau's *Le Maître à danser* in 1725. Pécour died in 1729 after an illustrious career during which he enjoyed greater recognition than any choreographer before him.

Pécour's widespread fame, which continued long after his death, was due not only to European acceptance of French culture but also to the proliferation of publications in dance. By far the largest number of the dances included in the early eighteenth-century flood of notated collections were social and theatrical dances by Louis Pécour. His best ballroom dances were republished many times and in many countries during the eighteenth century. They were enjoyed for their choreographic flow, their musicality, and their continuing originality within a highly systematized step vocabulary.

Pécour also choreographed for numerous revivals of Lully's works and collaborated on new works with the various composers who sought to succeed Lully. Some of his dances to music by such composers as Pascal Colasse, Louis de Lully, Marin Marais, and André Cardinal Destouches are extant. The composer with whom Pécour enjoyed his greatest successes, however, was André Campra.

Campra, a Frenchman of Italian descent, was born in 1660. His early musical associations were not with the theater but with the church; in 1694, he was director of music at Notre Dame in Paris. But Campra was drawn to the theater and in 1697, his first opéra-ballet, *L'Europe Galante,* was produced at the Opéra. *L'Europe Galante* was immediately successful and Campra's talent as a theatrical composer was firmly established. The dances for *L'Europe Galante,* several of which survive, were choreographed by Pécour. The work became the model for future developments in a new genre, the opéra-ballet.

André Campra. 1660-1774
Bibliothèque Nationale, Paris.

The works referred to as opéra-ballets were originally known simply as ballets, which nowadays refers to theatrical entertainments involving music, dance, and scenic effects, but without verses. However, verses were an essential ingredient of the opéra-ballet, as they were in the tragédie-lyrique. The tragédie-lyrique developed a serious and heroic plot, while the opéra-ballet consisted of independent sections of a light diverting nature. A motley of scenes could be hung upon such titles as *Carnaval de Venise, L'Europe Galante,* or *Les Festes Vénitiennes,* one of Campra's and Pécour's greatest successes, first produced in 1710. In this work, from which not only the music but several dances survive, there are Spanish entrées, dances for peasants, harlequins, and a "maître à danser" who had to sing as well as dance.

Campra had a long and successful theatrical career, the majority of his later works being tragédies-lyriques and opéra-ballets. The last productions of new works by Campra took place a few years before his death in 1744.

FOOTNOTES

1. For a discussion of Lully's influence and the theatrical genres of the period see James R. Anthony, *French Baroque Music* (New York: W. W. Norton and Company Inc., 1974, rev. ed. 1977).
2. Charles A. Sainte-Beuve, *Portraits of the Seventeenth Century*, trans. Katharine P. Wormsley, 2 vols. (New York: Frederick Ungar Publishing Co., 1964), II, p. 108.
3. Régine Kunzle, "The Illustrious Unknown Choreographer," *Dance Scope* (New York), vol. 8 no. 2, 1974, p. 32 and vol. 9 no. 1, 1974/75, p. 30.
4. Marie-Françoise Christout, *Le Ballet de cour de Louis XIV*, (Paris: Editions A. & J. Picard, 1967), p. 163.
5. Kunzle, "The Illustrious Unknown Choreographer."
6. Molière, "Avertissement pour les Fâcheux," *Oeuvres Complètes*, ed. Maurice Rat, 2 vols. (Paris: Bibliothèque de la Pléiade, 1956), I, p. 399.
7. Richard Oliver, "Molière's Contribution to the Lyric Stage," *Musical Quarterly* (New York), vol. 33, July 1947, pp. 350-364.
8. See Anthony, *French Baroque Music*, for further information, and complete listings of: ballets de cour, tragédies-lyriques with music by Lully, and Molière's comédies-ballets.
9. Anthony, *French Baroque Music*, p. 99.
10. Marcelle Benoit, ed., *Musiques de cour* (Paris: Editions A. & J. Picard, 1971), p. 115.
11. Kunzle, "The Illustrious Unknown Choreographer." Reproduced by kind permission of *Dance Scope*.
12. P[ierre] Rameau, *Le Maître à danser* (Paris: Chez Jean Villete, 1725), trans. John Essex, *The Dancing Master* (London, 1728), Preface, p. xxii. The words of Rameau, unless otherwise stated, are all from Essex's translation.
13. Essex, *The Dancing Master*, Preface, pp. xxiii, xxiv.
14. Benoit, *Musiques de cour*, see the year 1680.

An unidentified dancer. George Chaffee collection, Harvard Theater Collection.

CHAPTER THREE

Dance Types and Theatrical Technique, 1650–1715

Dance types

Theatrical
noble
style

No choreographies from original productions with music by Lully are known to have survived, but many dances composed for revivals of his works exist in the early eighteenth-century publications. The dance types used by Lully and his successors are contrasted in quality and atmosphere. Further, within each one there is variety. With these reservations in mind some general remarks may serve to introduce the most popular.

The most majestic of the dances is the entrée grave. The examples found in notation are technically complex dances for men. The music, with its dotted rhythms, is strong and commanding, perhaps reminiscent of the slow opening of an overture in the French style. Another dance which seems to have been used primarily, although not exclusively, for the male technique is the loure, or gigue lente. The other dance types were used equally for men and women, who, when dancing together, generally performed the same steps. Duets for two women or two men were common.

Louis Lestang. Rameau writes that L'Etang was a dancer of great nobility and precision, and that he and Pécour excelled among the male dancers at the Opéra under Beauchamp. The two dancers were also well versed in the manners of polite society and were welcomed in the residences of the greatest lords and ladies. Print by Trouvain. Bibliothèque Nationale, Paris.

Of the triple-time dances (those with three beats in a measure), the sarabandes are quite diverse in character. They are, on the whole, strong and calm with a sustained quality. The lengthy chaconnes and passacailles are largely represented by solos for men and women. There are no choreographies for groups to serve as examples of the chaconnes that were used for large scale finales, the position of the chaconne in most of the tragédies-lyriques and opéra-ballets. The menuet is, by comparison, gentle but nevertheless builds excitement in the cross-rhythm between steps and music. Its faster version, the passepied, is swift but still gracious.

Of the lively duple-time dances (those with two beats in a measure), the bourrée and rigaudon are virtually indistinguishable musically and choreographically. The gavotte is more spacious, with a slightly slower tempo. The liveliest of all dances are the gigues and canaries, which contain the greatest proportion of springing steps. In close relation to the gigue is the forlane, which has a slightly calmer, more beguiling quality.

Spanish entrées

Spanish entrées were very popular and various dance types were suitable for them, among which were loures, chaconnes, and sarabandes. Numerous portraits show dancers holding castanets (see pp.132,143), and their use in some of the entrées espagnoles is probably essential to authenticity.[1]

Character style

In addition to their use for purely noble choreographies—dances employing only the orthodox steps and the regulated arm motions of the noble style[2]—some of the musical forms were also used for dances of a character nature. A good example of a dance for this type is the "Chacoon for a Harlequin." In this dance, steps from the basic vocabulary are used, combined with head and arm motions characteristic of Harlequin.

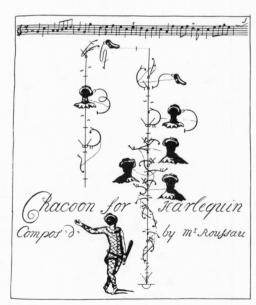

A figure from *Chacoon for a Harlequin,*
F. le Rousseau. The British Library, London.

The following is a guide to Lully's use, over a thirty-year span, of different dance types in the various genres. His successors used the same types, with the addition of the forlane.

Table of Dance Types[3]

Between 1653 and 1663: *ballet de cour*	The bourrée, gavotte, and sarabande predominate. Also found are the courante, gigue, gaillarde, and chaconne.
Between 1664 and 1672: *ballet de cour and* *comédie-ballet*	The menuet appears most frequently; the bourrée, gavotte, and sarabande remain as popular as before. Also found are the courante, gigue, canarie, gaillarde, and chaconne.
Between 1673 and 1687: *tragédie-lyrique and* *ballet de cour*	The menuet is now overwhelmingly predominant, the number of gavottes has doubled, the bourrée, sarabande, and canarie remain constant, the gigue is more popular, and the number of chaconnes, which provided large scale finales, has increased considerably. Also found are the loure, passepied, and passacaille. Lully wrote an occasional pavane and allemande. Any rigaudons in his scores are untitled.

Professional dancing at the Opéra

Pécour and Campra reaped the benefit of the inspired work of their predecessors at the Opéra: Lully, Beauchamp, and the other dancing masters who had worked there from its inception in 1672. These artists had established a renowned orchestra and a group of highly accomplished professional dancers, both male and female.

From the content of the notated dances it is evident that the demands made upon professional male dancers who performed in the noble style were considerable. Through the embellishment of the basic steps of court dances a purely theatrical vocabulary had been evolved. The elaborate dances for men were interspersed with cabrioles (springs in which the legs are beaten together while in the air) and successions of pirouettes (turns with the body supported on one foot) which had long been a part of the professional performer's equipment. In dances in the noble style, however, such tours de force had to be performed with elegance and apparent ease. Choreographically, even the most virtuosic steps were not stressed, but merely slipped into the rhythmic flow of the dance. The audience, most of whom danced themselves, would have been kinesthetically aware of the difficulties they were watching and able to appreciate apparent ease in a performer.

Such technical display was outside the range of female dancers, perhaps because it would not have appeared seemly, or simply because the costumes hampered movement. After 1672, the intermingling of courtiers and professional dancers in performances had declined. Thus for a number of years at the Opéra, female roles in the noble style were taken by boys en travesti, but by the 1680s, professional female dancers were successfully introduced to the stage to take these roles. The most outstanding were Mlles. de la Fontaine and Subligny. A great advance in female virtuoso technique, especially in the incorporation of pirouettes, took place in the early eighteenth century. Pécour's dances published in 1712 were far more complex than those published in 1704.

Marie-Thérèse Perdou de Subligny, 1666-1736. Bibliothèque Nationale, Paris.

Jean Balon (Ballon), 1676-1739. Bibliothèque Nationale, Paris.

A strangely static quality often characterizes the portraiture of dancers of this period.

In his Preface, Rameau describes the attributes of stars of the Paris Opéra who danced for Louis Pécour. One of the greatest was Marcel, who rose to fame because he could sing well enough to take the role of the dancing master in *Les Festes Vénitiennes:*

The Rise of Marcel's Reputation is an Epocha remarkable enough in the Opera. Campra, who of all the Successors of Lully in Composition of Musick, has obliged the Theatre with a Number of fine Performances brought on the Venetian Feasts. There was a very singular Scene in this Ballat, in which a Dancing-Master in a Song boasts of all the Advantages of his Art; and as at the same Time he performed the different Characters of Dancing in the Ballets, and had a small Voice and a good Taste of Singing, he undertook this Flight, and succeeded so well in it, that from that Time he engaged the Publick to observe with more Attention his Talent for Dancing, where he has constantly maintained what could be expected from him. I may say that the double Dance which he performed and does now every Day with Blondy, is like a Picture in which the Likenesses are so just and the Colours so lively, that one cannot forbear admiring them.[4]

Blondy was Beauchamp's nephew and pupil. The following "Entrée de deux homme" may be the "double Dance" referred to by Rameau. The first two figures of the dance are given on this one, rather crowded, page of notation.

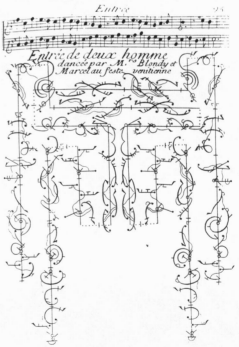

Nouveau Recüeil de dance de Mr Pécour. Graudrau, Paris, 1712.

The succeeding pages combine Rameau's descriptions of other dancers with title pages of dances they performed.[5]

[Ballon] had a great deal of Judgment and a prodigious Activity: He was for many Years the Pleasure and Admiration of all Spectators, which Merit of his was recompensed by the Honour he had of being the first Master to Lewis the Fifteenth, our august Monarch, the Love of his People, and the Hopes of all Arts.

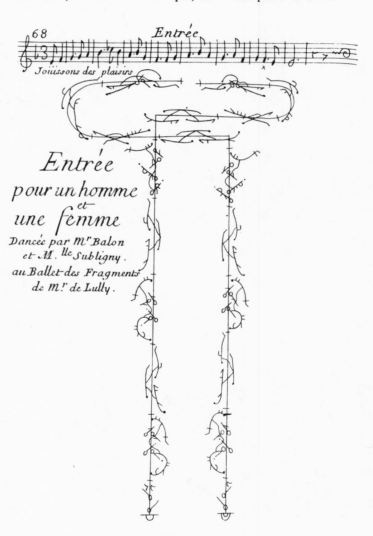

Recüeil de dances de M. Pécour. Feuillet, Paris, 1704.

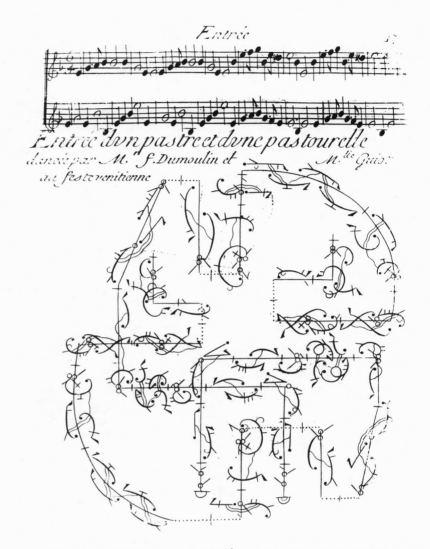

Nouveau recüeil de dance de Mr Pécour. Gaudrau, Paris, 1712.

DUMOULIN, the Youngest of the four Brothers, who are all very deserving, and who at this Time distinguish themselves in several Characters, was the Person that came the nearest up to Balon, and who in some measure afforded the Publick some Consolation. He had the Advantage at first of being the Partner in a double Dance with Mademoiselle Guiot, who was an excellent Dancer, and by his successful Attempts made himself capable of figuring with the incomparable Mademoiselle Prevoit [Prévost].

'TIS here that I wish it in my Power to pay that just Tribute of Praise her Merit calls for. In one single Dance of hers are contained all the Rules we are able to give on our Art, and she puts them in Practice with such Grace, Justness, and Activity, that she may be looked on as a Prodigy in this Kind. She justly deserves to be regarded as Terpsichore the Muse, whom the Ancients made to precide over Dancing, and has all the Advantages over Proteus in the the Fable. She at Pleasure assumes all manner of Shapes, with this Difference only, that Proteus oftentimes made use of them to frighten curious Mortals that came to consult him, and she to inchant the greedy Eyes of those that look on her; and to gain the Applause of every Body, which excites a noble Emulation among the other Women Dancers.

Nouveau recüeil de dance de Mr Pécour. Gaudrau, Paris, 1712.

The next generation of stars at the opera included the great Louis Dupré 1697–1774, Marie-Anne Cupis de Carmargo 1710–1770, a pupil of the illustrious Prévost so eloquently described above, and Carmargo's great rival, Marie Sallé 1707–1756.

FOOTNOTES

1. Raoul Auger Feuillet, *Chorégraphie* (Paris: 1700), p. 100. The examples of castanet rhythms in primary dance sources are limited.
2. For some information about early eighteenth-century experiments in dramatic dancing see F. Derra de Moroda, "The Ballet Masters Before, at the Time of, and After J.G. Noverre," *Chigiana* (Florence), vol. 29-30 (n.s.no. 9-10), 1972/73.
3. Helen Meredith Ellis (Little), "The Dances of J.B. Lully." (Unpublished Ph.D. diss., Stanford Univ., 1967). In compiling her lists of Lully's dance music Dr. Ellis included only the pieces designated as a dance type by title.
4. John Essex, *The Dancing Master* (London, 1728), Preface, p. xxvii.
5. The excerpts quoted on the pages of illustrations are from Essex, *The Dancing Master*, Preface.

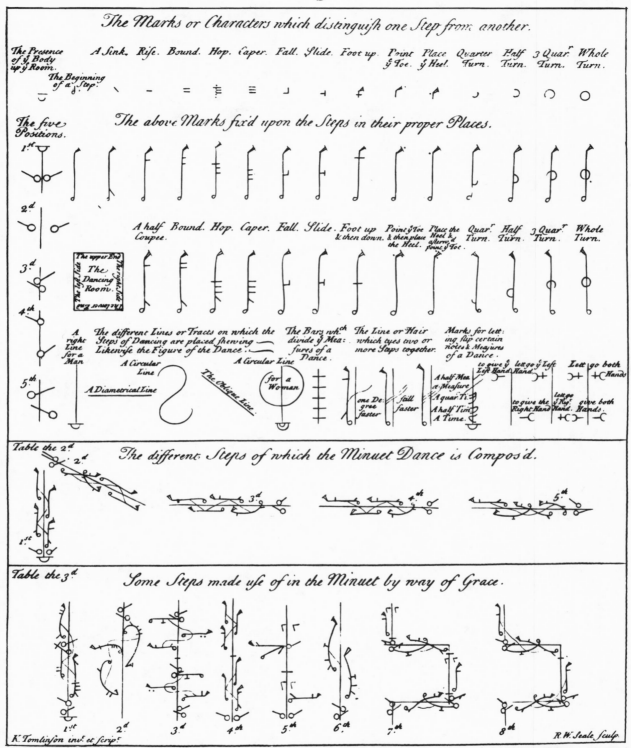

From *The Art of Dancing* by Kellom Tomlinson

CHAPTER FOUR

The Dancing Masters and Their Books, 1623–1725
Feuillet, Rameau, and Tomlinson.

In the early seventeenth century, a change of fashion and taste manifested itself. The fashions in dress were more flowing than those admired previously and were reflected in a fluid, unostentatious dance style. François de Lauze describes the new style in his book, *Apologie de la danse,* 1623, and he is the only master to do so.[1] From de Lauze's descriptions, it is impossible to reconstruct the steps with confidence, but he indicates quite clearly that the foundations for the dance technique to be developed by Louis's masters were already established.[2] The dance in the new style given by de Lauze is the courante, the dance Louis was to enjoy the most, for it would provide ample opportunity for the King to display the grandeur of his royal presence. The courante was to be the basis for lessons in the noble style for a century or more—even after the dance had lost its place of favor to the menuet.[3]

The next publication on dance technique did not appear until 1700. Due to the lack of direct documentation during the seventy-seven-year interim, only certain facts and some flavor of seventeenth-century dance can be elicited: from music; costume and stage design; the cast listings given in livrets; and the writings which express the opinions of contemporary commentators. It is possible, however, that a greater understanding of the early eighteenth-century manuals will shed some retrospective light on seventeenth-century developments.

The masters of the Académie Royale de Danse had two major tasks: to improve the level of dancing, and to establish sound theoretical principles for the art. Whether their work as a body expanded or stultified dance is open to speculation because what they might have accomplished is unrecorded. In the late 1670s, however, Louis entrusted Beauchamp, then director of the Académie, with the invention of a notation for dance and it is possible that Beauchamp had to codify steps and movements before he could proceed with this work. To him are attributed the systematization of the five positions of the feet, and the regulation of the formal arm motions.[4]

A mystery surrounds Beauchamp's notation because it was another master, Raoul Auger Feuillet, who, in 1700, actually published it in his book, *Chorégraphie ou l'art de décrire la danse par caractères, figures, et signes démonstratifs.* This notation is the first known completed system to record dance steps and movements with abstract symbols. In 1704, Beauchamp filed a petition against Feuillet for infringement of his work. Beauchamp claimed that some thirty years earlier Louis had told him to devise the notation, a task he completed within five years. Beauchamp lost his case and was advised to apply for letters of patent on his own behalf, but there is no record that he did so.[5] The question remains why he never promoted his own system. It is possible that it was not sufficiently finished, or perhaps he did not wish to undertake the enormous work involved in preparing it for publication.

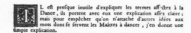

The title page of the first edition of Feuillet's *Choréographie*, 1700.

Feuillet himself makes no reference to Beauchamp, but two masters who published their own books on the notation after Feuillet's exclusive privilège expired in 1706 were eager to give Beauchamp full credit. John Weaver wrote in the Preface to his *Orchesography*, 1706 (a translation of *Chorégraphie*):

... to do Justice to Mons. Beauchamp, we must attribute to him the Invention of this Art... But as no Art was ever invented and perfected at once, so it remain'd for Mons. Feuillet, to raise the compleat and finish'd Superstructure on Mons. Beauchamp's Foundation.[6]

And P. Siris, in the Preface to *The Art of Dancing* (a paraphrase of *Chorégraphie*), stated:

It is to this last Gentleman [Feuillet] that France is endebted for The Art of demonstrating Dancing by Characters and Figures, which he publish'd about six Years since; but 'tis to Monsieur Beauchamp, nevertheless, that the Invention of this Art is wholly owing. This I can assure you, on my Word, since he himself taught me the

Grounds of it above Eighteen Years ago, but tho' through an unaccountable Negligence he delay'd the publishing of it from Time to Time, it must needs be no small concern to him to see that another has all the Honour and Advantage of what cost him so much Study and Labour.[7]

In 1712, another master, Monsieur Gaudrau, commented in the Preface to his new collection of dances by Pécour:

It is to Mr. Beauchamps, composer of ballets for the King and for the Royal Academy, that we are indebted for the invention of this new Art. And the late M. Feuillet profiting by his inspiration gave entirely his own publication to La chorégraphie.[8]

When *Chorégraphie* was published in 1700,[9] Feuillet was about forty years old and, to judge from his subsequent publications, spent much of his time notating until his death at the age of fifty.

Chorégraphie

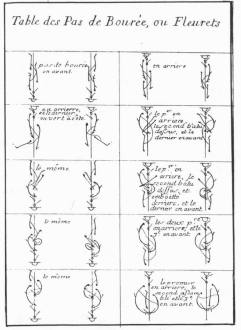

A page from Feuillet's *Chorégraphie*.

Chorégraphie, a work of beautiful detail, includes a section of forty pages, each containing an average of twelve diagrams of steps. At first glance, it seems that the vocabulary of steps was enormous, but Feuillet is showing every possible variation of each step as well as the different ways of notating each variation. Thus there are ninety-four examples of pas de bourrée, each drawn to account separately for execution with the left or the right foot. With the book are bound two collections of dances. The first of these comprises fifteen dances by Feuillet, devised to illustrate the use of the notation and provide examples for other masters. Feuillet's compositions are theatrical solos and duets of increasing complexity, culminating in a "Balet de neuf danseurs," a large portion of which is a beautiful study in double symmetry (see p. 96). The second collection contains nine ballroom dances by Louis Pécour.

In the same year, Feuillet published separately two more ball-room dances by Pécour: *La Pavane des saisons* and *Le Passepied nouveau*, the latter notated at Pécour's request. In this publication Feuillet promised a volume of theatrical dances by Pécour and also requested that:

Dancing masters in the Provinces and foreign Courts who wish to have ballets and other dances set to an air should send me the music, and I will send them an appropriate composition.[10]

In 1701, Pécour composed a loure, to music by Campra, called *Aimable vainqueur*, which Feuillet published. It became the most beloved of all the eighteenth-century danses à deux and was reprinted many times. Rameau also included it in his *Abbregé* (to which Pécour contributed an approbation), but his and Feuillet's versions differ in a few measures. The alterations may have been introduced and preferred by Pécour himself.

Recueils

In 1702, Feuillet published the first of an annual collection of ballroom dances. Consisting of two, three, or four dances, each collection was scheduled to appear in November in readiness for the coming season. Thus the publication of 1702 contained new dances for the year 1703. Also in 1702, Feuillet was urged to publish another dance by Pécour, *L'Allemande*, which had been performed that year in the theater by Mlle. Subligny and M. Ballon in the ballet *Fragments de Mr de Lully*. This lively dance joined *Aimable vainqueur* as a continuing ballroom favorite.

The output of a few dances in two years does not suggest enormous labor, but Feuillet was occupied in other ways, as he explained in the collection for the year 1704:

It has been impossible up to now to publish the promised works of M. Pécour because in addition to my ordinary occupations I have been obliged to compose and write several ballets requested by foreign courts; however, as the works of M. Pécour are well under way I hope I shall not delay in satisfying the great number of people who have waited for them so long.[11]

Feuillet was true to his word; the *Recueil de dances de M^r. Pécour* appeared in 1704 and contained his last apology for the delay:

. . . people will stop blaming me if they consider that the greatest number of the dances it contains were danced at the Opéra at different times and by different people, and it took an immense amount of work to put them into notation. [12]

This large collection consists of thirty-five dances and amounts to two hundred and twenty-eight notated pages, preceded by a

Traité de la cadance. This was the last sizeable book Feuillet was to publish apart from his *Recueil de contredanses* in 1706.

The annual collections of danses à deux, with an occasional danse à quatre, continued regularly until the 7th, 8th, and 9th collections, all having the publication date 1709. These were intended for the years 1709, 1710, and 1711. While the first two could still be had "chez l'Auteur," the last appeared "chez le Sr Dezais," to whom Feuillet bequeathed his works and privilège to publish. The volume states in the Preface:

M. Feuillet was born with a happy genius, of rare talents, and with marvelous aptitudes for his art, aided by various mathematical understandings. Upheld with a labor of twenty-nine years, he produced excellent pieces of chorégraphie with such success and an approval so general that they have carried his reputation to the borders of foreign countries. After having reduced his understandings to certain rules and having perfected that just described, he died, the 14th of June this year, being only fifty years old. [13]

With a publication date of 1709 for the 1711 collection, Feuillet's death would presumably have been June 14, 1709. Dezais perpetuated the annual collections until at least 1725. Compositions by Pécour continued to appear, but more often the dances are by Dezais himself and by Jean Ballon, the famous dancer of the Opéra.

P[ierre] Rameau

It is thought that P. Rameau, as he designated himself, was Pierre Rameau, the son of a Parisian dancer, Georges Rameau. In 1705, Pierre Rameau was employed at the Opéra in Lyon where, on May 23, he married Elizabeth la Haye.[14] On the title page of his first book, *Le Maître à danser* (Paris, 1725), Rameau states that he was "Maître à danser des Pages de Sa Majesté Catholique la Reine d'Espagne". Rameau's second book, *Abbregé de la nouvelle méthode,* was also published in 1725, and here Rameau describes himself as "Maître à Danser Ordinaire de la Maison de Sa Majesté Catholique, la Reine seconde Douairriere d'Espagne".[15]

Le Maître à danser

Le Maître à danser (translated in 1728 by one of England's foremost masters, John Essex)[16] contains the clearest and most detailed descriptions available of the structure and execution of the basic steps used in social and theatrical dance. These are preceded by instructions upon carriage, from which can be deduced the desired style of motion, bows and courtesies, and ballroom etiquette. Rameau leaves the important question of the relationship between steps and music for *Abbregé de la nouvelle méthode,* in which he deals primarily with the dance notation. The second part of this book is a collection of Pécour's most popular and durable social dances.

Abbregé

Books abroad

Early in the eighteenth century, theoretical books on dance began to be published in Germany: in Leipzig in 1705, *I.H.P. Maître de Danse oder Tantz-Meister*; in 1713, Samuel Behren's

L'Art de Bien danser oder: Die Kunst wohl zu Tanzen; and, in 1717, Gottfried Taubert's monumental 1176-page *Rechtschaffener Tantzmeister*. Although almost all the most fashionable European courts employed a French dancing master, it seems that only in England did the resident masters regularly publish their own compositions. Elsewhere dances from France were usually copied, the established favorites appearing many times in books published in Germany, Italy, Spain, Russia, and also in England.

England

The French dances became popular in England following the restoration of Charles II in 1660. The English nobility and upper classes, unlike their French counterparts, were actively involved in the affairs of their country and did not find dance to be such an important pastime. However, dance instruction was accepted as one of the best methods to acquire the social graces necessary for a man of affairs. Every cultured Englishman was expected to dance at least a minuet with a good grace and air, and to be well-versed in the etiquette of polite society. Thus Lord Chesterfield wrote to his son, Philip Stanhope, who began dance tutelage at the age of thirteen:

As you will be often under the necessity of dancing a minuet, I would have you dance it very well. Remember that the graceful motion of the arms, the giving your hand, and the putting on and pulling off your hat genteelly are the material parts of a gentleman's dancing. But the greatest advantage of dancing well is that it necessarily teaches you to present yourself, to sit, stand, and walk genteelly; all of which are of real importance to a man of fashion.[17]

Janssens: Charles II Dancing in the Hague. Here the King is dancing what is generally assumed to be a courante. Reproduced by gracious permission of Her Majesty the Queen.

The Dancing Masters and Their Books, 1623-1725

During his exile, King Charles had been a frequent guest at the French court and had absorbed much of its atmosphere. After his return to England, the new French dances became established at court, in fashionable society, and in entertainments. However, the first champion of French dance and dancers in the English theater was another talented amateur, the Duke of Monmouth, the King's illegitimate son, born in 1649.[18]

English masters

Although many French masters were employed in England, English masters of high repute also flourished, such as Josias Priest who choreographed the operas of Henry Purcell, beginning with *Dido and Aeneas* in 1688. Another English master of note was John Weaver (1673-1760) whom the court dancing master, Mr. Isaac, encouraged to translate Feuillet's theoretical works. Weaver was also a prolific and erudite author in his own right, and a highly influential figure in the dancing profession. Although he wrote on many aspects of his art, Weaver's theatrical interests did not lie primarily with the orthodox technique of the French noble style.[19]

A NEW
COLLECTION
O F
DANCES

Containing a great Number of the best

Ball and Stage Dances:

Composed by Monsieur L'ABBE, *Dancing-Master to Their Royal Highnesses, the Three Young Princesses.*

That have been performed both in *Drury-Lane* and *Lincoln's-Inn-Fields*, by the best Dancers, *viz.*

Monsieur BALON,	Mrs. ELFORD,
Mons' L'ABBE,	Mrs. SANTLOW,
Mons' LA GARDE,	Mrs. BULLOCK,
Mons' DUPRE,	Mrs. YOUNGER.
Mons' DESNOYER,	

A Work very Useful to all Masters, and other Persons that apply themselves to Dancing.

Recollected, put in Characters, and engraved, by Monsieur. ROUSSAU, Dancing-Master.

To be Sold at Mr. *Barreau's*, Book-binder in *Lumbard-Court, Seven Dials*; and at Mr. *Roussau's* in *York-street* near *St. James's Square*. Price 2s 5.

The first dance in Roussau's undated collection provides interesting evidence of French dancers performing for a king of England. Bodleian Library, Oxford.

While Rameau's *Le Maître à danser* was certainly the model for many subsequent European publications, one book was being prepared in England at exactly the same time Rameau was writing his. Kellom Tomlinson suffered the agonizing experience of writing a book and, before it could be printed, witnessing the publication of another similar in content. *The Art of Dancing* was completed in 1724, but it was not until 1735 that a total of one hundred and sixty-nine subscribers had donated sufficient funds to support its publication in London.

In the Preface, Tomlinson relates how he was shocked to read the following advertisement in Mist's *Journal* of January 1728:

Next Week will be published the Dancing-Master or The Art of Dancing explain'd by Monsieur Rameau. [20]

This was the first Tomlinson knew of Rameau's work, and his feelings upon seeing its contents can easily be imagined. When *The Art of Dancing* was eventually published seven years later, each part of the book included a statement signed by two persons affirming Tomlinson's claim that he had written his book without knowledge of Rameau's.

Tomlinson's beautiful publication could be had from the picturesque London address "the Red and Gold Flower Pot next Door to Edward's Coffee-House, over against the Bull and Gate, in High-Holbourn." The book is unique in its combination of text, notation, and figures of dances, most of the plates showing music at the top, notated spatial patterns, and one or two dancers in motion.

Besides the numerous titled persons who subscribed to Tomlinson's work, there were also a number of well-known professionals: John Rich, Esq., "Master of the Theaters Royal in Lincoln's-Inn-Fields, and Covent-Garden"; the dancing master John Weaver; Rameau's translator, John Essex; M. L'Abbé, "Dancing-Master to their Royal Highnesses the young Princesses"; and one of London's most famous dancers, Mrs. Santlow.

Compared with Rameau's text, Tomlinson's is less explicit and concise but more humane. He expresses his emotions over professional successes and frustrations and occasional exasperation at his less talented amateur pupils. In his Preface, Tomlinson explains, in characteristic style, how it was that he came to be known professionally by three different names:

During the Time of my Apprenticeship I went generally by the Name of Kellom, a Corruption of Kenelm my true Christian Name; as it is very common for young Persons to be called Mr. John, Mr. William, and the like, without the Addition of their Sur-name. At the Expiration of my Apprenticeship, several of my Friends out of Respect called me by my Sur-name of Tomlinson; but, being unwilling to decline the Advantage I might probably receive from the

Reputation of having learned the Art of Dancing under so great a Master as Mr. Caverley, I chose rather to retain the Name of Kellom, by which I had been so universally known to have been under his Instruction. This Duplicity of Appellation turned afterwards to my great Disadvantage: many of the Nobility and Gentry, who would have had their Children taught by Mr. Kellom, refusing to employ Mr. Tomlinson tho' recommended to them; and many, who would have employed Mr. Tomlinson, rejecting Mr. Kellom. To prevent which Confusion for the future, I shall acknowledge my self obliged to those, who, instead of either singly, shall be pleased to call me by both conjunctly, Kellom Tomlinson.

Tomlinson further tells something of his early career. Between 1707 and 1714 he was the apprentice of Mr. Thomas Caverley and also studied "the theatrical way" with a famous dancer, Mr. Cherrier. Later Tomlinson became active in the theater. In 1717, his composition, "The Submission," "was performed by Monsieur and Mademoiselle Salle, the two French Children, on the Theater in Lincoln's-Inn-Fields, to very considerable Audiences, every Night, for a whole Week together." "The Submission" was one of six dances composed between 1715 and 1720: "All which I composed, wrote in Characters, and published, for the Improvement of the Art of Dancing."

Recapitulation

The dance notation as published by Feuillet was widely accepted in spite of its limitations as a shorthand system. A balanced view of its scope was expressed by an English master, Mr. E. Pemberton:

The Generall Approbation the Characters of Dancing has met with in most parts of Europe is a sufficient Demonstration of its Usefulness, since no person who has applyed himself to Studye it but what has acknowledg'd himself much Improv'd by this Art.
It were to be wish'd that those Masters (who either thro Prejudice or Mistaken Notions) have not yet attain'd to it would consider it as necessary as the Notes of Musick.
The only Objection that seems to be of Weight is that ye Characters will not teach a particular manner of Dancing. This in some part must be allowed, & the same may be objected against Musick or even Common Printing, but sure no one for that reason will pretend that those Arts are unnecessary, especially for an Instructor.[21]

There is no doubt that notation greatly facilitated the masters' business: the publication of the new social dances enabled masters to obtain them through the mail, written in a reliable form; the publication of the best theatrical dances, notably by Pécour, enabled masters to study them and keep abreast of the latest developments in the orthodox technique. There was also the gratifying thought that the art of dancing, of which they were justifiably proud, would be preserved for posterity.

Soame Jenyns in his poem, *The Art of Dancing*, 1729, speaks of these advantages:

Long was the Dancing Art unfix'd and free;
Hence lost in Error and Uncertainty:
No Precepts did it mind, or Rules obey,
But ev'ry Master taught a diff'rent Way:
Hence, ere each new-born Dance was fully try'd,
The lovely Product, ev'n in blooming, dy'd:
Thro' various Hands in wild Confusion toss'd,
Its Steps were alter'd and its Beauties lost:
Till FEUILLET at length, Great Name! arose,
And did the Dance in Characters compose:
Each lovely Grace by certain Marks he taught,
And ev'ry Step in lasting Volumes wrote.
Hence o'er the World this pleasing Art shall spread,
And ev'ry Dance in ev'ry Clime be read;
By distant Masters shall each Step be seen,
Tho' Mountains rise and Oceans roar between.[22]

FOOTNOTES

1. For information about books published previously see the first section of general bibliography at the conclusion of this book.

2. For instance, the turnout of the legs from the hips, some of the basic steps, and the quality of motion.

3. Wendy Hilton, "A Dance for Kings: The 17th-Century French Courante," *Early Music* (London), April 1977.

4. P[ierre] Rameau, *Le Maître à danser* (Paris: Chez Jean Villete, 1725), trans. John Essex, *The Dancing Master* (London, 1728). Rameau: pp. 9, 195.

5. For an account of what has been ascertained about this case, see P.J.S. Richardson, "The Beauchamps Mystery," *The Dancing Times* (London), March 1947, p. 229 and April 1947, p. 351; also the excellent article by Friderica Derra de Moroda, "Chorégraphie," *The Book Collector* (London), Winter 1967; also Régine Kunzle, "The Unknown Illustrious Choreographer," *Dance Scope* (New York), vol. 9 no. 1, 1974/75.

6. John Weaver, *Orchesography. Or the Art of Dancing* (London: Printed by H. Meere for the Author, 1706), Preface.

7. P. Siris, *The Art of Dancing* (London: Printed for the Author, 1706), Preface.

8. M^r. Gaudrau, *Nouveau recüeil de dance de bal et celle de ballet* (Paris: Chez le Sieur Dezais, 1712).

9. Many modern writers give the date of publication of *Chorégraphie* as 1699. The privilège was registered on 13 December 1699, Colbert's signature followed by "Achevé d'imprimer pour la premiere fois le 31. Decembre 1699." The first edition is dated 1700.

10. Raoul Auger Feuillet, *Le Passepied nouveau* (Paris: Chez le Sieur Feuillet, 1700).

11. Feuillet, *IIme Recüeil de danses de bal* (Paris: Chez le Sieur Feuillet, 1703).

12. Feuillet, *Recueil de dances de M^r. Pécour* (Paris: Chez le Sieur Feuillet, 1704).

13. Feuillet, *IX Recueil de danses pour l'annee 1711* (Paris: Chez le Sr Dezais, 1709), Preface.

14. Léon Vallas, *Un Siècle de musique et de théatre 1688-1789* (Lyon: Chez P. Masson, Libraire, 1932), p. 167.

15. Rameau, *Abbregé de la nouvelle méthode dans l'art d'écrire, ou de tracer toutes sortes de danses de ville* (Paris: Chez l'Auteur, 1725).

16. John Essex, *The Dancing Master: Or, The Whole Art and Mystery of Dancing Explained,* Done from the French of Monsieur Rameau (London, 1728). A second edition appeared in 1731, followed by a second issue of this edition also dated 1731. Some of the plates in this issue, however, bear the date 1732 or 1733.

17. The Earl of Chesterfield, *Letters to His Son*, ed. Oliver H. Leigh, 2 vols. (New York: Tudor Publishing Co., n.d.), I, p. 120.

18. Ifan Kyrle Fletcher, "Ballet in England 1660-1740." IN: *Famed for Dance: Essays on the Theory and Practice of Theatrical Dance in England* (New York: The New York Public Library, 1960).

19. For an idea of the scope of Weaver's interest, here is a list of some of his works:

    An Essay Towards an History of Dancing, 1712.
    The Loves of Mars and Venus; A Dramatick Entertainment of Dancing, 1717.
    Anatomical and Mechanical Lectures upon Dancing, 1721.
    The History of the Mimes and Pantomimes, 1728.

20. Kellom Tomlinson, *The Art of Dancing* (London: Printed for the Author, 1735), Preface. All succeeding quotations are from this source.

21. E. Pemberton, *The Pastorall, Mr. Isaac's New Dance* (London: Printed for I. Walsh, 1713), Prefatory page before notation.

22. Soame Jenyns, *The Art of Dancing, A Poem* (London: Printed by W. P. and sold by J. Roberts, 1729), pp. 25-26.

PART TWO

An Analysis of The French Noble Style of Dance and its Notation

Introduction to The Analysis of Eighteenth–Century Dance Sources

SOURCES

The analysis is based upon the works by Feuillet and Rameau, and the English translations of them by John Weaver and John Essex. The analysis of the dance notation is based upon three works by Feuillet: *Chorégraphie*, 1700; the second edition of 1701, which was augmented by a short *Supplément des tables*; and the *Traité de la cadance*, which prefaced his *Recueil de dances de Mr Pécour*, 1704.

In the present text *Chorégraphie* refers to Feuillet's book, chorégraphie to the system of notation it explains. (In current French the word means dance notation in a comprehensive sense.) Feuillet's instructions also include signs and symbols representing some components used exclusively in dances for the theater. These are outside the scope of this text, which covers those components used in both theatrical and social dances.

Rameau's two books were published in 1725. The first, *Le Maître à danser*, deals largely with the execution of steps. Its contents are collated with Feuillet throughout the following text. In his second book, *Abbregé de la nouvelle méthode dans l'art d'écrire, ou de tracer toutes sortes de danses de ville*—which will be referred to as *Abbregé*—Rameau points out the limitations of the existing notation system and proposes improvements upon it. Some of the new signs he developed to replace those used by Feuillet are introduced into the main body of this text when they clarify Feuillet's system, while some others are given in footnotes.

Feuillet's theoretical writings were translated into English by John Weaver and published in 1706: *Chorégraphie* under the title *Orchesography*, and *Traité de la cadance* as *A Small Treatise on Time and Cadence in Dancing*. Rameau's *Le Maître à danser* was translated by John Essex, and published in 1728 as *The Dancing Master*. Quotations from Feuillet and Rameau are given in the words of Weaver's and Essex's translations, with the exception of those from *Abbregé* which have been translated by the author. Each quote is followed by a page reference to the original French work as well as to its English translation. *The Art of Dancing* (1735), by Kellom Tomlinson, is used as an adjunct to the French masters' texts.

Table of French Books used in the Analysis

Raoul Auger Feuillet.

Feu. 1 Chorégraphie ou l'art de décrire la dance, par caractères, figures et signes démonstratifs, avec lesquels on apprend facilement de soy-même toutes sortes de dances. Ouvrage très-utile aux maîtres à dancer et à toutes les personnes qui s'appliquent à la dance. Par M. Feuillet. . .Paris, l'auteur, 1700.*

Feu. 1a Supplément des tables, Chorégraphie, Paris, 1701.

Feu. 2 Traité de la cadance. In: Recueil de dances contenant un très grand nombres, des meillieures entrées de ballet de Mr Pécour . . . Recüeilles et mises au jour par Mr Feüillet M^c de dance. A Paris, chez l'auteur, 1704.**

P. Rameau.

Ram. 1 Le maître à danser qui enseigne la manière de faire tous les differens pas de danse dans toute la regularité de l'art, et de conduire les bras à chaque pas. Enrichi de figures en taille-douce, servant de démonstration pour tous les differens mouvemens. . .Paris, J. Villette, 1725.*

Ram. 2 Abbregé de la nouvelle méthode dans l'art d'écrire, ou de tracer toutes sortes de danses de ville. . .Paris, l'auteur, 1725.**

Facsimile editions (U.S.A. and England):
  *   Broude Bros. 56 West 45th St., New York, N.Y. 10036

  ** Gregg International Publications, Dance Books Ltd., 9 Cecil Court, London, England WC2N 4 EZ

All the editions are hardcover. The Broude editions are exceptionally handsome and justifiably costly; the approximate size of the original is retained. The Gregg editions are smaller and less expensive.

Table of English Books used in the Analysis

Raoul Auger Feuillet.

Wea. 1
> Orchesography or the art of dancing, by characters and demonstrative figures. . .Being an exact and just translation from the French of Monsieur Feuillet. By John Weaver. London, H. Meere for the author, 1706.**,***

Wea. 2
> A small treatise of time and cadence in dancing. . .shewing how steps, and their movements, agree with the notes, and divisions of the notes, in each measure. (Translated by John Weaver.) London, H. Meere for the author, 1706.**,***

P. Rameau.

Ess.
> The dancing-master: or, the art and mystery of dancing explained . . . Done from the French of Monsieur Rameau, by J. Essex, dancing-master. London, J. Essex and J. Brotherton, 1728. ***

Kellom Tomlinson.

Tom.
> The art of dancing explained by reading and figures; whereby the manner of performing the steps is made easy by a new and familiar method: being the original work, first designed in the year 1724, and now published by Kellom Tomlinson, dancing-master. . .London, the author, 1735.**,***

Facsimile Editions (U.S.A. and England):

**   See previous page.

***   John Essex's translation of Rameau's *Le Maître à danser* is not available in facsimile. The British Library, London, England, and the Sibley Library at the Eastman School of Music, Rochester, New York, are among the libraries which own copies. A modern translation, *The Dancing Master*, made and published by Cyril W. Beaumont, London, 1931, is available from Dance Horizons, 1801 East 26th Street, Brooklyn, N.Y. 11229.

TECHNICAL ILLUSTRATIONS

Dancers

Rameau's engravings for *Le Maître à danser*, which are executed with an unsophisticated technique, are intended to illustrate a particular technical point. Each pertains to only one part of the body with the remainder often carelessly and crudely depicted. Selection of the most accurate and kinesthetically evocative of Rameau's engravings has been made, although occasionally examples from an edition of Essex's translation have been substituted. The plates in Tomlinson's *The Art of Dancing* are done by a variety of artists, and have greater aesthetic merit than those of Rameau. Tomlinson groups his illustrations in two sections at the conclusion of his work: Books I and II relating to Book the First and Book the Second of his text. Examples from *The Art of Dancing* are used frequently in the present text.

Illustrations from other sources have been incorporated when the author has found the plates provided by Rameau and Tomlinson insufficient. Most of these additional illustrations relate to subtleties of carriage and deportment. Occasionally, a verbal description from Rameau will be combined with an illustration from Tomlinson, or the reverse, or either may be combined with an outside source.

In Rameau's work, illustrations are referred to as "Figures," in Tomlinson's as "Plates." The term plate will be used here to avoid confusion with the use of figure, which is a spatial pattern forming part of a dance.

Beauchamp-Feuillet Notation

Notators of the eighteenth century wrote with quill pens, and there are distinctive differences between the "hand" of one notator and another. The Beauchamp-Feuillet notation in this analysis has been drawn with a modern graphic tool—the rapidograph pen—chosen for its reliability and clarity. Notated dance figures from eighteenth-century sources are frequently introduced for technical purposes. When such material has been extracted it is boxed-in to indicate that it is an incomplete reproduction of the original.

Labanotation

The author's text, combined with the Beauchamp-Feuillet notation, is intended to be as self-sufficient as possible. The addition of Labanotation in Appendix 1 is for those already familiar with the Laban system. Numbers inserted into the text direct those concerned to the numbered examples in this Appendix. Each number is preceded by an L, for example, L10.

TERMINOLOGY

The technical terms employed are from the above-listed eighteenth-century sources. In establishing definitions, nineteenth-century ballet terminology has been avoided altogether. Although much of nineteenth-century terminology derived from the earlier period, meanings changed with changes in dance technique.

Eighteenth-century usage and spelling were far from standardized. (The same is true in music history and musical terms are here used sparingly.) To avoid entanglement in each author's idiosyncracies the terms used most frequently have been selected. Those quoted directly from the original sources are printed in italic type in the headings that follow; those terms supplied by the author appear in text type. Otherwise, original spellings have been modernized in the running text, and in the author's translations.

STRUCTURE OF THE ANALYSIS

The analysis may be divided into three sections. Following a survey of the components of the dance in Chapter Five, the first section continues as follows. The system of chorégraphie is explained in Chapters Six through Eight: Chapter Six, the notation of the leg and foot motions; Chapter Seven, the notation of arm motions; Chapter Eight, the notation of meter.

The second section comprises three chapters. In Chapter Nine, the information in the previous four chapters is combined in the study of the dance steps. Chapter Ten covers complex rhythmic situations, and Chapter Eleven, questions of tempi. In Chapter Twelve, the analysis concludes with matters of etiquette and ballroom procedure.

Although Chapters Six and Seven both deal with the limbs, each has a different approach. The symbols and signs representing motions of the lower limbs are somewhat self-explanatory, but those representing the arm motions are not. In Chapter Seven, therefore, it has been necessary to combine a full description of the arm motions with the explanation of the notation. While this enhances the stylistic picture of the dance, it might also push some students beyond their capabilities. The chapter is intended to be read for information but utilized only at the point a performing student feels ready to incorporate arm motions with the steps given in Chapter Nine.

CHAPTER FIVE

A Survey of the Components of the Dance

This chapter is designed to bring into perspective the most important principles of eighteenth-century dance in the noble style, and to define some of the terms most frequently employed to describe it. As with any school of dance, certain components are essential to its distinctiveness as an art form. They must be approached freshly, without preconceptions from other dance disciplines. The discussion in this chapter will give a rounded picture of eighteenth-century dance—its structure, style, and technique as defined by the dancing masters. Additional explanations and terms have been added by the author.

In the Survey, the components are grouped as follows: the carriage of the body; the step structure; the actions and paths of the limbs in space; and spatial and metric patterns. These sections should be reread from time to time as students progress through the succeeding chapters. For performing students, exercises to develop style and technique are given in Appendix ii. Study of these should begin after reading the Survey.

Feuillet and Rameau do not always provide concise definitions of technical terms. When they do, their explanations have been excerpted and printed opposite the author's analysis of their complete texts.

**BASIC DISPOSITION
OF THE BODY**

Both Rameau and Tomlinson begin their books with instructions on how to stand graciously and impressively when in company:

Before I proceed to treat on Motion, I apprehend it to be necessary to consider that Grace and Air so highly requisite in our Position, when we stand in Company; for, having formed a true Notion of this, there remains nothing farther to be observed, when we enter upon the Stage of Life, either in Walking or Dancing, than to preserve the same. *(Tom. p. 3)*

The Gentleman

A fashion plate by Bonnart. Late seventeenth century.
Bibliothèque Nationale, Paris.

The Head must be upright, without being stiff; the Shoulders falling back, which extends the Breast, and gives a greater Grace to the Body; the Arms hanging by the Side, the Hands neither quite open nor shut, the Waste steady, the Legs extended, and the Feet turned outwards. . .I hope after all these Precautions, no one will be so ridiculous to be stiff or formal, which ought to be avoided as much as Affectation; a just Carriage requiring nothing more than a natural, free, and easy Air, which is to be only gained by Dancing. *(Ram. 1 p. 2; Ess. p. 2)*

A Survey of the Components of the Dance

Madame de Sevigné. After a painting in the
Chateau de Bussy-Rabutin.

. . .I have made an Observation, which seems to me very just, on
the Manner of carrying the Head; which is, that a Woman, how
graceful soever she may be in her Deportment, may be differently judged of: For Example; if she holds it upright, and the
Body well disposed, without Affectation, or too much Boldness,
they say there goes a stately Lady; if she carries it negligently,
they accuse her of carelessness; if she pokes her Head forward, of
Indolence; and in short, if she stoops, of Thoughtlessness, or
want of Assurance. *(Ram. 1 p. 40; Ess. p. 23)*

BASIC DISPOSITION OF THE BODY WHEN DANCING

A Woman . . . in dancing . . . holds her Petticoats with her Thumb and Fore-finger, the Arms extended by the Side of the Body, the Hands turned outwards, without spreading the Petticoats out, or letting them fall in. *(Ram. 1 p. 103; Ess. p. 58)*

Plate: Tom. B.II. P.VI.

A Survey of the Components of the Dance

BASIC DISPOSITION
OF THE BODY
WHEN DANCING

Carriage

In dancing, the carriage of the torso and, for the most part, the head was that of everyday deportment, as illustrated on the previous pages. When the arms were at rest they were held easily by the sides, the woman's resting gently on her skirt, the man's held slightly away from his coat. (L1)

Women's fashion sometimes and in some places adopted extremes that affected their dance technique: notably height of heel and width of skirt. Men's dress remained more or less constant as far as maneuverability went, and the dance technique will be analyzed with their clothes and shoes in mind.

Turnout of
the Legs

In dancing, the legs were rotated outward from the hip joint to an angle of approximately forty-five degrees. Some illustrations in books on dancing and deportment imply a larger angle, but this is probably from lack of skill in drawing. (See almost all of Rameau's plates.) In social dancing, a greater degree of turnout would have been found inelegant. Professional dancers had long used a ninety-degree turnout when performing in the grotesque style. Professional dancers in the noble style emulated the nobility. Most significantly the notation symbols show the feet at forty-five degrees. (L2)

toe
heel

Left foot   Right foot

The Feet When
Bearing Weight

During the greater part of all dances the weight of the body was supported by the ball of one foot.

Pointe du Pied
Toe

The pointe referred to the ball of the foot when it alone supported the body (L3), and to the toe when it was placed on the ground without bearing weight. (When standing on the ball of the foot the exact degree of rise might be affected by the height of heel worn.) When on pointe, the instep was flexible, the ankle joint not locked or rigid.

Equilibre

. . .apporter le corps sur le pied droit en vous élevant sur la pointe du pied. . .ce que l'on peut appeler pour lors équilibre, parce que le corps n'est supporté que d'un seul pied. (Ram. 1 p. 74)

*Equilibrium
or Balance*

. . .rising upon the Toes of the right Foot. . .which. . .we may call the Equilibrium or Balance, because the Body is only supported by one Foot. (Ess. p. 42)

Equilibrium. From plate: Ram. 1 p. 74.

Pointing the toe on the floor.
From plate: Tom. B.I. P.XIV.

The foot in the air (a leg gesture).
From plate: Tom. B.I. P.XV.

A Survey of the Components of the Dance

| [Demi] pointe | In nineteenth-century ballet, standing on pointe referred to standing on the tips of the toes with the aid of blocked pointe shoes. Therefore, in order not to mislead dancers of today, [demi] pointe will be used in this text when the ball of the foot is bearing weight. When standing on [demi] pointe, the knees were straight, the thigh muscles pulled upward, the legs well braced. |

Equilibre
Equilibrium

The body supported on one foot only, on the [demi] pointe, with the upright carriage of the torso maintained.

The position shown opposite was passed through, not held, and the two stretched legs firmly established the center line of the body for purposes of aplomb. This position will be referred to by the author's term, position of equilibrium (pos. of eq.).
When the free leg is not close beside the other, heel beside heel as in the position of equilibrium, the term balance will be used in place of equilibrium.

The Feet When
Free of Weight

While pointing the toe upon the floor, making leg gestures (motions of the limb in space), or springing, the feet were held in certain relationships to the legs. In all leg gestures, except when the feet were in positions close together as explained below, the insteps were extended easily to continue the line of the leg. The toes would follow the line of the shoe and probably remain relaxed inside it. (L4, 5) (In some of Rameau's plates not specifically concerned with the feet, a leg gesture in an open position is drawn with the ankle apparently flexed, the foot pointing somewhat upward. Such an angular position is totally opposed to the prescribed ideals of baroque elegance and no instructions indicating its desirability were given.)

In positions with the feet close together and the body supported by one foot only, the foot of the gesturing leg is usually flexed. (L6,7)

STRUCTURE OF
THE DANCE STEPS

Positions

Positions, est ce qui marque tous les differens endroits où on peut poser les pieds en dançant. (Feu. 1 p. 2)

Positions

Positions, are the different Placings of the Feet in Dancing. (Wea. 1 p. 2)

Pas

Pas, est ce qui marche d'un lieu en un autre. (Feu. 1 p. 2)

Steps

Steps, are the Motions of the Feet from one place to another. (Wea. 1 p. 2)

Pas Simples

J'appelle Pas simple lorsqu'un Pas est seul. . .(Feu. 1 p. 46)

Simple Steps

A simple Step, is that which is alone. . .(Wea. 1 p. 44)

Pas Composez

Pas composez sont comme quand deux ou plusieurs sont joints ensemble, par une liaison, qui pour lors ne sont plus reputez que pour seul. . .(Feu. 1 p. 46)

Compound Steps

A compound Step, is, where two or more Steps are join'd together by a Line, and which then are to be reputed as one Step only. . .(Wea. 1 p. 44)

A Survey of the Components of the Dance

STRUCTURE OF
THE DANCE STEPS

Positions

There were five positions: two in which the feet were apart the length of the dancer's foot, and three in which the feet were together. Their purpose was to specify the direction and dimension of steps. To enable balance to be maintained most easily steps were carefully placed, their length proportionate to the dancer's height. (L8)

Pas
Steps

A step was the passage of the foot forward, backward, or sideward from one of the five positions to another, concluding with the full transference of weight to the moving foot.

Pas Simples
Simple Steps

Basically, dances were composed of groups of single steps. The first single step in each group was given an accent by an action of the knees and ankles known as a "movement."

Pas Marchés
Walking Steps

The so-called walking steps were the single steps within a group, unadorned by a "movement." They were usually made on [demi] pointe.

Pas Composez
Compound Steps

A composite step-unit consisted of more than a single step and sometimes more than one "movement." In most dance types one pas composé equalled one measure of music, the units ranging from two to four single steps. The first single step was combined with a "movement" to mark the first beat, almost always the strongest beat, in a measure of music.

Tems

A temps (this modern spelling will be used in the text) was a "movement" without a change of weight from one foot to the other, made to mark the "Time" or first beat in a measure.

A temps was also a step-unit beginning with a "movement" made without a change of weight, followed only by one single step and usually taking one measure of music to complete.

Contre-tems
Contretems

Although not defined by the masters, the term contretemps must have referred to a sprung "movement" without a change of weight, because pas composés which began with such a "movement" were named "contre-tems." A temps marks the "Time" on the rise, a contretemps marks the "Time" on the landing.

Step-unit

Step-unit is the author's term for pas composés and temps.

Step-pattern

The author's term for a combination of two or more step-units which do not form a complete "sentence."

Step-sequence

The author's term for a sequence of step-units which reaches a point of conclusion; a complete "sentence."

ACTIONS MADE
IN THE STEP-UNITS

Pliez

Plié, est quand on plie les genoux. (Feu. 1 p. 2)

Sinkings

Sinkings, are the Bendings of the Knees. (Wea. 1 p. 2)

From plate: Ram. 1 p. 216.

Elevez

Elevé, est quand on les étend. (Feu. 1 p. 2)

Risings

Risings, are when we rise from a Sink, or erect our selves. (Wea. 1 p. 2)

Mouvement
Movement

. . .one Sink and Rise, which is what we call a Movement. . .(Tom. p. 27)

Sauts

Sauté, est lorsqu'on s'éleve en l'air. (Feu. 1 p. 2)

Springings

Springing, is a rising or leaping from the Ground. (Wea. 1 p. 2)

Glissez

Glissé, est quand le pied en marchant glisse à terre. (Feu. 1 p. 2)

Slidings

Slidings, are when, in moving, the Foot slides on the Ground. (Wea. 1 p. 2)

Tombez

Tombé, est lorsque le corps est hors de son équilibre, & qu'il tombe par son propre poids. (Feu. 1 p. 2)

Fallings

Fallings, are when the Body, being out of its proper Poise, falls by its own Weight. (Wea. 1 p. 2)

ACTIONS MADE
IN THE STEP-UNITS

Pliez
Sinkings

The combination of bending and rising provided accents within the step-units. A sink was a bending usually of both knees, the feet in any of the five positions with the heel of the supporting leg, or legs, firmly on the ground. (L9)

Bend

The term bend, in more general use today, will be used in preference to "sink."

Elevez
Risings

A rise was a straightening of the knees following a bend. On completing the rise, the legs were braced, the thigh muscles pulled upward. It was extended whenever possible onto [demi] pointe with the insteps strong and flexible. (L10)

Mouvement
Movement

A "movement" was a bending of the knees followed by a rise, the rise being either a straightening of the knees (which could be extended by lifting the heels and standing on [demi] pointe), or a rise into the air in a spring. (L11) The "movements" created accents which usually coincided with the accented beats in the music. When they did not, it was for the purpose of producing a cross-rhythm between dance and music. A "movement" might or might not coincide with a change of weight.

"Movement"

The term "movement" is used solely in this sense throughout the analysis. Motion will be used for the more general sense of the word.

Sauts
Springings

A spring was a bending of the knees and a rise into the air. This could be done from and returning to one or both feet. When landing, the [demi] pointe touched the ground first, and the lowering of the heel, which continued into the ensuing bend, was controlled by strength in the instep. Most springs were primarily actions of the insteps and were evenly timed upward and downward. (It seems that when a series was being executed, the heels were not required to be fully lowered to the ground, the instep initiating the leverage.) Springs did not rise very high, especially when executed by ladies.

Glissez
Slidings

A slide denoted that a single step should be made with a slow sustained quality. The ball of the foot slid gently along the floor, without taking weight, on its way to one of the five positions where the weight was transferred.

Tombez
Fallings

In falling steps, the actions comprising a "movement" were reversed, the rise coming before the bend. The fall was brought about by a slight shift in the torso, resulting in apparent loss of balance which would only be regained during the single step following the fall.

Tournements	Tourné, est lorsqu'on tourne d'un côté ou d'un autre. (Feu. 1 p. 2)
Turnings	Turnings, are when the Body turns either one way or the other. (Wea. 1 p. 2)
Ouvertures de Jambes	L'Ouverture de jambe, est une action, que la jambe fait pour montrer l'agilité qu'il faut avoir en conservant le corps dans son équilibre, pendant qu'on se tient sur l'autre. . .(Ram. 1 p. 187)
Opening of the Leg	The Opening of the Leg is an Action which the Leg performs to shew the Agility requisite to keep the Body in its Equilibrium or Poize while one stands on the Other Leg. . . (Ess. p. 109)
Rond de Jambe	(Feu. 1 p. 54 in notated Table de Coupés)
Cabriolles	Cabriolle, est quand en sautant, les jambes battent l'une contre l'autre. (Feu. 1 p. 2)
Capers	Capers, are when in rising or leaping from the Ground, one Leg beats against the other, which we call Cutting. (Wea. 1 p. 2)

Tournements *Turnings*	There were two kinds of turn. One was made simply for the purpose of changing direction in space when stepping. The other, the pirouette, was made for its own sake. Court and theatrical dances contained pirouettes made on two feet, usually rotating only a quarter or half turn. But some theatrical dances, especially those for men, contained turns made on one foot, or during a spring into the air, usually completing one whole turn and sometimes two.
Tortillez *Wavings*	Wavings were inward and outward rotations of the leg from the hip, led by similar motions of the foot from the ankle. They were seldom, if ever, used in social dances, and neither Rameau nor Tomlinson described them.
Ouvertures *de Jambes* *Opening of* *the Leg*	The body was supported by one leg while the other, slightly raised, made a circular figure from the hip, opening from front to side. In social dances, this leg gesture stayed close to the ground. (L12)
Rond de Jambe	A circular action of the lower leg. Rarely, if ever, used in social dances.
Battements *Beats*	This term seems to have had two meanings: (1) A motion of the leg, or legs, made when standing or springing. (2) The contact of the legs brought about by this motion. The body was supported by one braced leg while the other, equally braced, opened and closed forward, backward, or sideward from the hip. (This use of the term could be likened to the beating of a bird's wing.) Small battements were made to move the leg around or against the supporting one in a rhythmic pattern. If the supporting leg bent, the beating leg bent also.
Cabriolles *Capers*	During a spring, the legs were held straight and beaten against each other by battements moving forward or backward from the hip. This action was usually used as an embellishment. Cabriolles were pas de ballet and the masters did not describe their performance in detail.

MOTIONS OF THE ARMS, SHOULDERS, AND HEAD

L'opposition
Opposition

From plate: Tom. B.I. P.XIII.

Elevation

From plate: Ram. 1 p. 188.

MOTIONS OF THE ARMS, SHOULDERS, AND HEAD

Arms

Motions of the arms paralleled those of the legs. The motion of the arm from the shoulder corresponded to the motion of the leg from the hip, the motion of the elbow to that of the knee, and of the wrist to that of the ankle.

Arm motions were also related to the disposition of the legs in space. Generally speaking:

Position of
Opposition

(1) The arms moved in a stylized opposition to the feet—the forward arm was opposite to the forward foot as is natural to preserve balance. This will be called the position of opposition [pos. of op.]

Position of
Elevation

(2) When the feet were side by side, the arms were elevated sideward. The hands were usually placed level with the pit of the stomach. This placement will be called the position of elevation [pos. of el.]

While there were one or two other specific placements, these were passed through rather than held.

Shoulder

A shading of the shoulder was often included when the arms moved in opposition: the shoulder of the "back" arm was drawn backward, bringing the other shoulder correspondingly forward in space.

Head

The head was sometimes rotated one eighth of a circle, inclined slightly, or both.

FIGURE
AND FORM

Figures

Figure, est de suivre un chemin tracé avec art. (Feu. 1 p. 2)

Figures

Figures, are Tracts made by Art, on which the Dancer is to move. (Wea. 1 p. 2)

Plate: Tom. B.I. P.XVI.

FIGURE
AND FORM

Spatial figures

The contour of dance figures was based on various combinations of circular and straight lines or paths. The essence of the use of space was symmetrical figuration. Dances were comprised of a number of varied figures, each of which usually equalled a musical reprise or strain.

Musical reprise or strain

A musical reprise or strain was a section of music, in dance music usually between four to sixteen measures in length, constituting a musical "sentence." (See Step-sequence p. 73)

Relationships of dance figures and musical strains

About sixty percent of dance music was in binary form, that is, having two strains. Each strain was played twice—AABB. Although the strains were repeated, the dance figures seldom were. Even when a figure and step-sequence was danced more than once, its spatial direction was almost always varied. For instance, a couple might progress up and down the room or stage for the initial performance, and across the room for the repeat. For choreographic purposes, a piece in binary form was often played twice. The two strains would be repeated both times, resulting in AABB, AABB. While some dance types usually had strains of uniform length, others did not, which produced considerable variety in the music of these types.

The rondeau (rondo) was a frequently used musical form for some dance types. In a rondeau there are several musical strains, the first of which keeps coming round again—for instance A B A C A B A. The thematic repetition notwithstanding, a dance figure was seldom repeated. A totally different musical structure used in certain dances was a kind of variation of considerable length, based upon a short ground bass or musical pattern A A' A''....

RHYTHM AND TIME

Cadences

Cadence, est la connoissance des differentes mesures, & des endtoits [endroits] qui marquent le plus dans les Airs. (Feu. 1 p. 2)

Cadence
or Time

Cadence or Time, is a right understanding of the different Measures, and Observation of the most remarkable places in the Tune. (Wea. 1 p. 2)

'Tis not enough that ev'ry Stander-by
No glaring Errors in your Steps can 'spy;
The Dance and Musick must so nicely meet,
Each Note must seem an Eccho to your Feet:
A nameless Grace must in each Movement dwell,
Which Words can ne'er express, nor Precepts tell; . . .
(*The Art of Dancing*, a Poem. Soame Jenyns, 1729, p. 32)

Cadance, qui fait l'ame de la danse. . .(Ram. 1 p. 96)

Cadence . . . is the very Soul of Dancing. (Ess. p. 54)

RHYTHM AND TIME

Cadence
or time

The term cadence covered the order and spirit of both the music and dance in a specific as well as a broad sense.

Basically, it meant knowing the meter of a piece (that is, the number of beats in each bar or measure), and being able to play and dance in time: for the musician this meant playing the music at a tempo (temps or speed) sympathetic to the dance and maintaining that speed throughout; for the dancer this meant keeping in time with the music.

Musicians made the meter clear by marking the strongest, most "remarkable" beats within a measure; dancers by defining the initial "movement" in each step-unit.

Vraye cadence
True cadence

In a measure with a ture cadence, the rhythmic stress provided by the initial "movement" in a step-unit was made on the first beat. The rhythmic stresses in dance and music therefore coincided. In the majority of dance types this was the basic relationship between step-unit and musical measure. For the dancer the rhythmic current between steps and music flowed sympathetically.

Fausse cadence
False cadence

In a measure with a false cadence, the rhythmic stresses in music and dance did not coincide. In dances structured this way throughout, a more intellectual grasp of the relationship of music and dance was required of the dancer.

Spirit

In its most profound sense the term cadence meant the spirit, the rhythmic flow which made music and dance alive, the nuances and subtleties of articulation, the dynamic textures of motions which created the mood of every piece.

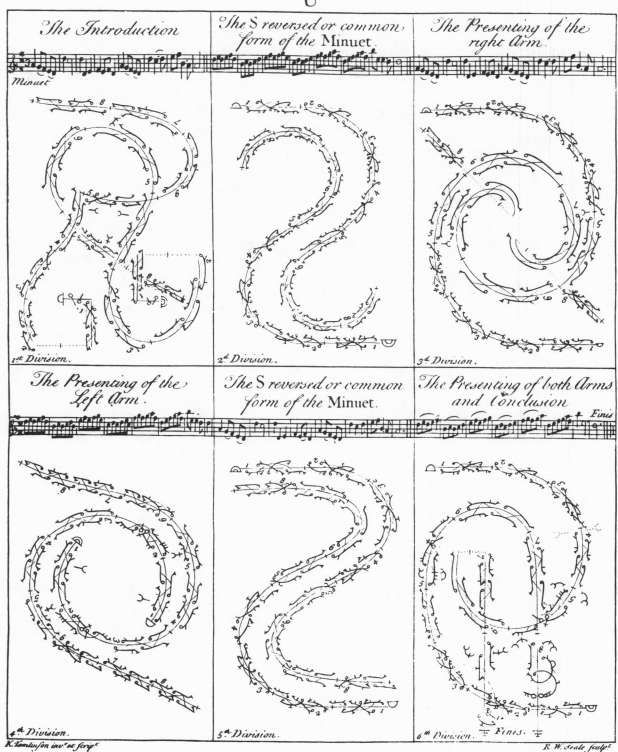

The minuet as notated by Kellom Tomlinson in *The Art of Dancing*.

CHAPTER SIX

The Beauchamp-Feuillet System of Chorégraphie
*The Representation of the Dancing Area, Spatial Figures,
the Music in Dance Scores, and Dancers*

DANCING AREA

*De la Salle ou Théâtre.
Of the Stage, Room, or School.
(Feu. 1 p. 3; Wea. 1 p. 3)*

In a baroque theater, the stage had more depth than width, and ideally the rooms in which dancing took place were also oblong. All ballroom dances were oriented toward the Presence—the person, or persons, of highest rank seated in the center at one end of the room.

In chorégraphie, each page represents one of these areas within which the figures and steps of the dance are drawn.

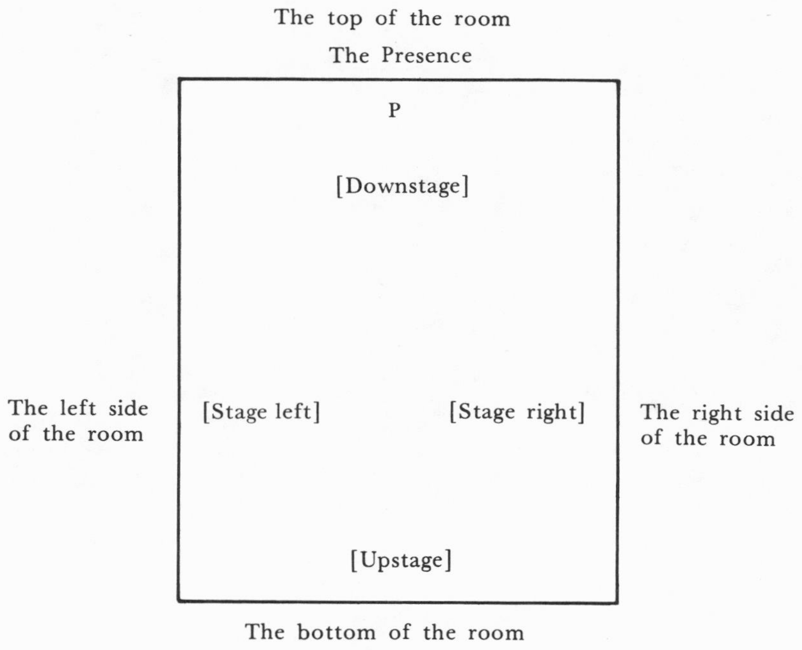

The top of the room

The Presence

P

[Downstage]

The left side
of the room

[Stage left]   [Stage right]

The right side
of the room

[Upstage]

The bottom of the room

The top of the page relates to the top of the room (downstage in the theater), the two sides to the sides of the room, and the bottom of the page to the bottom of the room, "where one places oneself in order to begin." *(Ram. 2 p. 2)*

A couple performing a *danse à deux* at a ball given in the *petit Parc* of Versailles during the latter part of the seventeenth century. See also the illustration in Chapter 12, p. 282. Dance Collection, New York Public Library.

But not all rooms were of an ideal shape, a point stressed by Tomlinson:

First then, you are to observe, that the Shape and Figure of Rooms differ exceedingly; for some are of a direct Square, others not square but oblong or longish, namely, when the two Sides are somewhat longer than the Top or Bottom, and various others that, in Reality, are of no Form at all; which renders Dancing extremely difficult and confused to those, who have not a just and true Idea of the Room, in its different Situations; because, if this be wanting, altho' they may perform very handsomely, at their own Houses, or in School with a Master, yet, in Assemblies or Rooms Abroad, they are as much disordered and at a Stand, as if in an Uninhabited Island. *(Tom. p. 18)*

However, direction of focus had to be chosen whatever the shape of the room, but "this is subservient to, and depends upon the Company, who must always be seated at the Presence or Upper End." *(Tom. p. 19)*

All ballroom, and most theatrical dances begin by moving in a straight line forward toward the Presence. A solo dancer stands on the center line of the room or stage; two persons must have the center line between them. Dances finish by moving down the room (or upstage) and end facing the Presence. Tomlinson has some further words of warning:

Dancers must have a particular Regard to the Presence and Bottom of the Room, where they begun, otherwise it is no Wonder that those, who are of a timorous and bashfull Nature, with the Fears of being out together with the various Turnings and Windings of some Dances, should be perplex'd and nonpluss'd; and this I have perceived to be the Case, when I have seen a Minuet begun at the Bottom of the Room, and ended at the Upper End. *(Tom. p. 20)*

In losing sight of the front, the dancers would find themselves not only finishing at the wrong end of the room, but with their backs to the Presence, an embarrassing breach of etiquette. Actually this is a common mishap even with experienced dancers. In the menuet, partners take hands and circle around looking at each other. The amount of circling is decided by the gentleman who, while regarding his lady, may only too easily lose sight of his situation in the room.

SPATIAL FIGURES

De la Figure.
Of the Figure.
(Feu. 1 p. 92; Wea. 1 p. 51)

Two types of figures are used in dancing:
Figure regulière. A regular figure. The dancers move symmetrically, making the same figure in opposing directions.

Figure irregulière. An irregular figure. The dancers make the same figure in the same direction.

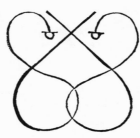 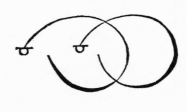

A regular figure   An irregular figure

Du Chemin.
Of the Tract.
(Feu. 1 p. 4; Wea. 1 p. 4)

Figures are described by geometric lines which form the tract. The tract shows the path, the line of travel of the dance. The lines which form the tract are:
Ligne droit. A right line. A straight line up or down the dancing area.
Ligne diamétrale. A diametrical line. A line from side to side.
Ligne oblique. An oblique line. A line from corner to corner.
Ligne circulaire. A circular line. A line making a curved path about the dancing area. Also *Ronde. A circle.* Feuillet does not separate this from a circular line, but Rameau does. *(Ram. 2 pl. 1)*

The geometric lines as combined by Feuillet.

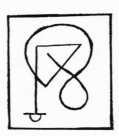

Start reading from the sign ⏝ which represents a dancer as explained on p. 94.

Ligne ponctuée. A pointed line. A dotted line, used when the forth-coming steps have to retrace the path just covered. *(Feu. 1 p. 42; Wea. 1 p. 40)*

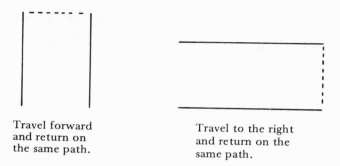

Travel forward
and return on
the same path.

Travel to the right
and return on the
same path.

A dotted line is also used when more than one dancer covers the same ground within a figure. This often causes a simple figure to appear alarmingly complex:

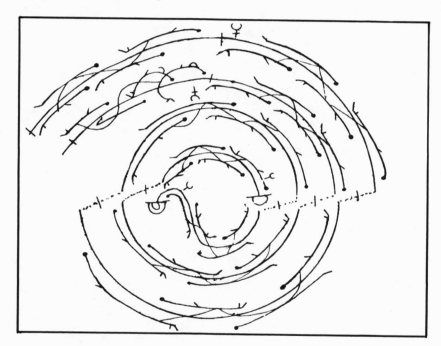

Part of a figure for two dancers from "Le Passepied" by Pécour. *Recueil de dances composées par M. Pécour.* Feuillet, Paris, 1700.

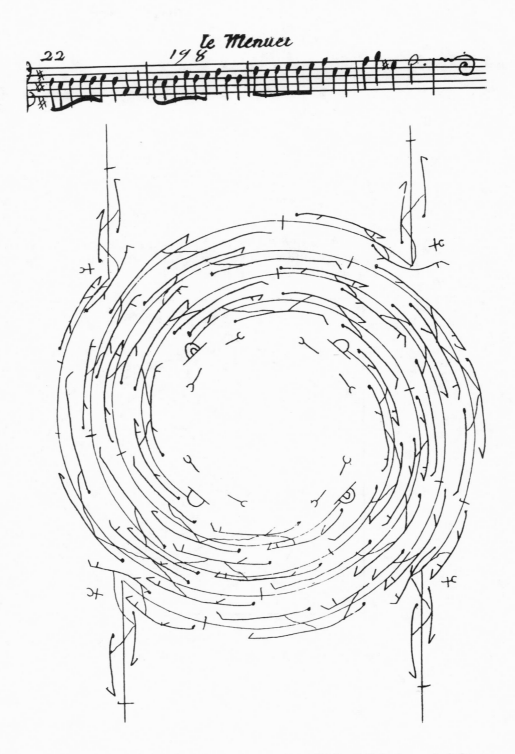

A figure from "Le Menuet à quatre." Anon. $V.^{me}$ *Recüeil de danses de bal pour l'année 1707.* Feuillet, Paris, 1706, p. 22.

The figure opposite is also misleading visually. The simple pattern it represents is that of four dancers holding hands, all making one circle on the same circumference.

In this situation there is no need for a dotted line:

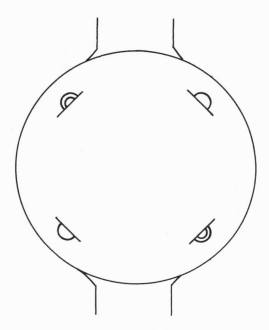

Here one dancer makes four circles, each of equal circumference. The tract must be drawn wider to show each circle, but the dotted lines joining them signify that the same ground is covered:

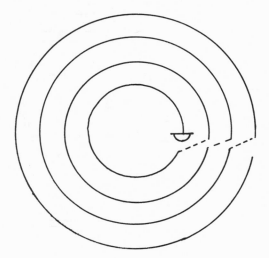

MUSICAL STAFF
IN DANCE SCORES

The music for each figure is placed at the top of the page and the tract is barred correspondingly:

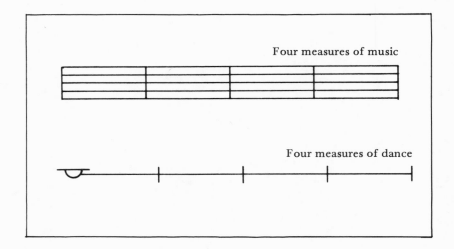

Four measures of music

Four measures of dance

If a dotted line is used in the tract, the bar line is placed along it.

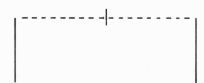

A double bar line denotes the conclusion of a musical strain. When dots are placed within those lines, the strain should be repeated:[1]

Play the strain once   Play the strain twice

Another sign which denotes a repeat is & .   This sign is usually used only when a group of measures is to be repeated from a point not indicated by a double bar line. For instance:

Play the strain through twice, then play the last four measures again

The Beauchamp-Feuillet System of Chorégraphie

French Violin Clef

In the first example above, the treble clef, which indicates the placement of the note G, encircles the second line of the five-line musical staff. In the second example, the clef places the G line at the bottom of the staff.

The airs in the French dance scores use the latter method, known as the French Violin Clef. Putting G on the bottom line of the staff facilitated the notation of music for the violin, permitting more notes in its range to fall within the staff. For instance:

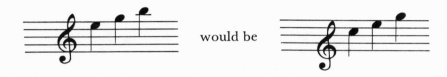

would be

Use of Sharps

Sharps are given twice if they lie within the staff. For instance, in the second example below there are two F sharps, one C sharp, and two G sharps, as opposed to current use shown in the first example.

Use of Flats

In dance music, keys involving more than two flats are rarely used. In the key of F major, signed only with B-flat, the sign is placed at the beginning of the staff. In the key of B-flat major which has two flats, B-flat and E-flat, the E-flat sign is not placed at the beginning of the staff but is interpolated at each occurrence.

REPRESENTATION
OF DANCERS

De la Présence du Corps.
The Presence of the Body.
(Feu. 1 p. 3; Wea. 1 p. 3)

The Posture or Presence of the Body, is to have respect to that part of the Room, to which the Face or Fore-part of the Body is directed. *(Feu. 1 p. 3; Wea. 1 p. 3)*

The sign for a man is ‿ . The sign for a woman ‿ has two half circles.[2] The line across the half circle represents the face or front of the body. The half circle describes the back and two sides.

These signs are usually placed only at the beginning of the tract on each page:

Forward	Backward
A man and woman ready to move forward up the room.	A man and woman ready to move backward down the room.

Sideward	Forward
The man ready to move to his left and the woman to her right.	The man ready to move forward to the left side of the room, the woman to the right side.

The woman normally stands to the right side of the man. In theatrical dances with two men or two women dancing together, a point (dot) is added to the sign on the woman's side:

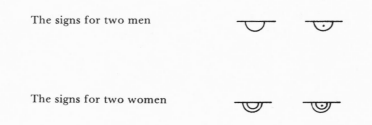

The signs for two men

The signs for two women

To identify a larger number of dancers, letters are added, those who figure together having the same letter:

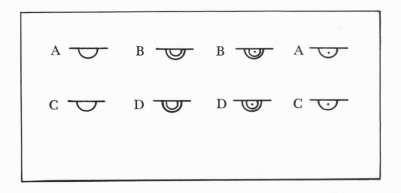

Here the men will figure together and the women will figure together. In his diagram illustrating this point, Feuillet gives the beginning of a tract for each of the above dancers: *(Feu. 1 p. 94; Wea. 1 p. 53)*

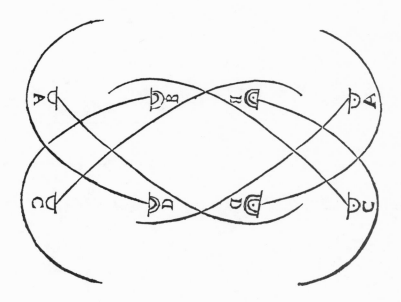

In a complex figure involving several dancers the letters and the dots may be repeated at the ends of the tracts, as in the example which follows:

Balet

à huit

A figure from "Balet de neuf Danseurs" by Feuillet. *Recueil de dances composées par M. Feuillet.* Paris, 1700.

Here, eight dancers are moving.

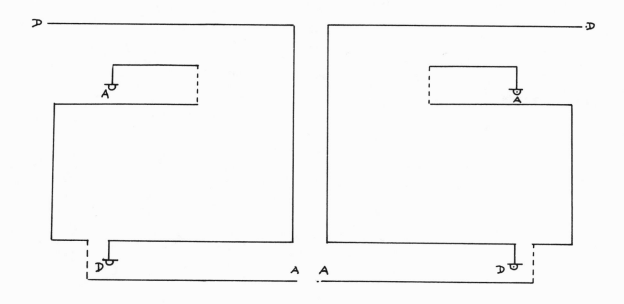

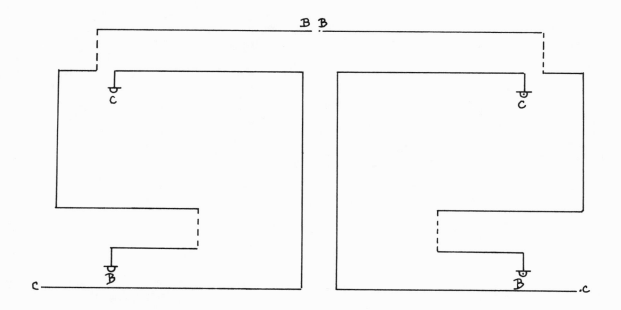

The tract of the figure opposite. This also serves to illustrate the initial stage of notating a dance. The tract was completed first and the steps added afterward.

THE SYMBOLS:
FOOT POSITIONS
AND STEPS

Foot Position Symbol

Des Positions.
Of the [Foot] Positions.
(Feu. 1 p. 6; Wea. 1 p. 6)

The symbols used in describing the dance steps are drawn alongside the tract, and are of two kinds: position symbols, which represent positions of the feet in relationship to each other; and step symbols, which show the motions of the legs from one of these positions to another, and the transference of weight from foot to foot.

The five positions of the feet were systematized by Pierre Beauchamp to "give a proportionate measure to the steps be it forward, backward or to the side; crossed in front or behind." *(Ram. 2 p. 5)* The feet are represented turned outward showing the degree of turnout used in dancing. The foot is symbolized in the following way:[3]

La pointe. The toe . . . . . .
La cheville. The ankle . . . . .
Le talon. The heel. . . . .

This diagram is not represented identically by Weaver who draws the dotted lines equidistant.

The white circle is the head of the symbol and represents the heel. The beginning of the line leaving the circle is the ankle, and the end of the line, the toe, or point of the foot.

Positions entières. Positions. (Whole). In whole positions both feet are shown:

Outside   Inside   Outside
                 of the foot

Demy position. A half position. Only one foot is shown. For instance:

The right foot

Des bonnes positions. Of true positions. The feet are uniformly placed and the legs equally turned outward. There are five true positions.

Des fausses positions. Of false positions. Both legs are turned inward, or placed parallel. The five false positions are not used in the noble style.

The five true positions of the feet are:

La première position. The first position. The feet are joined together, the heels touching. (L13)

La deuxième position. The second position. The feet are open on a diametrical line, "both Legs asunder, which ought not to be at a greater Distance than the Length of the Foot. . . ." *(Ess. p. 8)* (L14)

La troisième position. The third position. The heel of one foot touches the ankle (instep) of the other. This position is call Emboëture *(Ram. 1 p. 15)*, Emboëté *(Feu. 1 p. 7)*, Inclos'd *(Wea. 1 p. 7)*. (L15)

La quatrième position. The fourth position. The feet are placed one in front of the other, crossed as in third position but with the heels one foot length apart. (L16)

La cinquième position. The fifth position. The feet are crossed so that the heel of one is just in front of the toe of the other. In this illustration the right foot is in front, the left behind. (L17)

The last three positions can be done with either foot in front.

Quite frequently a foot position is used with the weight of the body supported by one foot only, the other foot raised slightly from the floor. These will be referred to as a given position "in the air," or if more descriptive in context, "off the floor."

Measuring of Steps

In the theory of the dance, each single step begins or finishes in first position, moving either to or from second, fourth, or fifth position. (Third position is only used for one or two special purposes or as a substitute for fifth position.)

Each step measured from heel to heel, should be no longer than the length of the dancer's foot, thereby keeping it proportionate to his height so that balance is most easily maintained.[4]

A step from first position to:

1st   2nd   4th   5th

A Step in Chorégraphie

A step symbol of normal size represents the length of two measured steps as given above, because in chorégraphie:

 A step forward or backward is from 4th pos. to 4th pos., passing 1st pos. halfway through (one length to 1st, one to 4th);

a step sideward is made from 2nd pos. to 5th pos., or the reverse, passing 1st pos. halfway through;

in a step from 4th pos. to 2nd or 5th pos., or the reverse, it is understood that the foot passes through 1st pos.

Fourth to 2nd pos.   Fourth to 5th pos.

In fact, the foot always passes through first position midway through a step unless otherwise indicated.

A step symbol therefore represents the passage of the foot forward, backward, or sideward from the starting position to the new position, and the completed transference of weight onto that foot.

STEP SYMBOL

The foot positions and the step symbols are not proportionate to one another.

A step forward with the right foot

(M)

The black pin marked A at the beginning of the symbol is known as the head. The line drawn from the black pin shows "the Motion, Figure and Largeness of the Step, as from A to D." *(Feu. 1 p. 9; Wea. 1 p. 9)* The letter B (M) shows the middle of the step, the significance of which is best expressed by Rameau.[5] The angled line at the end of the symbol is equivalent to a foot position symbol. D marks the heel, C the ankle, and E the toe. The line shows the foot in the finishing position after the motion of the leg.

Before any initial step, a starting position is shown by foot position symbols. In the first example below, the dot signifies that the stepping foot bears no weight. Only the toe touches the floor: (This will be explained on p. 112.)

A step forward from 4th to 4th pos. The step symbol represents the length of two measured steps. (L18)

A step forward from 1st to 4th pos. This step symbol represents the length of one measured step. (L19)

The distance traveled is the same in both instances but in the first example the leg has twice as far to go.

Although a step length should be proportioned according to height, the amount of ground to be covered in a dance figure sometimes dictates the length of step. Upon occasion a long step symbol is used to indicate unusually long steps. More often than not, however, normal-size step symbols are used (L20), it being left to the reader's intelligence to adapt the size of the steps to the requirements of the figure. Also, when dancing with a lady, the gentleman must adapt the length of his steps to hers.

Note the angle for the foot in the following examples:

Backward steps

Steps for
the left foot

Steps for
the right foot

Sideward steps

crossed [6]

open

to the right

2nd to 5th

5th to 2nd

open

crossed

to the left

5th to 2nd

2nd to 5th

PLACING SYMBOLS ALONG THE TRACT

In forward and backward steps, the symbols are drawn on each side of the tract, the right foot to the right and the left foot to the left. In sideward steps, the symbols are placed above and below the tract, the front foot above and the back foot below.

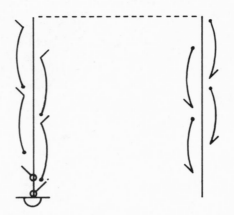

A man standing in 4th pos. Four steps forward followed by four backward.[7] (L21)

Series of Steps

In a series of steps, the symbols overlap by one half, since first position is passed midway through a step forward, backward, or to the side: (L22)

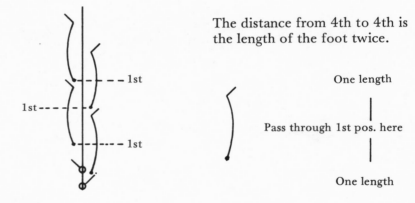

The distance from 4th to 4th is the length of the foot twice.

One length

Pass through 1st pos. here

One length

In sideward steps, this theory results in a very misleading visual image. In the example below, the left foot (above the tract) appears to move far beyond the right foot. In fact, it moves only as far as fifth position: (L23)

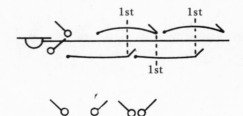

The distance from 2nd to 5th is also the length of the foot twice.[8]

One length from 2nd to 1st   One length from 1st to 5th

In a series of sideward steps not all will be placed directly to the side. To maintain a straight path, some open steps must be placed just in front of, or behind, the line of travel. Only when the front/back relationship of the feet is to be changed is the open step placed in an exact second position:

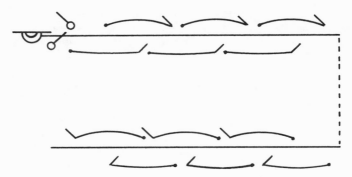

Begin in 5th, the L ft. in front, the R behind. This relationship will be maintained throughout. The R ft. steps to 2nd and the L to 5th and so on, until the R ft. steps to 5th, through 1st, to begin the return journey.

When the front/back relationship of the feet is changed during sideward steps, the step symbols must cross the tract:

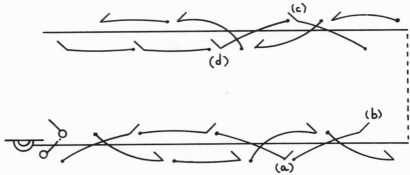

The R ft. steps to an exact 2nd, but as the L has to move to 5th behind, the R crosses the tract to become the front foot. During the next two steps this relationship is kept. In the remaining steps, those which should be placed in an exact 2nd pos. are marked (a) to (d). The sequence finishes with the weight on the L ft. (L24)

A sideward step is occasionally shown by an angled step symbol that finishes level with the previous one: (Note in the second example below that a step to fifth position is shown by the foot portion of the step symbol placed across the tract.) *(Feu. 1 p. 43; Wea. 1 p. 42)*

Step to 4th then 2nd (L25)   Step to 5th then 2nd   (L26)

Stepping Sideward on a Forward Tract

A short series of steps from side to side can be written on a vertical line. Remember that the L ft. moves to 1st before stepping to 2nd pos.: (L27)

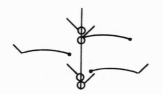

This sequence does not move forward. It ends in the place in which it began.

Du Pas Simple et du Pas Composé. Of Simple and Compound Steps. (Feu. 1 p. 46; Wea. 1 p. 44)

A simple Step, is that which is alone. . . and a compound Step, is, where two or more Steps are join'd together by a Line, and which then are to be reputed as one Step only. *(Feu. 1 p. 46; Wea. 1 p. 44)*

Composite step-units (pas composés) usually equal one measure of the music and are placed between the bar lines upon the tract. They embody two to four single steps. A line of "liaison" is drawn from the center of one step symbol to the next within the group, which forms them into a single unit:

Two single steps   Three steps   Four steps

Below is the opening figure of Pécour's ballroom dance, "La Bourré d'Achille", the first dance which students should study on completion of the present text.

Observe the number of single steps in each of the eight measures. In measures 1-2, and 5-6, there are three single steps; in measures 3 and 7, two single steps. The single steps in each group are linked by a line of liaison. While the above measures all contain a pas composé, measures 4 and 8 contain only one single step. This single step and the actions which accompany it comprise a temps.

la Bourée d'Achille.

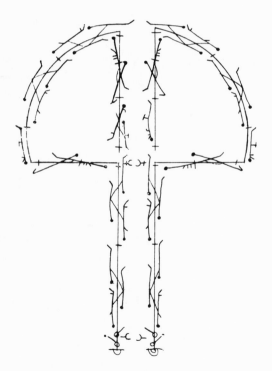

Recueil de dances composées par M. Pécour. Feuillet, Paris, 1700.

A step is shown terminating in a foot position when it is not to include full transference of weight but is to finish with the body supported equally on both feet in any of the five positions. The dancer does not travel.

Steps ending on both feet:

To 1st pos. (L28)

Sometimes notated thus

To 2nd from 5th behind (L29)

To 3rd behind from 4th in front (L30)

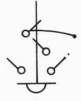

To 4th in front from 4th behind (L31)

To 5th in front from 2nd (L32)

Note that step symbols representing steps to first or third position culminate in foot position symbols regardless of whether the weight is fully transferred or held on both feet. The context will usually show which is intended. (The alternative notation of the step to first position, ending with a line for the foot, is seldom used and has the same meaning as the first example above.)

When two steps finish in a position, the notated position refers to the second step, not the first:

The R ft. steps forward
to 4th and then the L
closes to 1st. (L33)

Step forward to 4th (R and
L) then close the R ft.
to 1st. (L34)

When step-units finish in first position, it is quite usual for the following unit to begin from both feet, as in a spring off both feet, or for the next single step to be made with the foot that closed.

In both the following examples, the third position relates to the second single step, not to the first step:

The R ft. steps backward
to 4th and the L encloses
in 3rd behind. (L35)

Step forward to 4th, to
3rd, to 4th. (L36)

The Beauchamp-Feuillet System of Chorégraphie

Du Pas
Of Steps.
(Feu. 1 p. 9; Wea. 1 p. 9)

Steps in dancing can be reduced to five kinds:

Un pas droit. A straight step. The leg, moved from the hip, progresses in a straight line forward or backward. (See also the sideward step below.) These symbols are usually curved:

Forward (L37)　　　　　　　　　Backward (L38)

Un pas ouvert. An open step. The leg, moved from the hip, makes an arc or half circle outward or inward:

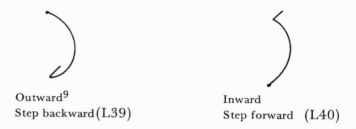

Outward[9]　　　　　　　　　　Inward
Step backward (L39)　　　　　　Step forward　(L40)

A step to the side with the leg opening directly to second position is called open or straight:

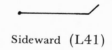

Sideward　(L41)

Un pas ronde. A round or circular step. Moved from the knee as well as from the hip, the lower part of the leg traces an outward or inward circular figure. These steps are seldom found in social dances:

Outward　　　　　　　　　　　Inward

Un pas tortillé. A waving step. Moved from the ankle as well as from the hip, the foot turns inward and outward a given number of times during the step. These steps are only found in theatrical dances:

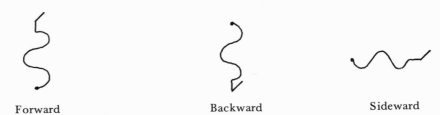

Forward   Backward   Sideward

Un pas battu. A beaten step. Moved from the hip and knee, or just from the hip. With both knees bent or straight, the beat is made by a part of the stepping foot hitting against a part of the supporting foot. The following symbols are not self-sufficient. Pas battu will be explained on p. 128:

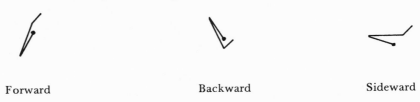

Forward   Backward   Sideward

USE OF SIGNS ON THE SYMBOLS

Signs representing the various actions the legs and feet may make in dancing are added to the symbols.

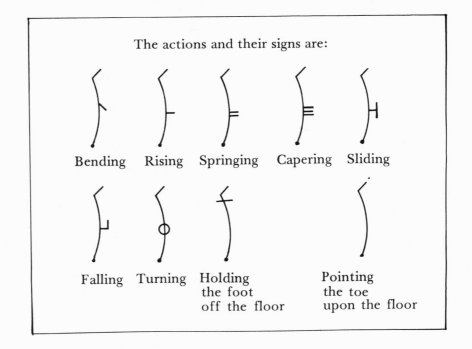

The actions and their signs are:

Bending   Rising   Springing   Capering   Sliding

Falling   Turning   Holding the foot off the floor   Pointing the toe upon the floor

PLACING THE SIGNS
ON STEP SYMBOLS

*Pour Poser les Signes en
Leurs Lieux et Places.
How to Place the Marks
in their Proper Order.
(Feu. 1 p. 13; Wea. 1 p. 14)*

For the purpose of placing the signs, the step symbols are divided into three sections. The placement of the signs within these sections indicates the relationship of action to step:

(1) The action takes place before stepping; that is before the stepping leg leaves the starting position.

(2) While stepping; that is while the leg is moving from the starting to the finishing position.

(3) After stepping; that is when the stepping leg has ceased to move, having reached the finishing position.

Because the step symbol represents the moving leg, signs placed within the first two sections of the symbol represent actions to be made with the body supported by the other leg.

Bending and rising signs refer to both legs although only one leg is notated:

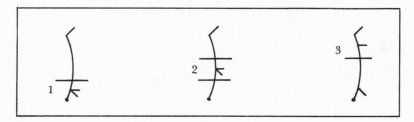

In the above examples the right leg, the moving leg, is symbolized with bending and rising signs. Only with the rise in the third example is the right leg the supporting leg, the weight of the body being then transferred to it. In all three examples, both legs will perform the actions of bending and rising (straightening the knees). The convention of a bending and a rising sign applying to both legs, although only one leg is shown, must constantly be borne in mind. The convention also applies to the springing, or rising into the air, sign.

PLACING THE SIGNS ON
FOOT POSITION SYMBOLS

*Comme les Positions
Peuvent avoir aussi les
mêmes Signes que les Pas.
Of Marking the Positions.
(Feu. 1 p. 21; Wea. 1 p. 23)*

All the signs can be used on foot position symbols except those for sliding and falling, actions made while the foot moves from one position to another. When more than one sign is on a position symbol, the one nearest the heel (o) must be read first.

SIGNS FOR THE
FOOT-OFF-THE-FLOOR
AND POINTING-THE-TOE

On the Step Symbols

Le Pied en l'Air.
The Foot Up.
(Feu. 1 p. 12; Wea. 1 p. 12)

To show that the foot is not to be placed on the floor but held low in the air, a line is drawn across the step symbol. This sign can be placed at the middle or at the end of a symbol:

When the line is at the end of the symbol, the foot must remain off the floor. (L42)

A line across the middle of the symbol is used when a particular action is in progress on the other (the supporting) foot. The action completed, the weight will be transferred onto the foot shown. (L43)

The foot-in-the-air will also be referred to as the foot-off-the-floor. (See Pl. 3 p. 70.)

Poser la Pointe du Pied
sans que le Corps y soit
Porté.
To Point the Foot.
(Feu. 1 p. 12; Wea. 1 p. 12)

A dot is put beyond the toe indicating that it alone should be placed on the floor. In an open position, the tip of the toe touches; in a closed position, the ball of the foot. The weight remains entirely on the other foot.[10]

The L ft. steps to 4th. The R "steps" to 4th but only the toe touches. (L44)

Here the R ft. remains off the floor. (L45)

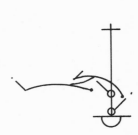

The R ft. steps to 5th. The L "steps" to 2nd but only the toe touches. (L46)

The Same Signs on the
Foot Position Symbols

The feet in 5th, the R raised off
the floor. (Usually used when both
knees are bent.) (L47)

Fourth position. (L48)

The feet in 4th, the weight supported on the front foot, the other
behind, on the toe. This is the starting position for almost all
dances. (L49)

SIGNS FOR BENDING
AND RISING

On the Step Symbols

As previously stated, all signs for bending and rising placed
upon the step symbols indicate that both legs, not just the one
shown, make these actions. Exceptions to this rule will be explained on p.115. Unless a specific gesture such as a circular step
(see p.118) is given for the stepping leg, all bends and rises occur
in first position.

Pas Plié.
A Sink.
(Feu. 1 p. 11; Wea. 1 p. 11)

The sign for bending is a short stroke inclining toward the head of the step symbol. It can be used in
any of the three sections of the step. The sign does
not show a specific degree of bend. (See p. 74.)

Bending before the step. The bend takes place before the foot
moves from the starting position:

*Plié avant
de marcher.
Sink before the
foot moves. (Feu. 1
p. 14; Wea. 1 p. 15)*

The starting position is 1st,
the body supported by the L ft.
Bend both knees and then move
the R ft. forward. (The knees
will stretch as the weight is
transferred.) (L50)

Rameau emphasizes the fact
that the bend is made before
the foot moves by placing a foot-
in-the-air sign after the bending
sign. Bend and then release the
foot from the floor and move it
forward. (L50)

Plié en marchant.
A sink in moving.

Bending during the step. The bend takes place while the stepping leg is moving. When the starting position is second, fourth, or fifth, the bend occurs as the stepping foot reaches first position midway through the step. In order to reach its full depth by this point, the bend must begin as the stepping foot moves. The bending sign is usually attached to the step symbol at the very beginning of the during-the-step section: (See p. 110.)

 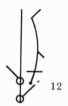

Release the R ft. from the floor, carry it to 1st pos. bending both knees, then step forward to 4th. (L51)

Plié après avoir marché. A sink after movement [moving].

Bending after the step. The bend takes place after the stepping foot has traveled to the finishing position, either during or after the transference of weight. A bending sign is seldom used at the end of a step symbol. When it is, the leg which has just been stepped "off," now free of weight, remains in the open position in order to execute the action indicated on the following symbol:

Step forward to 4th with the L, step forward to 4th with the R and bend. The L leg bends also, remaining in 4th pos. behind. The weight will be on both feet. (Some exceptions, where the leg is held in 4th pos. in-the-air with the knee stretched, will be found in the step-units.) (L52)

Pas Elevé.[13]
A Rise.
(Feu. 1 p. 11; Wea. 1 p. 11)

The sign for rising is a short, straight stroke which can be placed at the beginning, middle, or end of a step symbol.

A rise straightens the knees after a bend; these two actions are virtually inseparable. The combination of bend and rise was known as a "movement" which, in straight steps, usually finishes in the position of equilibrium. (*Ram. 1 p. 74.* See p. 70.) A rise should be extended whenever possible onto [demi] pointe. This could be clearly indicated by placing a dot beside the rising sign. (A dot beside every rising sign on a page produces a very startling result and perhaps for this reason it was seldom used.) Rising onto [demi] pointe is confusingly described by Rameau as "raising the toe".

Plié et élevé avant de marcher. Sink and rise before the foot moves. (Feu. 1 p. 14; Wea. 1 p. 16)

A "movement" before the step. In the following diagram, the dotted line is the author's:

Position of
equilibrium
(pos. of eq.)   First position

The starting position is 1st, the body supported on the L ft. Bend, then rise in equilibrium on [demi] pointe on the L, stretching both knees. Afterward, step forward on the R ft. (L53)

Plié et élevé en marchant. Sink and rise in moving.

A "movement" made during the step. Bend and rise in first position halfway through the step. The bend starts as the foot moves: (L54)

Pos. of eq.   First position

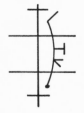

When more than one sign is placed in the middle section of a step symbol, the bending and rising signs are drawn first.

Elevé après avoir marché. Sink in moving, rise after the movement.

A "movement" when the rise is at the end of the step. The "movement" is begun with the weight on one leg and finished during its transference to the other: (L55)

A bend "during the step" and a rise "after the step." Stand in 4th, carry the stepping leg to 1st, bending both knees. Continue to 4th with the knees still bent, then transfer the weight to the R ft., simultaneously stretching both knees. The other foot usually comes to the pos. of eq.; this motion is shown by the next step symbol, as in the next example.

The Beauchamp-Feuillet System of Chorégraphie

The preceding example is an instance of the notation not providing all the necessary information. Many step-units begin with this step and "movement," performed with the following additional details: (L56)

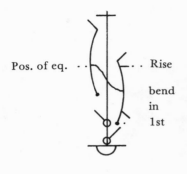

Pos. of eq. · · Rise

bend
in
1st

When the stepping foot reaches the finishing position, the ball of the foot should be put on the ground, the heel slightly raised, the knees still bent. (See p. 68.) Then simultaneously transfer the weight and stretch the knees. Generally, the next step brings the other foot through the pos. of eq. (It is important to read the symbols with continuity.)

After a rise, any plain steps which follow will be made at that level, the heel lowering at the end of the step-unit. (L57)

A combination of two "movements"

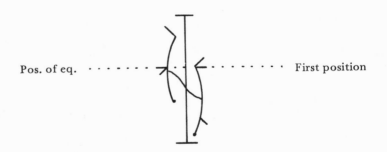

Pos. of eq. · · · · · · · · · · · · · First position

Perform the first step as in the previous examples until the pos. of eq. is reached. Then execute the bend and rise onto [demi] pointe written on the second step symbol. (L58)

Exception to the Rule That Bending and Rising Signs upon Step Symbols Apply to Both Legs

When only one leg should bend and stretch, a half position is used to depict the supporting foot. Its head is joined to the head of the step symbol by a line to show that they occur simultaneously:

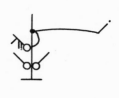

The L remains straight, the R bends and then straightens as it returns to 2nd pos. where the toe touches the floor. (L59)

Bend and rise on the L as the R, remaining straight, moves to 2nd pos. (L60)

Signs for Bending and Rising on the Position Symbols

When placed upon half positions, the signs refer to the given leg only, unlike their use on a step symbol where they apply to both legs, even though only one is shown:

Bend and rise on the L leg

Bend and rise on both legs

SIGNS FOR SLIDING AND FALLING

Pas Glissé.
A Slide.
(Feu. 1 p. 11; Wea. 1 p. 12)

These signs are placed only on the step symbols since they are actions made while the foot is moving.

The sign for sliding is a straight stroke with another perpendicular at its extremity. It is placed in the middle of the step symbol denoting that the ball of the foot slides gently along the floor. The foot bears no weight during a slide.

Starting in 4th, bend and rise in 1st; slide the R toward 4th (the ball of the foot barely on the floor), then put the weight onto it. (L61)

Standing on the L ft., bring the R to 1st and slide it to 4th "pointing the toe." The weight is retained on the L ft. throughout. (L62)

Slide the L ft. as above on the second step. (L63)

Do not transfer the weight after the slide. (L63)

Pas Tombé.
A Falling Step.
(Feu. 1 p. 11; Wea. 1 p. 12)

 The sign for falling is a straight stroke joined at right angles with another, pointing toward the foot upon which the weight will "fall." It is used in the middle of the step symbol.

In a fall, the knees bend with a suggestion of collapse. The fall is brought about by a slight shift of the torso from the support of one foot on [demi] pointe, producing an impression of lost balance. In a falling step the "movement" is reversed, the rise preceding the bend. In this case, the rise sign is placed at the beginning of the step symbol, although in practice this is often taken as understood.

The following example is for theory only:

Take an open step to 2nd with the R, both legs braced. Rise on the R to [demi] pointe, the body on balance. Moving the torso rightward, draw the L ft. toward 5th behind and "fall" onto it. The body will only fully recover balance on an ensuing step.

USE OF THE DOT (POINT)

The foot can have contact with the floor when supporting the body or when placed or moving without bearing weight. The sole of the foot may be touching the floor, or just the toe, or the heel. These parts of the foot can be indicated by a dot placed appropriately beside the symbols and signs.

Some of Feuillet's examples fail to make his intentions quite clear. Only the two uses of the dot already explained, and one other, given below, are used frequently:

 Positions of the feet with the weight on one foot, the toe of the other touching the floor.

 Steps finishing with the toe placed on the floor.

 Rise onto [demi]pointe on both feet.

TURNING

De la Manière
que l'on Doit Tenir
le Livre pour
Déchiffrer Dances qui
sont Ecrites.
How to Hold the Book
or Paper, to Decipher
Written Dances.
(Feu. 1 p. 33; Wea. 1 p. 33)

When turning steps are read, the relationship of the book to the dancing area must never be altered. When the turn is less than a whole, the reader must in effect move around the book in order to read what is written next. To achieve this when holding it, he must adjust the book in relation to himself while moving. "You must observe always to hold the upper end of the Book against the upper end of the Room." *(Feu. 1 p. 33; Wea. 1 p. 34)*

The lazy reader who has remained seated will find that the book is in the correct relationship to him, but not to the room—the top is now the bottom.

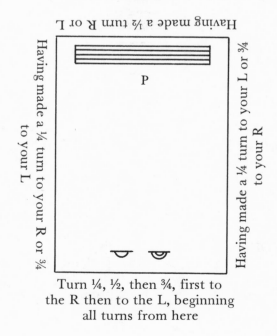

Turn ¼, ½, then ¾, first to the R then to the L, beginning all turns from here

The reader must hold the book in both hands adjusting it in front of himself with each turn.

Hold the book and walk a complete circle in a clockwise direction. In order to follow the symbols it will be necessary to keep the book's relationship to the room:

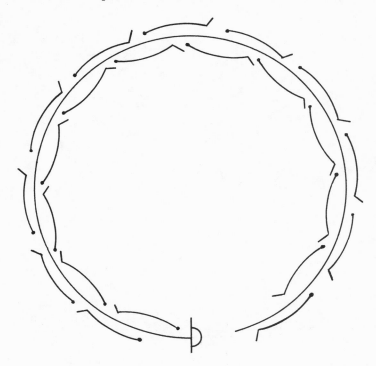

Walking forward

SIGN FOR TURNING

Tourné.
Turn.
(Feu. 1 p. 12; Wea. 1 p. 13)

Sign for Turning on
the Foot Positions

There are two reasons for turning: to introduce a virtuosic feat, as a pirouette; to change direction in space during a step-unit. Turns are generally made on rising. In pirouettes the turn will continue after rising. In steps made with a bend and rise and a change of direction, the rise and turn will be completed simultaneously. Turns made while springing are completed in the air.

A turn is shown by a circle or part of a circle which must be read from its earliest point of contact with a symbol. In a whole turn, a dot indicates from which side of the symbol the turn sign should be read.

In the following examples, the dot by the toe means that the body will be supported by the foot on [demi]pointe:

| A whole turn, a whole circle | | One turn to the R on the R ft. |
| A ¾ turn, a ¾ circle | | A ¾ turn to the L on the L ft. |

A ½ turn,
a ½ circle

A ½ turn to the R on
the R ft.

A ½ turn to the L on
the R ft.

The next three examples are used frequently. At the end of
the turn the front/back relationship of the feet in fifth position
will be reversed:

A ½ turn, a
½ circle

A ½ turn to the L on
both feet in 5th. (L64)

A ½ turn to the R on
both feet

A ¼ turn, a
¼ circle

A ¼ turn to the R on
both feet

The sign for an eighth of a turn is given below.

Remember to read the half circle for a half turn from its
point of contact nearest the beginning of the symbol. Follow all
turning signs around from their point of contact with the symbol.[14]

Turning Sign on
the Step Symbols

The turning sign is placed where there is room on a step symbol, for instance: if the bend and rise occur during the step, the
turning sign is placed first; if they occur before the step, the
turning sign follows.

When reading the examples below, remember to turn the book,
turn yourself, and bend the knees. The remainder of the step
symbol and those that follow may then be read. When performing, however, the turn should not be completed on the bend
but distributed between the bend and the rise. Only if the
"movement" is made on one foot should the turn be made while
rising.

Turns made to change direction in space:

Make an 1/8 turn, a "half quarter
turn" to the L, stepping forward
on the R toward the corner.
(Weaver only) (L65)

Make a ¼ turn to the L
on the R ft. Step to 5th
front on the L, and to 2nd
on the R. (L66)

Make a ½ turn to the R
on the L ft. Then three backward steps R, L, R toward
the top of the room. (L67)

Make a ½ turn to the R
on the R ft. Then three
forward steps L, R, L toward
the bottom of the room. (L68)

Make a ½ turn to the R on the L ft. Step to 5th front on the R,
to 2nd on the L, and 5th front on the R. (L69)

SIGN FOR SPRINGING

Given two feet, five kinds of springs are possible; a spring from:
(1)   one foot to the other foot
(2)   one foot to two feet
(3)   two feet to one foot
(4)   one foot to the same foot
(5)   two feet to two feet.

Rameau refers to most of the above types merely as springs, with
the exception of the jeté. Even today there is no universally
accepted terminology for each of the five types. Those most
commonly used are:

17th-18th century dance	19th-century ballet	Labanotation
(1) Jeté/Bound	Jeté	Leap
(2) Assemblé/Close	Assemblé	Assemblé
(3) Sissonne[15]	Sissonne	Sissonne
(4) Sauter à cloche pied,[16]/Hop	Temps levé	Hop
(5) ——	——	Jump

Remarques sur les Sauts.
Observations upon Springings.
(Feu. 1 p. 15; Wea. 1 p. 16)

Basically, springs which travel or involve specific instructions for a stepping leg are written on the step symbols; those which do not travel are written on the position symbols.

Pas Sauté.
A Spring.
(Feu. 1 p. 11; Wea. 1 p. 11)

The sign for springing—rising into the air—is two short parallel straight strokes.

With few exceptions springs land with the supporting knee, or knees, bent. In the notation, the bend will usually appear on the following step or foot position symbol.

Springs from One Foot to the Other

Sauté et retombé
sur la jambe qui marche.
A bound.
(Feu. 1 p. 15; Wea. 1 p. 17)

Both legs bend as the stepping leg reaches first position, then spring off the L ft. onto the R.[17] (L70)

A jeté can be written on a foot position when the foot to be sprung onto has already been moved to the receiving position. (L71)

Springs from One Foot to Two Feet

There was no special term for this kind of spring—which usually involves the motion of the free foot from an open to a closed position—except "close" or "pas assemblé." Feuillet chooses to think of this as akin to the jeté; springing onto the foot:

Spring off the L ft. and land on both feet, the R closing into 1st. (L72)

As the spring actually takes off from the left foot, Rameau uses a half position symbol to show this more clearly.[18] He also explains that it would be better if the step symbol were curved since the leg should move out to the side during the spring.

Springs from One Foot
to the Same Foot

Sauté et retombé
sur l'autre jambe
que celle qui marche.
A hop.
(Feu. 1 p. 15; Wea. 1 p. 17)

 Bend, spring off, and land on the R ft.

 The same on the L.

The ensuing bend will be shown on the following symbol.

A hop is written on a step symbol when the stepping leg is moving from one position to another:

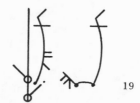

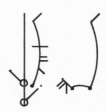

A hop on the L ft. while carrying the R to 4th. (L73)

The same followed by a step onto the R. (L74)

The hop followed by two steps (on [demi] pointe). (L75)

Modification of the Hop

In some instances, springs which are really hops are modified and taken off two feet instead of one:

In a true hop, the signs are placed in the middle of the symbol; spring off one foot. (L76)

In a modified hop, the signs are placed at the beginning of the symbol; spring off both feet. (L77)

The placement of the signs at the beginning of the symbol is the only indication of this modification.

If a turn is to be made, the turning sign will be placed before the other symbols as below in example (a), or after them as in example (b). If the spring is off one foot, the turn sign is placed first: (L78)

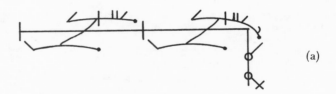

(a)

If the spring is off two feet, the bending and springing signs are first: (L79)

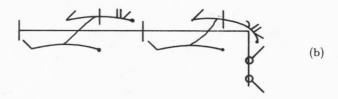

(b)

The step preceding the spring ends on the left foot in second position, the dancer facing stage right. In example (a), the spring is off the left foot making a quarter turn while in the air. In example (b), the placement of the signs at the beginning of the symbol modifies the previous step to second position. The weight should not be fully transferred to the left foot; it is equally distributed on both.

Springs from Two Feet to One Foot

There was no special term for this type of spring. In the first example below, the left foot, which finishes off the floor in front, should probably be flexed. There are no specific instructions describing a foot-off-the-floor in third or fifth position in front:

The feet in 5th, the L in front. Spring off both feet and land on the R, the L off the floor in front, both knees bent. (L80)

The feet in 5th as above. Spring off both feet and land on the R, the L finishing in 4th behind, off the floor, the leg straight. (L81)

Bend in 4th on both feet. Spring off both feet, landing on the R foot in 3rd behind. (L82)

A spring from two feet to one foot taken from a closed position is usually preceded by a spring from one foot to two feet, the bending sign being written on the end of the first spring rather than on the beginning of the second:

The feet in 3rd with the R in front, the L off the floor. Spring off the R, landing in 5th, the L in front. The bending sign is written on this foot position. Spring off both feet and land on the L, the R off the floor in 5th behind, the instep stretched. (L83)

Springs from Two Feet to Two Feet

There was no special term for this kind of spring. When springing without changing the foot position there is no need to show a landing position:

Spring in 1st pos. (L84)

The same with a whole turn in the air to the R. (Theatrical dances only.) (L85)

Spring in 5th pos. (L86)

If these springs are to be made traveling, a "line of connection" joins the position symbols:

Spring forward in 1st pos. (L87)

When springing and changing the foot position, the finishing position must be added:

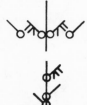

A spring from 1st to 2nd pos. (L88)

from 4th to 3rd pos. (L89)

from 4th to 4th pos. (L90)

from 5th to 5th pos. (L91)

Spring from 1st to 2nd, traveling forward. (L92)

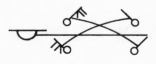

Spring from 4th to 4th, traveling sideward; the feet changing their front/back relationship. (L93)

Here step symbols are combined with position symbols. (L93)

The Beauchamp-Feuillet System of Chorégraphie

Changes of position when the feet move simultaneously away from first to an open position are usually written on step symbols:

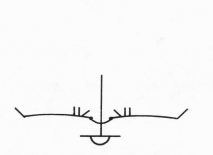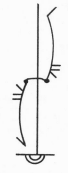

Spring from 1st to 2nd. (L94)   Spring from 1st to 4th. (L95)

SIGN FOR CAPERING
(THEATRICAL DANCES ONLY)

Pas Cabriolle.
A Caper.
(Feu. 1 p. 11; Wea. 1 p. 11)

The sign for capering is three short straight strokes: one added to the springing sign when a beat is added to the spring.

SIGN FOR WAVING
(THEATRICAL DANCES ONLY)

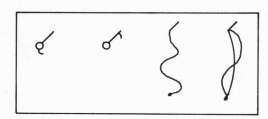

A little hook is attached to the toe or heel of the position symbols. No specific sign is used on the step symbol which is itself "waved." Occasionally a wavy line is drawn across the symbol.

SINGLE STEPS WITH BEATS

Pas Battus.
Beaten Steps.
(Feu. 1 p. 45; Wea. 1 p. 43)

Many steps are ornamented with little beats made by the stepping leg around or against the supporting one. The path of the step symbol shows the path of the beat and the relationship of the feet.

Both bends and rises can be so ornamented. The rule of bending and rising signs upon step symbols still applies; normally, beats on a bend are made with a bent leg and those on a rise with a straight one. However, in a series of beats made while bending, the beating leg must be stretched when opening to the side.

The terminology of pas battus is not consistent but a theoretical picture does emerge. Beats are made:

Dessus. Above.   A beat in which the foot passes from the back, beats in front, and returns to the back.

Dessous. Below.   The reverse of the above.

Devant. Before.   The foot begins forward in an open position, beats in front, and returns to the starting position.

Derrière. Behind.   The reverse of the above.

Beats are made with the feet in three relationships:

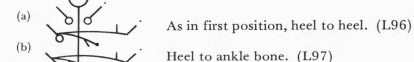

(a)   As in first position, heel to heel. (L96)

(b)   Heel to ankle bone. (L97)

(c)   As in third position, heel to instep. (L98)

The degree of crossing in beats varies according to context, tempo, the number made, and the bend or stretch of the legs. Depending upon the type of beat and any modifying factors, different parts of the legs and feet make contact:

(a) A côté. To the side. (Heel to heel.)

The step symbol touches the head (o) of the foot position symbol:

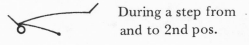

During a step from and to 2nd pos.

During a step forward.

(b) *Contre la cheville. Against the ankle.* (Heel to ankle.)
The step symbol touches the beginning of the line for the foot just beyond the head:

From the back and returning to step in 4th pos.

Derrière le talon. Behind the heel. (Heel to ankle with the foot passing behind.)
The step symbol crosses as far as in the above but there is no actual contact between the symbols, just as the heel will not touch the ankle due to the forty-five-degree turnout:

From the front and returning to step in 4th pos.

(c) *Sur le cou de pied. On the instep.* (Heel to instep.)
The step symbol passes through the middle of the line for the foot:

From 4th front and returning to step forward. (Most frequently made with bent knees.)

Single Beats

Single beats are most common when the stepping leg is to return to the starting position:

The R ft. moves from
4th front to 4th front.
The beat is on the instep,
the cou de pied. (L99)

The L ft. moves from
4th back to 4th back.
The beat is behind the
heel. (L100)

When the foot position has already been clearly established, a beat can be shown by step symbols alone: (Examples from *Feu. 1 p. 54.*)

This beat (which follows a rise) is made with straight knees "behind the heel." The calves will make contact. (L101)

Written without the half position symbol. (L101)

The same backward with a beat on the cou de pied. (L102)

Written without the half position symbol. (L102)

Complex Beats

Sometimes steps are elaborated by two beats:

Pas battu derrière et devant. Behind and before. (Behind the heel and against the ankle.)

On the second step, beat behind and before with straight legs. (L103)

In the most complex theatrical dances, three, four, or five beats are found.

FOOTNOTES

1. In English dance scores the dots are seldom used.

2. Rameau's signs for the man and woman are ⌣ , ⊒ . *(Ram. 2 Pl. 1)* The two straight lines for the woman were probably easier to engrave than the two half circles used by Feuillet.

3. Rameau for the most part uses black pins instead of white.

4. In fourth position the crossing of the feet is represented equal to third position, i.e. the heels opposite the insteps. With the turnout of the legs, this is the most stabilizing placement of the feet in forward and backward steps.

5. M = milieu (middle). This is the moment "when the two heels are near to each other," i.e. the stepping foot is passing through first position in the air. *(Ram. 2 p. 8.)*

6. The stepping foot can cross into fifth position either in front or behind.

7. It is understood that the stepping foot will move into first position in the air before the first step backward.

8. Weaver's diagrams, "To move to the second Position and afterwards to the fifth," are inaccurate according to the system; the symbols do not overlap as in Feuillet's diagrams. *(Feu. 1 p. 43; Wea. 1 p. 42)*

9. In Feuillet and Weaver the foot is incorrectly drawn in this example.

10. Rameau uses a dart (∨) instead of a dot.

11. Rameau's full diagram. *(Ram. 2 p. 86, No. 4)*

12. Rameau's full diagram. *(Ram. 2 p. 86 No. 3)*

13. In *Abbregé* Rameau uses the term "élevé" to mean a rise without a preceding bend, and "relevé," a rise following a bend. *(Ram. 2 p. 97)* His sign for élevé is ⌐ .

14. Rameau detaches all turn signs from the step symbols in order to place them more accurately, "because it is only in rising that one should turn: thus to represent this in the way it should be done, the sign to turn is above the one to rise and not at the beginning of one to represent the step." *(Ram. 2 p. 52)* Rameau's turning signs are ↶ a whole turn, ↷ a half turn, and ↶ a quarter turn. Like the step symbols, these signs are read from the black pin.

15. Pas de Sissonne was the name of a pas composé containing two springs, one of which was a spring from two feet to one foot; later called a sissonne.

16. Rameau uses this term once only, in the contretemps de menuet.

17. In his explanation, Feuillet (not Weaver) places the signs together in the middle of the step symbol. This seems a more accurate way to describe this "movement" but it is not often used by any notator, including Feuillet. Both ways fulfill "When there is a Mark of a Spring upon a Step, and no Mark for the holding up of the Foot after it, it shews, that the Spring is to be made with [onto] the Foot that moves." *(Feu. 1 p. 15; Wea. 1 p. 16)*

18. *Ram. 2 p. 88, No. 18 & p. 98.*

19. Rameau uses a half position symbol for a hop. *(Ram. 2 p. 62 No. 4.)*

A lady of quality dancing. Dance Collection, New York Public Library.

CHAPTER SEVEN

The Theory of the Arm Motions and Their Notation

PRELIMINARIES

*Des Ports de Bras, et de
Leurs Mouvemens.
Of the Different Movements
of the Arms.
(Feu. 1 p. 97; Wea. 1 p. 55)*

*Des Differens Mouvemens
des Bras.
Of the Different Movements
of the Arms.
(Ram. 1 p. 200; Ess. 1 p. 117)*

Although provision was made for notating the arm motions, they are included in the dance score only when something specific or unusual is required. In orthodox dances everyone knew the appropriate movements for each step, and also, according to Feuillet, there was a certain freedom of choice dependent upon the taste of the individual performer:

Altho' the Carriage and Movement of the Arms depend more upon the Fancy [Goût] of the Performer, than on any certain Rules, I shall nevertheless lay down some Examples, which will explain, by demonstrative Characters, the different Motion of the Arms in Dancing; or at least, will inform you what Characters to make Use of in describing the Motion of the Arms, to the Movement of each Step. *(Feu. 1 p. 97; Wea. 1 p. 55)*

But some rules were established governing the arm motions:

. . .every Body knows that Monsieur Beauchamp was one of the first that introduced them, and laid down Rules, and from thence the Desires of so many Persons of both Sexes have arose to practise them to add to all the other Graces, for which they are obliged to him and some other extraordinary Masters. *(Ram. 1 p. 195; Ess. p. 114)*

The arm symbols and lines of motion show the motions and positions of the arms in a very rudimentary way. The symbol for the arm is a straight line with a perpendicular stroke across the end representing the top of the arm joining the shoulder, marked A. The other end of the line, which is the wrist or the extremity of the arm including the hand, is marked C:

The middle of the line, marked B, is the elbow which is distinguished by Weaver (but not Feuillet) with a short straight stroke:

To show a bend in one of these joints, the arm symbol is bent at the appropriate place:

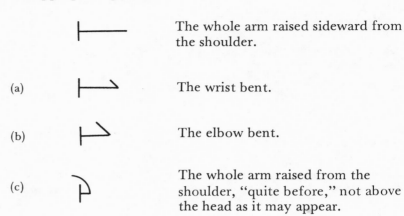

The whole arm raised sideward from the shoulder.

(a)   The wrist bent.

(b)   The elbow bent.

(c)   The whole arm raised from the shoulder, "quite before," not above the head as it may appear.

It will be seen that the symbols do not indicate clearly the direction of the limb: visually it could be either forward or upward depending on the viewpoint. Seen as if from above, the limb appears to point in a forward direction, but viewed as though from behind, it seems to point upward. However, Rameau describes positions (a) and (b) as the limbs directed upward, whereas of (c) Feuillet says "the arm quite before oneself."

Because of such ambiguities, it is necessary to know the motions of the arms in order to understand the symbols. These are best described by Rameau; Tomlinson is confusing as well as too brief on this subject. But both agree that to move the arms well is to reveal a fine dancer:

As the Grace of the Body. . .depends on the moving the Arms well, one cannot take too much Precaution to understand how to dispose them first, that they may move with all necessary Freedom. *(Ram. 1 p. 197; Ess. p. 115)*

The Correspondence of the Legs and Arms in Dancing is a Point of so nice a Nature that any Awkwardness or improper Movements therein would destroy the Beauty of the whole, since that Dancing cannot be good which is decrepid or lame in any of its Parts. . .so that in fine it is the very Polish and finishing Stroke. *(Tom. p. 153)*

Grouping of the Fingers

Many illustrations show the fingers held close together with the thumb placed on the outer joint of the first finger. It is true that the thumb should not stick out in a strained and ugly fashion, but Rameau does not recommend dancing with the fingers held in such a restricted position:

I have also represented the Hands neither open nor shut, that the Movements of the Wrist and Elbow may be performed with all Ease and Freedom; whereas if the Thumb was to touch one of the Fingers, it would make the Motion more stiff. *(Ram. 1 p. 199; Ess. p. 116)* (L104)

Arms By the Side
Before Dancing

The Palms or Insides of the Hands are to our Side in a genteel easy Shape or Fashion, the whole Arms hanging from under the Shoulders without Force downwards, or too much Relaxation upwards, but natural and easy in a Readiness for the Elevation. *(Tom. p. 153)* (L105)

De la Position des Bras et de l'Elévation qu'ils Doivent Avoir. Of the Position of the Arms and their Proper Elevation. (Ram. 1 p. 197; Ess. p. 115)

From plate: Ram. 1 p. 11.

From plate: Ram. 1 p. 197.
The elevation of the arms (palms up)
(L106)

From plate: Ram. 1 p. 216.
The elevation of the arms (palms down)
(L107, 108)

To begin their motion the arms must be elevated sideward "to the Height of the Pit of the Stomach." *(Ram. 1 p. 197; Ess. p. 115)* The height of the arms may be altered slightly for individuals:

INDEED a good Master knows how to dispose them properly according to the Make of his Scholar, to raise them higher if of low Stature, and if Tall to bring them down to an Equality with the Hips; but if the Subject is of a just Proportion, he should keep them out even with the Pit of his Stomach: A Remark I have known to be made by the most able Masters of this Age. *(Ram. 1 p. 195; Ess. p. 114)*

Position of Elevation
[Pos. of el.] in Chorégraphie

Viewed from behind:

The left arm   ———⊢ ⊢———   The right arm

The above is how Feuillet represents the elevation of the arms which is, of course, too high. More accurately the lines should slope:

⋀ ⋀

**Preliminary Motion
of the Arms**

The arms now raised in the position of elevation with the palms facing upward (according to Rameau), or forward to the Presence (according to Tomlinson), they make their first motion— rising and falling a little, while rotating inward until the palms face downward: (L109)

. . .the Turn of the Wrists and Palms of the Hands downwards in a slow and even Motion inwards, or forwards. . . greatly resembling the Fall of a Feather or the Coming down of a Bird, their Fall is so smooth and easy; and it is a wonderful Grace to Dancing when well performed. *(Tom. p. 154)*

This preliminary downward motion coincides with a preliminary bending of the knees.

Tomlinson implies that all dances begin with the arms placed in the position of elevation, the palms up, but Rameau generally relates this symmetrical placing to the first and second positions of the feet where they too are side by side. Since most dances begin from fourth position, the arms would be more suitably placed in the position of opposition. (See p. 140.) Whatever the preparatory position of the arms, the preliminary motion is downward to the position of elevation, palms down, in the manner so beautifully described by Tomlinson.

In the position of elevation, palms up, the line of the whole arm to the fingertips should be very slightly curved. When the palms face downward as the knees bend, the arms should be virtually straight, held without strain or rigidity but with some strength.

NOTATED MOTIONS OF THE ARMS

Feuillet gives five notated circular motions of the wrist, elbow, and whole arm from the shoulder. The positions in the motions of the wrists given below, will serve to clarify the more detailed explanations which follow.

Small motions, approximately a half turn:

(1)	From *Below upwards*	Made from the pos. of el., palms down, to the pos. of el., palms up.
(2)	From *Above downwards*	Made from the pos. of el., palms up, to the pos. of el., palms down.

Whole turns:

(3)	*Round upwards*	Beginning and ending in the pos. of el., palms down.
(4)	*Round downwards*	
(5)	*Round downwards*	Beginning and ending in the pos. of el., palms up.

The arms in motion trace circular paths either upward or downward, inward or outward. In chorégraphie, these paths are shown by curved lines joined to the end of the arm symbols which represent the starting position. (The finishing position becomes the starting position of the next symbol.) In the following explanations, positions will be clarified by directions for the facing of the palm.

De la Manière de Prendre des Mouvemens du Poignet.
Of the Manner of Moving the Wrist.
(Ram. 1 p. 203; Ess. p. 119)

The motions of the wrist necessitate small rotations of the hand and of the arm from the shoulder. The arm remains in the position of elevation apart from a very slight rise and fall. In the examples below, drawn for the right wrist only, the symbol shows the arm in the starting position. The circular line joined to the arm symbol represents, rather haphazardly, the circular motion of the wrist. The finishing position is read from the starting position of the next motion:

Below upwards

From the starting position, the pos. of el., palm down, circle the hand from the wrist until the palm faces just short of straight upward, in the pos. of el., palm up. (L110)

Above downwards

From the pos. of el., palm up, circle the hand from the wrist until the palm faces downward. The reverse of the above. (L111)

Round upwards

Circle the hand as in below upwards, but continue the motion until the palm returns to the pos. of el., palm down. (L112)

Round downwards

(a) Retrace the path of the above motion. (L113)

Round downwards

(b) Begin as in above downwards, but continue the motion until the hand returns to the starting position. (L114)

Sometimes two motions are written on one symbol:

A motion from below upwards and one from above downwards.

*Du Mouvement du Coude
et de l'Epaule.
Of the Movement of the
Elbow and the Shoulder.
(Ram. 1 p. 206; Ess. p. 121)*

To accomplish motions of the elbow, the lower part of the arm circles from the elbow, the height of the upper arm remaining more or less constant. These motions necessitate small rotations of the arm from the shoulder and sympathetic motions of the wrist:

. . .when you bend with the Elbow and the Wrists move with them, which prevents the Arms from being stiff and gives them a great Grace; but yet the Wrists must not be bent too much, for that would look extravagant. *(Ram. 1 p. 206; Ess. p. 121)*

The following examples depict the right arm only:

Below upwards

From the starting position, the pos. of el., palm down, circle the lower part of the arm from the elbow, finishing in the raised position shown on p. 140. (L115)

(When the lower part of the arm is directed inward in front of the body, the palm faces it from a distance of about eight inches.)

Above downwards

From the above finishing position, retrace the same path. (L116)

Round upwards

Circle as in below upwards, but continue the motion until the palm again faces downward. (L117)

Round downwards

(a) Retrace the path of the above motion. (L118)

Round downwards

(b) Begin as in above downwards, but continue the motion until the arm returns to the starting position. (L119)

Double movements are also written for the elbow:

A motion from below upwards followed by one from above downwards.

Rameau says of ballroom steps, that motions of the arms from the shoulder are seldom used. Feuillet gives symbols for motions which were only used in theatrical dances. (See *Feu. 1 p. 99.*)

PRINCIPAL USE OF THE ARMS

De l'Opposition des Bras aux Pieds.
Of the Opposition of the Arms to the Legs.
(Ram. 1 p. 210; Ess. p. 123)

Of all the Movements in Dancing, Opposition or the Contrast of the Arm to the Leg is the most natural to us, and the least regarded: For Example; to see different Persons walk, you will find that when they step with the right Foot forward, the left Arm will naturally oppose it, which seems to be a certain Rule. *(Ess. p. 123)*

Plate: Ess. 1731 edition, first issue p. 128.

(L120)

The Body is upright, the Head is turned aside to the opposite Arm, which is the Right and is bent before; the Hand raised to the Height of the Shoulder and a little forwards, the left Arm extended and drawn a little back, but raised to the Pit of the Stomach; the Body rested on the left Foot, and the right Heel off the Ground ready to make a Step. *(Ram. 1 p. 211; Ess. p. 124)*

The position of opposition used in baroque dance is extremely difficult for people of today to achieve, and can only look convincing if the carriage of the body is correct in terms of baroque deportment. (At the time, for men at least, a similar principle of balance applied to some positions of the arms in fencing.)

The position of opposition is generally reached with a motion of the elbow from below upwards, made by the arm in opposition to the forward foot. In forward steps, this is the foot stepped onto; in backward steps, the foot stepped off, and in sideward steps, either, depending upon the sequence.

To balance the motion of the elbow from below upwards, the wrist of the other arm simultaneously makes a complimentary motion from below upwards while remaining in the position of elevation.

Changing the Opposition

The opposition is generally changed by returning both arms from above downwards to the position of elevation, palms down, after which the other arm will be raised in opposition from below upwards; the lower arm turning simultaneously from the wrist: (In the following two examples, the notation is read from the bottom up.)

The left arm is raised into opposition and the right wrist turns. Both arms return to the pos. of el., palms down. The right arm is raised into opposition and the left wrist turns.

Sometimes the same arm will be raised again, making a whole turn followed by a half turn:

The right arm is raised, continues the path outward and is raised again, finally returning inward to the pos. of el., palm down. The wrist of the left arm makes complementary motions.

Though I have said that these Movements should be made together, I repeat it again that they should be taken with a great deal of Ease and Freedom: And for the readier Performance of them, I would advise you to stand before a Glass and move your Arms as I have directed, and if you have any Taste you will perceive your Faults, and by consequence mend. *(Ram. 1 p. 212; Ess. p. 124)*

Sometimes the arm in opposition is lowered through an outward circle:

(1) When two oppositions are made within one step-unit, the first arm opens outward to the position of elevation, palm down, and continues into a circle as the other arm is raised for the second opposition.

(2) When an arm is in opposition and must be raised again in the following step-unit, a complete circle starting outward will be made, the arms passing through the position of elevation, palms down.

When an arm is in opposition and a springing step follows, requiring the arm to be lowered to the position of elevation on the landing, it seems most sympathetic if the arm follows the shortest, most direct path from one position to the other.

In the following explanations, the opposition of the arms will sometimes be referred to by the author's term, "the position of opposition," and the abbreviation, pos. of opp.

When moving into opposition as described on p. 140, the arms should work independently, making quite different actions. There is usually a strong tendency for the motion of the wrist in the lower arm to emulate the inward motion from the elbow of the opposing arm. This can best be avoided by beginning the motion of the elbow before moving the lower arm. Make sure the circle inward from the elbow is full enough, the hand passing in front of the body at a distance of some eight inches. Do not bring it too close.

Once the arm is raised, make sure the elbow is not dropped so that a sharp angle results.　　　　NO

Instead, achieve a curved line by supporting the elbow slightly.　　　　YES

But be careful to relax the support when lowering the arm from above downwards; otherwise another sharp angle will appear during the motion.　　　　NO

Do not allow the wrist motions to become too exaggerated, but also avoid stiff, motionless hands and fingers. To make impressive arm motions, a surprising amount of concealed strength is required.

Other Placements
of the Arms in Relationship
to the Foot Positions

The following remarks are general and will not apply to the arm motions in all contexts. Depending upon the total content of a step-unit and the way in which units are combined, one rule of placement may outweigh another.

When the feet are side by side, as in first or second position, the arms will be to the side of the body:

  The pos. of el., palms up or down

  As above

or

Both arms raised from the elbows corresponding to the bend of both knees, the weight on both feet.

Both arms raised from the shoulders corresponding to the leg raised from the hip.

Plate: Ess. 1731, first issue p. 152.

Plate: Ram. 1 p. 168

When one foot is forward of the other, as in third, fourth, or fifth position, the arms will generally be raised in opposition.

  The Position of Opposition

In this picture of a theatrical dancer the arms are beautifully placed, the high arm opposing the forward foot. The torso is fluid but centered, producing an impression of grace, vitality, strength, and ease. The situation of the head, turned 1/8, is a position passed through during a motion of the head, rather than an assumed pose.

The arm motions will be further discussed at the end of Chapter Eight, and with each step-unit in Chapter Nine.

SHOULDERS AND HEAD

There were no signs or symbols for the very small and subtle motions of the shoulders and head.

Shading the Shoulder

Rameau incorporates this action into a few step-units. To shade the shoulder, the dancer drew the shoulder parallel to the front foot slightly backward, thereby bringing the other into opposition. The resulting rotation of the upper chest would probably have amounted to 1/16 or a little more.

Shading was used on some forward and sideward steps. When incorporated into the position of opposition, it caused the raised arm to move a little more forward in space and the lower arm backward. (L121)

Motions of the Head

Rameau gives some small rotations and inclinations of the head when describing the arm motions for one or two step-units, but for the most part the head should be held straight "without any suggestion of Stiffness." The direction of the gaze will be dictated by the dance figure, partners either looking toward the Presence, at each other, or along the line of travel. The head could be rotated up to 1/8 so that dancers could maintain direct or indirect contact with each other or complement the step being performed. In a choice between step and partner, the latter would take precedence. The use of shading and motions of the head will be discussed as they occur in individual step-units. (L122)

AUTHOR'S NOTES

It is better to leave these subtle motions until the basic arm motions and an easy bearing of the head have become second nature, even when performing complex sequences. This is especially so for dancers used to moving in a nineteenth-century style. When shading the shoulder, think of drawing the shoulder backward rather than of bringing the other forward. This will broaden the appearance. A strong center line through the torso should always be maintained.

**PLACING THE ARM
SYMBOLS ALONG
THE TRACT**

The arm symbols are placed to the right and left of the tract when traveling forward and backward, but when traveling sideward, both are shown above the tract.

When the arms move consecutively, the symbols are placed accordingly along the tract:

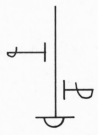

When they move simultaneously, the symbols are level and joined by a line which passes across the tract linking them below the shoulder area:

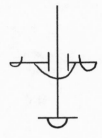

The necessity for this link becomes obvious when traveling sideward where the symbols must always be placed side by side:

(1)   (2)   (3)   (4)

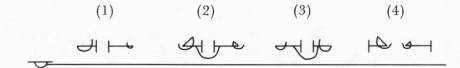

(1) Circle the L from the elbow and the R from the wrist consecutively.
(2) Circle the L from the elbow and the R from the wrist simultaneously.
(3) Circle the R from the elbow and the L from the wrist simultaneously.
(4) Circle the R from the elbow and the L from the wrist consecutively.

TAKING HANDS

Feuillet and Weaver explain this most clearly:

For giving the Hands in Dancing.

YOU will know when to give the Hand, by a small *Crescent* or *half Circle* at the end of a little Barr or Stroke, which is to be plac'd on the fide of the *Tract*, viz. when it is on the right fide of the *Tract*, it fhews, that you muft give the right Hand ; and when on the left, it fhews the left Hand is to be given ; and when there is one on each fide, both Hands muft then be given.

To give the right Hand.   To give the left Hand.   To give both Hands.

      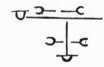

When you have thus given one Hand or both, you are not to quit Hands, 'till you find the fame Marks cut through with another little Stroke, which fhews, that in that place the Hands are to let go.

To let go one Hand.   To let go both Hands.

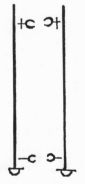   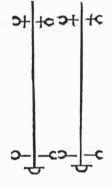

To give one Hand.   To give both Hands.

However, the precise directions and levels of the arms are not indicated.

When one hand is given, the symbols represent the usual manner of holding hands when dancing or when leading the lady on other occasions in everyday life. The arms will be to the side, but lower than the symbols suggest:

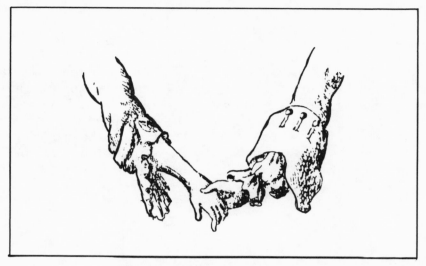

Plate: Ess. 1731, second issue p. 48.

When both hands are given, the symbols must have been meant to represent a position with both arms forward of the body. Otherwise the dancers would be pressed—somewhat in advance of their time—chest to chest!

CHAPTER EIGHT

The Notation of Meter in Chorégraphie

De la Mesure ou Cadence.
Of Time, Measure or Cadence.
(Feu. 1 p. 87; Wea. 1 p. 47)

Traité de la Cadence.
Of Time.
(Ram. 2 p. 103; Tom. p. 141)

Traité de la Cadence.
A Small Treatise of
Time and Cadence in Dancing
(Feu. 2; Wea. 2)

Although the terms Cadence and Temps (Tems)[1] were used synonymously, at least in reference to meter, musical theorists also attributed to Cadence an indefinable quality and spirit. These broader connotations of Cadence will be discussed in Chapter Eleven. The present chapter is concerned only with meter and the manner in which the musical relationships of the steps and actions are indicated in chorégraphie and in the verbal descriptions of Rameau and Tomlinson.

METER OR TIME

A measure of dance constituted differing numbers of single steps and actions combined to form a unit. In the majority of dances, one of these step-units equals one measure of music in duple- or triple-time.

Duple- ("Common"[2]) and
Triple-Time or -Meter

Duple-time has two beats per measure, and triple-time has three:

It is first then to be observ'd, that in the general Rule for Measures and Time in Musick, two sorts of Movements are only made use of, viz. Common Time, and Triple Time, for on these depend all the rest; some of which are quicker, and some slower, yet all to be beat as Common and Triple Time. *(Feu. 2 p. 1; Wea. 2 p. 3)*

Quadruple-Time

Tomlinson gives a further explanation of duple- and triple-time, adding:

From the former of these [duple] flow very slow Entrees . . . call'd, Quadruple or of two Times on Account of their Slowness or admitting of a suppos'd Bar in the Middle of the said Measure. *(Tom. p. 143)*

In duple- or triple-time one step-unit equals one measure of music. In quadruple-time two step-units equal one measure of music; the music is notated as duple-time but performed more slowly. There were two kinds of quadruple-time, as will be seen in the table on p. 155.

Musical note values and their rests:

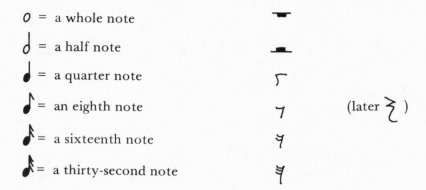

o = a whole note

$\textit{d}$ = a half note

$\textit{J}$ = a quarter note

$\textit{♪}$ = an eighth note   (later ξ)

$\textit{♪}$ = a sixteenth note

$\textit{♪}$ = a thirty-second note

In musical notation, the beats in a measure are represented by specific note values. In one piece, each beat may have the value of a half note while in another, a quarter note. A dot placed after a note increases its value by one half. For instance, a dotted half note:

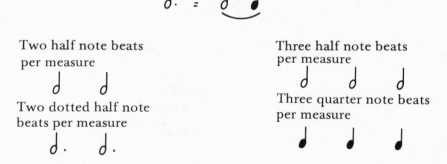

Two half note beats
per measure

Two dotted half note
beats per measure

Three half note beats
per measure

Three quarter note beats
per measure

TIME VALUES OF SINGLE STEPS COMPRISING PAS COMPOSES (STEP-UNITS)

Duple- and Triple-time
or -meter

In the dance notation, the step symbols relate to the beats in a measure.

In pas composés, the line of liaison joining the single steps is used to explain their relative values in time. Step symbols joined by a single liaison have equal value, and the basic units for duple- and triple-time are:

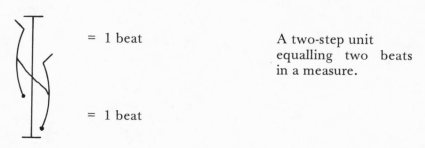

= 1 beat

= 1 beat

A two-step unit
equalling two beats
in a measure.

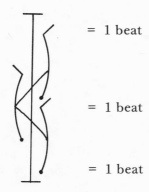

= 1 beat

A three-step unit
equalling three beats
in a measure.

= 1 beat

= 1 beat

A step symbol which is not quite joined by the line of liaison has twice the time value of one that is joined. This can show the timing of a two-step unit in triple-time:

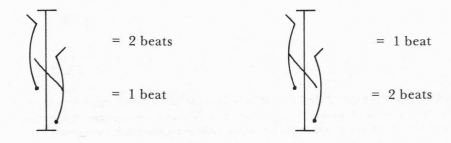

= 2 beats   = 1 beat

= 1 beat   = 2 beats

Not all notators, including Feuillet, always make use of this provision.

A double liaison halves the value in time of each step symbol so joined. This can be used to show the timing of a three-step unit equalling two beats in a measure:

= the second beat

= the second half of the first beat

= the first half of the first beat

Single steps at double-speed usually occur during the first beat in a measure. Here a four-step unit equals three beats in a measure:

= the third beat

= the second beat

= the second half of the first beat

= the first half of the first beat

In the next example, a four-step unit equals two beats in a measure. The notation, however, lacks precision. Perhaps the first beat should be divided not into two, but into three:

= the second beat

= the last third of the first beat

= the second third of the first beat

= the first third of the first beat

Another interpretation, more sympathetic to performance, is:

= the second beat

= one half of the first beat

= one quarter of the first beat

= one quarter of the first beat

RESTS

These uses of the line of liaison are the only indications of time values in chorégraphie apart from rests, which, like the step symbols, do not relate to specific note values but to the beats in a measure:[3]

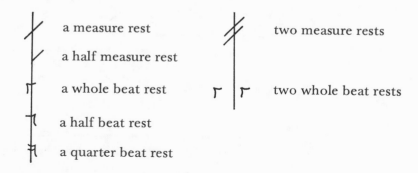

A single step symbol which equals only the first beat in a measure should be followed by a rest, or rests, during which you wait "without dancing."

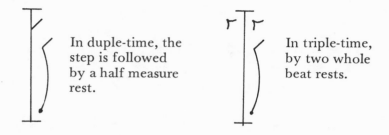

Rests are often taken as understood by notators.

UPBEAT (S) FOR ANACRUSIS, DOWNBEAT

In today's conventional music theory, the upbeat is the unaccented beat at the end of a measure which leads to the downbeat, the first, and usually the strongest beat within a measure. The downbeats must figure among Feuillet's and Tomlinson's "most remarkable" places in a musical strain.

The bend in the first "movement" in a step-unit corresponds to the upbeat, the rise to the downbeat (although in a sprung "movement" the landing from the spring marks the downbeat). These "remarkable" moments in music and dance are moved toward, reached, then moved away from, in a ceaseless, rhythmic ebb and flow. For the immediate purposes (until Chapter Eleven) it will be necessary to establish, rather pedantically, the musical beats in the different dance types, and the relationship of the step-units to them.

DANCE TYPES FROM FRENCH SOURCES

The following dance types are contained in the notated French dance collections of the early eighteenth century which have come to light. In the table, the time signature 2 means two half notes per measure, 3 refers to three quarter notes per measure. Time signatures probably refer to note values rather than speed; it will be noticed, for example, that both fast and slow gigues (loures) are written with a $\frac{6}{4}$ time signature.

When dances are not titled, they can sometimes be identified as belonging to one of the types listed below. Happily, a number do exist which cannot be packed tidily into any category.

Dance Types			
Dances in duple- ("common") time with one step-unit per measure		**Dances in triple-time with one step-unit per measure**	
Dance	Usual Time Signature	Dance	Usual Time Signature
Allemande Bourrée Gavotte Rigaudon Gaillarde Pavane	2	Sarabande	3 or $\frac{3}{2}$
		Chaconne Passacaille	3
[Compound] duple-time			
Canarie	$\frac{6}{8}$		
Gigue Forlane	$\frac{6}{4}$		
Dances in quadruple-time with two step-units per measure		**Dances in triple-time with one step-unit per two measures**	
Entrée Grave	2 or C	Menuet	3
Gavotte (gravement)	2	Passepied	$\frac{3}{8}$
Loure or Gigue Lente	$\frac{6}{4}$	**With one long and one short step-unit per measure**	
		Courante	$\frac{3}{2}$

The masters do not differentiate between duple- and [compound] duple-time.

Loures are sometimes written in 3, two measures equalling one of $\frac{6}{4}$. Passepieds may be found in $\frac{6}{8}$, one measure equalling two of $\frac{3}{8}$. Menuets may be found in $\frac{6}{4}$, one measure equalling two measures of $\frac{3}{4}$.

Step-units Related to the Musical Measures		
Beats per Measure	Usual Time Signature	Step-units per measure and the levels upon which the single steps and actions move
Three beats Three half notes per measure	**TRIPLE-TIME** $\frac{3}{2}$ ♩ ♩ ♩	One step-unit per measure moving on the half note level.
Three quarter notes per measure	3 ♩ ♩ ♩	One step-unit per measure moving on the quarter note level. (Exceptions: the menuet and passepied, which will be discussed on p. 191.)
Two beats Two half notes per measure	**DUPLE- (COMMON) TIME** 2 ♩ ♩ / ♩ ♩ ♩ ♩	One step-unit per measure moving on the half or the quarter note level.
Two dotted half notes per measure	**[COMPOUND] DUPLE-TIME** $\frac{6}{4}$ ♩. ♩. / ♩ ♩ ♩ ♩ ♩ ♩	One step-unit per measure moving on the dotted half note or the quarter note level.
Two dotted quarter notes per measure	$\frac{6}{8}$ ♩. ♩. / ♫♫ ♫♫	One step-unit per measure moving on the dotted quarter or eighth note level.
Two half notes per measure	**QUADRUPLE-TIME** 2 ♩ ♩ ♩ ♩ / ♫♫♫ ♫♫♫	Two step-units per measure moving on the quarter note or the eighth note level.
Two dotted half notes per measure	$\frac{6}{4}$ ♩. ♩. / ♩ ♩ ♩ ♩ ♩ ♩	Two step-units per measure moving on the quarter note level.

**TIMING OF THE
INITIAL ACTION IN
A STEP-UNIT**

The first action in a step-unit is usually the bending of the knees in a "movement:"

The Tune or Cadence is expressed two Ways in Dancing; that is to say, the Steps which are sinking and rising, are raised in the Cadence; but those of jumping fall in it: Therefore the Movement ought to be taken before. *(Ram. 1 p. 97; Ess. p. 55)*

Almost all step-units can be rhythmically adapted for use in the different dance types. Unfortunately, chorégraphie does not convey the precise relationships of the single steps or the "movements" to the music. Aware of this deficiency, Feuillet and Rameau give tables relating step-units to music by numbers, and when these are combined with descriptions by Rameau and Tomlinson, a very full picture of the time values of steps in both duple- and triple-time emerges.

The necessity for these explanations arises partly from the separation of the step-units by bar lines:

This clearly shows the unit and the measure of music to which it relates, but precludes the placement of some of the actions in their correct relationship to the musical measure.

The first single step in a measure must culminate on the downbeat with the transference of weight. Therefore the motion of the stepping foot from the starting position with any accompanying action must be made on the upbeat of the preceding musical measure. This means that in chorégraphie the first action (or actions) on the first step symbol within a measure relates not to the first beat of the measure within which it appears but to the upbeat in the previous measure:

Thus this   means this   in time.

The action, a bend in this example, occurs not on the downbeat but on the upbeat. In reading the notation, this fact must be kept in mind constantly.

The appearance of a bending sign at the beginning of a measure in chorégraphie has misled many scholars. However, Rameau says quite clearly:

The Sink ought to be made properly, the Rise in Cadence. . .When I say that the Sink must be made properly, I mean that a Person should sink at the End of the Time, [measure] to rise again as the Time [first beat of the next measure] is beat, which in Terms of Dancing is called Cadence. *(Ram. 1 p. 134; Ess. p. 76)*

After bending, the following rise or landing from a spring will mark the first beat in the next measure:

The first Note or Beginning of a Bar is the Time or Mark the Dancer must hit; . . . whether it be done by a Rise upon the Toe, a Hop, or any other Step, it matters not, in that it is to be observed, the Rise from a Sink beats Time in Dancing. *(Tom. p. 146)*

Without the use of bar lines, the step symbols would continue to overlap, and all the signs upon them would be accurately placed in relationship to time and to the steps. For this reason Rameau eliminates the bar lines, using an M (measure) beside the action to be made on the downbeat:

Feuillet's separation of each step-unit by bar lines causes the bends to appear to coincide with the downbeats.

Rameau's modification: no bar lines.

If the step symbols were drawn in their correct relationship to the music, the bends would be accurately placed on the upbeats, the rises on the downbeats, but the unit would not be contained within the measure.

Rameau's solution has its drawbacks when reading a score, especially when the page is crowded, because without the landmarks of bar lines it is difficult to distinguish the step-units.

Conflict of "Rests" and "Movements"

Feuillet uses rests in relation to the single steps, even when "movements" are added, because rests are one of the few ways to establish the meter of a dance in chorégraphie:

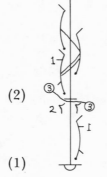

This example could be either in duple- or triple-time but for the rests. Their presence does not alter the upbeat/downbeat relationship of the following "movement."

Beat 3 in measure (1) is given as a rest; in measure (2), however, the bending sign and the step symbol direct the dancer to bend and pass the foot forward to 1st pos. on beat 3 of the previous measure.

The rest on beat 2 in measure (1) is a rest in the sense of absence of motion but not in the sense of absence of effort, since the dancer is balancing on one foot. Only when a rest lasts a measure or more can it be defined in the latter sense.

RELATING STEP-UNITS TO THE MUSICAL MEASURE

Feuillet

Feuillet gives numerous tables relating one step-unit to one measure of duple- and triple-time. He indicates by numbers the beats in a measure upon which the single steps will culminate and also the accented points of arrival of some of the "movements." *(Feu. 2)*

Rameau

In *Abbregé* Rameau compiles tables in which he defines the step/music relationships in great detail, but he employs so many numbers that only occasionally do they coincide with the musical beats.

Tomlinson

The verbal descriptions given by Tomlinson are usually for triple-meter. When he discusses step-units in "Common Time," Tomlinson counts four in a measure:

Common Time, for Instance, is of four Notes to the Bar or Measure. . .and the Rise or Beginning of the Step, in Dancing, from a Sink always marks Time to the Tune, as well as the fourth or last Note is in the Sink or Preparative for the Rise or beating Time to the succeeding Step. . . . *(Tom. p. 144)*

In the following chapter on the step-units, the author's tables will match the French "deux temps" to Tomlinson's descriptions:

Tomlinson		W.H.	
1		Beat 1	
2			and
3		beat 2	
4			and

Almost all the nineteen step-units which, according to Rameau, form the basic step vocabulary of the dance could be used in almost all the dance types listed on p. 154. In the analysis in Chapter Nine, the step-units are discussed in duple- and triple-meter. These metric values apply to all the duple- and triple-time dances which have one step-unit per measure. The author relates the steps and actions in a step-unit to the musical beats as in the following examples:

Triple-time   Duple-time

3	= bend then		
		and =	bend then
and	= place the foot		place the foot
1	= rise	1 =	rise
2	= step	and =	step
3	= step/bend etc.	2 =	step

In the text, the term "timing" is used for the general relationship of a step-unit to duple- or triple-meter.

The note upon which the actions which precede the measure is made is, for want of a better term, referred to here as the upbeat. In triple-time the upbeat is also a beat, whereas in duple-time it is not. The word "and" indicates a division of the note; as in this $\frac{3}{2}$ example:

$$3 = \text{𝅗𝅥}$$

divided into:

$$3 = \text{♩} = \text{bend then}$$
$$\text{and} = \text{♩} = \text{place the foot} \Big\} = \text{𝅗𝅥}$$

Note Values and Beats

In Chapter Nine, specific note values are used only occasionally to avoid confusion with beats: a beat may be represented by a different note value in dance types with the same meter, or in different pieces of the same type. For instance, a sarabande might be in $\frac{3}{2}$, a half note representing a beat; or in $\frac{3}{[4]}$, a quarter note representing a beat.

In order that the text accompanying the numbers may be as concise as possible a hyphen or, occasionally, a slash is used. For example:

> step-bend = make these two actions simultaneously
> step/bend = make these two actions consecutively

Rhythmic Complexities

Chapter Ten deals with some rhythmic complexities of the menuet, passepied, and gavotte, the basic steps of which are given in Chapter Nine. It also introduces [compound] duple-time and quadruple-time dances. Peforming students will be directed to Chapter Ten at several points in Chapter Nine, when their knowledge of the step-units is sufficiently advanced.

RELATIONSHIP OF ARM MOTIONS TO THE "MOVEMENTS"

The arms move in rhythmic sympathy with the "movements," their motions usually ending on the downbeat. If the starting position is the position of elevation, palms up, the arms will rotate inward to the position of elevation, palms down, as the knees bend on the upbeat. They will then circle inward and upward to reach the position of opposition on the downbeat. (See pp. 136, 140 for these arm positions.)

If, however, the preceding step should conclude with the arms raised in the position of opposition, they will usually circle inward and downward to reach the position of elevation, palms down, on the downbeat. Or, if another opposition follows, the raised arm will lower outward and make a circle of the wrist from below upwards, the other arm being raised simultaneously into opposition, on the downbeat. (It should be remembered that the position of elevation is lower than the position of opposition.)

Table Relating the Arm Motions in General to the Music

Music:	Arms reach:	"Movements"
Upbeat	The position of elevation (palms down)	Bend the knees.
Downbeat	The position of elevation (palms up)	Straighten, or bend if landing from a spring.
	The position of opposition or	
	The position of elevation (palms down) if	
	(a) The preceding step-unit concluded with the arms in the position of opposition,	
	(b) the step-unit required only a motion of the wrists.	

Author's References to
the Arm Motions

In the following chapters, the arm motions will be described as succinctly as possible, presuming a thorough grasp of the theory given in Chapter Seven. Making the position of opposition may be indicated simply by the instruction to "oppose." Lowering to the position of elevation will be qualified by:

inward   = take an inward circular path from the elbow

outward   = take an outward circular path from the elbow

directly   = take the shortest path

Rameau's directions regarding paths are often insufficient, and sometimes the author has given instructions based on the theory of the arm motions and practical application. No page references are given for the arm motions because they can be found easily in *Le Maître à danser,* Part Two.

Modifying the Arm Motions

In a sequence of steps, it will often be found that the regular arm motion for a step-unit must be modified because of the context. Sometimes the juxtaposition of step-units results in what can only be described as a multitude of motions. Individual taste must finally determine which motions to retain and which to discard. Simplicity without loss of rhythmic vitality should be the goal.

FOOTNOTES

1. Tems or Time is used by the masters with a variety of meaning. The term may refer to meter, speed, the first beat in a measure, any beat in a measure, or a whole measure itself. In steps, it refers to a "movement" without a change of weight made to mark the "Time" or first beat in a measure.
2. In today's conventional music theory, common time is four beats in a measure. The common time given by Weaver and Tomlinson has two beats per measure. The note representing the beat is most commonly a half note. (Note values are given on p. 150)
3. See *Ram. 2 p. 23* for his modifications of the black pins which equate step symbols to the specific musical note values. Also *p. 25* for rests.

A plate from *The Art of Dancing.* Kellom Tomlinson, London, 1735.

CHAPTER NINE

The Steps and Their General Performance in Duple- and Triple-Meter

In the step vocabulary of the dance described by Rameau, there are nineteen basic step-units. A step-unit (the author's term) is any combination of single steps or other actions which are grouped to equal a musical measure. Almost all the units can be danced in duple- or triple-time and appropriately used in the different dance types listed on p. 154. Definitions of the two kinds of step-unit, the temps and pas-composé, are given on p. 73. Modern spelling is used in the following table.

Table of Step-units As They Relate to the Musical Measure

Temps: Equalling one Measure (A half in quadruple time)[1]
   Temps de courante
   Pirouette

Pas Composés: Equalling one Measure (A half in quadruple time)
   Pas coupé
   Glissades: two *coupés* combined to fill a measure
   Pas de bourrée or *Fleuret*
   Contretemps de gavotte
                   de chaconne
                           ballonné
   Pas de sissonne
   Jetés:
   Chassés: two or three combined to fill a measure
   Pas tombé
   Pas de courante: used only in *courantes*[2]

Pas Composés: Equalling two Musical Measures (One in quadruple time)
   Pas de rigaudon: duple-time only
   Pas échappé
   Pas de gaillarde
   Pas balancé
   Pas de menuet:
   Contretemps de menuet: used only in menuets and passepieds

A Step of Punctuation: Equalling the First Beat in a Measure
   Pas assemblé

Table of Steps in the Order in Which They Will Be Analyzed (given in Rameau's original spelling)

Single Steps Without "Movements" Used in *Temps* and *Pas Composés*

    Pas marché   *Pas glissé*

Single Steps With "Movements" Used in *Pas Composés*

    Demi-coupé   *Jetté*   *Demi-jetté*

Pas Composés Beginning With a *Demi-coupé*

    Pas coupé   *Glissades*   *Pas de Bourée*
    Pas de Menuet   *Pas balancé*

Step-units Called *Temps*

    Tems de Courante   *Tems*   *Pirouette*

Step-units Called *Contretemps*

    Contre-tems de Gavotte   *Contre-tems de Chaconne*
    Contre-tems du Menuet   *Contre-tems balonné*

Step-units Composed Mainly of Springs

    Pas assemblé   *Pas de Sisonne*   *Pas de Rigaudon*
    Jettez   *Jettez chassez*   *Chassez*

Step-units With an Element of Collapse

    Pas tombé   *Pas de Gaillarde*   *Pas échapez*

Preliminary Bends in Step-units

In theory, almost all step-units begin with a bend and finish with the knees straight. In practice, the end of one unit flows into the bend of the next, leading to the downbeat. Rameau stresses the importance of a sufficiently deep bend:

But as to the Sinks they should always be made full, especially at first learning, because they render a Dance more agreeable; whereas when they are not, the Steps are hardly to be distinguished, and the Dance seems stiff and dry. *(Ram. 1 p. 173; Ess. p. 102)*

SINGLE STEPS WITHOUT "MOVEMENTS" USED IN TEMPS AND PAS COMPOSES

*Pas Marché sur la
Pointe du Pied.
March on the Toes.
(Ram. 1 p. 76 in the pas
de menuet; Ess. p. 43)*

A pas marché is a walking step generally made on [demi] pointe. The legs must be held straight throughout, the thigh muscles pulled upward.

*Pas Glissé.
A Slide.
(Ram. 1 p. 133 in the Coupe;
Ess. p. 76)*

A pas glissé is a walking step made as above but with a slow sustained quality. It is done by sliding the ball of the foot gently along the floor toward the finishing position.

SINGLE STEPS WITH "MOVEMENTS" USED IN PAS COMPOSES

*Le Demi-coupé.
The Half Coupee.
(Ram. 1 p. 71; Ess. p. 41)*

The main use of the demi-coupé is to emphasize the first beat in a measure of music by bending the knees on the upbeat and rising and stepping on the downbeat. Rhythmically exciting performances are largely dependent upon the dancers' execution of this step. Almost all the non-springing pas composés begin with a demi-coupé:

It is, first of all, to be observed, that the Half Coupee. . .is originally nothing more than a single Step, made with either Foot, from one Place to another with the additional Ornament of a Movement or Bending or Rising of the Knees in Time to Music. *(Tom. p. 25)*

A demi-coupé consists of one "movement" made during a single step. According to Rameau it is not a step-unit in its own right since it does not equal one measure of music: "The demi-coupé being only part of a pas composé such as a coupé, pas de bourée, and others, one calls it demi." *(Ram. 2 p. 32)* (L123)

Rameau rightly stresses the importance of the demi-coupé. Almost all the step-units used most frequently begin with one. The demi-coupé requires a detailed and lengthy explanation, but once this basic single step and "movement" has been mastered, step-units which begin with a demi-coupé can be learned easily.

In *Le Maître à danser* Rameau gives a reasonably clear description of the demi-coupé, illustrated by the following four plates:

As no bent Step can be made without the Movement of the Knee, and as commonly all those Steps which are composed of many Steps, begin with half Coupees, whether it be with the right or left Leg, its no matter; but supposing it to be with the Right, the left Foot must be foremost, in the fourth Position, and the Body rests upon it, as represented by this first Figure, which hath the Body rested forwards upon it, the Right being ready to move, having nothing but the Toes placed on the Ground.

Therefore, to begin this half Coupee, you bring the right Foot up to the Left, in the first Position, and bend both Knees equally together, keeping the Body on the left Foot, as shown by the second Figure, which hath both the Feet close together, the Body all the while on the Left. . .the Right off the Ground, both the Knees equally bent, and turned outwards, the Waste steady, and the Head upright. *(Ram. 1 p. 71; Ess. p. 41)*

From plates: Ram. 1 pp. 71-72.

In this Sink you carry the right Foot before you, without rising, to the Fourth Position, as this third Figure shews; and at the same Time bring the Body forwards on it, rising upon the Toes of the right Foot. . .with an extended Knee, and bringing the left Foot close up. . .with its Knee extended also, as the fourth Figure represents, which for that reason we may call the Equilibrium or Balance, because the Body is only supported by one Foot. Afterwards you let the Heel down to the Ground, which makes an End of this Step. *(Ram. 1 p. 72; Ess. p. 42)*

From plates: Ess. 1731, second issue, p. 42.

The demi-coupé can finish in two ways:

(1) When followed by another "movement," it concludes with a lowering of the heel (which is usually combined with the next bend).

(2) When followed by a pas marché, the rise is the conclusion.

Preparation for the rise

A question is often asked concerning the preparation for the rise in the demi-coupé: If the rise is to be made onto [demi] pointe, should the foot be placed into the stepping position with the heel already raised, or should the whole foot be flat on the ground, the heel (of the shoe) being lifted only upon the straightening of the knee?

In Essex's plate the heel appears to be raised, and many other engravings clearly show the heel raised. To perform the demi-coupé in this way seems better stylistically; the alternative of rising from the flat foot tends to be jerky and labored, and sequences of steps progress in a bumpy manner. The placing of the foot with the heel raised is used throughout this book.

From plate: Ess. 1731, second issue, p. 42.

The rise

The rise onto [demi] pointe in the demi-coupé is not indicated in dance scores although there is provision for it—a dot beside the rising sign meaning rise onto the toes. Perhaps the writing of a dot beside each rising sign was avoided as much for the reader's sake as for the notator's, but there was also some leeway concerning the degree of rise when dancing in a ballroom: "...and it [the Half Coupee] is most amiable, when executed in that gentle and graceful Manner it ought to be, whether upon the Toe or Heel." *(Tom. p. 25)* Here "Heel" means the whole foot flat on the floor.

Tomlinson often mentions the two alternatives, but Rameau leaves no doubt that a rise onto [demi] pointe was desirable and used whenever possible. Unless a modifying leg gesture is given, the rise in a demi-coupé finishes in the position of equilibrium.

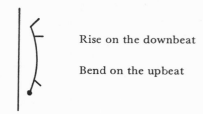

Rise on the downbeat

Bend on the upbeat

In his *Traité de la cadence (Ram. 2 p. 108)*, Rameau provides a detailed account of the upbeat/downbeat relationship of the demi-coupé. Rameau says that the note which precedes the measure, the upbeat, is used to lift the stepping foot, while bending the knees, and to pass it to the finishing position. The rise is then made on the downbeat, on [demi]pointe. Rameau adds the precise instruction to "remain on the pointe. . .for the space of time of the quarter note."

Rameau is specifically discussing the pas de menuet but his remarks apply to the demi-coupé in all contexts. His revelation that the process of rising should not take the full duration of the downbeat is of the utmost importance. If the rise is completed one half or three quarters of the way through the first beat (depending on the pas composé), the performance gains in vitality; the dancer has time to emphasize the beat with a subtle pause in the position of equilibrium.

Rameau's description of his next notated example is even clearer:

The first note [the downbeat] is given as a rise; that is to show you that the bend and passage of the foot [to fourth position] should be done before the measure begins so as to be ready to rise on the first beat. *(Ram. 2 p. 109)*

In order to rise as the downbeat sounds, the dancer must ensure that the passage of the foot to the stepping position takes place on the second half of the upbeat. This is especially true of dances in slow triple-time when the performers' desire to achieve a legato quality often results in their steps dragging along just behind the beat.

Duple-time		Triple-time	
and	= bend then place the foot	3	= bend then
1	= rise, in pos. of eq.	and	= place the foot
		1	= rise in the pos. of eq.

ARMS

The use of the arms in a demi-coupé will often depend upon the preceding step, but generally opposition is used on the rise, the arms lowering inward on the next bend. The arm motions coordinate with the "movements" as follows:

First half of the upbeat	As the knees bend, the arms will be in the pos. of el., palms down.
Second half of the upbeat	As the foot is passed into the stepping position, the opposite arm, having begun to move from below upwards when the foot moves, will reach a point about midway toward opposition, the palm facing the body just above waist level.
On the first half, or three quarters, of the downbeat	As the knees stretch, the arm reaches the pos. of opp., the lower arm turning simultaneously from the wrist from below upwards.

If another demi-coupé follows, return the arms from above downwards to reach the pos. of el., palms down, as the knees complete their next bend on the first half of the upbeat.

AUTHOR'S NOTES

Keep the weight of the body forward and:

First half of the upbeat	COMPLETE the bending of both knees BEFORE MOVING THE STEPPING FOOT FROM FIRST POSITION.
Second half of the upbeat	STAY DOWN while placing the foot into the stepping position, the heel of the STEPPING foot raised SLIGHTLY but the heel of the supporting foot PRESSED FIRMLY TO THE FLOOR. Transfer some weight to the stepping foot as soon as it touches the floor. BOTH knees are still bent.
The first half, or three quarters, of the downbeat	Stretching BOTH knees, WITHOUT RAISING THE HEEL OF THE STEPPING FOOT HIGHER, transfer the weight onto the stepping foot, bringing the other foot to 1st pos. in the air, flexing the ankle so that the foot is held parallel to the floor. Do not twist the foot, or allow the big toe to strain upward into the air.

Make sure that the arm motions correspond with the bends and rises. In order to arrive at the pos. of opp. on the downbeat, the arm motion MUST be begun on the second half of the upbeat.

Now hold the position of equilibrium to ensure that the body is well placed, the torso upright, the muscles of the pelvis firm, the rib cage lifted and full of air. The shoulders, arms, and hands must be without strain. The head is level and held with ease. Feel a plumb line through the center of the body, the backs of both legs pulling downward toward the floor. The raised heel is therefore not pushing away from the floor but pulling toward it. The dancer, especially a man, should have solidity, giving the impression that he owns the ground upon which he is standing.

EXERCISE Practice a series of demi-coupés without arm motions. Each demi-coupé should take two beats of music. This exercise will establish the upbeat/downbeat relationship of the first demi-coupé and prepare the student for two demi-coupés in succession which occur in some pas de menuet. Work either without music or to a bourrée: start slowly and increase to metronome marking MM ♩. = 50. (L124)

Bend,
place
the foot, Rise

Bend,
place
the foot, Rise

Bend,
place
the foot, Rise

Demi-coupé en arrière The same as the demi-coupé forward but traveling backward. (L125)

ARMS The foot that is stepped off is opposed, which means that if the left foot is making the step backward, the left arm will be raised to oppose the right foot.
Do not practice the demi-coupé backward until p. 173.

Demi-coupé de côté Bend in 1st pos. as usual and step and rise in 2nd with the R ft. (L126)

The leg stepped off will probably not move to the pos. of eq. with emphasis since it is more propitious for balance to move it in gently from 2nd pos. and to bypass the lst pos. for the following single step.

ARMS Various, depending upon the step sequence.

Here the leg stepped off does move to the pos. of eq.

Bend in lst and step and rise in 5th front on the L ft., the R in the pos. of eq. (L127)

ARMS Usually opposition is used.

Note. All demi-coupés are made with the bend in first position unless a modifying factor is introduced.

The Demi-coupé Alone in a Measure

Generally used as part of a pas composé, the demi-coupé is sometimes made alone in a measure. (L128, 129)

As discussed in Chapter Eight, the notation does not visually depict the true relationship of the "movement" to the measure.

Duple-time			Triple-time		
and	=	bend then	3	=	bend then
		place the foot	and	=	place the foot
1	=	rise in pos. of eq.	1	=	rise in pos. of eq.
and	=	hold	2	=	hold
2	=	hold			

Although Rameau does not refer to it as such, Tomlinson feels that the demi-coupé is indeed a step-unit, even though it does not take a whole measure to complete:

The Half Coupee, which, tho' no more than a single Step, is, however, a Step, because it generally takes up a Measure, but more especially in Tunes of triple Time; and it is made by a smooth and easy Bending of the Knees, rising in a slow and gentle Motion from thence; which Rising, as I have said, is upon the first Note of the Measure, the Weight of the Body being supported by the Foot that made the Step, during the Counting of the second and third Notes of the Bar. . . The graceful Posture of the Dancer's Standing adds not a little to the Beauty of this Step, who, till the Time be expired, is to wait or rest; by which it is evident, that the Half Coupee, tho' a single Step, is equal, in Value, to any compound Step whatsoever, whether of two, three, four, or more Steps in a Measure. *(Tom. p. 29)*

Here the rise should probably be onto the whole foot as Tomlinson gives no directions for lowering the heel.

AUTHOR'S NOTES

Although not specifically indicated, it seems reasonable to assume that, in the theater at any rate, dancers would have taken the rise onto [demi] pointe, remaining there to display their ability to balance during the following rest or absence of motion. (L130, 131) In any case, to practice demi-coupés rising onto [demi] pointe is an excellent exercise for aplomb. The following may now be added to the daily routine.

EXERCISE

Practice a series of demi-coupés forward (later with arm motions) to a sarabande. When these begin to feel secure, practice a series backward. When forward is changed to backward without pause, the arm in opposition must circle outward as the forward/backward path is reversed.

Demi-coupés Which Do Not Finish in the Position of Equilibrium

Although the rise in a demi-coupé almost always finishes in the position of equilibrium, on some occasions the free leg either is momentarily retained in an open position, or makes a more deliberate gesture which will be seen in the notation. The former is not shown by the notation symbols but is indicated in written descriptions.

Le Jetté.
The Bound.
(Ram. 1 p. 162; Ess. p. 95)

The jeté consists of one single step and one sprung "movement." A jeté is sometimes used as the last single step in a pas composé. (L132)

The jeté is a very small spring from one foot to the other, performed primarily by an action of the instep:

As Rising consists in the greater or less Strength of the Instep, so this Step depends on it to be performed with Activity, (légèreté). *(Ram. 1 p. 163; Ess. p. 95)*

In theory, a jeté is made by bending (as in the demi-coupé) and springing off the supporting leg onto the [demi] pointe of the stepping leg. After arriving on the [demi] pointe, the heel is immediately lowered to the ground, to complete the jeté. However, this lowering coincides with the bend of the next "movement." Thus in practice, the jeté will end by flowing downward through the foot into the bend. (L133)

TIME AND ARMS

These will be discussed as the jeté occurs in individual pas composés.

AUTHOR'S NOTES

A jeté is a step that is sprung rather than walked. The instep must be very resilient. Do not brush the foot along the floor or make leg gestures. The supporting leg stretches only enough to facilitate the push off into the air. Remember that the spring is very small.

Le Demi-jetté.[3]
The Half Bound.

The demi-jeté is like a jeté but made with an even smaller spring, the dancer scarcely leaving the ground. According to Rameau, it is used more frequently than the jeté because the last single step of a pas composé should not be too accentuated. Tomlinson says that the choice of jeté or demi-jeté will depend upon the character of the dance being performed. (L134)

The demi-jeté does not seem to have acquired this name until after 1700 because Feuillet refers to it with the illuminating description, "Jetté sans sauter ou demy coupé en l'Air" [A jeté without jumping or a demi-coupé into the air]. *(Feu. 1a)* The demi-jeté is also known by other names. In *Le Maître à danser*, Rameau seems uncertain what to call it, using upon occasion the terms "demi-coupé échappé" or "jetté échapé", but in *Abbregé* he has settled for "demi-jetté" on the grounds that the "movement" is only half sprung. *(Ram. 2 p. 24)*

Feuillet does not provide a special sign for a half spring. He sometimes notates the demi-jeté with its "movement" halfway through the step where it occurs, but in most pas composés he notates it as a demi-coupé. As the latter is used at the beginning of a pas composé and the demi-jeté at the end, this convention was no doubt acceptable. Rameau improved the situation by modifying the springing sign:

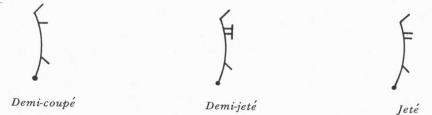

Demi-coupé   Demi-jeté   Jeté

The demi-jeté must be sufficiently animated within its small scope. The decision to perform it with emphasis on the rise, as in a demi-coupé, or on the landing, as in a jeté, must be made by the individual; no instructions are given on this point. In physical terms the difference is very slight, but in the courante, where the demi-jeté is used frequently, this decision is important.

TIME AND ARMS

These will be discussed as the demi-jeté occurs in individual pas composés.

AUTHOR'S NOTES

A pas composé ending with a demi-jeté should be more animated than one ending with a pas marché. But the idea that the spring is "demi" often results in a lifeless, flat performance, producing just the opposite effect from the one intended. To avoid this, give a very animated rebound out of the preliminary bend, using the ankle and the strength of the instep. From this, arrive with LIFE on the [demi] pointe of the stepping leg, coming down through the instep to lower the heel. If the emphasis is up, as in a demi-coupé, pause MOMENTARILY on [demi]pointe.

GROUPING OF THE STEP-UNITS

In the following pages, the step-units are grouped into two sections under five headings:

Section 1

Pas Composés Beginning With a Demi-coupé: a transference of weight in a single step, combined with a "movement."

Step-units Called Temps: units beginning with a "movement" made on the foot already supporting the body.

Step-units Called Contretemps: units beginning with a sprung "movement" off and on to the foot already supporting the body (a hop).

Section 2

Step-units Composed Mainly of Springs: springs other than the hop.

Step-units With an Element of Collapse: the knees bend with a slightly more collapsed quality than in other units.

The majority of step-units can be performed *en avant* (forward), *en arrière* (backward), and *de côté* (sideward). When made sideward, the first single step may be an open step to second position or a crossed step to fifth position, depending upon the direction of travel, and which foot is making the step.

In addition, a few units have several variations, the basic structure of the unit being retained.

SHORT STUDY GUIDE FOR PERFORMING STUDENTS

In the following study of the step-units, performing students should follow a slightly different route for a while from those reading for theory only. For theory it is best to present each step-unit with all its variations, but for the performing student this is not an efficient system. Readers who intend to perform must acquire a functional knowledge of the basic steps before concerning themselves with the variations. The following is a progressive order suitable for classroom study:

Having mastered these five step-units sufficiently well to perform them with ease in any direction, students can return to p.178 and pursue the chapter including all the variations. Reading material in Beauchamp-Feuillet notation is given in the Study Guide as soon as possible for the rhythmic and spatial study of step-sequences. Performing students should now turn to p. 184.

STEP-UNITS
Section 1

**THE STEP-UNITS BEGINNING
WITH A DEMI-COUPE**

Coupés: Units of Two
Single Steps

Le Coupé.
The Coupee.
(Ram. 1 p. 133; Ess. p. 76)

This pas composé consists of one "movement" and two single steps: the first a demi-coupé, the second a slow, sustained sliding step. It is used in both duple- and triple-time and does not provide a change of foot for the following step-unit.

Rameau describes two ways of performing this coupé, the first easier than the second which, however, corresponds to the notation. In both, the demi-coupé finishes as usual on the [demi] pointe, after which the dancer may either:
(1) Lower the heel, then bend the knees while sliding the foot to the finishing position before transferring the weight onto it.
(2) Remain on [demi] pointe, slide the ball of the foot to the finishing position, then transfer the weight to it and lower the heel. (L135)
The second method is used throughout this book.

Not all coupés are notated with sliding signs and Rameau calls his example with a slide "coupé soutenue" and the one without "coupé simple":

Coupé soutenue   *Coupé simple*

A coupé made forward is usually a coupé soutenue, and one made backward or to the side a coupé simple. In the coupé simple the foot will be passed just above the ground. (L136)

TIME

Duple-time		Triple-time	
and	= bend then place the foot	3	= bend then
1	= rise in pos. of eq.	and	= place the foot
and	= slide	1	= rise in pos. of eq.
2	= transfer the weight	and	= slide
and	= lower the heel flowing into the bend/place the foot, etc.	2	= transfer the weight
		and	= lower the heel flowing into the bend, etc.

ARMS

Coupé en avant

(L137)

Begin in opposition. Lower the arms inward or outward on the bend for the demi-coupé, hold the pos. of el., and then oppose the second single step.

Coupé en arrière

(L138)

The coupé backward has two oppositions. The first opposes the supporting foot on the bend for the demi-coupé, the other the second single step. Change the opposition by lowering the raised arm outward as the other lifts.

Coupé de côté

(L139)

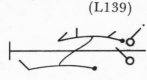

Oppose the demi-coupé then lower the arms outward on the second single step. Rameau also suggests using only a motion of the wrists from below upwards on the demi-coupé. Remember to be in 1st pos. when bending, and when in the pos. of eq.

(L140)

Rameau gives this sideward coupé only in conjunction with glissades.(See p. 170.)

AUTHOR'S NOTES

Perform the demi-coupé as on p.   . It will be executed as usual, taking the upbeat and part of the downbeat. Remember that it is only halfway through the second single step that the sustained quality which characterizes the coupé is introduced. For instance, in a coupé forward, the slide occurs only from first position toward fourth position. DO NOT ANTICIPATE the slide by dragging the foot INTO first when completing the demi-coupé.

Variations of the Coupé

The single steps of the coupé can be varied in several ways without altering its value in time:

Coupé battu (Ram. 1 p. 136; Ess. p. 77)

There are also Coupees with a Beat often used in Ball Dancing; For Example; you make your Half Coupee forwards with the right Leg, and the Left comes up striking the Calf of the Right and retires back to the fourth Position. *(Ram. 1 p. 136; Ess. p. 77)* The beat is made with both legs straight. (L141)

TIME

In triple-time:	one	and	two	three
Beat of the leg:		beat		
In duple-time:	one	and	two	and

ARMS

Oppose the demi-coupé on the step and rise, shading the right shoulder. Maintain this position during the beat of the foot.

Coupé avec ouverture de jambe (Ram. 1 p. 136; Ess. p. 77)

In this coupé the second single step becomes a leg gesture, passing slightly forward from 1st pos. and opening to the side, the foot remaining off the ground. (L142)

TIME

This coupé is often done with a beat behind and before. (L143) The first beat would probably be done on the rise in the demi-coupé:

In triple-time:	one	and	etc.
Beats of the leg:	beat	beat	
In duple-time:	one	and	etc.

ARMS

Begin in 4th pos., the arms in opposition. Lower them outward on the bend for the demi-coupé. Maintain this position during the opening of the leg.

Coupé avec tour (ronde) de jambe
(Feu. 1, Tables of Coupés)

This being essentially a theatrical step, Rameau mentions it only in passing. (L144)

Coupé sans poser le corps
(Ram. 1 p. 232; Ess. p. 125)

The second single step finishes with the toe just touching the ground. (L145)

ARMS

The arms are in opposition. Lower them outward to the pos. of el., palms up, on the demi-coupé and hold that position.

The rules governing the arm motions will often be modified by the step-unit preceding and following the coupé. (See Chapter Eight) When a coupé finishes with the foot off the floor or with the toe "pointed," a change of foot for the following step-unit will be provided since the weight is not transferred on the second single step.

EXERCISE

For coupés in duple- and triple-meter.

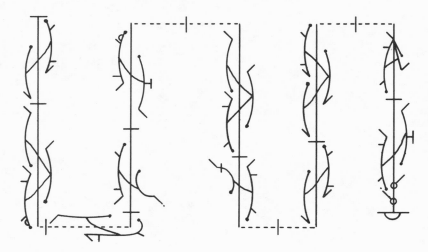

Coupé à Deux Mouvements.
Coupee with Two Movements.
(Ram. 1 p. 139; Ess. p. 80)

This coupé has a second "movement," a demi-jeté, made during the second single step. (L146)

It is imaginatively described by Rameau:

This Step is one of the most graceful and gay of all the different Steps that have been invented, for the Variety of its Movements, which are easy and give a great Grace when understood. . . .it is composed but of two Steps, and those two Steps contain two different Movements. The First is sinking on one Foot and making a Step with the other and rising on it, [demi-coupé] which obliges you to do it gracefully. The Second is sinking on that Foot, and rising with more Life to fall on the other with a half Bound, which makes this Step gay and airy. *(Ram. 1 p. 139; Ess. p. 80)*

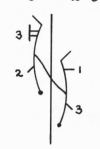

Ram. 2 p. 104, No. 6
The numbers are edited.

Triple-time

3 = bend then
and = place the foot
1 = rise in pos. of eq.
2 = bend
and = half spring
3 = land-bend

Feuillet's table could mean this also but suggests another possibility which is compatible with the sarabande rhythm: (L147)

3 = bend then
and = place the foot
1 = rise in pos. of eq.
and = bend/half spring
2 = land on [demi] pointe-and flow
3 = into the next bend, etc.

Duple-time

and = bend then
      place the foot
1 = rise in pos. of eq.
and = bend/half spring
2 = land on [demi] pointe- and
      flow into the next bend, etc.

ARMS

Some very subtle uses of the arms, head, and body are obviously essential in a true performance of this coupé. It is best to allow Rameau to convey these almost intangible qualities:

Therefore when you take your first Step, which is a half Coupee well rested upon, at that Time you let both Arms turn a little downwards, and make a half Movement with the Wrists and Elbows, beginning from below upwards; which ought to be attended with a small Inclination of the Body and Head imperceptibly and without Affectation; but when you take your second Movement. . .in beginning your Sink your Arms extend and at the same Instant have a little Motion from the Shoulder in falling, and in rising the Body recovers as well as the Head, which ought to be held a little back, which gives a majestik Air, and makes a perfect Union of the Movement both of the Legs and Arms as well as the Head and Body. *(Ram. 1 p. 236; Ess. p. 138)*

Remember to rebound out of the bend of the demi-jeté. In a series, do not miss the placing of the foot in the demi-coupé which maintains the difference between the two "movements."

Coupé à deux mouvements de côté

 (L148)

Rameau does not mention this open, sideward coupé.

 (L149)

Rameau gives the following arm motion for this crossed, sideward coupé:

ARMS

. . .making those Movements of the Arms from below upwards; but lower them a little in taking your second Movement and raise them in finishing, and also make a small Inclination of the Body and Head, observing if you go from the right the Head should be half turned [an eighth] that Way. All these Observations have a wonderful Effect in Dancing, and shew both Life and Judgment. *(Ram. 1 p. 238; Ess. p. 139)*

Glissade.
The Slip.
(Ram. 1 p. 138; Ess. p. 79)

Coupés made smoothly, but quickly, so that two equal one measure of music, are called glissades. The demi-coupés are taken in second position and the pas glissés in third, or fifth, front or behind. They can be used in duple- or triple-time and are generally followed by another glissade or coupé taking a whole measure.[4] Sometimes a demi-jeté is used instead of a demi-coupé.

TIME

Duple-time. There are no tables for the timing of glissades, but two are included in a sequence analyzed by Rameau. Rameau notates them with his demi-jeté sign, and this execution is more compatible with their usual fast tempo. *(Ram. 2 p. 107)*

Make two coupés twice as quickly. (See the coupé in duple-time on p. 177.) The rises will occur on beats 1 and 2 in a measure. (L150)

Triple-time. From dances it can be seen that in triple-time the first glissade usually takes one beat and the second, two. (L151)

ARMS

At most, small motions of the wrists would accompany such quick "movements" of the insteps, but no motion seems preferable. Instructions are not given on this point.

Pas de Bourrée:
Units of Three Single Steps

Le Pas de Bourée.
The Boree with
Two Movements.
(Ram. 1 p. 122; Ess. p. 70)

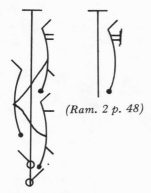

(Ram. 2 p. 48)

(Tom. Pl. E)

According to Rameau, this is the "true" pas de bourrée. It has two "movements" and three single steps: a demi-coupé, a pas marché, and a demi-jeté. It can be used in duple- or triple-time. It rarely appears in French dance scores, having been replaced by the fleuret, which uses only the first "movement," but is found frequently in dances published in England.

Feuillet does not include a table of this pas de bourrée, so it must have been out of fashion in France by 1700. Rameau describes it briefly: "The Boree is composed of two Movements, viz. a half Coupee, a Walk on the Toes, and a half Bound, which makes the second Movement and is the Extent of the Step." *(Ram. 2 p. 49)* Tomlinson calls the second "movement" a demi-coupé, not a demi-jeté, saying it should be made without leaving the floor, but he notates it with a springing sign.

TIME

There are no tables showing the timing of this pas composé, only Tomlinson's directions for triple-time. (L152)

3	=	bend then	3	=	bend then
and	=	place the foot	and	=	place the foot
1	=	rise in pos. of eq.	1	=	rise in pos. of eq.
2	=	step	and	=	step
and	=	bend/half spring	2	=	bend
3	=	land-bend, etc.	and	=	half spring
			3	=	land-bend, etc.

ARMS

No motions are given for this pas de bourrée but those for the pas de bourrée vite seem applicable: oppose on the demi-coupé and extend on the demi-jeté.

Fleuret.
The Borée Step or Fleuret.
(Ram. 1 p. 122; Ess. p. 70)

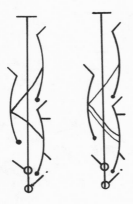

This pas de bourrée has one "movement" and three single steps: a demi-coupé, followed by two pas marchés made on [demi] pointe. The fleuret is used more frequently than any other step-unit; it travels well and provides a change of foot for the next step-unit.

TIME

Tomlinson says one single step should be made on each beat in a measure of triple-time. (L153) The use of a double liaison in notated examples indicates an alternative:

3 = bend then	3 = bend then
and = place the foot	and = place the foot
1 = rise in pos. of eq.	1 = rise in pos. of eq.
2 = step	and = step
3 = step-bend, etc.	2 = step

In duple-time Feuillet's table indicates: (L154)

and = bend then
        place the foot
1 = rise in pos. of eq.
and = step
2 = step

Remember that in duple-time the fleuret will not always be notated with a double liaison as it should be.

Fleuret en arrière

(L155)

ARMS

Fleuret en avant and en arrière. One opposition is made on the demi-coupé; lower inward on the following bend.

AUTHOR'S NOTES

Make sure the demi-coupé is made in time and that the arm in opposition is raised with the straightening of the knees. When making fleurets backward, do not lean backward. In the second example in triple-time, the lowering of the heel must be especially well controlled.

The Steps and Their General Performance in Duple- and Triple-Meter

Fleurets de Côté

Rameau only gives verbal instructions for the first two examples below. The others can be found notated in Feuillet and Weaver: *(Feu. 1 pp. 64-65; Wea. 1 tables 17 & 18)*

Dessus et dessous. Before and behind

The demi-coupé is placed in 5th pos. in front, the first pas marché in 2nd, the second pas marché in 5th pos. behind. (L156)

Remember to bend in 1st pos. and rise in the pos. of eq.

ARMS

Opposition on the demi-coupé, lowering outward on the first pas marché, make another opposition on the third pas marché. If turning, use the same motions, "...which produces two Oppositions in this Step, but sometimes they are not both made because of the Connexion of another Step that follows, and which alters the Rule." *(Ram. 1 p. 225; Ess. p. 131)*

Dessous et dessus. Behind and before

The demi-coupé is placed in 5th behind, the first pas marché in 2nd, the second pas marché in 5th front. (L157)

ARMS

Rameau gives no directions for these step-units.

Dessus. Before

The demi-coupé is placed in 5th front, the first pas marché in 2nd, the second pas marché in 5th front.

Derrière. Behind

The demi-coupé is placed in 5th behind, the first pas marché in 2nd, the second pas marché in 5th behind.

In the following example, the foot released of weight is not moved immediately to the position of equilibrium. It moves smoothly to fifth position bypassing first position:

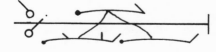

The demi-coupé is placed in 2nd, the first pas marché in 5th front, the second pas marché in 2nd.

For pas de bourrée (fleurets) en avant, en arrière, and de côté. Do not use arm motions until the steps are secure. Practice to a bourrée for duple-meter, and a sarabande for triple-meter.

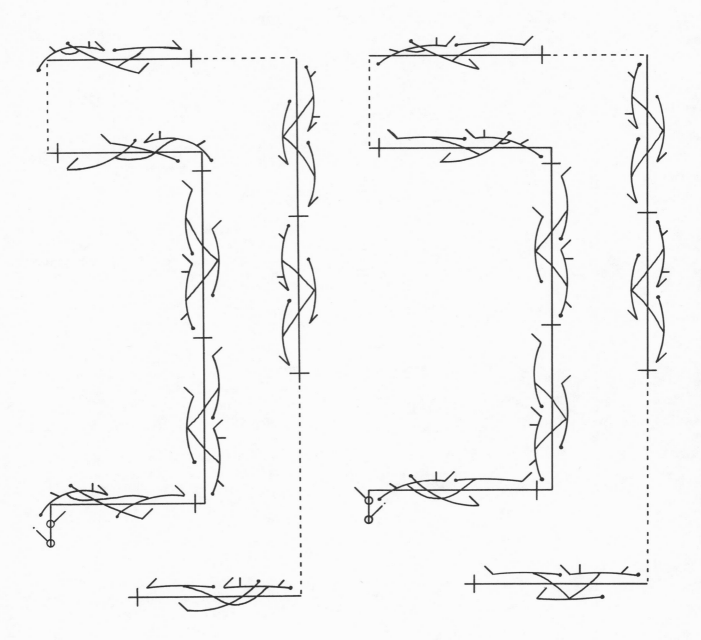

The Steps and Their General Performance in Duple- and Triple-Meter

Some Variations of the
Pas de Bourrée or Fleuret

D'autres. . .de côté (Ram. 1 p. 125; Ess. p. 71)

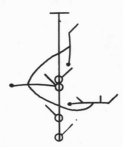

The demi-coupé is placed in 2nd pos., the first pas marché in 3rd behind, the second pas marché in 4th front "sliding" the foot. (Feuillet does not notate this "glisser de pied.") (L158)

ARMS

Finish the previous step with the arm in opposition. Lower inward on the demi-coupé shading the shoulder slightly, hold for the first pas marché, oppose the second pas marché.

Pas de bourée emboëté. Closed boree (Ram. 1 p. 128; Ess. p. 73)

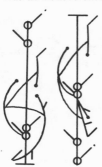

This pas de bourrée is characterized by a tiny pause made after the circular pas marché into 3rd pos. (L159, 160)

It is often performed with a battu behind the heel during the demi-coupé. (L161)

The half Coupee must be made backwards in the fourth Position, the second Step quickly follows in the Third, and you remain a little in this Position on the Toes of both Feet with the Knees extended; then let the foremost Foot slide to the fourth Position. *(Ram. 1 p. 128; Ess. p. 73)*

TIME

There are no tables for the timing of this pas de bourrée but it would not differ from the fleuret, apart from the pause on the first pas marché. The battu is done on the upbeat, taking some of the time usually used for placing the foot in the single step of the demi-coupé.

ARMS

There are two oppositions: one on the demi-coupé and one on the second pas marché. During the first pas marché the arms remain still. The one in opposition lowers outward as the next opposition is made with the other arm.

AUTHOR'S NOTES

Make sure that the first pas marché closes quickly and tightly into third position, for it is here that the slight, barely perceptible pause is made.

Pas de bourée ouvert.   Open boree (Ram. 1 p. 126; Ess. p. 72)

The first rise in this pas is not made onto [demi]pointe. It has a second rise which is taken onto [demi] pointe. This rise is unusual in that the heel is raised without a preliminary bending and stretching of the knees, an action for which Feuillet has no special term nor sign.

The pas is described, beginning with the right foot, by Rameau in *Le Maître à danser*:

> In rising on the Right, the Left follows in the first Position while the right Foot rests intirely [sic] on the Ground; then step with the left Foot in the second Position setting the Heel first down, and when the Body rests on this Foot, rise on the Toes, which brings up the Right, which slides behind the Left in the third Position and makes an End of the Step: But when you make another with the left Foot, you must set down the right Heel and sink upon it. *(Ram. 1 p. 126; Ess. p. 72)* (L162)

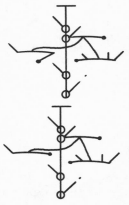

In *Abbregé*, Rameau gives a pas de bourée ouvert in notation without instructions. Compared with the above description, it omits only the final lifting of the heel. Rameau has a special sign for the final rise but he does not use it here. Feuillet gives no example called pas de bourrée ouvert but his tables in *Chorégraphie* include one identical in content to Rameau's notation, the passage of the foot to first position before the first pas marché being shown by the second step symbol, as the foot cannot move out unless first brought in.

The question remains: Do the notated pas de bourrée, which are used frequently, represent the one described verbally by Rameau? If not, the symbols should be interpreted as a fleuret made into second position—with the rise on [demi] pointe—second, and third position behind. (L163) (See also the Double Bouree. *Tom. p. 115)*

ARMS

Begin in opposition. Lower inward to pos. of el., palms down, on the demi-coupé, and oppose the third single step.

Pas de bourée vite
ou quatre pas. Pas de bourée
double. Pas de bourée à
deux mouvements. Quick bouree
or the boree with four steps.
(Ram. 1 p. 229; Ess. p. 74)

Rameau says there were many different terms for this step-unit which is included with pas de bourée. In fact, it may have been difficult to categorize since it has four single steps instead of three, like other pas de bourée:

This pas de bourée consists of four single steps and two "movements": a demi-coupé, two pas marchés, and a demi-jeté. It can be used in duple- or triple-time and does not provide a change of foot for the following step-unit. (L164)

There are the usual differences of opinion about the last single step. It is notated by Feuillet and Tomlinson with a springing sign and by Rameau with his demi-jeté sign.

TIME

Tomlinson says that the differences between this step-unit and the fleuret are: only one beat is allowed for the first two single steps; and a bound must be added after the third single step. Feuillet's tables do not include the pas de bourée vite. From available evidence the best timing appears to be:

Triple-time

3	=	bend
and	=	place the foot
1	=	rise in pos. of eq.
and	=	step
2	=	step-bend
and	=	spring
3	=	land-bend, etc.

ARMS

Pas de bourée vite de côté

When making this pas de bourée forward use opposition on the demi-coupé. Hold the position during the pas marchés, then lower the arms outward to the pos. of el., palms up, on the jeté.

(L165)

When moving sideward, use opposition on the demi-coupé. During the pas marchés lower the arms outward to the pos. of el., palms up. Lower and raise the arms slightly, ending in the pos. of el., palms down, on landing from the jeté.

EXERCISE   For pas de bourreé de côté, vite, and emboëté.

Recueil de dances composées de Mr Pécour. Feuillet, Paris, 1704. p. 79.

The music is by Lully from the tragédie-lyrique, *Persée*, first produced in 1682.

Pas de Menuet: Units of
four single steps

Pas de menuet can only be used in menuets and passepieds, where they equal two measures of music. They always begin with a demi-coupé onto the right foot whether traveling forward, backward, or to the right or left. Therefore, pas de menuet to the right will begin with a demi-coupé to second position, and those to the left with a demi-coupé to fifth position.

*Pas de Menuet à Deux
Mouvements.
Minuet Step of Two
Movements.
(Ram. 1 p. 77; Ess. p. 44)*

Other masters, especially Tomlinson, use other names for this step:

Minuet step of two movements; One and a fleuret; French minuet step; The new minuet step (Tom. p. 104)

This pas de menuet has two "movements" and four single steps: two demi-coupés and two pas marchés made on [demi] pointe. (L166)

TIME

Rameau explains that the two measures of music may, "for the better Apprehension. . .be divided into three equal Parts; the First for the first half Coupee, the Second for the Second, and the Third for the two Walks, which ought to take up no longer Time than a half Coupee." *(Ram. 1 p. 78; Ess. p. 44)* These divisions are not 1 2/ 3 4/ 5 6 but:

6 1/	2 3/	4 5
Demi-coupé	Demi-coupé	Step step
bend rise	bend rise	

Here there is a cross-rhythm between music and dance. The accents in the music are on the first and fourth of the six quarter notes (the first beat in each measure), while in the pas de menuet the accents made by the rises in the demi-coupés occur on the first and third quarter notes:

According to Rameau, the first measure, in which the stresses in music and step coincide, has a true cadence. The second measure has a false cadence. (See *Ram. 1 p. 97*)

Pas de menuet à deux
mouvements en arrière

To facilitate the execution of this step when traveling backward, the leg stepped off is held in 4th pos. in the air on the rise in the first demi-coupé. It then comes to 1st pos. as usual on the following bend.

Pas de menuet à deux
mouvements de côté

For traveling to the left:

Rameau gives these positions for the four single steps, but they appear differently in various dances because the pas marchés may be crossed in front or behind.

For traveling to the right:

Rameau does not specify 5th front or behind for the two crossed pas marchés. They are generally notated crossed behind.

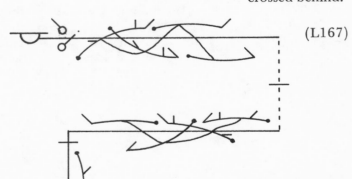

(L167)

The first demi-coupé in a pas de menuet leftward is frequently made in 5th pos. behind.

EXERCISE   For pas de menuet en avant, en arrière, and de côté.

AUTHOR'S NOTES

Through a daily practice of the exercises, the routine bending and rising and precise placing of the feet should have been established. Now, some qualities more requisite of art than science should begin to be explored. To be expressively differentiated and to reflect the music to which they are being danced, the step-units must be articulated with varied expressiveness.

The motions of the insteps provide the greatest possibility for articulation. The insteps can "breathe": the rise an inhaling, the lowering of the heel a controlled exhaling. In slow dances, the breaths will be deeper than in fast dances, and within dances, the "slower" step-units need deeper breaths. (Slower step-units have the fewest single steps per measure.)

Repeat all the step-sequences studied so far, exploring the possibilities for subtle articulation in the insteps when lowering the heel. For now, it is sufficient to develop a slow exhaling through the instep in the pas de bourrée in triple-time, the pas de menuet, the balancé, and the coupé. The step-sequences should be practiced to different pieces of music of the same dance types, for each piece will suggest a different articulation to the dancer.

To aid the control in the instep, other parts of the body—with the exception of the shoulders—should pull imperceptibly upward while the heel is being lowered. In controlling the lowering of the heel, which is usually closely connected to the bend of the following "movement," care must be taken not to exaggerate to the point of being late for the ensuing rise.

Pas de Menuet à
Trois Mouvements.
Minuet Step of
Three Movements.
(Ram. 1 p. 76; Ess. p. 43)

This pas composé consists of three "movements" and four single steps: two demi-coupés, one pas marché, and a demi-jeté. It is notated by Feuillet and Tomlinson as a demi-coupé and by Rameau as a demi-jeté. This pas de menuet was usually made traveling only forward or to the left.

In France, this pas de menuet was no longer commonly danced in ballroom menuets, although still used in passepieds. Rameau merely gives its structure before proceeding to the pas de menuet à deux mouvements which had replaced it. Fortunately Tomlinson deals with it in some detail since it had just come into fashion in England. (L168)

TIME

Tomlinson describes the pas traveling to the left (counting two measures of triple-time):

(L169)

Measure (1)	3 = bend and place the foot then:
	1 = the first Step with the right Foot to be made upon the Toe to the first Note;
	2 = the second is in the coming down of the Heel and Sink upon the right Foot. . .
	3 = the Rising or Receiving of the Weight. . . [upon the left] marks the third Note of the first Measure. . .
Measure (2) [4]	1 = the right Foot. . .behind the left, is the third Step, and marks Time to the first Note in the second Measure;
[5]	2 = the second Note is in the Sink upon the said right Foot, preparing for the fourth and last Step that is made, in rising and
[6]	3 = stepping sideways. . .upon the left Foot, to the third Note. *(Tom. p. 111)*

Here there is the same cross-rhythm as in Rameau's directions for the pas de menuet à deux mouvements. The final single step (the demi-jeté) is not rhythmically strong, but lively and inconsequential in this pas de menuet.

The two pas de menuet described below were not in fasion at the time Rameau and Tomlinson wrote. No timing is given in the sources under discussion.

Pas de Menuet à un Seul Mouvement. [One "Movement"]. (Feu. 1a)

Neither Rameau nor Tomlinson mention this pas which consists of one "movement" and four single steps: a demi-coupé, and three pas marchés.

Pas de Menuet à Deux Mouvements à la Bohëmiènne. Minuet Step. (Feu. 1a; Wea. 1 p. 42)

Rameau does not mention this pas de menuet which consists of two "movements" and four single steps: a demi-coupé, two pas marchés, and a demi-coupé or demi-jeté. Tomlinson gives both versions, but no further information because:

They are now rarely, if ever, practised amongst Persons of the first Rank, and seem to be, for the present, intirely [sic] laid aside; not as being ungraceful, or that the Dancer could not give Pleasure to the Beholders, or raise to himself a Reputation, in their Performance, but merely through Alteration of Fashion, which varies in this Respect, as in Dressing, etc. *(Tom. p. 104)*

These two menuet steps appear frequently, however, in dances published in England in the early eighteenth century.

ARMS

De la manière du faire
les bras de menuet.
Of the Manner of moving
the Arms in a Minuet.
(Ram. 1 p. 99; Ess. p. 56)

The arm motions are for the gentleman only:

The Manner of moving the Arms gracefully in a Menuet, is as necessary as that of the Feet; because they move with the Body, and are its greatest Ornament.

THEREFORE the Arms ought to hang by the Side of the Body, as this first Figure represents; the Hands neither open nor shut: For if the Thumb was to press one of the Fingers, that would shew a determined Motion, which would cause the upper Joints to look stiff, and prevent that easy Motion which the Arms ought to have. *(Ram. 1 p. 99; Ess. p. 56)*

From this starting position the arms move in a discreet and subtle manner very difficult to describe. The arms motions must be very fluid. (L170)

The Arms. . .fall almost to the Bottom of the Coat-Pocket. . . the Hands turned in.	6 = bend	hands in
the Elbows bend a little, raising the Hands imperceptibly.	1 = rise	bend the elbows
	2 = bend	
open them very easily, extending them with a Grace to the End of the Menuet Step, and so on during the Course of your Menuet, in every Step you take, whether it be backwards, forwards, or sideways. *(Ess. pp. 56-57)*	3 = rise	rotate and lower
	4 = step	
	5 = step	continue to lower

AUTHOR'S NOTES

Keep the arm motions small. The hands should do nothing except remain relaxed. Concentrate on lifting the elbows first and then rotating and lowering the arms.

From plates: Ram. 1 pp. 99-101.

Le Balancé.
Of Ballances.
(Ram. 1 p. 153; Ess. p. 89)

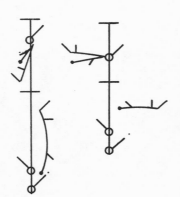

This pas composé has two "movements" and two single steps: two demi-coupés made either forward and backward or from side to side. It takes two measures of music in duple- or triple-time and is often used at the opening or conclusion of a strain. It neither travels nor provides a change of foot for the following step-unit.

Rameau prefers the balancé made forward and backward (L171), which has a shading of the shoulders and a complimentary use of the arms, and it is this balancé that he describes. The path of the step symbol in the second demi-coupé suggests a pas battu but Rameau makes it clear that the foot merely moves forward to first position in order to step backward again.

The demi-coupé is made forward, the leg stepped off remaining in the air in fourth position. Afterward, the heel is lowered and the back leg moves simultaneously to first position in the air. This motion will flow without pause into the bend of the following "movement." Rameau's description of the second demi-coupé goes as far as the rise, the leg stepped off remaining in fourth position in front. Presumably the conclusion will be the same as in the demi-coupé forward.

Although Rameau prefers the forward/backward balancé, it is the balancé de côté which is usually found in dances. For a description of the balancé de côté, Tomlinson must be consulted. He combines his description with instructions for its performance in triple-time: (L172)

The Balance is compos'd of two plain Steps, to which are added two Movements or Sinkings and Risings. . .the Rising or Receiving of the Weight upon the Toe or Heel marks Time to the first Note; and, if upon the Toe, the second is in the Coming down of the Heel; or, if made upon the Heel, it is in the tight Holding of the Knee leaving the left Toe upon the Point . . . The third Note, which concludes the first Measure and part of the Step, is in the Sink that prepares for the second Step of the Balance. *(Tom. p. 118)*

TIME

Tomlinson is clearly giving two ways:

  3 = bend and
 and = place the foot
  1 = rise onto [demi]pointe   or the whole foot
  2 = lower the heel   or hold

Tomlinson gives precise instructions as to the disposition of the gesturing leg on count 2 in the balancé onto flat foot, but none if the rise is to be taken onto [demi]pointe. It would seem reasonable to hold the leg in the open position on the rise and bring it to first position on the lowering of the heel, thus conforming to Rameau's instructions for the balancé forward and backward. (See Author's Notes.)

Feuillet does not give a table for the timing of the balancé. Rameau's table in triple-time seems to bear out Tomlinson's instruction to rest on the second beat, whereas his directions for the balancé forward and backward confirm the lowering of the heel on that beat. *(Ram. 2 p. 104, No. 3)*

ARMS

The step-unit preceding a balancé should be one in which the arms can finish in opposition. *(Ram. 1 p. 247; Ess. p. 145)*

Balancé en avant. The arms in opposition. Lower them inward to the pos. of el. on the bend and make another opposition on the demi-coupé with a shading of the shoulder. Hold the opposition during the demi-coupé backward, turning the head a little and inclining it slightly as you bend. The head lifts again as you rise.

Balancé de côté. The arms in opposition. Lower them inward to the pos. of el. on the rise of the first demi-coupé and hold this position.

AUTHOR'S NOTES

Having completed the rise in the demi-coupé keep the thigh muscles pulled upward in order to maintain the position, or to help control the lowering of the heel. The lowering of the heel and the carriage of the free leg to first position should melt into the following bend. In the demi-coupé backward it seems better to leave the free leg in fourth position in the air until the bend, as in the pas de menuet en arrière.

Suggested performance of the balancé in duple-time: (L173)

and =	bend then place the foot	
1 =	rise onto [demi]pointe	or the whole foot
and =	hold	
2 =	lower the heel	or continue to hold

For changing direction in space. Read the inner boxes first.

The Steps and Their General Performance in Duple- and Triple-Meter

Step-units beginning with a bend and rise without a change of weight were called temps. The "movement" had the same timing as the "movement" combined with a single step in the demi-coupé. The following two examples are for theory only:

The demi-coupé takes the upbeat/downbeat, the single step the remainder of the measure.

The bend and rise take the upbeat/downbeat as above, the slide and transference of weight the rest of the measure. Here one step symbol containing the "movement" as well as the step has the same value in time as the two step symbols in the above coupé.

*Tems de Courante
ou Pas Grave.
Courante Step.
(Ram.1 p. 115; Ess. p. 66)*

This temps consists of one "movement" and a single sliding step. It takes one measure of duple- or triple-time and provides a change of foot for the following step-unit. It is often used to open a section, or on the half or full cadence measures.[5]

(Ram. 2 p. 86)

Rameau gives the simplest and clearest account of the temps de courante when describing the arm motions. It is presented on the following pages. (L174)

The Body in this first Figure is rested on the right Foot in the fourth Position, the left Heel off the Floor, the Toes only down and by consequence ready to make a Step, the left Arm opposite to the right Foot, and the right Arm extended, the Hand outwards; and the Writing forming a half Circle is to shew the Course the Arm is to take.

To begin this Step, the left Foot must be brought up to the Right, in which Approach turn the Elbow as represented by these Words, The Turn of the Elbow from above downwards, which forms the half circle, and you trace the Turn which the Arm makes from above downwards, as these other Words, The Turn of the Wrist, shew the Movement of the right Wrist.

The second Figure shews how low one ought to sink. The Body rests on the right Foot, the left Foot off the Ground, both the Heels close together, and the Arms turned downwards of equal Height. (*Ram. 1 pp. 215-216; Ess. pp. 126-127*)

From plates: Ess. 1731, first issue, pp. 126-127.

The third Figure shews how to rise after having sunk, (which one may call in Equilibrium) the Body being rested on the Toes of the right Foot, the left Leg extended as well as the Right with its Foot off the Ground, and the Hands open.

From plates: Ess. 1731, first issue, pp. 127-128.

The Fourth is designed to shew the Opposition to the left Foot making a Step forwards, to the which sliding in the fourth Position the right Arm forms its Contrast, the Step and Movement of the Arms ending together.

But as one cannot be too careful in moving the Arms in Dancing, and as all depends on the Beginning, I beg Attention to this Figure, in which the right Arm is opposed to the left Foot which is placed before; the right Arm extended and drawn back as well as the Shoulder, which makes the Opposition just and according to Rule. *(Ram. 1 pp. 217-218; Ess. pp. 127-128)*

The temps de courante "occupies in its duration one measure of two or three time." *(Ram. 2 p. 28)*

Triple-time

        3 = bend then
    and = begin to rise
        1 = finish the rise in pos. of eq.
    and = slide
        2 = transfer the weight
    and = lower heel flowing into the bend (L174)

Duple-time

    and = bend then
              begin to rise
        1 = finish the rise in pos. of eq.
    and = slide
        2 = transfer the weight
    and = lower the heel flowing into the next bend
              begin to rise, etc. (L175)

Temps de courante en arrière

Rameau does not refer to a temps de courante backward but gives one in his examples in *Abbregé*. *(Ram. 2 p. 29, No. 7)* (L176)

There is no account of the arm motions but no doubt they move in opposition as in the temps de courante en avant.

Temps de courante de côté

Rameau says this temps de courante is generally preceded by a pas de bourrée (fleuret) dessus et dessous (before and behind) which finishes with the last single step placed into third position behind. (L177) Note the placing of the signs at the beginning of the symbol, indicating a bend on both feet in third position. Rameau explains this clearly:

For Example, when you make a Boree step before and behind, with the left Foot going to the Right, the right Foot becomes foremost; from thence you sink on both Legs equally, and rising from thence with both Legs well extended, slide the right Foot aside in the second Position. *(Ram. p. 118; Ess. p. 68)*

ARMS	As this is an open sideward step, Rameau gives no opposition, "the Arms being open, and the Hands turned . . ." [see pl. 1 p. 136] just before, in sinking they must be turned downwards [see pl. 2 p.136] and in rising and finishing the Step a little Motion of the Elbow and Wrist from below upwards, which brings them again into their former Situation." *(Ram. 1 p. 221; Ess. p. 129)*

AUTHOR'S NOTES

For the first time, the author is moved to suggest a slightly different performance from that conveyed by Rameau. Years of performing, and watching others perform the temps de courante, have revealed that its climax is the pas glissé with opposition of the arms on the second beat. Everything leads to this moment of arrival: the dancer's weight newly transferred to the stepping foot, the back foot remaining momentarily on the toe without weight, and the arms in opposition.

This does not mean that the "movement" no longer marks the first beat. Technically a temps requires great strength in the supporting leg and instep and, as in all slow steps, the danger lies in letting the "movement" drag behind the beat. In the temps de courante, most dancers take a moment of sleep at the bottom of the bend. DO NOT DO THIS. Instead REBOUND from the bend with sustained liveliness in the instep but blend the final moment of the rise into the slide. Everything is now leading toward the arrival of the body on the stepping leg and an infinitesimal moment of stillness on the second beat, a stillness filled not with sleep but with fulfilled alertness. The Royal Presence has arrived, assured and majestic (without a hint of pomposity—unless you choose to play a pompous person).

EXERCISE

For pas de bourrée, pas coupés, and temps de courante en avant and en arrière, with pas balancés de côté. Practice to bourrées and sarabandes. The outer tract is written in duple-meter. The inner alternative measures are for triple-meter.

ARMS

Two places require special attention when traveling forward. Both occur at the conclusion of a pas coupé:

Measure (2) Oppose the pas glissé in the pas coupé (do not anticipate), open outward as in the previous exercise.

Measure (4) Maintain the opposition while bending the knees, and lower inward to the pos. of el., palms down, on straightening the knees in the following demi-coupé.

Pas coupés en arrière require two oppositions.
Change by opening the raised arm outward.

EXERCISE

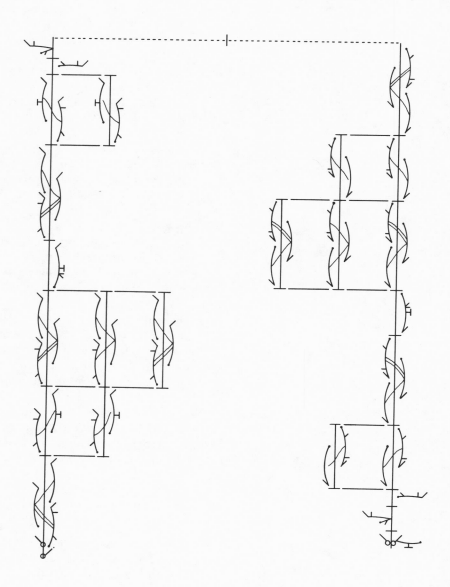

Tems.
Pointings.
(Ram. 1 p. 119; Ess. p. 68)

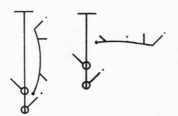

The temps consists of one "movement" and a modified single step: the toe touching the floor without taking weight. Here the term temps refers to the type of "movement," not a step-unit, since a temps does not equal a whole measure of music. Coincidentally with the rise, the toes of the stepping leg are placed upon the floor and in time, a temps compares with the demi-coupé alone in a measure. (See p.172.) (L178,179)

TIME

Duple-time

and = bend then
      begin to rise
  1 = finish the rise
and
    = hold
  2

Triple-time

  3 = bend
and = begin to rise
  1 = finish the rise
  2 = hold

Pointings are also made backward:

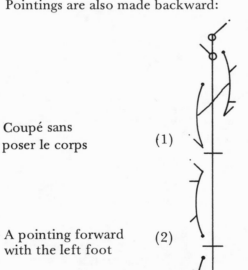

The arms use simple opposition.

Coupé sans
poser le corps   (1)

Oppose the demi-coupé (L arm up) on the first beat.

A pointing forward
with the left foot   (2)

Oppose the pointing on the first beat.

and one backward   (3)

Oppose the pointing on the first beat.

Temps de Courante and a Demi-jeté

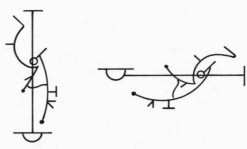

The combination of temps de courante and demi-jeté is used in menuets, made forward or sideward. Rameau provides a table in *Abbregé* which shows that the demi-jeté has the same time value as in the pas de menuet à trois mouvements.

		3	= bend then
Measure (1)		and	= begin to rise
		1	= finish rising
		2	
		3	= slide
Measure (2)	[4]	1	= transfer the weight
	[5]	2	= bend
		and	= spring (demi-jeté)
	[6]	3	= land-bend
		and	= begin to rise, etc.

EXERCISE

For menuet.

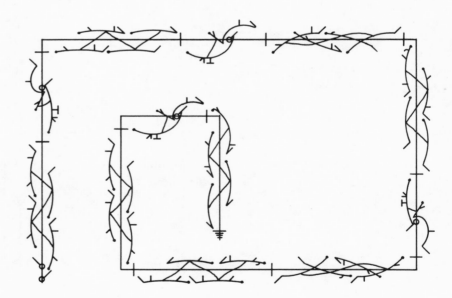

Des Pirouettez.
Of Pirouettes.
(Ram. 1 p. 148; Ess. p. 86)

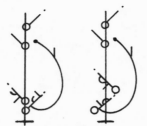

A quarter-turn   A half-turn

This temps[6] consists of one "movement" and a pivot on [demi] pointe(s). It equals one measure of music in duple- or triple-time. A pirouette does not travel, nor often result in a change of foot for the next step-unit. (L180,181)

In social dances, pirouettes were generally made on both feet, turning either a quarter- or a half-turn, usually finishing with the weight on one foot:

Suppose it then to be made with the right Foot in a quarter Turn to the Right, sink on the left Foot the Right being off the Ground, and as the. . .Knee bends the right Foot that is off the Ground forms a half Circle; and setting down its Toe behind the left Leg in the third Position to rise on the Toes, you make a quarter Turn. *(Ram. 1 p. 148; Ess. p. 86)*

Tomlinson says that the turn should be made with "the Weight of the Body resting mostly upon that Foot which at first supported the Weight." *(Tom. p. 91)* Rameau continues:

When you have risen and made the quarter or half Turn, the Heel of the Foot on which the Body rested must be set down to be the more firm to take another. *(Ram. 1 p. 149; Ess. p. 87)*

TIME

The bend and rise take the upbeat and downbeat; the heel is lowered on the upbeat. The turn takes the intervening beat. At the conclusion the moving foot rests on the ball of the foot in third position.

Duple-time

and	= bend then place the foot
1	= rise on both feet
and 2	= turn
and	= lower heel-bend, etc.

Triple-time

3	= bend then
and	= place the foot
1	= rise on both feet
2	= turn
3	= lower heel-bend, etc.

The placing of the foot into a closed position resembles a demi-coupé: both knees bent, the ball of the stepping foot on the floor.

ARMS

On the step preceding the pirouette the arm on the subsequent turning side should be raised from the elbow; this may or may not be in opposition. During the turn the arm will return to this position having made a circle outward from the elbow to facilitate the turn. If a different step-unit follows, it may not be necessary to complete the circle.

Pirouette on Both Feet
from Fourth Position
to Fourth Position

 Stand in 4th pos. with the right foot in front, the weight on both feet. Bend and rise and make a quarter-turn toward the back foot—the front and back foot are reversed. The 4th pos. must be exact, otherwise the feet will finish somewhere between 4th and 2nd pos. (L182)

AUTHOR'S NOTES

Make sure the rise BEGINS in time, but also that it blends slightly into the turn so that the effect is smooth and level. Open the arm to LEAD THE TURN, taking care to raise it again in time if another turn follows. Be sure to straighten the knees on the turn, but not to rise too high on the feet.

EXERCISE

For pirouettes in duple- and triple-time.

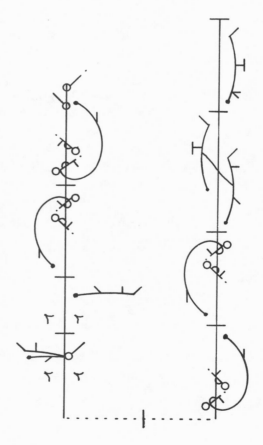

ARMS	Measures in triple-time:

Measures in triple-time:
(1) full circle
(2) full circle
(3) lower inward on 1,
(4) hold, up on upbeat for turn
(5) full circle
(6) full circle
(7) down inward on 1, oppose
    2, open and
(8) oppose slowly on 2.

Turns with a Spring

A turn with a spring is most frequently encountered beginning in first position, the weight on both feet:

Two quarter-turn pirouettes to the right, beginning in 1st pos. The right leg will finish circling and close after the spring and turn have been completed.

This type of turn is sometimes used in ballroom dances. Rameau clearly describes one method:

Being in the second or fourth Position, for it is taken equally from either, and the Body on one Foot, the Toes of the other on the Ground, you sink with both Knees and rise with a Hop on the Foot whereon the Body rested; but in making the Hop, the Leg of that Foot which was but pointed on the Ground, extends, following the Body in the Turn it makes either to the Right or Left. If you are to turn to the Right you sink and hop on the left Foot, and the right Leg and Arm are extended; and the same with the other Leg and Arm if you turn to the Left. *(Ram. 1 p. 152; Ess. p. 88)*

TIME

The supporting knee may remain bent as the right leg completes the circle to second, or the left knee may straighten as the right leg circles. The former seems preferable to achieve the level, smooth motion which seems essential to a pirouette.

Duple-time		Triple-time	
and	= bend then spring and turn	3	= bend
1	= land	and	= spring and turn
and	= complete opening of the leg	1	= land
2	= close	2	= complete opening of the leg
and	= spring and turn	3	= close, etc.

THE STEP-UNITS
CALLED CONTRE-TEMS

The Gavotte comes originally from the Lyonnois and Dauphiny, and 'tis from thence we borrowed that Number of Contretems we have in Dancing, introduced by the Pains and Care of the many great Masters we have had, to whom we are obliged for having embellished these Steps with all the Graces they appear at this Time. *(Ram. 1 p. 131; Ess. p. 75)*

Contretemps begin with a hop: a spring from one foot onto the same foot. Therefore, as in temps, the initial "movement" is made without a transference of weight. In step-units beginning with a spring the landing coincides with the downbeat, thereby serving the same rhythmic function as the rise in the demi-coupé. The preliminary bend is as deep as that used in the demi-coupé. The hop should be made with vitality, rising straight up into the air, landing in almost the same spot; it should scarcely travel.

Contre-tems de Gavotte
ou Contre-tems en Avant.
Contretems of the Gavotte or
Contretems Forwards.
(Ram. 1 p. 166; Ess. p. 97)

A hop
followed
by a step.

When the hop is followed by a pas marché, the two are written on one step symbol. This notation does not always represent the desired relationship between the motion of the stepping leg and the spring, but Rameau additionally provides detailed descriptions of the various types of contretemps.

This pas composé consists of one sprung "movement" and two single steps: a hop and two pas marchés on the [demi] pointes. It can be used in duple- or triple-time and does not provide a change of foot for the next step-unit. (L183)

Begin in 4th pos., the toe of the back foot touching the floor. Bend in 1st pos., the foot in the air, to hop and carry the stepping leg forward to 4th pos. off the floor with the knee straight. When landing from the hop, use a soft bend but make a little rebound up out of it, to transfer the weight onto the stretched forward leg for a pas marché on [demi] pointe. The rebound is a very slight action of the instep but it gives great animation to this contretemps, which concludes with a second pas marché on [demi] pointe.

ARMS   The arms are in opposition. On the hop, lower them directly to
                                the pos. of el.

                                Contre-tems en arrière

                                During the hop, the stepping leg should be raised in
                                front, the knee stretched. Not until landing will it
                                be carried bent through 1st pos. to 4th pos. behind,
                                stretched for the first pas marché. The raising of
                                the leg forward is not shown by the notation. (L184)

TIME   Tomlinson gives the contretemps in duple-time:

                                The Hop certainly marks the first Note or what we call
                                Time. . .viz. the Spring or Hop. . .beats Time to the first of
                                the four Notes; the second Note is counted in the setting
                                down or receiving the Weight of the Body upon the left
                                Foot, after its having advanced the length of a Step. . .and
                                the third Note is counted, when the right Foot receives the
                                Body, as before, and finishes. The remaining fourth Note,
                                as has been said, is in the Sink which prepares for the suc-
                                ceeding Step. *(Tom. p. 63)* (L183)

                                    and = bend then
                                               spring (hop)
                                      1 = land
                                    and = step
                                      2 = step
                                    and = lower heel-bend, etc.

                                            Triple-time

             3 = bend then   3 = bend-then
           and = spring (hop)   and = spring (hop)
             1 = land   1 = land
             2 = step   and = step
             3 = step-bend   2 = step
           and = spring, etc.   3 = lower heel-bend
                    (L185)   and = spring (hop), etc. (L186)

ARMS   The same as for the contretemps en avant.

Contre-tems de côté (croisée). Crossed contretems. (Ram. 1 p. 168; Ess. p. 99)

In this contretemps the two pas marchés are placed: into fifth (or third) position in front or behind; into second position. It begins in second position with the weight on both feet (L187), although Rameau says that many people do begin from one, but in his opinion: "the Body does not seem so firm, and the Leg moves too quick; besides, it has not so good a Grace." *(Ram. 1 p. 169; Ess. p. 100)* If the contretemps croisée is made from one foot, he says that care should be taken not to bring the stepping foot from second into fifth too quickly. (L187,188)

ARMS The arms are in the pos. of el., palms up. On the bend, raise both arms inward from the elbows, then straighten them during the hop, finishing with the arm toward which you are traveling slightly higher (see p. 143), the palms facing front. The head turns 1/8 in the same direction, unless partners pass, in which case they will look at one another.

Contre-tems ouvert ou contre-tems de chaconne. Chaconne or open contretems. (Ram. 1 p. 170; Ess. p. 100)

In this contretemps, the two pas marchés are placed: into second position; into fifth (or third) position in front or behind. Rameau gives fourth or third as the starting position. (L189)

In a series of contretemps ouvert it is usual to end the first one in fifth (or third) behind, the next one in front, and so on.

TIME As in contretemps en avant.

ARMS The arms are in opposition. On the hop, lower them directly to the pos. of el., palms down, and then oppose the second pas marché.

EXERCISE

For contretemps de gavotte en avant. Practice one pas de bourrée and one contretemps de gavotte alternately, to a bourrée and a sarabande. Make sure only two, not three, pas marchés follow the hop in the contretemps. The sequence will result in a change of foot for each repetition.

ARMS

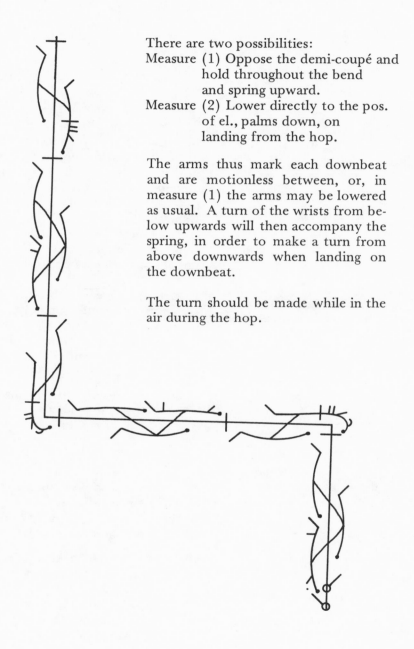

There are two possibilities:
Measure (1) Oppose the demi-coupé and
hold throughout the bend
and spring upward.
Measure (2) Lower directly to the pos.
of el., palms down, on
landing from the hop.

The arms thus mark each downbeat and are motionless between, or, in measure (1) the arms may be lowered as usual. A turn of the wrists from below upwards will then accompany the spring, in order to make a turn from above downwards when landing on the downbeat.

The turn should be made while in the air during the hop.

Contre-tems de Menuet.
Contretems or Composed
Hops of the Menuet.
(Ram. 1 p. 104; Ess. p. 59)

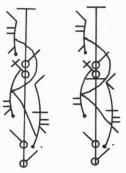

In $\frac{6}{4}$ time   In $\frac{3}{4}$ time   (L190)

This pas composé consists of three sprung "movements" and two single steps: basically a hop, a pas marché, a hop, and a jeté. It is used in menuets and passepieds, taking the time of a pas de menuet. The first hop is always upon the left foot.

The second bend is sometimes written on the first step symbol, sometimes on the second.

In this contretemps the stepping leg remains in first position during the first hop, only passing to fourth position on the second beat. This is clearly described by Rameau and Tomlinson but not by the notation. It is probably for this reason that Rameau says that the first "movement" is made "before the step," although the foot has already moved as far as first position. He uses, here only, the term "sauter à cloche pied" for this initial hop. *(Ram. 1 p. 105)*

TIME

Rameau provides a table for the timing of this rather complex step-unit but unfortunately, one crucial number is omitted. *(Ram. 2 p. 104 No. 4)* Nevertheless, combined with a good description from Tomlinson, it is very helpful. The moot points are the step and bend on beats 2 and 3:

6	=	bend on L
and	=	hop (right remains in 1st pos.)
1	=	land-bend on L
2	=	"step" forward (rising to 4th, both feet flat on floor) or carry the R ft. to 4th, both knees still bent.
3	=	(bend) or place the R ft. in 4th, both knees still bent
and	=	hop (modified, the spring is off both feet)
4	=	land on R (bend a little), L in 3rd behind in the air
5	=	bend more
and	=	spring forward (jeté)
6	=	land-bend on L, etc.

On beat 2 (or 3) the weight should be shifted so that it is slightly forward on the right foot rather than equally distributed on both feet. The bend on beats 4 and 5 should be one smooth continuous motion. The jeté, therefore, is timed as in the pas de menuet à trois mouvements.

In a contretemps de menuet there are two stresses. They occur on counts 1 and 4 when landing from the first two springs. There is therefore no cross-rhythm between music and dance.

ARMS	There are no arm motions in a contretemps de menuet.

Contretemps de menuet en arrière

This step-unit is not described and is seldom used in dances. Perhaps it was difficult for the woman to execute if her dress had even a slight train, or in the increasingly voluminous skirts of eighteenth-century fashions.

In the following menuet sequence, a contretemps de menuet backward is used in the second measure. (Turn the book around to read this figure.) The directions of the symbols show that the legs should follow slightly curved paths, opening outward. In Rameau's notated version of the sequence this contretemps is replaced by a balancé. *(Ram. 2, Part 2, p. 50)*

In the version below, the music is notated in $\frac{6}{4}$, one measure equalling one step-unit. In *Abbregé*, Rameau bars the music in the more usual 3, two measures equalling one step-unit.

EXERCISE	For contretemps de menuet.

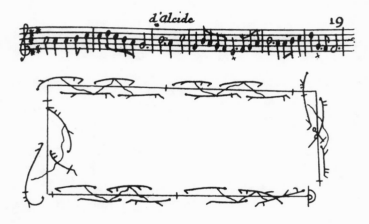

VIIe Recueil de dances de bal pour l'année 1709. Feuillet, Paris, 1709, p. 19.

A six-measure sequence, from a ballroom danse à deux, "Le Menuet d'Alcide," by Pécour. The music is by Louis de Lully and Marais from the tragédie-lyrique, *Alcide*, 1693.

EXERCISE

For steps used in the menuet and passepied. The passepied was a quick menuet.

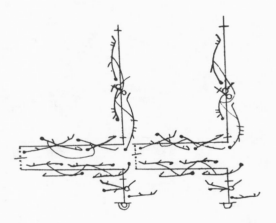

Recueil de dances composées par M. Pécour. Feuillet, Paris, 1700.

A figure from "Le Passepied," a danse à deux by Pécour. The composer of the music is anonymous. The music, which consists of four strains each of which is repeated, is played twice, with all repeats both times.

Performing students should now turn to Chapter 10, p.239 and study the section on the hemiola in the menuet and passepied.

*Contre-tems à Deux
Mouvements ou
Contre-tems Balonné.
Contretems or Composed
Hop of Two Movements.
(Ram. 1 p. 171; Ess. p. 101)*

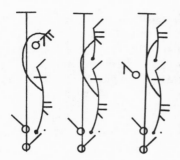

This lively pas composé consists of two sprung "movements" and one single step: a hop and a demi-jeté. It equals one measure of duple- or triple-time and provides a change of foot for the following step-unit. In such a lively step-unit a jeté seems more appropriate than a demi-jeté. (L191)

This Step is composed of two different Movements. . .to sink and hop on one Foot, and then to sink on the same Foot and throw the Body on the other. *(Ram. 1 p. 172; Ess. p. 101)*

During the hop the stepping leg is raised, extended as in the previous contretemps; therefore, when moving forward or sideward it is in position for the jeté, which is notated in various ways. In example (1) above, it is given on a half position since the foot has already moved to fourth. In example (2)[7] the small step symbol suggests that the jeté travels slightly further. In example (3) the half position for the left foot makes it clear that only the left knee bends after the hop. Example (1) is generally used.

TIME

Feuillet's Tables:

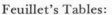

Duple-time

Each spring equals a half measure, the landing from the hop coinciding with the first beat, the landing from the jeté with the second: (L191)

and = bend then
      spring (hop)
  1 = land-bend
and = spring (jeté)
  2 = land-bend
and = spring
  1 = land-bend, etc.

Triple-time

When two springs are made in one measure of triple-time, the first landing is made with straight knees; the bend is delayed until the second beat: (L192)

  3 = bend then
and = spring (hop)
  1 = land (bend very slightly)
  2 = bend/spring (jeté)
  3 = land-bend and spring,
      etc.

ARMS	Opposition on the hop, the head turned slightly in the direction of the raised arm. Maintain the opposition as you alight on the ball of the foot in the jeté, then lower the arms directly as you lower the heel and bend in the next "movement." The head will return to normal at some point in the jeté.

Contre-tems balonné en arrière

The hop will be made with the stepping leg raised in front, and then passed through first position for the jeté. This is similar to the contretemps de gavotte en arrière described on p.213. (L193)

ARMS	Rameau is confusing on this point but seems to be saying that there should be two oppositions during this step-unit as in the coupé en arrière. Therefore, oppose the leg raised in front during the hop and change the opposition for the jeté, probably by opening the raised arm while bringing the other inward and up.

Contre-tems balonné de côté

When the contretemps ballonné is made de côté, it is generally preceded by a fleuret. (L194)

ARMS	Motions of the wrists are sufficient.
AUTHOR'S NOTES	The use of the insteps must be resilient throughout. In triple-time, allow the knee to bend slightly when landing on beat 1 and CONTINUE SMOOTHLY into a deeper bend on beat 2.

STEP-UNITS
Section 2

STEP-UNITS COMPOSED MAINLY OF SPRINGS

Before studying this group of step-units, reviewing the theory of notating springs on pp.121-125 is suggested.

Pas Assemblé.
Close or Jump.
(Ram. 2 p. 59;.Tom. p. 37)

The assemblé consists of one foot moving from an open to a closed position combined with a "movement." It is a punctuation step comparable to a full stop or period, and has the value of the first beat in a measure. Since the pas assemblé usually finishes on both feet, the following step-unit can be taken with either foot. It does not travel.

Although not indicated by the straight path of the step symbol, the moving leg should open to the side during the spring. *(Ram. 2 p. 98)*

Rameau does not describe the pas assemblé as an entity in *Le Maître à danser*, only in *Abbregé*. A pas assemblé is the closing of one foot to the other from an open to a closed position. It is done while bending and rising or while bending and springing.

Tomlinson names the former, "Close on the Ground": (L195)

The Body. . .thrown into the Air by the Spring of the Instep, I mean no higher than you can rise without quitting the Ground with your Instep or Toe. *(Tom. p. 37)* (L196)

The sprung pas assemblé Tomlinson calls a close, or jump, in which you "spring quite off from the Floor." He begins his "Close" from third position, opening to second position on the bend and spring, and finishing in first position, or in the reverse third (front or back).

Pas assemblé en arrière

An exact reversal of the pas assemblé en avant. (L197)

TIME

This Step in Dancing much resembles a Period or Full Stop in Letters; for, as that closes or shuts up a Sentence, the Close in Dancing does the very same in Music, since nothing is more frequent than, at the End of a Strain in the Tune, to find the Strain or Couplet of the Dance to conclude in this Step, as also at other remarkable Places of the Music. . . .

This Step generally takes up a Measure, that is to say, with the Time you Rest you stand still [after the pas]; For Instance, to the Tune of triple Time the Close is performed to the first of the three Notes, and the second and third are counted during the Time you rest; but to Tunes of common Time, as Marches, Gavots, Rigadoons, etc. this Step and Time it is to rest sometimes are a Measure and at others not, as having a plain Step or Walk added thereto, which said Close and Step together fill up the Time. *(Tom. p. 39)*

Triple-time (L198)

> 3 = bend then
> and = spring
> 1 = land-bend (assemblé)
> 2 = hold (keeping knees bent)
> 3 = hold/spring, etc.

Duple-time (L199)

> and = bend then spring
> 1 = land-bend (assemblé)
> and
> 2 = hold (keeping knees bent)
> and = hold/spring, etc.

ARMS

The arm motions are not indicated. A turn of the wrists from above downwards to reach the pos. of el. on the landing is appropriate.

Performing students should now turn to p. 246 and add the Gavotte to their daily studies.

222

Pas de Sissonne.
The Sissonne Step.
(Ram. 1 p. 156; Ess. p. 91)

A pas composé consisting of two sprung "movements": a pas assemblé and a spring from two feet to one. It equals one measure of music in duple- or triple-time and can result in a change of foot for the following step-unit. It travels just far enough to accommodate the change of foot position.

The pas de sissonne generally begins and ends in third or fifth position. Writers usually mention third while notators use fifth.

Pas de sissonne en avant

Make a sprung pas assemblé from 5th or 3rd pos., the back foot in the air. Spring and close in 5th, reversing the front and back foot. Then spring off both feet, landing on the front foot, the back foot in 5th or 3rd pos. in the air. (L200)

The angle of the free foot in relation to the leg at the end of a pas de sissonne is not specified. When held in a closed position in front, the principle that the knees and ankles are flexed at the same time seems to hold good, but when in a closed position behind, it seems preferable to point the free foot to some extent.

ARMS

Begin in opposition. Change the opposition to oppose the front foot in the assemblé. Lower inward to coincide with the landing from the second spring.

Pas de sissonne en arrière

This is an exact reversal of the above: make the pas assemblé, taking the front foot behind, then spring off both feet, landing on the back foot, the front in 3rd or 5th pos. in the air. (L201)

TIME

Rameau gives a description of this pas in triple-time which he calls pas de sissonne coupé since it is interrupted by a slight pause:

. . .at the first Hop you fall on both Feet, without bending the Knees; but then you sink afterwards to make the second Hop, which may be called the Sissonne Coupee, because there is a Rest made to sink at the second Hop. *(Ram. 1 p. 158; Ess. p. 92)* (L202)

ARMS

The same as for the pas de sissonne en avant.

Duple-time			Triple-time		
and	=	bend then spring	3	=	bend
1	=	land-bend	and	=	spring
and	=	spring	1	=	land
2	=	land-bend	2	=	bend
and	=	spring, etc.	and	=	spring
			3	=	land-bend
			and	=	spring

Sometimes the pas de sissonne concludes differently:

(1) The back foot passes to the front and is raised again on the second spring. (L203)
(2) The front foot passes to the back and is raised again on the second spring. (L203)
(3) The pas de sissonne often ends with the leg extended in 4th pos. behind in the air. (L204)

ARMS

None of these variants alter the opposition given for the basic pas de sissonne.

Performing students should turn to p.247 and add the gigue to their daily studies.

EXERCISE   For pas de sissonne in [compound] duple-, duple-, and triple-meter.

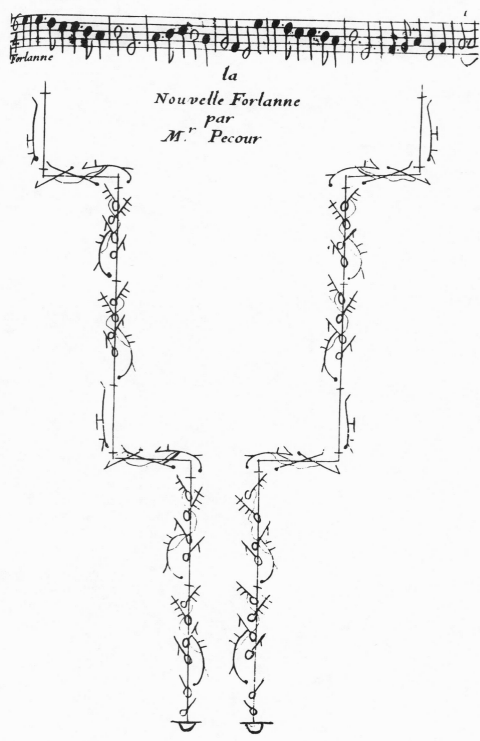

IX Recueil de dances pour l'année 1711. Feuillet-Dezais, Paris, 1709.

Pas de Rigaudon.
Rigaudon Step.
(Ram. 1 p. 159; Ess. p. 93)

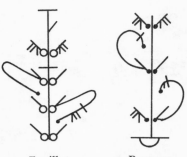

Feuillet   Rameau.

This lively and highly individual pas composé consists of two sprung "movements" and two sharp, slightly circular leg gestures. It takes one and a half measures in duple-time, followed by a rest or single step. The pas de rigaudon does not travel and finishes with the weight on both feet. The leg gestures circle outward as shown in Rameau's notation. (L205)

The degree of bend when making this pas is very slight: "This Step. . .has no Movements in it that require a great deal of Strength; for properly speaking 'tis but a Play of the Instep which engages the other Joints to make some Motion." *(Ram. 1 p. 252; Ess. p. 149)*

Descriptions of the pas de rigaudon are especially obscure since it contains two types of spring for which there were no specific terms: a spring from two feet to one foot and a spring from two feet to two feet. On the leg gestures there should be small deviations forward on the outward path. In *Abbregé,* Rameau explains that the leg gestures should be slightly circular *(Ram. 2 p. 101)*, and his notation given on the right above shows in which direction the small circular leg gestures move. (L205)

Begin from 1st pos., bend the knees slightly and spring off both feet, landing with one foot in the air in 2nd pos; the raised leg should be straight, the supporting one bent. Then close the raised leg sharply to 1st pos., straightening the supporting leg which is immediately raised to 2nd pos. in the air; both knees stay straight. Then close the raised leg to 1st pos., simultaneously bending the knees in order to spring off and onto both feet.

TIME

The pas de rigaudon is used only in duple-time. Rameau makes the surprising statement that the whole step-unit equals one measure, although it is clear from the notation that the second spring lands on the downbeat of a second measure:

	and	=	bend then spring
(1)	1	=	land on one foot
	and	=	close and raise the other leg
	2	=	close-bend
	and	=	spring
(2)	1	=	land-bend
	and / 2	=	hold
	and	=	spring, etc.

ARMS

In the pas de rigaudon, the wrists move in sympathy with the insteps: once from below upwards on the first spring, and then from above downwards on the last spring.

AUTHOR'S NOTES

For students new to dancing, the pas de rigaudon presents special difficulties. The leg gestures will tend to be much too high. Keep the feet JUST off the floor. The toes will tend to point directly upward, especially on the second leg gesture. Slide the foot out to second position before lifting it from the floor. The body will tend to wobble instead of remaining unaffected by the fast activity of the legs. To avoid this, hold the torso firmly.

EXERCISE

For pas de rigaudon in duple- and [compound] duple-meter.

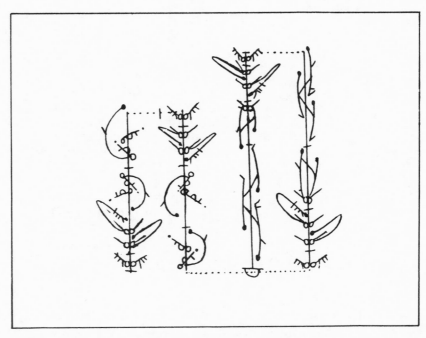

Recueil de dances composées par M. Feuillet. Feuillet, Paris, 1700.

"Rigaudon de la Paix." Sixteen measures of the man's side.

Jettés ou Demies Cabrioles.
Bounds or Half Capers.
(Ram. 1 p. 162; Ess. p. 95)

ARMS

The jeté is analyzed on p.173. One spring lands on each beat. Two or three are combined to fill a measure of duple- or triple-time. Half capers belong to theatrical dances.

Begin in the pos. of el., palms up. Make a circle of the wrists from above downwards on the first jeté in a measure. If the arms are in opposition in the previous step-unit, lower to the pos. of el., palms down, on the downbeat.

Jetté Chassé.
Bounds en Chasez.
(Ram. 1 p. 178; Ess. p. 105)

Chassés are step-units in which one foot chases or drives away the other. They begin and end in open positions of the feet. A jeté chassé consists of one sprung "movement" and a simultaneous gesture of the leg into an open position in the air. Like the jeté, two or three are combined to fill a measure. Jetés chassés do not travel. A sequence of jetés chassés "ought to follow one another without any Interruption, as well as the Ballance of a Pendulum." *(Ram. 1 p. 179; Ess. p. 105)* For instance, with the body supported by the left foot, the right in 4th pos. in front in the air, make a jeté onto the right foot in 3rd pos. which chases the left foot away to 4th pos. behind in the air. Then reverse the process. (L206)

TIME

Two or three jetés chassés are combined to fill a measure of duple- or triple-time. One spring lands on each beat.

ARMS

One opposition is made on the first jeté chassé in each measure.

For jetés chassés, contretemps de côté, pas de sissonne, and pas de bourrée emboëté.

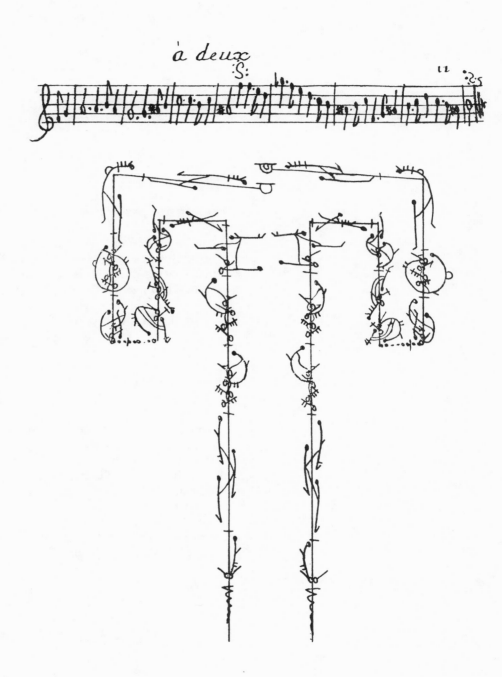

Recueil de dances composées par M. Feuillet. Feuillet, Paris, 1700.

The closing page of Feuillet's "Gigue à deux." The music is from Lully's tragédie-lyrique, *Roland*, 1685.

Des Chasséz.
Chasses.
(Ram. 1 p. 175; Ess. p. 71)

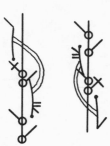

This traveling pas composé begins and ends with the weight on both feet in an open position. It consists of a small sprung "movement" from two feet to one, quickly followed by the placement of the free foot into an open position. Two or three are combined to fill a measure of duple- or triple-time. (L207,208)

The degree of bend is shallow, the action being mainly from the insteps: "This Step is fluent, because in springing you gain Ground to perform the Figure the Dance requires; it is gay when several are made together, for one appears to be always off the Ground, and yet with only a half Spring." *(Ram. 1 p. 177; Ess. p. 104)*

This chassé is one of the least sophisticated steps found in the serious style of dance:

It is a Step frequently found in Tunes of common Time, not much unlike what we often see Boys perform in Play, when they run along, and, in rising from a Sink, knock or beat one Heel against the other, lighting in the fourth Position, with the Knees bent, continuing the same, perhaps, the Length of a Street or Field. *(Tom. p. 72)*

Chassés are made sideward from second position or forward or backward from fourth position. Rameau describes them sideward to the left, the preceding step, generally a coupé, having finished in second position:

. . .you Sink on both Legs and rise with a half Spring or Hop, that is to say, slipping on the Ground; and in taking this Movement on both Feet, the right Leg approaches the Left to fall in its Place; therefore by consequence the Chassée drives it farther off in the second Position, which ought to be performed very quick; because you fall again on the Right first, and the left Leg is placed quickly in the second Position, which makes it appear as if a Person lighted on both Feet. *(Ram. 1 p. 175; Ess. p. 103)*

Chassés de côté

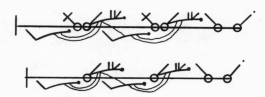

These chassés are the most frequently used. (L209)

TIME

Tomlinson writes briefly on duple-time and seems to indicate:

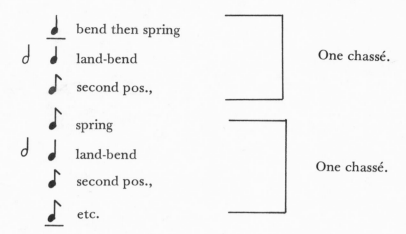

bend then spring

land-bend

second pos.,

One chassé.

spring

land-bend

second pos.,

etc.

One chassé.

ARMS

On chassés sideward: at the end of the preceding step-unit, bend both arms from the elbow (as in the contretemps croisée on p. 214.) Extend them during the first "movement" to the pos. of el., palms down. Usually the last chassé in a series is followed by a turn, in which case the arm will be raised in readiness. (See Pirouettes, p.210.) In a long sequence of chassés, a motion of the wrists may be introduced on the first chassé of each measure to prevent stiffness.

AUTHOR'S NOTES

Although this step-unit is most commonly used in duple-time, it is found in triple-time dances. No timing is indicated but the division of each beat into a triplet[8] works well: (L210)

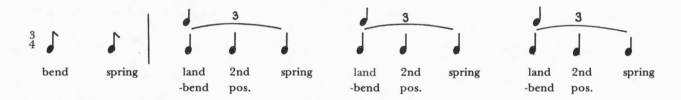

$\frac{3}{4}$ bend spring | land -bend 2nd pos. spring land -bend 2nd pos. spring land -bend 2nd pos. spring

STEP-UNITS WITH AN ELEMENT OF COLLAPSE

Pas Tombé.
Falling Step.
(Ram. 1 p. 142; Ess. p. 82)

In these Step-units the knees bend without the usual control. As Rameau expresses it: "the Knees bend as if their Strength failed them. . . ." *(Ram. 1 p. 142; Ess. p. 82)*

This pas composé consists of two "movements" and two single steps: a falling step and a demi-jeté. The first "movement" is reversed, the rise coming before the bend. The pas tombé equals one measure of duple- or triple-time. It does not provide a change of foot for the following step-unit.

Pas tombé de côté.

The characteristics of the pas tombé are the reversed "movement," the use of the body which causes the "fall," and the relatively collapsed quality of the bend.

The preceding step-unit must finish in an open position with the foot supporting the weight flat upon the floor, the leg well braced. The other leg will be on the toe or in the air. If on the toe, the leg will be lifted slightly as a rise is made by the supporting foot.

After rising onto [demi] pointe, the body must be held momentarily on balance, then the weight shifted slightly beyond the supporting leg until balance is lost. To save the situation, the raised leg moves into a closed position, catches weight, bends and pushes off into a jeté which enables balance to be fully restored.

Rameau describes this pas in detail. (L211) Standing on the L ft. in 2nd pos., rise on balance, then shift the weight slightly leftward until balance is lost, fall onto the R ft. in 5th pos. behind and spring onto the L ft. in 2nd pos. Rameau fails to clarify, however, whether the whole torso or just the pelvic girdle should be shifted. This question will be discussed in the teaching notes on p.235.

Pas tombé en avant

This pas is not described by Rameau.

The pas tombé is often preceded by a coupé but more often by an old form of the pas de gaillarde. In fact, these two units are virtually inseparable. The single step before a pas tombé must be concluded with the leg braced, ready for the rise which replaces the usual bend on the upbeat.

TIME AND ARMS

These will be given with the following pas de gaillarde.

Pas de Gaillarde.
Gaillard Step.
(Ram. 1 p. 142; Ess. p. 82)

Rameau's pas de gaillarde[9] is a combination of an older pas de gaillarde and the pas tombé. The older pas is given by Feuillet, and described by Tomlinson with a sprung pas assemblé.

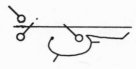

This pas composé has one "movement" and one single step: a pas assemblé and a pas marché. It equals one measure of music in duple- or triple-time and provides a change of foot for the following step-unit. (L212)

In the pas assemblé, the foot closes to first position in the air, "disengaged and at Liberty to perform the succeeding plain straight Step or Walk." *(Tom. p. 48)* The pas de gaillarde is also often notated with the weight on both feet at the end of the pas assemblé.

Pas de Gaillarde
Described by Rameau

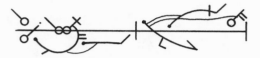

This pas consists of three "movements" and four single steps: a pas assemblé, a pas marché, a pas tombé,[10] and a demi-jeté. It equals two measures of music in duple- (rarely triple-) time and provides a change of foot for the following step-unit. (L213)

In effect, this pas de gaillarde is a combination of the pas de gaillarde and the pas tombé previously described.

TIME

One essential feature of the pas tombé is the reversed "movement": the rise takes place on the upbeat, the "fall" on the downbeat.

Tomlinson's account[11] for triple-time can be compared with notations of the pas de gaillarde in loures, in which one measure of $\frac{6}{4}$ time is considered as two of triple-time. (L214)

Triple-time

(Loure, 1 measure $\frac{6}{4}$ = 2 in $\frac{3}{4}$)

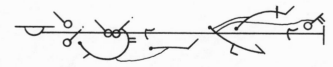

Although quarter-note rests are used, only eighth-note pauses are possible. In measure (1) the step that arrives on count 3 must be anticipated, and in measure (2) no allowance has been made, as usual, for the "movement."

♩ Bend and spring,

𝅗𝅥. ♩ land-bend

♩ rest, begin to step

♩ step, rise and shift

𝅗𝅥. ♩ fall,

♩ rest/spring

♩ land-bend/spring, etc.

Any following pas de gaillardes will begin from the finishing position (first).

Duple-time

For the performance of the pas de gaillarde in duple-time, there is Rameau's table. *(Ram. 2 p. 105 No. 6)* (L215)

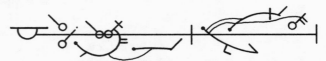

Comparing Rameau's table with the little Tomlinson says, there seem to be two possible interpretations:

♩ Bend/spring

𝅗𝅥. ♩ land-bend

♩   step

𝅗𝅥. ♩ step   rise

♩ rise/shift   shift,

𝅗𝅥. ♩ "fall"

♩ spring,

𝅗𝅥. ♩ land-bend

♩ spring, etc.

The Steps and Their General Performance in Duple- and Triple-Meter

ARMS

Begin in the pos. of el., palms down. On landing from the assemblé, the arms have arrived at the pos. of el., palms up. On the step to second position they return to the former position. On the fall, the arms move in sympathy with the legs by falling below the pos. of el., returning upward to it on the jeté.

AUTHOR'S NOTES

The pas tombé sideward is one of the most interesting step-units since it involves an action within the torso. Unfortunately, Rameau fails to convey exactly what this action, a move into the direction of travel, should be. In theory, there are three possibilities:

(1) Only the upper torso can be inclined or tilted. This does not result in the raised leg being drawn under the body as Rameau specifies. In fact, it has the opposite effect. The author has therefore rejected this possibility.

(2) Only the pelvic girdle can be shifted. This results in a curve of the upper torso toward the raised leg which then may be drawn under the body. If performed in this way, the upper torso should be well supported as it tilts—up and over, not dropped.

(3) The whole torso can be shifted in one piece (insofar as this is possible). The author prefers this solution.

When falling naturally, one tries to save oneself by pulling the torso upward. To incorporate this idea into the pas tombé, lift within the torso during the shift sideward, feeling momentarily suspended—off balance—before you fall. (Of course, total control is maintained throughout so that the shift does not go beyond hope of recovery!)

The arm position shown in Pl.2 p.143 is most compatible with the pas tombé. It is an extension of Rameau's lift from the shoulders, conforming to the lift of the leg from the hip. If used, this position should be reached on the rise and held during the shift, possibly until landing from the jeté. (L215)

For the greatest effect in the pas tombé, the RISE AND SHIFT MUST BE WELL DIFFERENTIATED. As they are performed in quick succession, this is hard to achieve. Practice by making the rise, holding the position, and afterward shifting until you HAVE to fall. The time between the two actions can gradually be lessened.

For pas de gaillarde in duple-, and [compound] duple-meter.

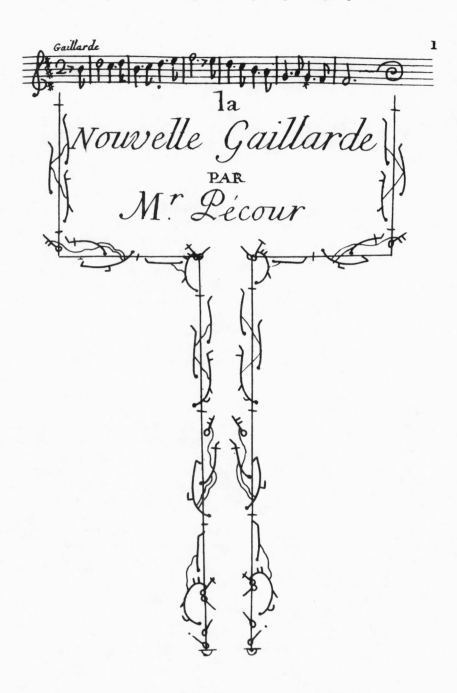

VIIe Recueil de dances de bal pour l'année 1709. Feuillet, Paris, 1709.

*Saillies ou Pas Echapez
des Deux Pieds.
Sallies or Starting Steps
of the Feet.
(Ram. 1 p. 183; Ess. p. 107)*

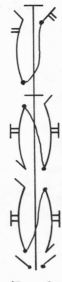

The pas echappé has two features in common with the pas tombé: reversed "movements" and bends made with a suggestion of collapse. It consists of three "movements" and three changes of foot position. The weight is equally distributed over both feet throughout. It takes one and a half measures in duple-time, followed by a rest or single step. It does not travel. As it ends on both feet, either foot is available for the following step-unit. (L216)

Rameau gives two starting positions for the pas echappé: in *Le Maître à danser,* fourth position; in *Abbregé,* first position.

(Ram. 2 p. 83, No. 5)

The first two changes are made by the feet passing each other in 1st pos. just clear of the floor, and spurting out to 4th for the bend. The third change is a sprung assemblé bringing the sequence to a close.

TIME

The pas echappé is not included by Feuillet or Tomlinson, and Rameau gives no timing for it. But it seems straightforward. The pas assemblé is followed by a half-measure rest.

ARMS

Oppose the first 4th pos., then hold the arms still until the assemblé when they should lower directly to the pos. of el., palms down.

FOOTNOTES

1. See p. 154.
2. See Wendy Hilton, "A Dance for Kings . . .", in the footnotes to Chapter Four.
3. No page references are given because Rameau does not deal with the demi-jeté separately, only as the concluding step of a pas composé.
4. There is a moot point of terminology here. Rameau calls this another glissade perhaps because it glides while other coupés de côté do not. It is more properly a coupé because it equals a whole measure of music.
5. Rameau describes this step-unit as sometimes beginning with a motion of the stepping leg to second position. From here the leg slides to fourth position for the transference of weight.
6. "This pas is properly a temps made on two feet or on one." *(Ram. 2 p. 52)*
7. See *Ram. 2 p. 88, No. 24.*
8. Musical term, not the modern dance term.
9. This bears no resemblance to galliard steps of the sixteenth century.
10. A pas tombé can be a single step as well as a pas composé.
11. He introduces his remarks by relating the timing to tunes such as "Forlanes and Jigs, etc." but then gives an explanation in triple-time.

A grand ball celebrating the birthday of Prince William III of Orange in 1689. Nürnberg, Germanisches Nationalmuseum.

CHAPTER TEN

The Steps in More Complex Metrical Situations

So far the study of the step-units has presented the steps in a general relationship to the triple-meter menuet and passepied, sarabande, chaconne, and passacaille, and the duple-meter bourrée, rigaudon, allemande, and gavotte. The duple pavane and gaillarde have also been covered, but these are dances rarely encountered in the period under discussion and should not be confused with their sixteenth-century predecessors.

Of the triple-time sarabande, chaconne, and passacaille, only music for the sarabande has been suggested for practice purposes because of the length of a typical chaconne or passacaille. Both are a kind of continuing variation over a short ground bass, or musical pattern. In his Preface, Tomlinson praises the performance of one of his pupils: "...Miss Frances, who, on the Theatre Royal in Little Lincoln's-Inn-Fields, performed the Passacaille de Scilla, consisting of above a thousand Measures or Steps, without making the least Mistake." The chaconnes and passacailles in French notated dance sources belong to the realm of the theater.

Of the dances listed above, the menuet and passepied, and the gavotte require a more detailed examination within the present context. This chapter will also discuss the use of the step-units in [compound] duple-, and quadruple-time dances, and the overlapping of musical and step-units in dances with a false cadence.

HEMIOLA IN THE MENUET AND PASSEPIED

The pas de menuet à deux and à trois mouvements have been discussed in Chapter Nine on pp. 191-195, and the contretemps de menuet on p. 216. The following remarks apply to both the menuet and the passepied. The dances used the same step-units, and the passepied was often referred to as a quick menuet.

Hemiola

The Greek word hemiola, or hemiolia, in music denotes three beats in the time of two. In a $\frac{3}{4}$ menuet, a hemiola may be written as a measure of $\frac{3}{2}$ shown in the top line below, or across the bar line as in the bottom line:

(The tie tying the two notes across the bar line means that the first note continues to sound for the duration of the second note. The bow is necessary because of the bar line.)

In a passepied in $\frac{3}{8}$ the hemiolas may be notated in $\frac{3}{4}$:

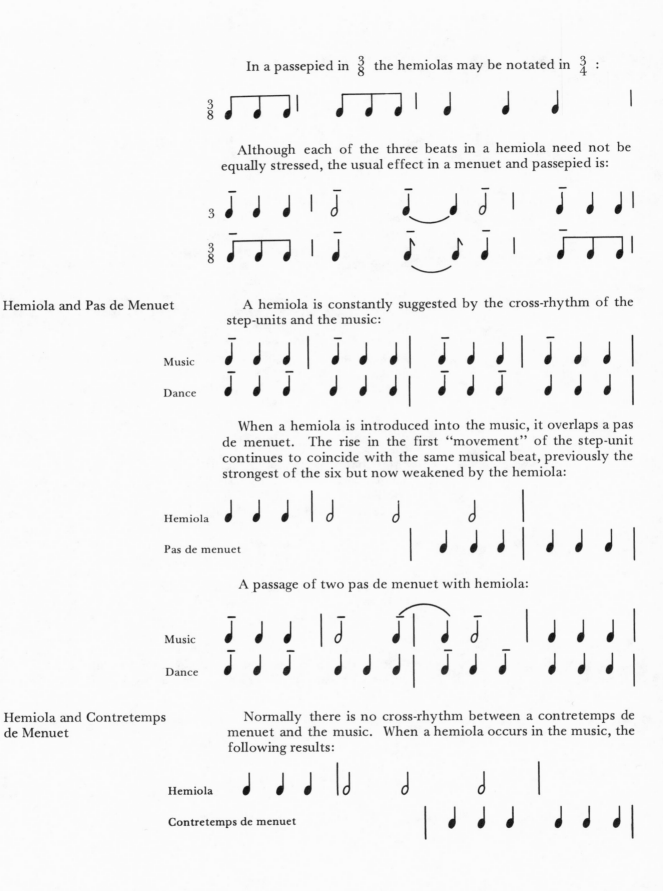

Although each of the three beats in a hemiola need not be equally stressed, the usual effect in a menuet and passepied is:

Hemiola and Pas de Menuet

A hemiola is constantly suggested by the cross-rhythm of the step-units and the music:

Music

Dance

When a hemiola is introduced into the music, it overlaps a pas de menuet. The rise in the first "movement" of the step-unit continues to coincide with the same musical beat, previously the strongest of the six but now weakened by the hemiola:

Hemiola

Pas de menuet

A passage of two pas de menuet with hemiola:

Music

Dance

Hemiola and Contretemps de Menuet

Normally there is no cross-rhythm between a contretemps de menuet and the music. When a hemiola occurs in the music, the following results:

Hemiola

Contretemps de menuet

The Steps in More Complex Metrical Situations

A passage of two contretemps de menuet with hemiola:

The passepied figure opposite has a hemiola in the fourth and fifth musical measures. A contretemps de menuet is introduced in the fifth measure:

Hemiola

Contretemps de menuet

A contretemps de menuet has the following rhythmic pattern in the last two of its three "movements" because of the long bending of the knees through beat 4 and half of beat 5:

If the second manner of performance suggested in Chapter Nine is adopted, the bend of the knees on the first beat is also modified. The result is difficult to render in musical notes because the stepping leg is moving even as the bend is held. Perhaps the best approximation is:

Two measures of $\frac{3}{8}$

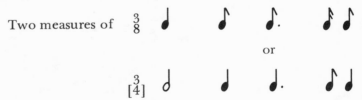

or

$[\frac{3}{4}]$

The rhythmic pattern of the contretemps de menuet is especially enjoyable when performed in conjunction with a rhythmic musical pattern often used in the formation of a hemiola toward the end of a strain as seen.

EXERCISE   For step-units in menuets and passepieds.

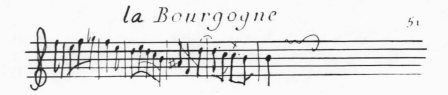

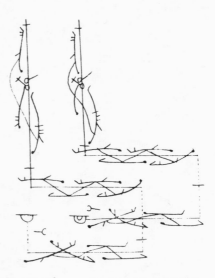

Recueil de dances composées par M. Pécour. Feuillet, Paris, 1700.

The conclusion of a figure from the passepied section of "La Bourgogne." The step-pattern should be practiced to menuet and passepied music. A pas de menuet backward and a pas balancé may be added. The uneven number of step-units will cause a different unit to coincide with a hemiola every time the pattern is repeated.

Performing students should now resume their study of Chapter Nine, p. 219.

Gavotte

The gavotte, like the bourrée and the rigaudon, is in duple-meter with two half notes in a measure. While the bourrée and the rigaudon have one quarter-note upbeat (sometimes divided into two eighth notes), the gavotte begins on the half bar, that is, in the middle of the measure.

In each example below, Feuillet shows that, as in all tunes which begin with "odd notes," the dancer should allow the notes which precede the first bar line to pass and land the spring on the first beat in the measure:

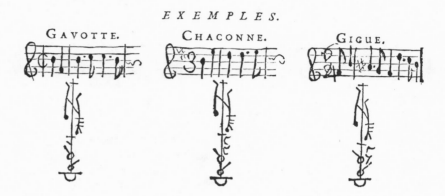

EXEMPLES.

GAVOTTE.   CHACONNE.   GIGUE.

Weaver translates Feuillet's explanation but does not include the notated examples. *(Feu. 1 p. 91; Wea. 1 p. 51)*

In the gavotte there is a conflicting emphasis between step-units and musical units. The former are contained within the measure while the latter cross the bar line. Below, the single steps of the units without the "movements" are related to the beats:

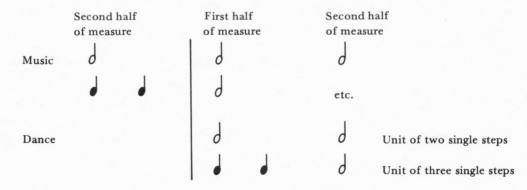

	Second half of measure	First half of measure	Second half of measure	
Music	♩ ♪ ♪	♩ ♩	♩ etc.	
Dance		♩ ♪ ♪	♩ ♩	Unit of two single steps
				Unit of three single steps

The gavotte does not, however, have a false cadence because the stresses coincide even though the units overlap. Here music and steps are related with a "movement"; the stresses coincide on the first beat in the measure:

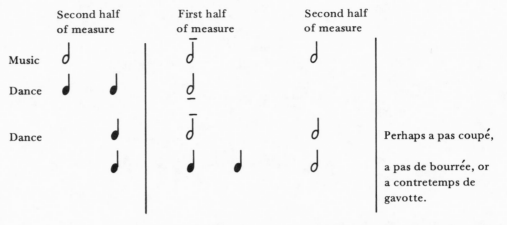

	Second half of measure	First half of measure	Second half of measure

The step-units relate to one measure of gavotte just as they do to one measure of bourrée, but the dancer will experience a "pull" between them and the musical unit. Gavotte music is almost invariably written in four-measure phrases, the strains being either four or eight measures long. In step-sequences, it is basic to use a pas assemblé every fourth measure to resolve the pull in the last measure of a phrase or strain. Steps and music relate:

EXERCISE

Practice the four-measure step-sequence of: contretemps de gavotte; pas de bourrée; contretemps de gavotte; pas assemblé.

AUTHOR'S NOTES

The pull between the musical units and the step-units is a conflict in which the musical unit usually wins in initial studies of the gavotte. The dancer will be drawn to mark the beginning of the music with the "movements," rather than the beginning of the measure:

The Steps in More Complex Metrical Situations

Until the ear becomes accustomed to the harmonic structure of the music, even the landmark of the pas assemblé may not be sufficient to ensure that the beginner knows whether the "movements" are marking the correct beats. An outside eye and ear may be necessary to confirm the marking of the first quarter note in a measure and not the third.

The gavotte, although lively, is also spacious. In performing the bourrée and rigaudon, the author is primarily aware of the feet moving whereas in the gavotte, the carriage and a proud use of the upper arm in the arm motions seem to predominate.

ARMS   The step-sequence in the previous exercise requires only one arm opposition. Begin with the feet in 1st pos., the arms in the pos. of eq., palms down. Oppose on the pas de bourrée, lower the arms directly to their original position on the landing from the hop in the contretemps. [Do not start to lower the arms as the rest of you goes up!] A turn of the wrists may mark the landing in the pas assemblé.

The most basic step combination for gavottes is a contretemps de gavotte and pas assemblé. It is used throughout Ballon's "Gavotte du Roy" (composed for the seven-year-old Louis XV), the first figure of which is reproduced on p. 21. This sequence presents no difficulties as the pas assemblé occurs so frequently, and a preparatory step is used to bridge the gap to the next step-unit:

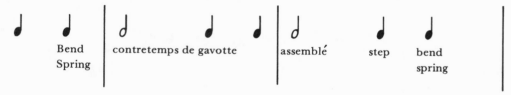

Bend Spring | contretemps de gavotte | assemblé | step | bend spring

The first figure of the "Gavotte de Seaux" which follows is a typically complex ballroom gavotte. In the most complex gavottes there may be no pas assemblés, but a continuous overlapping of the units.

Familiarity with the gavotte transforms what may be at first a puzzling experience into a delectable one.

For step-sequences to gavottes.

XIIe Recueil de danses pour l'année 1714. Dezais, Paris. p. 3.

Performing students should now turn to Chapter Nine, p. 223.

Gigue and Forlane (Forlana)

The performance of step-units containing more than two single steps is not explained by the masters because they do not differentiate between duple- and [compound] duple-time. Units of two single steps are performed with the two steps and two beats coinciding and should present no difficulties to students by now familiar with their performance in duple-time.

However, with two beats in a measure each with a triple division, there are too many notes for units with three single steps, such as pas de bourrée. The problem is one of distribution.

Obviously the two beats should be marked, the "movement" occurring on the upbeat/downbeat as usual with the first single step. A pause on the second note will further emphasize the downbeat. The first pas marché should probably occur on the third note so that the final pas marché can take place on the second beat, and the next bend should probably coincide with this pas marché:

Pas de bourrée	Contretemps de gavotte

(2) 4 = bend
    5
    6 = place the foot
 	
(1) 1 = rise in pos. of eq.
    2
    3 = step
(2) 4 = step/bend
    5
    6 = place the foot
	Following the hop which lands on the downbeat, the same modifications should be followed as in the pas de bourrée.

EXERCISE

To a gigue or forlane, practice a series of pas de bourrée until they move with a secure rhythmic flow. Then do three pas de bourrée and one contretemps de gavotte. Then a contretemps de gavotte alternating with a pas de bourrée. Finally, add a pas coupé from time to time.

Structure

Unlike the dances studied so far, consisting of musical strains which are repeated, the music of a forlane generally has strains built basically of two-measure segments, each of which repeats. The strains are seldom repeated consecutively although some may recur as the piece progresses. A common device was to use the first strain as the conclusion of a forlane.

The sophisticated French gigues under discussion tend to have strains of different lengths. The opening nine-measure figure of Feuillet's "Gigue à deux," given opposite, should now be studied. Although most beautiful as a danse à deux because of the symmetrical patterns, it is also effective as a solo.

This dance is one of the rare examples in which the dance figures and step-sequences, as well as the musical strains, are repeated. The dance consists of a nine-measure strain played twice, followed by a four-measure passage forming a bridge to the second strain. The second strain, which consists of eight measures, is then performed twice. The dance concludes with a repetition of the last four musical measures, but with a different step-sequence. The device of repeating the final measures of a strain was a common one. The repeated section was called a *petite reprise*.

ARMS

Measure (1) Oppose
      (2) oppose
      (3) oppose, hold
      (4) lower directly to the pos. of el., palms down
      (5) oppose, hold
      (6) a full circle outward beginning on beat 1 and finishing in opposition on beat 4 is effective
      (7) lower directly to the pos. of el., palms down
      (8) hold
      (9) oppose.

AUTHOR'S NOTES

In the quick [compound] duple-time dances the pas de bourrée should feel as though they are traveling smoothly and swiftly. Their performance should not be pedantic but have a feeling of disciplined freedom. To achieve smooth swiftness, the knees must be well braced on the demi-coupé and first pas marché. If the dancer experiences a bobbing up and down at this moment, the knees are giving way. The feeling of swift travel should be achieved by the carriage of the body, not by attempting over-long steps, especially when traveling forward. Control in the insteps and the quality of the bend will prevent too sharp an effect on the second beat (note 4).

EXERCISE   For step-sequences in [compound] duple-time.

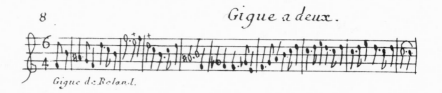

Gigue a deux

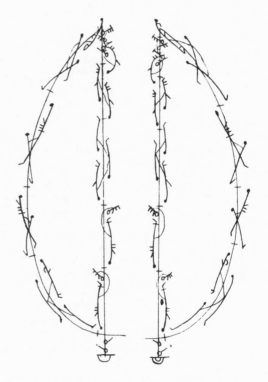

Recueil de dances composées par M. Feuillet. Feuillet, Paris, 1700.

The music is by Lully from the tragédie-lyrique, *Roland*, 1685.

Note: The two jetés in measure (4) land on the first and fourth quarter notes. Performing students should now resume their study of Chapter Nine, p. 225.

OVERLAPPING OF STEP- AND MUSICAL UNITS IN A FALSE CADENCE

The practice of overlapping step- and musical units in [compound] duple-time dances was obviously enjoyed. Here, unlike the gavotte, the stresses in the units do not coincide:

Music   𝅗𝅥. | 𝅗𝅥.

Dance | 𝅗𝅥.   𝅗𝅥.

The notation of such dances involves either the units of the music or of the choreography crossing the bar line. From extant examples the musical units were apparently interrupted by bar lines and the stressed beat placed on the half bar. The music in the "Venitienne" on p.252 is from Campra's *Le Carnaval de Venise*, 1699, and is barred similarly in the orchestral score.

In the score of one dance, the step-units cross the bar line but only because the step/music relationship changes halfway through the piece. The dance is "La Contredanse," a gigue, the third figure of which is given opposite. During the first two figures of this dance, the step-units equal a measure of music as usual. At the beginning of the third figure, a single step equalling a half measure is injected, which causes all subsequent step-units to begin on the half bar.

AUTHOR'S NOTES

Most students have some difficulty mastering the overlapping of step-units and musical units. One method is to begin performing pas de bourrée, making sure that the final single step (and the bend of the following "movement") coincides with the strongest musical beat. When the pas de bourrée feel secure, perform a pas coupé instead of the second pas de bourrée in every group of four. Follow each pas coupé with a contretemps de gavotte. Finally, perform the four-measure sequence of: pas de bourrée, pas coupé, contretemps de gavotte, temps de courante. Take great care not to hurry the temps de courante.

Having securely established the feeling of dancing the unstressed conclusion of a step-unit against the stressed musical beat, become bolder in establishing the stress of the "movement" on the weaker of the two musical beats within the measure.

EXERCISES   For step-sequences with a false cadence.

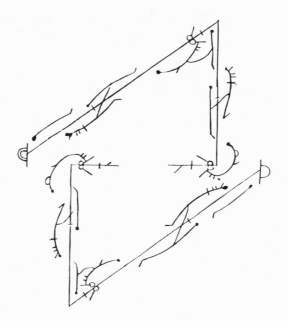

Recueil de dances composées par M. Pécour.   Feuillet, Paris, 1700.

The music, by Lully, was used as part of the ballet which augmented Cavalli's opera, *Serse*, when it was given in Paris in 1660.

Perform a contretemps de gavotte, pas assemblé, and a pas simple to a gigue, landing from each spring on the first beat of the measure as usual. After the fourth time through, add another single step, equalling a half measure of music. Then perform the sequence landing from the springs on the second half-note beat in each measure.

SCENE IV.

LEANDRE, ISABELLE.

Une Troupe d'Esclavons, d'Armeniens & de Bohemiennes, viennent dans la Place S. Marc, prendre part aux plaisirs du Carnaval

Here the music appears to be wrongly barred. However, the bar lines correspond to those in the dance score, and it is possible that the barring in the musical score was intended to coincide with the notation of the step-units.

Part of "La Venitienne" from the ballet, *Le Carnaval de Venise*, Campra, 1699, in *partition reduite*. Ballard, Paris, 17—.

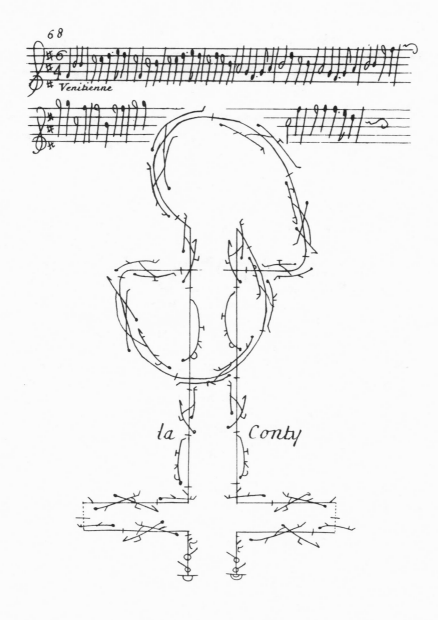

Recueil de dances composées par M. Pécour. Feuillet, Paris, 1700.

"La Conty" was a popular danse à deux. In the first four measures the cross-rhythm of step- and musical unit is made even harder to achieve by Pécour's unusual step-pattern.

SOME DANCE TYPES WHICH ARE PRIMARILY THEATRICAL

Canarie(s)

The remainder of this chapter deals with complex dance types, the extant examples of which contain pas de ballet: the lively [compound] duple-time canarie, and the lofty quadruple-time loure and entrée grave. The comments will not extend beyond theoretical discussion.

In canaries, the music begins on the half bar, the step-unit with the measure:

The available canaries are complex theatrical dances, generally for men. One very elaborate dance for a woman is extant, although it was apparently never performed at the Opéra. This is the "Gigue pour une femme," by Pécour, the first figure of which is given opposite. (Canaries are frequently titled gigue in music and dance scores.) The music for Pécour's dance is a canarie from *Alcide*, 1693, by Louis de Lully and Marin Marais. The dance is unusually long for a solo, always excepting chaconnes and passacailles.

With the music beginning on the half bar and the step-unit on the first beat in a measure, the canarie has a certain similarity to the gavotte in the pull between step- and musical units. The canaries move more swiftly, however, and there are no places of outstanding repose. In the dance mentioned above, there are teasing pauses of a half measure from time to time, which serve only to increase the liveliness and wit of Pécour's composition.

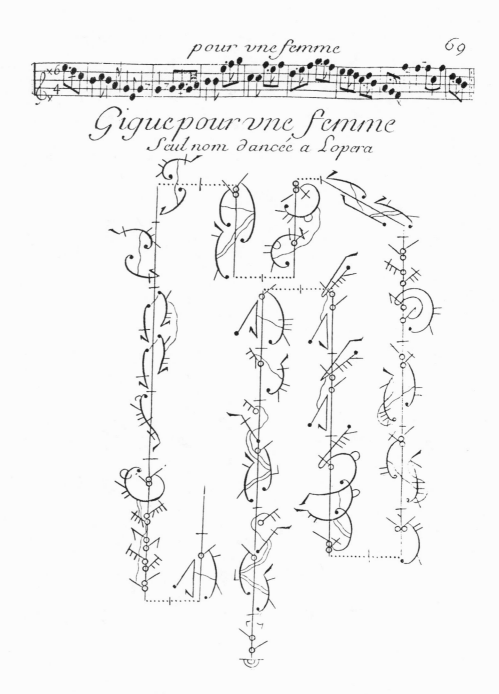

Gigue pour vne femme
Seul nom dancée a Lopera

The music, titled "Canarie," is by Louis de Lully and Marin Marais from *Alcide*, 1693.

Nouveau recüeil de dance de M. Pécour. Gaudrau, Paris, 1712.

Dances in Quadruple-Time:
Loure (Gigue Lente) and
Entrée Grave

Loure, Gigue Lente

In quadruple-time dances, two step-units are danced to the time of one measure of music.

In the seventeenth and eighteenth centuries, the names "Loure" and "Gigue Lente" (in English "Louvre" or "Slow Jigg") were synonymous. Like that of a fast gigue, the music for a slow gigue is usually in $\frac{6}{4}$ time, but for the dancer, an imaginary bar line divides each measure because two step-units are contained within one measure of music:

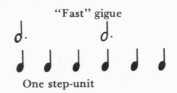

One step-unit

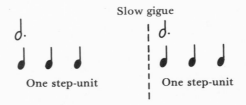

One step-unit | One step-unit

The two step-units are danced as though to two measures of triple-time, the initial "movement" of the two units coinciding with the two dotted half-note beats. The dancer must be aware of the swing of the duple beat, and of the triple-meter of the step-units. (As mentioned on p. 154 a $\frac{6}{4}$ quadruple-time loure was sometimes notated in $\frac{3}{4}$.)

Around the turn of the seventeenth century a new kind of loure appeared in which the triple-meter was more predominant than the duple-meter. The most famous of these was the air "Aimable vainqueur" from Campra's opera *Hesionne*, 1700. The music is in triple-time and the choreographies which accompany it, two theatrical solos for a man and the ballroom dance, "Aimable vainqueur," have one step-unit per measure.

The first figure of a gigue lente.

Recueil de dances de Mr Pécour. Feuillet, Paris, 1704.

The music is from Campra's *Hesionne*, 1700.

The theatrical entrées grave for male dancers are the most noble and majestic of all the dances. Each measure contains two step-units, the initial "movements" coinciding with the two half-note beats in a measure:

A duple-time dance with
one step-unit per measure

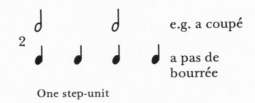

One step-unit

A quadruple-time dance;
two step-units per measure

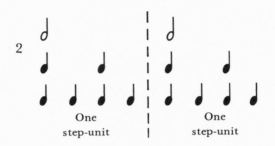

One step-unit   One step-unit

In quadruple-time dances, there is an underlying liveliness produced by the speed at which the two step-units per measure must be executed. The overall quality, however, is one of grandeur because of the slow swing of the duple beat. The grandeur is especially apparent in the entrée grave because of the strong, dotted rhythms which characterize the music.

In reaching a satisfactory performance tempo for a quadruple-time dance, the quickest, most complex choreographic step-patterns must not appear ridiculously fast, nor must the duple swing become funereal.

The fascinating and very beautiful worlds of the loure and entrée grave need a detailed exploration beyond the boundaries of the present text. Both dance types require in their interpreters the quality of "cadence" developed to the highest level of sensitivity. Cadence, in the sense of "quality of movement," the swing of a dance and its music, is discussed in the following chapter.

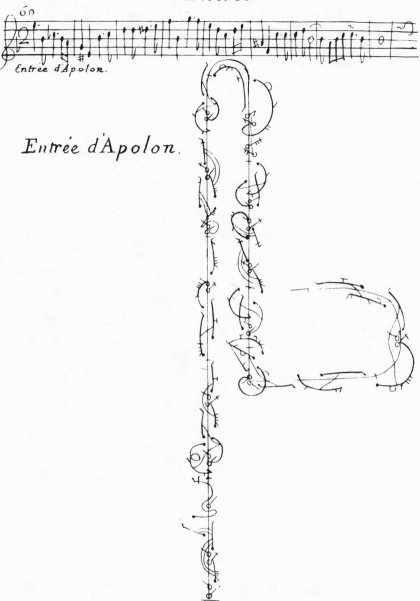

Recueil de dances composées par M. Feuillet. Feuillet, Paris, 1700.

The opening figure of Feuillet's dance, composed to music from Lully's *Le Triomphe de l'amour*, 1681.

A rather languid dancing master playing his kit or pochette, the small stringed instrument used by dancing masters to accompany their pupils' lessons. The instruments were called pochettes because they were small enough to be carried in a pocket. George Chaffee collection, Harvard Theater Collection.

CHAPTER ELEVEN

Step-sequences, Tempi, and Expression

Cadence or Rhythm

Dancers with a true ear for cadence express the rhythm and spirit of the music in every motion. The term cadence was used to denote rhythm in the broadest sense. The difference between temporal rhythm and one more fundamental to life is well defined by Suzanne Langer:

There have been countless studies of rhythm, based on the notion of periodicity, or regular recurrence of events. It is true that the elementary rhythmic functions of life have regularly recurrent phases: heartbeat, breath, and the simpler metabolisms. But the obviousness of these repetitions has caused people to regard them as the essence of rhythm, which they are not. The ticking of a clock is repetitious and regular, but not in itself rhythmic; the listening ear hears rhythms *in* the succession of equal ticks, the human mind organizes them into a temporal form.

The essence of rhythm is the preparation of a new event by the ending of a previous one. A person who moves rhythmically need not repeat a single motion exactly. His movements, however, must be complete gestures, so that one can sense a beginning, intent, and consummation, and see in the last stage of one the condition and indeed the rise of another. Rhythm is the setting-up of new tensions by the resolution of former ones. They need not be of equal duration at all; but the situation that begets the new crisis must be inherent in the denouement of its forerunner.[1]

Rhythm in the latter sense is a gift which makes distinctive the performances of musicians and dancers who possess it. Its innate, instinctive quality is described in the following definition of cadence:

The CADENCE, Is a quality of good music, which gives to those who listen to it, a lively feeling of the measure, so that they remark it, and perceive it fall justly, without reflecting on it, as it were thro' instinct. This quality is particularly requisite in the airs for dancing. . . .[2]

When both musicians and dancers possess this quality the arts of music and dance are truly united, as Tomlinson says:

. . .the natural Effect of good Dancing adorn'd with all its Beauties, is that the Music seems to inspire the Dancing, and the latter the former; and the Concurrence of both is so requisite to charm those who behold them, that each of them in some Measure suffers from a Separation.[3]

This is the ideal, but Tomlinson reveals that then, just as now, many musicians lacked a reliable sense of speed and many dancers were without musical awareness. Tomlinson becomes irate with such dancers:

. . .it may be of Service to such as have but indifferent Ears. . .to hearken to the Tune, that they may know the Time in which the Dance is to be perform'd;. . . the Music [musicians] rarely fail of beating Time to the Tune they are playing, or at least ought not, because hearing the beating or striking of the Toe or Heel against the Floor are visible and certain Marks of the Dancers commencing.[4]

The dancers were entirely dependent upon the musicians for establishing and maintaining a tempo. After describing the bows before dancing, Rameau leaves his dancers awaiting the beginning of the music, their attention directed toward the Presence, the musicians seated behind them. (See p. 282.) Coming after these elegant bows, the rather down-to-earth method of having the leading musician beat out a measure with his foot was at least a very positive way of setting the tempo and ensuring that everyone started together. The dance then began with a preparatory bending of the knees which coincided with the upbeat, if the music had one. If not, the dancers alone had an upbeat in the preliminary bending of the knees.

Having started, it seems the next problem was keeping together:

. . .if the Partner with whom we dance be a good Performer, we should take Care to keep our Steps and Figure agreeable with theirs; and I am of opinion, if a Person has the least Notion of the Steps he is performing, it will be very easy for him to observe, whether they begin and end together, which I believe may be useful in Dancing.[5]

Tomlinson felt that the best way for partners to keep in time with each other was for both to listen to the music and so keep in time with that, but:

. . .that itself is uncertain, nothing being more common than the hearing of a Tune begun in one Time, and, before it is ended, to be near as fast again; which renders it impossible for the best Dancers whatsoever to dance as they ought.[6]

If all went well: ". . .the Dancers, sure of the Time they dance to, perform not only with Pleasure and Ease to themselves, but also give a double Satisfaction to the Spectators."[7]

Mood and Tempo

Among the masters under discussion, only Tomlinson touches on the characters and relative tempi of the dance types. The adjectives which he used were intended to convey the quality and mood of the types, of which the tempo is but one aspect. Following is a table of the relative speeds Tomlinson discusses in his text, including the manner in which the "Time" of a "Bar" (or measure) should be beaten by a musician with his foot. Each group of dances is listed from the slowest to the quickest.

Usual "Odd Notes" [Upbeats]	Beating. One bar Duple-time	Step-units per bar	Dance types	Relative tempi
	down up ♩ ♩ ♩ ♩	2	Entree (quadruple)	"Very slow. . . Grave"
On ½ bar ♩ ♩		1	Gavot ⎫	"Rather more solemn and grave" than
♩		1	Galliard ⎬	
♩		1	Allemaigne ⎫	
♩		1	Bourée ⎬	these
♩		1	Rigadoon ⎭	
♪ ♩ 𝅗𝅥. 𝅗𝅥.		2	Louvre or slow Jig (quadruple)	"Grave"
♪ ♩ 𝅗𝅥. 𝅗𝅥.		1	Jig ⎫	
		1	Forlane ⎬	"Light and airy"
On ½ bar ♪ ♪♪♩ 𝅗𝅥. 𝅗𝅥.		1	Canary	"Very brisk"

Triple-time

	Beating. One bar	Step-units per bar	Dance types	Relative tempi
♪	down up 𝅗𝅥 𝅗𝅥 𝅗𝅥	1 long 1 short ⎫	Courante	"Very solemn and grave"
	♩ ♩ ♩	1, 1, 1 ⎬	Sarabande, Passacaille, Chaconne	Less grave and "every one a Degree lighter"

Two bars*

	Beating	Step-units per bar	Dance types	Relative tempi
	down up ♩ ♩ ♩ | ♩ ♩ ♩	1 in two bars	Minuet, Passepied ⎬	Each one "still brisker"
♪	♪♪♪ | ♪♪♪			

* Tomlinson says that menuets begin with "odd notes" but that passepieds never do. Since the reverse is usually true the author takes this to be a slip on his part.

Evocative as the quality and tempo adjectives are, their application in many of today's musical performances by performers unfamiliar with the choreographies shows that to the modern mind the tempo-adjectives suggest something more excessive than originally intended. Did "brisk" really imply the nervous rushing which characterizes so many current performances of bourrées and other "lively" duple-time dance music? With such fast tempi the dancer dashes through the steps, deprived of any opportunity for phrasing and nuance. Conversely, how slow was "very slow"? Certainly "noble" did not imply the pomposity so often heard in performances of the slower triple-time dance music: the sarabandes, courantes, and even the menuets. A study of the ideals of eighteenth-century deportment and the content of the choreographies proves this widespread concept to be false.

Using the performance of the step-units comprising the dances for information about the tempi and character of music and dance here presumes in the researcher a dance technique equal to that of the best eighteenth-century performers, both "amateur" and professional.

Tempi and Character Suggested by Step-sequences

Any indications for the tempo suitable to a dance type should be viewed only as a general guide. Not all pieces within a type move best at an identical speed, nor is there an absolutely correct tempo for any one piece. Rather there is an *area* of tempo within which all the elements can best be realized. The search is for the expression and style of a piece, its character or "quality of movement."

Every court dance requires nobility and liveliness (mental as well as physical) from the performers; all the dances embody these qualities in varying degrees. The choreographies reveal that even the liveliest dances contain some temps de courante and coupés soutenus, the slowest and stateliest of the step-units, while the solemn and serious dances contain springing steps.

Almost all the dances, whatever their meter or type, could be composed from any of the step-units, except the most highly regulated of the menuets and passepieds. Therefore, the varied articulation needed to characterize every dance and its music is far wider in scope than might be supposed. In seeking to establish an area of tempo, the mechanics of performing the choreography is of some help. For instance, if the arm motions feel and look rushed, the tempo is obviously too fast.

In footwork, the most conclusive answers are provided in duple-time dances simply because of the mechanics of jumping—the body can defy gravity only for a limited amount of time—within the aesthetics of eighteenth-century springing. In the duple- and [compound] duple-time pieces, the sprung step-units are made with an even bounce upward and downward. If too slow, they will appear sluggish and labored; if too fast, the resilient bounce is lost. Taken to either extreme, the aesthetic quality of lively yet easy springing will be destroyed. There is still, however, a range of possible tempi. Not every duple-time type was always given the same tempo indication: the gavotte, for example, was usually considered a little slower than the bourrée.

In triple-time dances, two-spring step-units are executed differently and cease to play such a determining role in establishing an area of tempo. Instead of a repeated even bounce, the two springs are separated by a controlled lowering of the heels before the bend for the second spring. This can be done in a fairly wide range of speed, the tempo controlled mainly by strength in the insteps, and still make aesthetic movement sense.

Tempi Measured by Mechanical Means

The forerunner of the modern metronome was a simple pendulum-type device. A weighted piece of string was hung from a fixed point and swung from side to side. The measuring principle was the length of the string: the shorter the string, the faster the swing. By using this device, or by measuring musical beats to the human pulse, eighteenth-century musical theorists devised tables of tempi, the majority of which pertain to dance music or closely related instrumental music.[8]

An early eighteenth-century treatise which includes tempo indications is Michel L'Affilard's *Principes très-faciles*, Paris, 1705. The *Principes*, a collection of dance songs, is primarily a treatise for singers and offers illuminating information on phrasing by placing marks where the singer should breathe. L'Affilard also provides a tempo indication at the beginning of each song.

There are differences of opinion about the correct interpretation of a pendulum swing. Was the tempo count taken from a swing one way, or a swing to and fro? In the former case, the resulting tempo would be twice as fast as in the latter. L'Affilard's term "vibration" seems to settle conclusively that he measured tempo by counting one swing of the pendulum *to and fro*. L'Affilard says that his music could be used for dancing if so desired. However, not all the songs have tempo indications suitable for the purpose.

AUTHOR'S NOTES

The author has matched a selection of L'Affilard's pieces to the early eighteenth-century choreographies. Included are the dance types used for step-practice in the present text. The basis for establishing tempi is L'Affilard's "vibration," a swing of the pendulum to and fro. The following table gives the resulting tempi from L'Affilard,[9] and suggests the areas of tempo (on a modern metronome) at which the author has found the choreographies to move best in performance.

Time or meter-signatures	L'Affilard's tempi	Author's approximate tempi
2 Gavotte	𝅗𝅥 = 60	𝅗𝅥 = 60
2 Bourrée	𝅗𝅥 = 60	𝅗𝅥 = 80
3 Menuet	♩ = 105	♩ = 105
6/8 Menuet	♪ = 114	♩ = 114
3/8 Passepied	♪ = 129	♪ = 129
3 Sarabande	♩ = 67	♩ = 69
6/4 Gigue	♩. = 58	♩. = 88
6/4 Canarie	♩. = 53	♩. = 80

Conclusions

In establishing an area of tempo for a dance and its music, a range of speed should be worked through, first for the mechanically possible and then for the aesthetically pleasing. To this end the piece should be studied by a group of proficient performers, so that a norm may be established—an area of tempo within which everyone feels free to find his own articulation and phrasing.

Too Slow   Too Fast

impossible   impossible

     possible   possible

Mechanically

       good   good

        best for:

        articulation
        phrasing
        speed
        harmonic rhythm
        ornamentation

Conclusions based upon seventeenth- and eighteenth-century music and dance theory must be tested by practical application. If a theoretical conclusion in trial has to be forced upon the dance and music to its obvious distortion, the theory should be reexamined. Robert Donington has expressed this ideal on behalf of musicology:

But of course, when musicology doesn't make useful sense you cut off the last three syllables and talk about music.[10]

FOOTNOTES

1. Suzanne Langer, *Feeling and Form* (New York: Charles Scribner's Sons, 1953).
2. J. J. Rouseau, *Dictionary of Music*, trans. William Waring (London, 1770), p. 49.
3. Kellom Tomlinson, *The Art of Dancing* (London, 1735), p. 151.
4. Tomlinson, *Art of Dancing*, p. 150.
5. Tomlinson, *Art of Dancing*, p. 150.
6. Tomlinson, *Art of Dancing*, pp. 150, 151.
7. Tomlinson, *Art of Dancing*, p. 151.
8. For further information about eighteenth-century musical theorists see Neal Zaslaw, "Materials for the Life and Works of Jean-Marie Leclair l'aíné." (Unpublished Ph.D. diss., Columbia University, 1970); also Erich Schwandt, "L'Affilard on the French Court Dances," *The Musical Quarterly* (New York), vol. 60, 1974, pp. 389-400.
9. Schwandt, "L'Affilard."
10. Robert Donington, "Rhythm and the Performer." (A lecture delivered at the International Bach Summer Sessions, New York, July 22, 1969.)

The placement of the hand on the hip is not part of the prescribed formal deportment for a lady. The pose may be characteristic of the theatrical, or fancy dress being worn. Yet, with her upright but relaxed carriage the position of the arm does not, as might be expected, detract from the elegant poise of this beautiful lady.

George Chaffee collection, Harvard Theater Collection.

CHAPTER TWELVE

Technique of Etiquette

Introduction

A dancing master taught his pupils the bows and courtesies and also the rules of conduct when in company. Although masters had a knowledge of such matters, some tended to execute the motions in a somewhat exaggerated fashion, quite contrary to the fashionable ideal of effective simplicity:

. . .a moderate Knowledge in the little Rules of Good-breeding gives a Man some Assurance, and makes him easy in all Companies. For Want of this, I have seen a Professor of a Liberal Science at a Loss to salute a Lady; and a most excellent Mathematician not able to determine whether he should stand or sit while my Lord drank to him.

It is the proper Business of a Dancing Master to regulate these Matters; tho' I take it to be a just Observation, that unless you add something of your own to what these fine Gentlemen teach you, and which they are wholly ignorant of themselves, you will much sooner get the Character of an Affected Fop, than a Well-bred Man.[1]

The use of the hat, the honours, the bows and courtesies are primarily useful today for dramatic productions. To many it may still come as a surprise to learn that gentlemen bowed without the handkerchief-in-hand flourishes and the waving about of hats so long considered the epitome of period deportment.[2] Such embellishments only revealed affectation, notably in fops who were conceited, foolish rather than witty, and vain of their showy and exaggerated dress.

Ladies and gentlemen of fashion were required to be completely poised, and no action in everyday life was left to chance. Yet the ultimate aim was to appear supremely natural. This ideal is expressed very simply in the following quotation from *The Spectator*:

Good breeding shows itself most. . .where it appears the least.[3]

The simplicity of early eighteenth-century honours is succinctly expressed by Joan Wildeblode and Peter Brinson:

The art of making a graceful bow no longer depended up-on the flowing gestures and deep obeisances. Rather it was an art which concealed art, for every action of the well-bred gentleman now expressed something of that refined reserve which for generations to come was to be the hall-mark of polite society. Every movement, as in a bow, was well-considered, exact, and without superfluity of gesture. Even the manner of taking off or replacing the hat, fol-lowed prescribed and carefully timed movements.[4]

Once the actor applies himself to the simple bows of a gentle-man, however, a problem becomes immediately apparent: it is far more difficult and, therefore, takes more application and time to make a simple bow strikingly than to impress an uneducated audience with an embellishment. Bows must be perfected and correctly applied. They revealed social background just as strongly as differences in speech. By an educated man they were made not as an act of servility, but as an expression of politeness and respect, and to display his education and quality. The fol-lowing is from Cyril Beaumont's translation of *Le Maître à danser* (Essex abbreviates this passage):

A very necessary matter for everyone, whatever their sta-tion, to be informed upon, is the correct manner of raising one's hat and making a graceful bow; but in general it is that which receives the least care, whereas everything shows that both should be done well. In the first place, this excites admiration in others for us and brings further advantages in its train. It inclines a person to show us con-sideration by regarding us as persons who have known how to profit from the education we have received.[5]

Rameau describes at great length how to bow well, insisting espe-cially upon a lack of affectation. He then points out the mistakes most commonly made by his pupils which could be paradigms for an actor's movement pattern in an unsophisticated role.

For ladies, Rameau stresses even more the need for modesty and lack of affectation in the ideal social demeanor. Beyond showing how the fan should be carried when walking and making a courtesy, he gives no specific instructions for its use, but with the emphasis placed upon lack of affectation in general, the fan should ideally be managed unobtrusively. Some comments on the "language of the fan" are given by Joan Wildebloode along with some of the gestures and their assumed meanings.[6] The pro-blem with many of the gestures is that they do not visually sug-gest their supposed meaning and are therefore meaningless to today's uninitiated audiences. The honours Rameau describes for ladies are even simpler than those for gentlemen, but require a good balance.

Honours, like greetings and partings today, punctuated life and were imbued with expression. Saint-Simon gives a vivid account of some dramatic events at Versailles in which honours were ex-changed with a variety of emotions. The King was anxious that

Mlle. de Blois, one of his illegitimate daughters, marry M. le Duc de Chartres, his nephew. De Chartres's mother, Madame (Liselotte), was extremely upset by this insult but the King, through devious means, achieved his purpose. The day the wedding was announced ended with the King's supper, which Saint-Simon described as follows:

The King seemed perfectly composed. Madame sat next M. de Chartres, but never so much as glanced at him, nor at Monsieur. Her eyes were full of tears, which fell from time to time, and every now and then she wiped them away, looking around all the while to see how others were affected. M. de Chartres's eyes were also very red, and neither he nor his mother ate much. I observed how courteously the King offered Madame the dishes that were placed before him and how ungraciously she refused, which did not in any way disturb his air of polite attention. It was much remarked that after they had left the table, the King made Madame a particularly low and impressive bow, at which she performed a pirouette so neat and swift that all he could see as he straightened himself, was her back retreating towards the door.

Next day, the entire Court called upon Monsieur, Madame, and M. le Duc de Chartres, but nothing was said. People merely made their bows and everything passed off in perfect silence.[7]

As will be seen later, bows were often made so frequently in company that walking and standing seem only occasionally to have interrupted them.

WALKING

Rameau describes the ideal way in which the gentlemen should walk. The heel of the stepping foot should touch the ground first, the knees boldly stretched, the legs slightly turned outward. Steps should not be uncomfortably long, and the speed of walking should be:

. . .neither too fast nor too slow; the last bordering on Indolence, and the other on Folly; therefore both Extreams ought to be avoided. I have already said that the Head ought to be upright, and the Waste steady, by which Means the Body will preserve an advantageous Situation. As to the Management of the Arms, let them hang easy by the Side of the Body, observing only, that when you advance with the right Foot, you make a small Motion with the left Arm forwards, which makes a small Contrast and Balance, and follows naturally. *(Ram. 1 p. 6; Ess. p. 4)*

Rameau's remarks for stepping also apply to ladies, although their steps should not be as bold as those of the gentlemen. Ladies must walk smoothly so that their skirts do not bob up and down, with:

. . .the Head upright, the Shoulders down. . .above all, without Affectation. *(Ram. 1 p. 41; Ess. p. 23)*

The Marquise de Caylus dressed for autumn. After Trouvain, 1694.

Technique of Etiquette

STANDING

The Gentleman

Some elegant postures for standing have been illustrated on pp. 66-67. Tomlinson adds another for the gentleman:

Plate: *The Rudiments of Genteel Behaviour.* F. Nivelon, 1737.

. . .when the Heel of the right or left Foot is inclosed or placed, without Weight, before the Ancle of that Foot by which the Poise is supported, the Hands being put between the Folds or Flaps of the Coat, or Waiste-coat, if the Coat is unbuttoned, with a natural and easy Fall of the Arms from the Shoulders, this produces a very modest and agreeable Posture, named the Third Position inclosed: Or, if the inclosed Foot be moved open from the other, sideways, to the Right or Left, about the Distance of half a Foot, or as far as, in setting it down to the Floor, the Weight of the Body resting on the contrary Foot is not disordered by it, with the Toes handsomely turning out, the Hat under one Arm, and the other in some agreeable Action, the Head also turning a little from the Foot on which the Poise rests, this we stile the Fourth Position open, and it may be very justly esteemed a most genteel and becoming Posture. *(Tom. p. 4)*

Both Rameau and Tomlinson describe a pose which Tomlinson says is suitable when among familiars, not superiors:

. . .for Conversation, or when we stand in Company. . . when the Weight rests as much on one Foot as the other, the Feet being considerably separated or open, the Knees straight, the Hands placed by the Side in a genteel Fall or natural Bend of the Wrists, and being in an agreeable Fashion or Shape about the Joint or Bend of the Hip, with the Head gracefully turning to the Right or Left [when conversing] , which compleats a most Heroic Posture. *(Tom. p. 4)*

The Lady

The lady's feet being hidden, she would place them so that her upright, but relaxed, carriage could be most easily maintained.

THE HAT AND HOW TO WEAR IT

The hat played an important part in a gentleman's formal life for he was constantly having to remove and replace it when bowing. It was generally worn, indoors as well as out, unless in the presence of the King and Queen or in certain more casual circumstances. When a gentleman was "uncovered" he would hold his hat underneath the left arm with the inside against his body.

By the turn of the seventeenth century, the three-cornered hat was in general use. Rameau gives instructions on how, and how not, to wear it:

[Wearing the hat correctly]
The most graceful Manner of wearing it, in my Opinion, is this: the Fore-part to be lower a small Matter than the Back-part. The Button ought to be on the left Side, and the Corner or Point of the Hat over the left Eye, which disengages the Face.

This contradicts some pictorial evidence where the point appears to be over the nose. Rameau continues:

[Incorrectly]
For to wear it quite back gives an awkward silly Air, and too much press'd down gives a melancholy or angry Look; whereas the Manner of wearing it, as I have shewn, seems both decent, modest and agreeable. *(Ram. 1 p. 28; Ess. p. 16)*

De la Manière d'ôter son Chapeau, et de le Remettre. Of the Manner of Taking off the Hat and Putting it on Again. (Ram. 1 p. 24; Ess. p. 14)

Raising the arm

Before a gentleman bows, he must remove his hat. (L217)

Grasp the hat by the "cocked Brim", never by the crown. When moving it, keep the arm sufficiently open so that the face is always visible. In a continuous motion, raise the right arm sideward to shoulder height, the hand open. Bend the elbow and carry the hand to the hat, placing the thumb against the forehead under the brim, the fingers above. As the thumb and fingers close, lift the hat very slightly by pressure of the thumb, and lower the arm diagonally right, stretching and unfolding it easily until down by the side, the inside of the hat facing forward.

In replacing the hat, the arm follows the same paths. (L218)

Rameau warns his readers to keep the head still when removing or replacing the hat. It should not tilt toward the hand. Secure the hat by pressing the brim once only. Do not clap the hand on the crown nor press the hat down so firmly that it would be hard to remove again, ". . .its use being only for an Ornament." (However, the "Ornament" does have to be secured at a fashionable angle, without fuss, on the first try.)

Bending the elbow

Arm by the side

From plates: Ram. 1 pp. 24-26.

BOWS AND COURTESIES

Des Révérences.
Of Honours.
(Ram. 1 pp. 22-60;
Ess. pp. 17-34)

There are three different bows and courtesies. The bows are quite complicated; a gentleman must coordinate the removing and replacing of his hat with the inclination of his body and, in most cases, a bending of one knee.

A lady has an easier time because she has only to turn her legs outward and bend, then straighten her knees while lowering and raising her gaze. She must keep her body and head upright and be careful not to wobble. The depth of the honour depends upon the rank of the person to whom it is directed, and the solemnity of the occasion. A profound courtesy requires the lady to bend her knees enough that the heels are forced to leave the floor, which does require a very good balance.

Before a bow is made, it must be clearly directed toward the person honoured:

It is also necessary to observe, when you bend the Body, not to incline the Head so much as to hide the Face, which is so much the more palpable Fault, because you put the Person in doubt whether or no it is him you salute; therefore before you begin the Bow, look the Person modestly in the Face, which is what we call directing your Bow before you make it. *(Ram. 1 p. 33; Ess. p. 19)*

To complete the honour, look once more at the person while rising. The inclination of the body in a bow and the bending of the knees in a courtesy will be "greater or less according to the Quality of the Person you salute." *(Ram. 1 p. 30; Ess. p. 17)*

A bow made when presenting a gift or handing something. *The Rudiments of Genteel Behaviour.* F. Nivelon, 1737.

Bows and Courtesies Forward

These are generally the first honours to be made upon entering a room, or when approaching someone to converse.

From plate: Ess. 1731, second issue p. 17.

For isolated practice begin in 3rd pos.

Direct the bow while removing the hat and sliding the front foot forward to 4th pos.;[8] the weight on the back foot, the front foot resting flat on the floor.

Bend the back knee, keeping the front one straight, at the same time inclining or bending the body forward from the waist while lowering the gaze. The arms are relaxed.[9]

When the body is inclined, the front heel may lift a little.

Punctuate the bow at its lowest point with a slight pause to show sufficient respect within the given circumstances.

Raise the body and the gaze, transferring the weight, when almost upright, to the front foot and close the back foot to 3rd pos. behind. (If another bow forward is to follow, which is unusual, the back foot will pass straight to 4th pos.)

The Rudiments of Genteel Behaviour.
F. Nivelon, 1737.

For isolated practice begin in 3rd pos.

Direct the courtesy sliding the front foot forward to 4th pos.; the weight on both feet, the position proportioned according to your height, so that balance can be kept easily.

Bend the knees sufficiently (depending upon the rank of the person) at the same time lowering the gaze with the head erect.

Punctuate the courtesy with a small pause at its lowest point to show sufficient respect within the given circumstances.

Rise again smoothly lifting the gaze toward the person.

**Passing Bows
and Courtesies**

These are used when walking in the street, promenading at leisure, moving through an assembled company, and to acknowledge complimentary remarks received in conversation when walking side by side. They resemble honours forward except that the upper torso is turned one eighth toward the person, the hips, legs, and feet maintaining their direction of progress. On nearing a person to whom a passing honour should be initiated or returned, the distance must be measured so that the bending can be directed diagonally forward.

Plate: Ess. 1731, second issue p. 18.

When walking in the street, direct the bow while removing the hat and sliding the foot nearest the person to 4th pos., the toe or the ball of the foot touching the ground, the upper torso turned toward the person.

Incline the body from the waist, lowering the gaze. (The twist causes a slight tilt sideways.)

Raise the body and the gaze, transferring the weight to the front foot to resume the interrupted walk, replacing the hat. When walking in the street about your business, the bow need only be very slight unless the person is of greatly superior rank, in which case Tomlinson suggests adding a bow backward.

When walking in fashionable promenades, the hat was usually carried casually under the left arm. If bowing to a person of superior rank, it should be taken in the right hand. Even in these leisurely circumstances, the bow would be made with all ceremony and style.

Plate: Ram. 1 p. 44.

Direct the courtesy, sliding the foot nearest the person forward to 4th pos., the weight on both feet, the upper torso turned toward the person.

Bend the knees, lowering the gaze, keeping the head erect.

Raise the body and gaze, transferring the weight to the front foot to resume the interrupted walk.

**Bows and Courtesies
Backward**

Of the three honours, these are the most ceremonious and respectful.

Plate: Tom. B.II. P.IV.

The hat has been removed and the bow directed. The feet are in 4th pos., the front foot free of weight, almost flat on the floor.

Move the front foot to 2nd pos., the heel touching the ground first for maximum steadiness.

With the weight equally distributed on both feet, bend the body forward from the waist, lowering the gaze.[10]

Punctuate the bow at its lowest point with a slight pause to show sufficient respect within the given circumstances.

Raise the body and the gaze, and transfer the weight to the foot that moved to 2nd pos., sliding the other to 3rd pos. behind.

Whether the front or back foot makes the first move to 2nd pos. depends on the context or on the path of travel forward or backward.

Start with the feet together and direct the courtesy.

Step into 2nd pos. and close the other foot to 1st pos.

Bend the knees "very low,"[10] at the same time lowering the gaze, the head erect.

Rise and direct the gaze toward the person.

Rameau says that if another courtesy backward is to follow, it should be made to the same side. But Tomlinson makes it clear that this will depend upon the circumstances for they may also be made from side to side to "preserve the same Ground."

If the courtesy must be made low, it may be necessary to lift the heels of the shoe from the floor. If so, they should be replaced as soon as possible while rising.

Bowing upon entering a room.

Philippe Mercier. The British Library, London.

SOME OCCASIONS FOR WHICH RAMEAU PRESCRIBES HONOURS

Upon Entering a Room or Assembly

When entering a room, remove the hat with the right hand, advance two or three steps to clear the door, slide the back foot forward to fourth position without transferring any weight, direct the bow, your gaze taking in the entire company, and make:
(1) a bow forward, followed by
(2) a bow backward.
The foot that closes to third position after the bow forward opens to second position for the bow backward.

Passing Through Assembled Company

When progressing through the room, make such passing honours as the disposition of the company demands. Here Tomlinson is most helpful:

And, in these Passing Honours, it must be noted, that no Regard is to be observed, with Respect to the Quality of the Person, but only Conveniency, in Relation to the Right or Left, as the Company first present themselves, as we pass along; nor, indeed, can it well be otherwise, because they are all to receive it, in their Turns. *(Tom. p. 13)*

If the company is thick, it may be necessary to take only two steps between each honour. (These follow the transference of weight onto the forward foot which concludes the honour.) The opposite foot will then slide forward for the next bow, a continuing progress made to one side and then the other so that no person is omitted.

Approaching Someone to Converse and Taking Leave

When wishing to speak with someone, approach, and make the same honours as upon entering the room, finishing with the weight supported by the front foot only. During the conversation, honours backward may be used "by way of Acknowledgement for some Favour or obliging thing spoken in our Praise." *(Tom. p. 7)* If these occur frequently during the conversation, they should be made from side to side "to Preserve the same Ground." *(Tom. p. 7)* When taking leave, make two honours backward, both to the same side depending upon the direction in which you intend to proceed.

Leaving a Room

Rameau gives no information, but Tomlinson says that two honours backward should be made to the same side as when taking leave in conversation. However, common sense should always prevail and in many instances it would be more convenient and appropriate to your position in space and in relation to the company to make one to each side.

Plate: Ram. 1 p. 1.

Rameau's depiction of a grand ball presided over by Louis XV. The King and the ladies are seated, the gentlemen shown standing for clarity. The couple to dance is represented twice. First making an honour to the King, and then standing, ready to begin the dance.

**PROCEDURES
BEFORE DANCING**

Before dancing begins, the company will be seated around the room in the places assigned them according to their rank. (See p. 282.)

Inviting a Person to Dance

Neither Rameau nor Tomlinson specify which honour should be used. In the presence of the King, the honour inviting a person to dance will be made from the center of the room. The person invited will join his or her partner and they will make an honour to the King. From Rameau's illustration this appears to be an honour forward.

If the King is not present, the honour of invitation will be made close to where the person is seated (being careful not to stand between that person and the Presence); then, without taking hands, partners move to the center of the room to make their honour forward.

Presenting the Hand

Following their honour to the Presence, the dancers must take some steps backward to the bottom of the room, where dancing begins and where the musicians are often placed. These steps must finish in fourth position, the front foot on the toe: the lady's left, the gentleman's right.

The gentleman, who has his gloves on, will remove his hat with the left hand, at the same time offering his right to the lady, looking at her.

Plate: Ram. 1 p. 61.

The lady puts her left hand in his while looking at him, then both face the Presence for the first bow. The giving of hands must be simple and unaffected, positive yet gracious and unhurried.

**HONOURS BEFORE
AND AFTER DANCING**

These consist of two honours backward, the first to the Presence, the second to your partner.(L219) It is possible that they were performed without music, for they are only given once with specific timing; Tomlinson puts them before the minuet, to eight measures of "Music or Flourish." However, this does provide a guide to their relative values which can be applied to their performance before all dances.

(In Tomlinson's examples, the first honour takes three measures, the following maneuvers, two measures, and the second honour, three measures. Most dances require further maneuvers which would take the same time as the first ones.)

Plate: Tom. B.II. P.II.

In Tomlinson's bow backward the gentleman stands in second position, his weight supported by one foot only.

The Gentleman	Bows backward	Both	The Lady	Courtesies backward

Place the R ft. into 2nd pos.

Step onto the L ft. in 2nd and close the R into 1st pos.*

bow to Presence

On rising transfer the weight to the R, slide the L just beyond 3rd behind, transfer the weight onto it and

On rising transfer the weight onto the R and

release hands

sliding the R just beyond 5th in front turning (shading) the body to the left, the R arm forward

sliding the L just beyond 5th in front turning (shading) the body to the right, the L arm forward

partners
shoulders are
almost back to
back *(Tom. B.II. P.III.)*

bend the left knee (slightly) and step onto the R turning to

bend the right knee (slightly) and step onto the L turning to

face partner

place the L ft. into 2nd pos.*

step onto the R ft. in 2nd and close the L into 1st pos.*

bow to partner

On rising close the R to 3rd pos. behind.

The honours after dancing finish here.

Dancers now maneuver into the starting position of the dance to be performed.

Continuing thus;

Slide the L just beyond 5th in front turning (shading) the body to the right, step onto it and turn left to face the Presence, placing the L into 2nd pos.

Slide the R just beyond 5th in front turning (shading) the body to the left, step onto it and turn right to face the Presence, placing the R into 2nd pos.

   Rameau leaves the dancers in second position but to begin most dances the outside foot (the one farthest from your partner) must then be placed into fourth position behind upon the toe:

If the hands are to be taken or the arms placed in opposition, do so when moving the foot.

The dancers now await the beginning of the music.

*These actions flow, their purpose being to bring partners face to face for their honour to each other.

Rameau instructs both persons to place their feet into second position for the first bow before dancing. As they are already holding hands, this will bring partners uncomfortably close, especially bearing in mind the increasing width of the lady's skirt during the eighteenth century. Since many of today's performances of these dances are unfortunately given by dancers who are not very experienced in the style and who have not had adequate rehearsal time, the author suggests that the woman use the other foot, or simply close the front foot into first position and omit the step to second position.

When making an honour, ladies must keep the torso AND THE HEAD upright while bending the knees and lowering the gaze. Gentlemen must keep the supporting leg or legs braced, and think of bending forward from the waist. The spine should form a curved line as in the illustration on p.277. AVOID STICKING THE BEHIND OUT AT A SHARP ANGLE. DO NOT LOWER THE HEAD SO FAR THAT THE AUDIENCE CAN SEE ONLY THE TOP OF IT. The arms should be RELAXED AND LOW.

Always take sufficient time to direct an honour. On the other hand, beware of being sluggish! Consider each one within the particular circumstances, formal or emotional, and so forth.

ETIQUETTE FOR VARIOUS BALLROOM OCCASIONS

Procedure at a State Ball in France

Rameau describes the King's Grand Ball in the time of Louis XV, but makes it clear that the procedure was established during the reign of Louis XIV. Although this would not be followed exactly in all places at all times, it sets an overall pattern for formal occasions in fashionable circles during the eighteenth century:

FIRST you must know, that nobody is admitted in the Ring but Princes and Princesses of the Blood; then Dukes and Peers, and Dutchesses; and after them, the other Lords and Ladies of the Court according to their Rank; the Ladies placed foremost, and the Lords behind them.
EVERY one being thus placed in Order, when his Majesty has a Mind the Ball should begin, he rises, and the whole Court does the same.
THE King places himself in the Part of the Room most proper for the Beginning of the Ball, (which is by the Musick Room). The late King used to dance with his Queen, and in her Absence his Majesty took out the first Princes of the Blood, and they placed themselves first, and after them every one in a Row according to their Rank; all the Lords on the left Side, and all the Ladies on the Right; and in this Order they made their Honours one before the other. Afterwards his Majesty and his Partner led up the Brawl [branle], which was danced wherever there were any Court Balls, all the Lords and Ladies fol-

lowing their Majesties, each on their Side; and at the End of the Strain, the King and Queen went to the Bottom, and the next Couple led up the Brawl in their Turn, and so successively till their Majesties came at the Top again: After which they danced the Gavotte in the same Order as the Brawl, every Couple going to the Bottom in their Turn; and then made the same Honours in parting as they did before they began to dance.

AFTERWARDS they danced double Dances; but formerly the Courant used to be danced after the Brawls: And Lewis the Fourteenth danced one better than any Person of his Court, as I shall give you an Account hereafter; but now the Menuet is danced after the Brawls.

THEREFORE after the King has danced the first Menuet, he goes to his Seat, and every Body then sits down; for while his Majesty is dancing, all stand: After which the Prince, who is to dance next, makes the King a low Bow, and then goes to the Queen or first Princess, and they make their Honours together before they begin to dance; and after the Menuet, they make the same Honours as before. Then this Lord makes a very low Bow to this Princess at parting from her, because nobody offers to reconduct her to the King.

AT the same Instant he advances two or three Steps, to address himself by a Bow to the Princess that is to dance next, to invite her to dance, and there waits for her to make their Honours together to the King, as shewn by the Figures (1), (2); then they descend a little lower, as represented by the Figures (3), (4), and make the usual Honours together before dancing, and dance a Menuet, and then make the same Honours again; afterwards he makes her a Bow backwards, taking his Leave, and goes to his Place; whilst the Lady observes the same Ceremonial to invite another Prince, and so to the End. But if his Majesty desires another Dance to be danced, one of the first Gentlemen of his Bed-Chamber speaks for it; but still the same Honours are observed. *(Ram. 1 p. 49; Ess. p. 28)*

Etiquette at
Well-Regulated Balls

Although the procedure at all well-regulated balls was based upon that of court balls, Rameau describes some differences. A "King and Queen" would be chosen but the company was not obliged to stand while they were dancing. Neither would the "Queen" await her second partner but approach him to make her courtesy of invitation. They would then make their way to the center of the room, without taking hands. After their dance, the gentleman would ask which lady the "Queen" wished him to invite next. Leaving her with a bow,[11] he would approach his next partner.

It seems that in these freer circumstances the person invited might be engaged in conversation. If so, the person making the invitation would perform an honour and return to the center of the room until the conversation could politely be concluded. A gentleman would then go and meet his partner but, presumably, a lady would await hers. After dancing, a lady was conducted back to her seat but a gentleman went alone, having made a bow[12] to his partner upon leaving her.

If you were invited to dance and did not wish to, it was impolite merely to refuse. First you must move to the center of the room and make the usual honour to the Presence. Then you could ask your partner to excuse you. If your partner insisted, you were obliged to dance even at the expense of making an utter fool of yourself. In such a situation, however, it would seem that your partner's manners were in need of improvement, since courtesy is essentially a consideration for the ease of others.

The other points given by Rameau sensibly fulfill the requirements of consideration. First, it would be impolite to occupy the seat of someone who is dancing since your presence would create an awkwardness on his or her return. Second, if you refused an invitation from someone, you could not then accept someone else's. Third, if you accepted an invitation, you had to invite the same person back when it became your turn to choose.

Essex says that, in England, these rules applied only in some places. He also adds an admonishment to the spectators:

It is rediculous to intimate any Man while he is dancing, or whilst the Musick is playing, to keep time, and play the Fool with your head, your hands, or your feet.[13]

Private Family Gatherings

Even if the company was composed only of relatives and friends, Rameau says the:

Same Ceremonial ought to be observed, as well as in Balls; that is, to know how to take a Person out to dance, by making their Honours properly, and returning them reciprocally. Above all, I recommend to young Persons, for whom these Dancings are often made, to observe these Rules that their Masters ought to have taught them, and to take a Pride in the Education they receive. *(Ram. 1 p. 59; Ess. p. 33)*

FOOTNOTES

1. *The Spectator*, 17 May 1711 (London: Buckley, 1712), vol. 1.
2. The very beautiful, flowing bow used earlier in the seventeenth century where the arm carying the hat does make a curved path in space is illustrated and described by Joan Wildebloode and Peter Brinson, *The Polite World* (London: Oxford University Press, 1965), see Pl. 8c and p. 264.
3. *The Spectator*, 17 July 1711.
4. Wildebloode-Brinson, *The Polite World*, p. 225.
5. P[ierre] Rameau, *The Dancing Master*, trans. Cyril W. Beaumont (London, the author, 1931), p. 13.
6. Wildebloode-Brinson, *The Polite World*, pp. 220-222 and 278-280.
7. Lucy Norton, ed. and trans. *Saint-Simon at Versailles* (New York: Harper, 1958), p. 8.
8. Tomlinson describes these slides as "scrapings."
9. ". . .the Arms naturally hanging under the Shoulders;" *(Tom. p. 14)* Actually the arm holding the hat is not quite relaxed but the other one should literally hang. (See p. 277.) This is of greatest importance stylistically.
10. Rameau says he has seen many people incline the body and at the same time draw the foot to second position, but he feels this to be less distinguished.
11. Not specified.
12. Presumably backward, as when taking leave in conversation.
13. "What we are to observe at a Ball." in: *The Rules of Civility* (London, 1722), pp. 154-158.

Le bal à la française (Almanach royal, 1682). Le Menuet de Strasbourg.

The dancer is reputedly Louis XIV after returning from a visit to Strasbourg. Through political means Louis had achieved the annexation of Strasbourg to France in 1681. The depiction of the ballroom scene is highly stylized. Bibliothèque Nationale, Paris.

CHAPTER THIRTEEN

The Menuet According to Rameau

Menuet Ordinaire

It is difficult to pinpoint exactly when a new dance became introduced, but from Lully's scores it is clear that the menuet was increasingly popular after 1664. The new dance was enthusiastically adopted by the French Court and consequently by fashionable society elsewhere. The menuet traveled as far as Russia, and also to America where it was taught by immigrant dancing masters.

The ballroom menuet for one couple, the menuet ordinaire, continued to be danced until the French Revolution (a period of more than one hundred and twenty years), and lingered elsewhere even after the downfall of the ancien régime in France. Of all the dances that were later revived in the nineteenth century, the menuet has probably suffered the most from subsequent choreographic corruptions. The menuet ordinaire will hereinafter be referred to simply as the menuet, and given its French spelling except when English sources are being quoted.

Documentation

The improvisatory aspects of the menuet rendered it difficult to document. In order to notate the dance, some masters, like Tomlinson, reduced it to a "just and regular Dance," thus concealing to the casual reader its essential flexibility. Others, like Rameau, introduced detail only where flexibility was not permissible. Most masters give Pécour's modifications of an earlier form of the menuet, probably the one notated by Tomlinson. *(Tom. Book II, Plate U)* Although not identical in every detail, the accounts show that throughout the eighteenth century the menuet was danced in basically the same form. This chapter analyzes the menuet ordinaire as notated by Rameau with supplementary information from Tomlinson.

Spatial Elements

The menuet, like all danses à deux, was performed by one couple alone before an audience of peers. The dance consists of an introduction and four figures performed in a set order:
Introduction
The Z Figure (the main figure)
The Presentation of Right Hands
The Presentation of Left Hands
The Z Figure
The Presentation of Both Hands

The Z figure (which originally traced an S) prescribes the spatial area of all the menuet figures:

In other figures this basic shape
is interrupted by an inner circling.

The two dancers face each other virtually throughout the dance, a distinguishing characteristic; in other danses à deux, the dancers' attention was frequently directed toward the spectators. In the menuet, the visual contact between partners can become quite intense although their facial expressions should remain open and modest.

Flexibility

The absolutely unique characteristic of the menuet among the other danses à deux is its flexibility. The main figure, the Z figure, can be repeated as often as the gentleman chooses. The menuet may be performed throughout with a basic pas de menuet or certain other steps substituted as embellishments.

In the menuet, the honours before dancing are performed to music, their duration being determined by the gentleman. When they are completed, the man may commence the dance within the measure of music being played.

HANDEL'S
Favourite MINUETS
from His
OPERAS & ORATORIOS
with those made for the
BALLS at COURT.
for the Harpsicord, German Flute,
Violin or Guitar.
BOOK. I.

London. Printed for I. Walsh in Catharine
Street in the Strand.

Of whom may be had
The British Miscellany, being the favourite Songs in the Pastoral call'd The Spring.
Thomas & Sally, and 14 Books of Select Songs by Dr. Arne.
Handel's Marches, 4 Books, Apollo's Banquet, Select Tunes, 4 Books,
Dragon of Wantley, Enchanter, Shepherds Lottery, Chaplet
Solomon, a Serenade, and Devil to Pay.

The British Library, London.

A minuet with an eight- followed by a twelve-measure strain.

The Menuet According to Rameau

Relationship of
Dance and Music

While the other danses à deux were composed to specific pieces of music, the menuet could be danced to any menuet air. In general, menuets written for dancing or purely instrumental purposes consist of strains of an even number of $\frac{3}{4}$ measures, grouped in pairs. Pécour's Z figure requires twelve, and it is quite usual to find music with an eight- followed by a twelve-measure strain. It was not, however, considered admirable for figures and strains to coincide. According to Tomlinson:

There is no limited Rule, as to its [the menuet's]...Relation to the Time of the Tune, since it may begin upon any that offers, as well within a Strain as upon the first Note or commencing thereof. It is the very same with Respect to its ending, for it matters not whether it breaks off upon the End of the first Strain of the Tune, the second, or in the Middle of either of them, provided it be in Time to the Music. *(Tom. p. 137)*

[By "in Time to the Music" Tomlinson means that each pas de menuet should commence on the first beat of the first measure in every pair.]

Instead of standing to wait the Close or Ending of a Strain of the Tune, begin upon the first Time that offers, in that it is much more genteel and shews the Dancer's Capacity and Ear in distinguishing of the Time, and from thence begets himself a good Opinion from the Beholders, who are apt to judge favourably of the following Part of his Performance; whereas the attending the concluding or finishing of a Strain has the contrary Effect.

He continues with some advice for the unmusical:

However the latter is by much the safer Way for those whose Ear is not very good, the concluding of a Strain of the Tune being much more remarkable than the middle Part; for, if they should happen to begin out of Time, it is a thousand to one if they recover it throughout the Dance. But on the other Hand, had they waited a remarkable Place of the Tune, and taken the Time at Beginning, they might have come off with Reputation and Applause; for many dance the Minuet Step in true and regular Time, tho' out of Time to the Music, which is occasioned by not hitting with it right at first; and not being able to recover it afterwards, they dance the whole Minuet out of Time. Their dancing on this Account loses its Effect upon the Beholders; for, if the Steps and the Notes do not perfectly agree, in their performing, one with another, they can produce no Harmony, and if no Harmony, no Pleasure to those they design to entertain. *(Tom. p. 124)*[1]

If the dance ends in the middle of a strain, the music can be concluded during the honours made after dancing.

Duration

The menuet can last as long as seven minutes, its duration largely dependent upon the number of times the gentleman chooses to repeat the Z figure. The Z figure is introduced into the dance twice: Rameau suggests five or six Z's be danced the first time, and three or four the second time; Tomlinson's total is four or six S's or Z's, but the shortest way, he says, is to perform the figure only once each time.

If the gentleman decides to make the maximum number of Z's suggested by Rameau to a menuet comprising two eight-measure strains, the dance will need at least twenty-two strains. [For performance today it is suggested that two menuet airs be combined so that some repetitions can be avoided. It is also suggested that only one or two Z figures be performed each time that figure occurs, and that the dance be organized to enable the commencement of figures and strains to coincide from time to time.]

Steps and Embellishments

Because the pas de menuet à deux mouvements (described on p. 191) was currently in fashion at the French court, Rameau uses it as the basic pas de menuet. For steps of embellishment he gives the pas balancé, the temps de courante and demi-jeté, and the contretemps de menuet. (See p. 216.) Where Rameau suggests the replacement of a basic pas de menuet with a step of embellishment will be indicated in the analytical descriptions of the dance figures to follow.

Relationship of the Basic Step to the Musical Measures

In performance, the menuet derives enormous strength, beneath its controlled surface, from the hypnotic cross-rhythm between dance and music. The stressed rise of the second demi-coupé in the step-unit occurs one beat before the downbeat of the second measure of the music:[2]

Honours Before Dancing the Menuet	Before dancing the menuet, the honours given on p.285 are performed with the following modifications: without holding hands and some distance apart, because on the initial pas de menuet the dancers move toward each other; and, following the rise from their honour to each other, the dancers must transfer the entire weight to the left foot. The right foot is then free to begin the first pas de menuet. The lady will be in first position, the man in second position with his hat already, or about to be, transferred to his left hand.
Hat	The manner in which the hat should be removed and replaced is given on p. 274. Rameau does not refer to the hat after his instructions for bowing, but Tomlinson offers some suggestions for its use in the presentation of right and left hands, and these will be incorporated into the explanations.
Arms	The arm motions in the menuet consist of the presentation and taking of hands as indicated and will be described in the dance figures. The special motion used by the gentleman at other times is described on p. 196. The way in which a lady places her hands on her skirt is shown on p. 68.
Degree of Technical Difficulty	The technical requirements of the menuet are not overly demanding, and older dancers could easily participate. But in its very simplicity, the menuet is all revealing. By the quality of a gentleman's dancing, the way in which he removes and replaces his hat and presents his hand to the lady, his breeding, education, and character might be judged:

The Minuet is one of the most graceful as well as difficult Dances to arrive at a Mastery of, through the Plainness of the Step and the Air and Address of the Body that are requisite to its Embellishment. *(Tom. p. 105)*

Du Menuet... *Of the Menuet.* *(Ram. 1 p. 84;* *Ess. p. 48)*	The following pages contain an analysis of the menuet figures as given by Rameau. In the diagrams, the tracts correspond to Rameau unless otherwise stated, while the notated steps have been added according to his or Essex's written instructions. Essex is sometimes clearer and more comprehensive than Rameau in his interpretation of the diagrams. The Author's Notes are continued in brackets. The list of steps which precedes each figure has been collated by the author. Discussion of analytical problems will be found on p. 308; letters placed in the text refer to this page.

THE DANCE

Introduction

Tomlinson calls the opening figure of the menuet the Introduction. Here the gentleman "hands or introduces the Lady into the Dance in the most agreeable Manner he possibly can." *(Tom. p. 125)* Rameau gives seven pas de menuet for the opening figure. (a)

In the following diagram, Rameau's first and second diagrams ("figures") are combined. *(Ram. 1 p. 84; Ess. p. 48)* The notated steps have been added by the author.

Steps for the man
One pas de menuet sideward to
his right
Two pas de menuet forward

Steps for the lady
One pas de menuet
sidward to her left
Two pas de menuet
forward

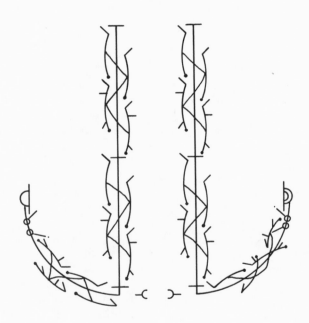

For the manner of taking hands, see p. 148.

[It seems best to take hands on count 5 of the first pas de menuet, turning to face the Presence on the bend on count 6. Perform smoothly, the actions blending together during counts 4, 5, and 6. The man must start his arm motion in plenty of time.]

At the beginning of the following pas de menuet dancers will transfer their attention from the Presence to each other.

The Menuet According to Rameau

Rameau's third diagram. *(Ram. 1, p. 86; Ess. p. 49)* Steps and numbers added by author.

Steps for the man	Steps for the lady
(1) Pas de menuet backward	Pas de menuet forward
(2) Pas de menuet to his right	Pas de menuet forward
(3) Pas de menuet forward	Pas de menuet forward
(4) Pas de menuet to his right	Pas de menuet to her right

Rameau's diagram is of necessity visually misleading. The dancers are closer than they appear to be because they hold hands until the end of pas de menuet (2). The actual tract covered is more neatly thus:

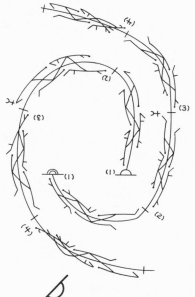

By the end of pas (3) the dancers face

The quarter turn which follows brings dancers to

The final pas de menuet is made sideward, the dancers traveling obliquely backward. (b) During the last pas de menuet, the hat should be replaced upon the head. [It should probably be returned to the right hand first.]

Of the final pas de menuet, Rameau says, "in making this step, the right Shoulders of both Parties are shaded from each other and the Head turned a little to the Left, looking at each other, which ought to be observed throughout the whole Course of the Menuet; but above all, without Affectation." *(Ram. 1 p. 86; Ess. p. 49)*

Having been shaded, the shoulders return to normal at the end of the pas de menuet.

[The spatial relationship of the dancers at the conclusion of the Introduction should be checked after working the following Z figure.]

Z Figure. The Principal
Figure of the Menuet
(Ram. 1 p. 87; Ess. p. 49)

Steps for the man and the lady
Two pas de menuet sideward to the left
Two pas de menuet forward
Two pas de menuet sideward to the right (c)

Rameau's Fourth Diagram
(Ram. 1 p. 87; Ess. p. 49)

The numbers have been added by the author.

Once again, Rameau's tract does not give an exact representation of the path dancers follow, since both cover the same ground at the top and bottom of the Z.

Also, in order not to collide in the middle of the Z, dancers must make a slightly curved path.

Rameau describes the figure thus:
To pursue the Figure as represented by this Plate, two Steps (2) must be on the left Side, with the Body upright; and in making two other Steps forwards at (3), the right Shoulders of both should be shaded, the Man always to let the Woman pass on the right Side of him, but both looking at each other; (What I call shading the Shoulder, is drawing it a little backwards, presenting the Body more full) but nevertheless still to make their Steps forward. *(Ram. 1 p. 87; Ess. p. 49)* (d)

[At the conclusion of the first and fifth pas de menuet, partners should be opposite each other.]

[Care should be taken that at (4) the shading of the shoulder does not become a small bow on bending the knees to begin the fourth pas de menuet.]

The temps de courante and demi-jeté can be used instead of a pas de menuet when passing each other, "but it must not be too often repeated, because that would look affected." *(Ram. 1 p. 96; Ess. p. 54)*

The Menuet According to Rameau

Varying the Z Figure
(Ram. 1 p. 94; Ess. p. 53)

Rameau gives a variation which can be used in the Z figure. One dancer may choose to make three pas de menuet forward instead of two, in which case the other dancer should also incorporate an extra step-unit so that finally the dancers will "conform to the Figure."

Steps for the man
Two pas de menuet to his left
Three pas de menuet forward

One pas de menuet to his right

One pas de menuet to his right

Steps for the lady
Two pas de menuet to her left
Two pas de menuet forward
One pas de menuet to her right
A temps de courante and demi-jeté
One pas de menuet to her right

When crossing in the Z, the gentleman makes three pas de menuet forward followed by one rightward. The lady, when turning after the two pas de menuet forward regularly used in the Z figure, will see that the gentleman is still going forward and, after making her first pas de menuet to the right, will incorporate a temps de courante and demi-jeté which scarcely travels. [A balancé would serve the same function.] The man will then catch his partner up at the end of his first pas de menuet rightward.

The dancers complete the Z with a pas de menuet rightward as usual. The incorporation of the extra step-unit adds two measures of music to the number used in the regular Z: 14 instead of 12.

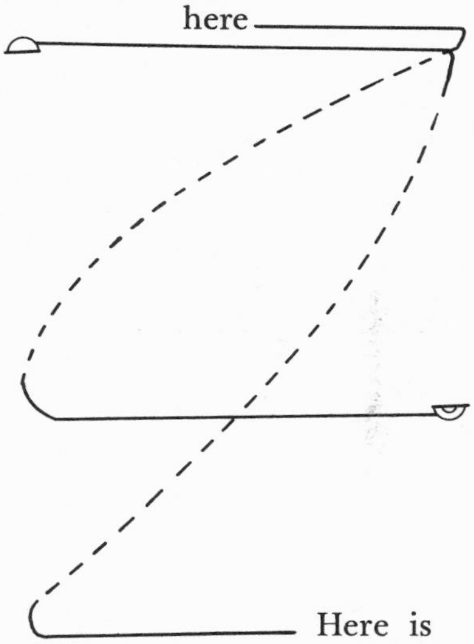

The lady finishes here

Here is where the gentleman finishes.

Presentation of Right and Left Hands

Although Tomlinson gives the Presentation of Right and Left Hands as two separate divisions of the menuet, it is more helpful in performance to view them as one continuous figure. When done this way, the pattern described by Rameau is seen to be a Z interrupted by an inner circling, first to the left and then to the right:

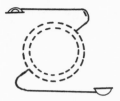

Presentation of Right Hands
(Ram. 1 p. 88; Ess. p. 50)

. . .which consists in the Ceremony of presenting or giving the right Hand; and in it there is no small Beauty and Air, as to the graceful and easy raising of it, in order to take Hands, and also the gentle and natural Fall on Letting them go. *(Tom. p. 128)*

The Figure

Steps for the man and the lady
Two pas de menuet to their left
One pas de menuet forward to take right hands
Ad. lib. while circling [forward steps, three are good]

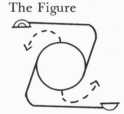

Rameau's [Fifth] Diagram
(Ram. 1 p. 88; Ess. p. 50)

Rameau's diagram does not show the beginning of this figure, which is identical to the first half of the Z figure. In his text, Rameau assumes this prior knowledge in his readers, mentioning the steps only as they relate to the arm motions:

. . .looking upon one another present your right Hand in your Step forward. But that you may the better apprehend it, when you are going over, that is, at the End of your last Step returning to the Left, raise your right Arm to the Height of your Breast. *(Ram. 1 p. 88; Ess. p. 50)* (e)

To warn the lady that the figure to be performed is the Presentation of Right Hands, and not another Z, the man must begin to raise his right arm at the end of the second pas de menuet to the left. If he delays too long, the lady may be forced into an awkward transition at the last moment or, even worse, dance right past him leaving him stranded.

The three pas de menuet, two leftward and one forward, bring the dancers to the commencement of the circle. (f)

Author's tract.

Embellishment: The temps de courante and demi-jeté, or a contretemps de menuet may replace the pas de menuet forward. (See *Ram. 1 p. 94* for some subtleties of performance.)

Tomlinson's moment of taking hands is indicated by the hand symbols.

The manner in which hands are presented is not described in detail. Rameau says that the right arms are raised sideward to chest height during the pas de menuet forward (the man having anticipated the motion). In Rameau's diagram the arms are raised with the palms facing downward. As hands are taken, the man's palm should probably be facing upward so the lady may place her hand in his, palm down. Her thumb will be under his hand. [While raising the right arms, make sure that the left arms remain down.]

Of the moment of taking hands, Rameau says: "The Head being turned to the right, looking at each other, you make a little Movement of the Wrist and Elbow raised up, with a slight Inclination in presenting the Hand." *(Ram. 1 p. 88; Ess. p. 50)* "The Movement of the Wrist and Elbow raised up" is ambiguous and may be interpreted in a variety of subtle ways. The "Inclination" presumably refers to the head and is likely to take care of itself as dancers approach, looking at each other.

Tomlinson recommends that the hat be taken off before hands are taken. He suggests doing so with the right hand and afterward transferring it to the left, but:

If it should be objected, that it is inconvenient and troublesome to take off the Hat with the right Hand, by Reason it must be changed to the left before the right can be at Liberty to present to the Lady; I answer, it is easy to be done; or it may be taken off with the left Hand as well as the right. *(Tom. p. 130)*

If the hat is removed with the right hand and transferred to the left [which is the more impressive way], it must be done during Rameau's two pas de menuet to the left. The use of the hat has the additional advantage of warning the lady that the figure is not to be another Z.

Having made the first three pas de menuet and taken hands, there remains the circling. The circle should be as wide as possible, the dancers holding their arms straight but not rigid, "pursuing their respective Tracts in taking as large a Circumference, as the joining of Hands will admit. . .at the full extent or Length of the Arms." *(Tom. pp. 129, 131)*

The Presentation of Right Hands.
Plate: Ram. 1 p. 88.

Rameau leaves the direction and number of steps unspecified, but there is nothing to suggest that they should be made other than forward. [While circling, the arms should not be allowed to bend and stretch out again due to faulty placement of the steps. The usual tendency is for the elbow to bend on the first demi-coupé in a pas de menuet. This can be avoided by crossing the right foot sufficiently in front of the left when stepping to fourth position.]

The circle holding right hands completed, the dancers release hands and make one pas de menuet, turning to the left at approximately:

See
Rameau's
diagram
opposite

The turn must be shallow, dancers avoiding the tendency to move too far out toward the corner.

On this final pas de menuet, the man transfers his hat to his right hand, the lady returns her hand to her skirt. [Allow the gaze to lead you around without straining the neck.]

The choice and use of embellishments may make a difference to the number of step-units needed to fulfill the circle and, therefore, the number of measures of music used. Probably one embellishment would have been thought tasteful.

Steps for the man and the lady
One pas de menuet forward to take hands
Ad. lib. while circling [forward steps]
One pas de menuet to their right

Rameau's [Sixth] Diagram
(*Ram. 1 p. 89; Ess. p. 50*)

Rameau's instructions are not too specific. He merely says: "present your left Hand, observing the same Ceremonial as in the Right, as shewn by this Figure." The pattern does not, however, begin with two pas de menuet leftward, as dancers are still well within the inner area of the Z. Presenting left hands begins with the pas de menuet forward, to take hands, performed on a circular path.

If dancers make their turn out from the right-hand circle correctly, they will be placed approximately here to make the pas de menuet forward to take left hands:

Author's tract.

Man ends
here

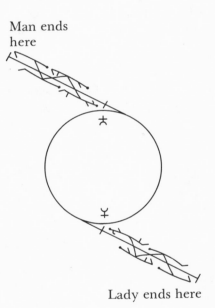

Lady ends here

From these positions in space make one pas de menuet forward circling and coming closer to take hands at its conclusion. Tomlinson's moment of taking hands confirms Rameau's diagram.

For the final pas de menuet, having completed the circle, dancers make one pas de menuet sideward to the right on the usual oblique path.

"And when you have let go the left Hand, you must make a Menuet Step aside to the right obliquely backwards." (*Ram. 1 p. 89; Ess. p. 50*)

"Hands are broke off or let go and, extended as they are, gently fall to their proper Places. The Hat is put on again with the right Hand." (*Tom. p. 132*)

The lady returns her left arm to her skirt.

Return of the Z Figure
(*Ram. 1 p. 89; Ess. p. 50*)

The conclusion of presenting left hands "brings you again into the principle Figure, which you continue for three or four Turns."

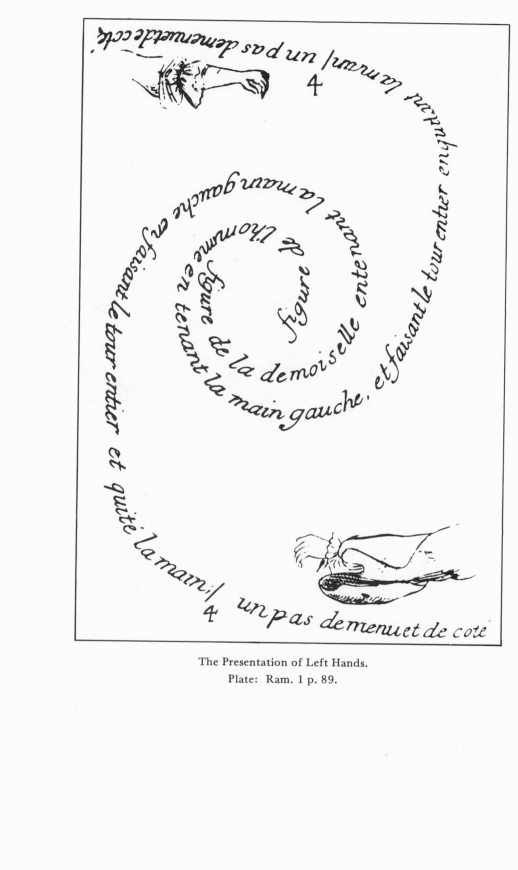

figure de l'homme en tenant la main gauche, et faisant le tour entier enquittant la main droit un pas demenuet de coté.

figure de la demoiselle entenant La main gauche en faisant le tour entier et quité la main; un pas demenuet de coté

4

4

The Presentation of Left Hands.
Plate: Ram. 1 p. 89.

Presentation of Both Hands
(*Ram. 1 p. 89; Ess. p. 50*)

Steps for the man and the lady
Two pas de menuet to their left
One pas de menuet forward
Ad. lib. while circling
One pas de menuet backward into the honours after dancing

Author's tract.

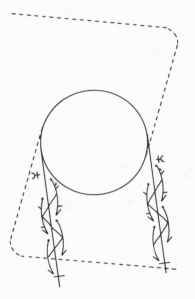

The honours after dancing. (See p. 285.)

That dancers begin this figure with two pas de menuet leftward is indicated visually. Dancers are shown approaching each other from the left corner having completed the Z figure in the right corner.

Both arms are presented in the pas de menuet forward, the arms being raised sideward and then brought forward with a *slight* inclination of the body toward your partner.

[While circling, dancers should make the pas de menuet forward but shade the right shoulders so that the torsos will be somewhat turned toward each other. The arms should form, as nearly as possible, a circle just below shoulder height.]

Circling should finish with dancers facing each other, still holding hands.

For the final pas de menuet, dancers make a pas de menuet backward away from the Presence, releasing the hand nearest the Presence as they turn on the first demi-coupé (the moment of turning is not specified).

The gentleman may remove his hat with his left hand as he travels backward, or wait until he has completed his pas de menuet. The lady replaces her right hand on her skirt. The hands which remain held are lowered on the first demi-coupé backward.

The Presentation of Both Hands.

Plate: Ess. 1731, second issue p. 50.

ANALYTICAL NOTES

(a) For the sixth pas de menuet of the opening figure Rameau says, "vous faites un pas de Menuet en avant" in his text (p. 86); but in his diagram (p. 86), "deux en avant." Essex corrects this in his diagram to "One forwards."

(b) Rameau's instructions for the seventh pas de menuet, the last in the opening figure, are: "un pas de Menuet du côté droit en arriere, qui vous remet en presence par le quart de tour que vous faites à votre premier pas, de ce pas de menuet de côté." This is more explicit than the mere, "Un pas en arriere qui vous mets en presence" in his diagram. (p. 86) Essex gives, ". . . a side Step slanting on the Right backwards, which sets them opposite to each other, by the quarter Turn made at the first step of the Menuet Step aside." (p. 49) In his diagram Essex gives, "One behind facing each other." (p. 49)

(c) Of the final pas de menuet in the Z figure Rameau refers readers to his diagram where he gives, "un en arriere du coté droit." In his diagram Essex gives the two pas de menuet necessary for the completion of a Z as "two backwards sideways to the right."

(d) The top and bottom of the Z figures are drawn slightly obliquely; a little more so in Rameau than in Essex.

(e) Rameau's instruction to raise the arm at the end of the second pas de menuet to the left, combined with the placement of the arms in his diagram may suggest that the motion should be completed by the time dancers reach the corner of the Z. This would leave dancers with motionless arms as they approach, contradicting Rameau's instructions ". . .en presentant la main lorsque vous avez fini votre pas de Menuet en revenant du côté gauche, & en allant à la Demoiselle, vous levez le bras droit." *(Ram. 1 p. 93)*

(f) The exact points where circling should begin becomes a problem when Rameau's "Figure pour presenter la main droit" is put into practice. From the commencement of the tract and the placement of the arms, it appears that right hands should be taken across the diagonal.

After a Z figure, however, dancers are too close to present and take right hands at this point where the verbal tract begins, without cramping the arm motion. Tomlinson's placement for the taking of right hands has therefore been incorporated as offering an approximate solution. The important aspects are elegant arm motions and an easy transition into the circling. The indicated point at which left hands should be taken is the same in Rameau and Tomlinson and there are no performance problems.

FOOTNOTES

1. The truth of Tomlinson's warning can unfortunately be seen in a film, "Menuett," produced by Insell Films, Munich, Germany, for which this author taught the dancers the menuet. Due to a postponement for the actual filming, she could not be present and the sound was incorrectly synchronized with the image. Dance and music are firstly two, then three beats apart, only coinciding correctly in the final pas de menuet. Copies of this film, made for educational purposes, have now been deposited in several archives. It is of a certain ironic comfort to know from Tomlinson that, in a most regrettable way, this film is indeed an "authentic" representation of some eighteenth-century performances of the menuet!

2. For a more detailed discussion of cross-rhythms in the dance, see Hemiola in the Menuet and Passepied, pp. 239-241.

Appendices

APPENDIX ONE
Labanotation Examples

The Labanotation examples are intended as illustrations of the text and should be read in conjunction with it. When they are reviewed out of context the keys should be reviewed also.

The examples are keyed into the text by numbers preceded by an L. They are given when new subject matter is introduced and include the author's full realization of the material, sometimes in advance of the text. This is necessary because chorégraphie is a shorthand system.

When reading the arm motions, which are fluid and continuous, any overlap of the symbols should be carefully observed.

The Labanotation conforms to current usage in 1978 as certified by the Dance Notation Bureau.

KEYS

Style

Steps
and Open Positions

$1 = \{$ Distance between feet (length of dancer's foot) is measured from heel to heel. In couple dances the man adjusts to the woman's foot length.

Gestures

Hands

Demi-Coupé

Time

Triple-time
No specific note values.

Duple-time

$\}$ see Glossary

Duple-time staff

GLOSSARY

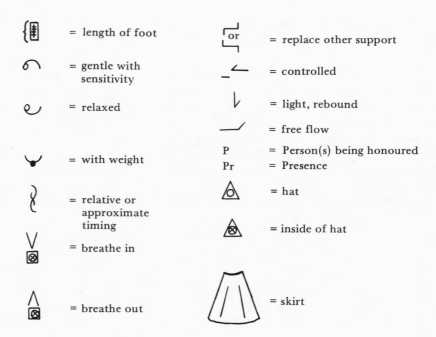

⟮▤	= length of foot
⌒	= gentle with sensitivity
℧	= relaxed
⌣	= with weight
⟩	= relative or approximate timing
V̲	= breathe in
Λ̲	= breathe out

⌐ or	= replace other support
⤙	= controlled
↓	= light, rebound
⌣	= free flow
P	= Person(s) being honoured
Pr	= Presence
△	= hat
⊗	= inside of hat
	= skirt

DEGREES OF BEND
IN STEP-UNITS

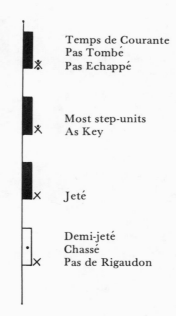

Temps de Courante
Pas Tombé
Pas Echappé

Most step-units
As Key

Jeté

Demi-jeté
Chassé
Pas de Rigaudon

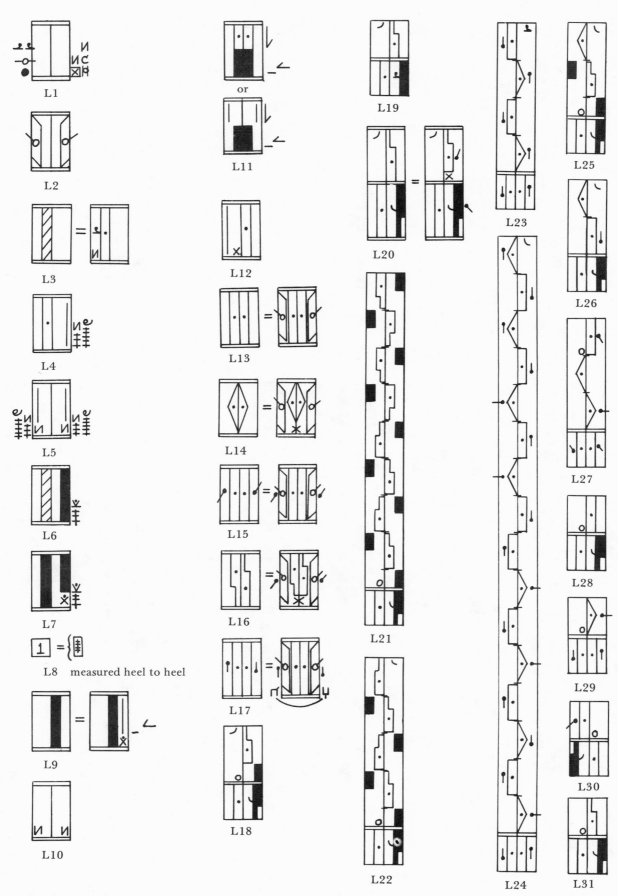

L1   L2   L3   L4   L5   L6   L7   L8   measured heel to heel   L9   L10   L11   L12   L13   L14   L15   L16   L17   L18   L19   L20   L21   L22   L23   L24   L25   L26   L27   L28   L29   L30   L31

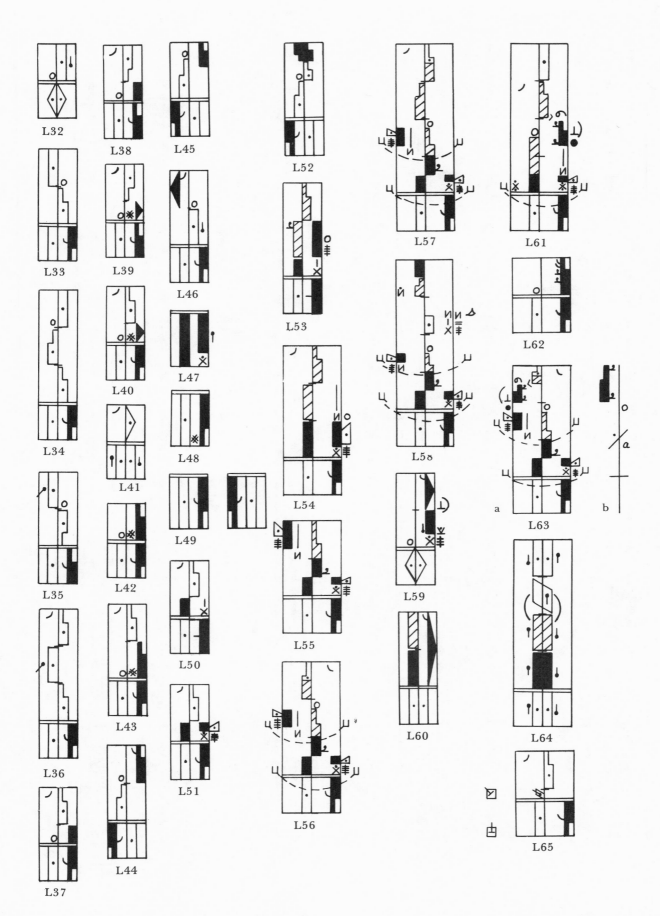

L32 L33 L34 L35 L36 L37 L38 L39 L40 L41 L42 L43 L44 L45 L46 L47 L48 L49 L50 L51 L52 L53 L54 L55 L56 L57 L58 L59 L60 L61 L62 L63 a b L64 L65

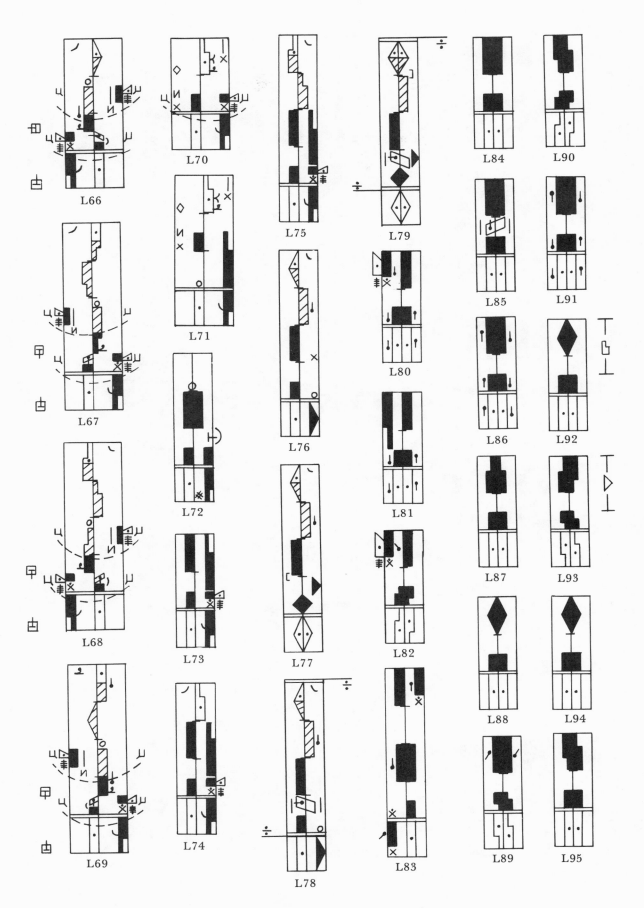

L66

L67

L68

L69

L70

L71

L72

L73

L74

L75

L76

L77

L78

L79

L80

L81

L82

L83

L84

L85

L86

L87

L88

L89

L90

L91

L92

L93

L94

L95

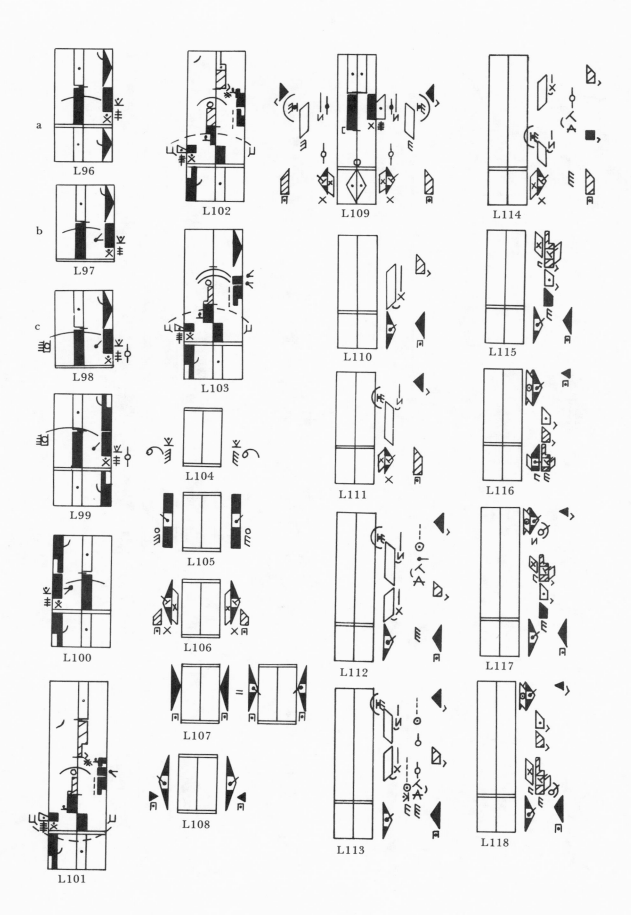

L96

L97

L98

L99

L100

L101

L102

L103

L104

L105

L106

L107

L108

L109

L110

L111

L112

L113

L114

L115

L116

L117

L118

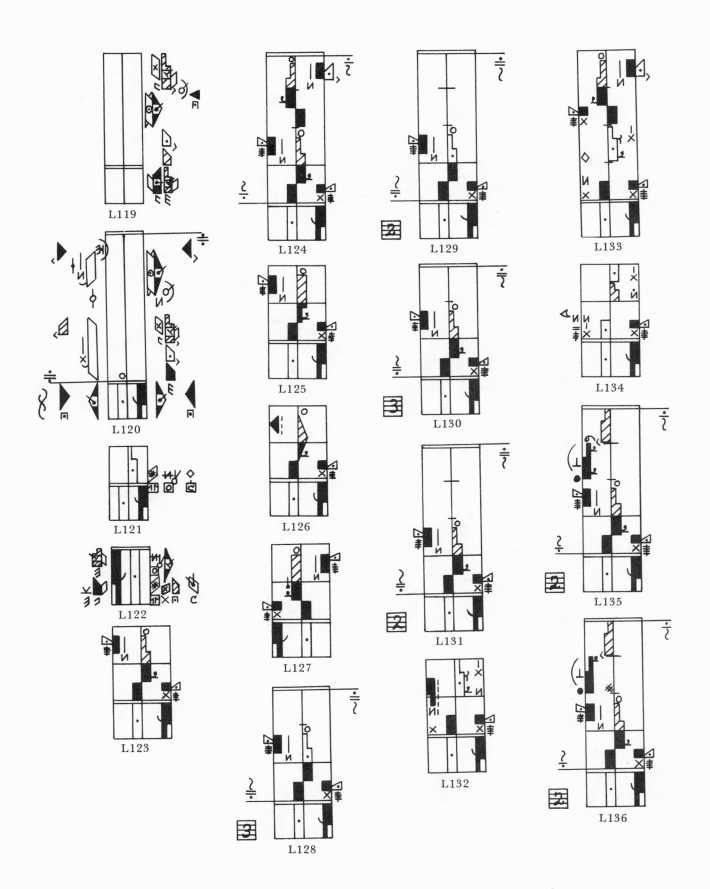

L119

L120

L121

L122

L123

L124

L125

L126

L127

L128

L129

L130

L131

L132

L133

L134

L135

L136

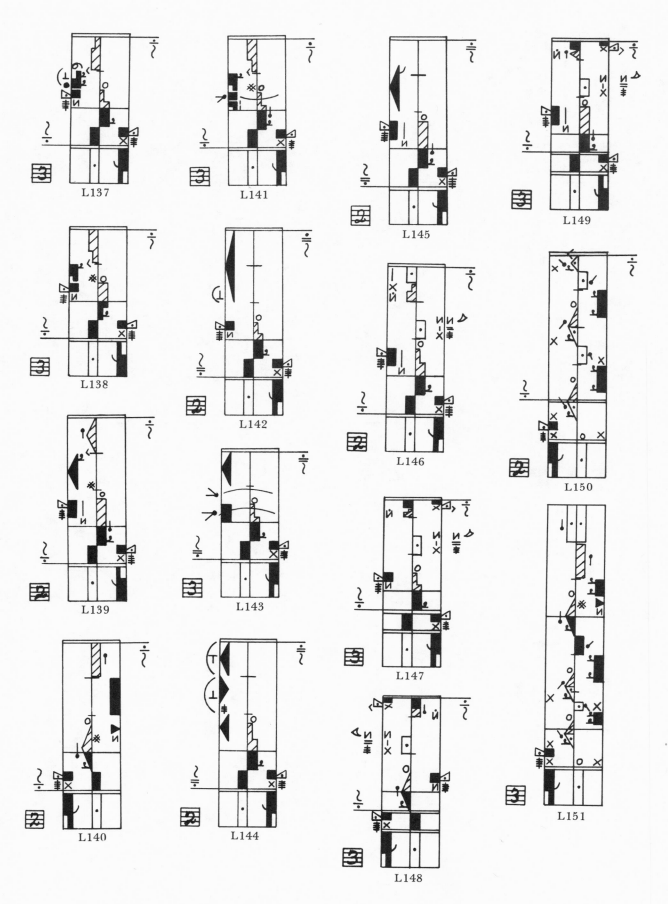

L137

L138

L139

L140

L141

L142

L143

L144

L145

L146

L147

L148

L149

L150

L151

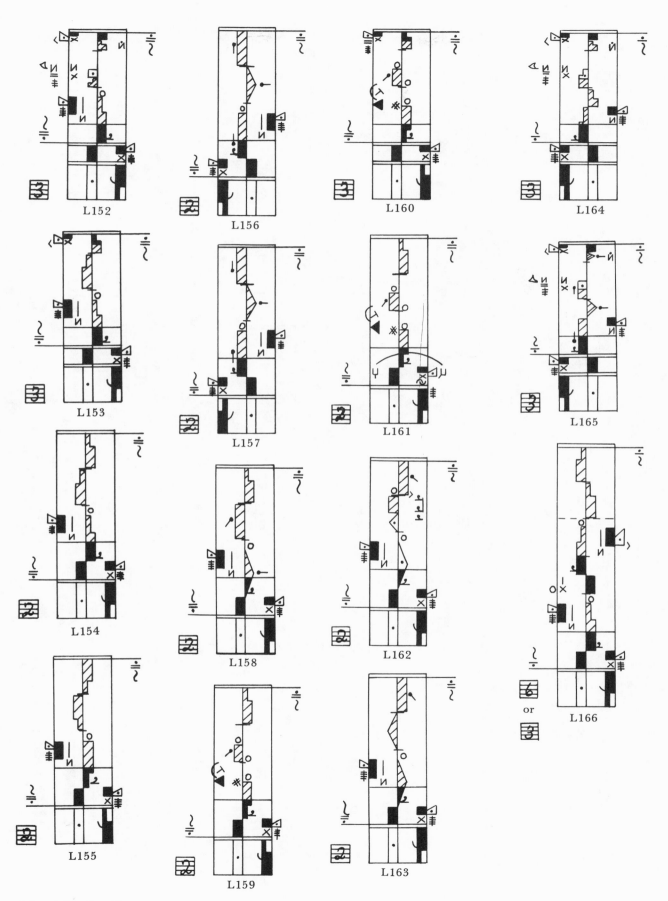

L152

L153

L154

L155

L156

L157

L158

L159

L160

L161

L162

L163

L164

L165

or

L166

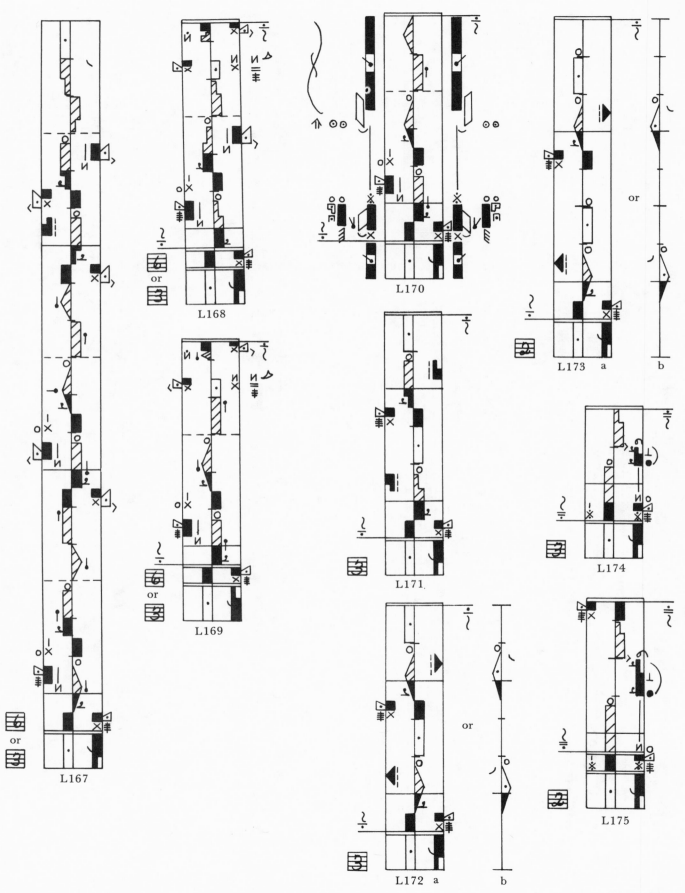

L167

L168

L169

L170

L171

L172 a   b

L173   a   b

L174

L175

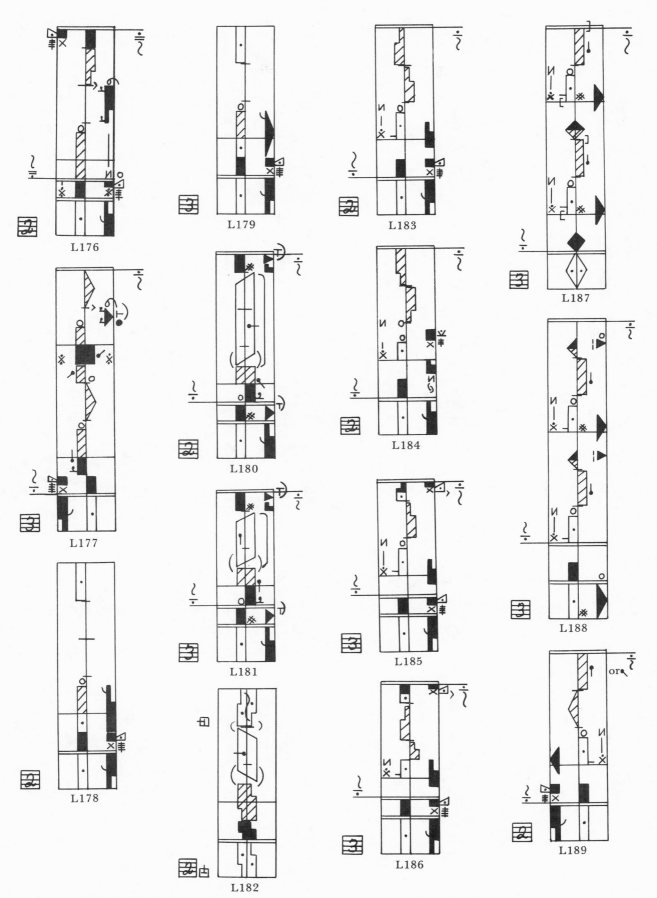

L176

L177

L178

L179

L180

L181

L182

L183

L184

L185

L186

L187

L188

L189

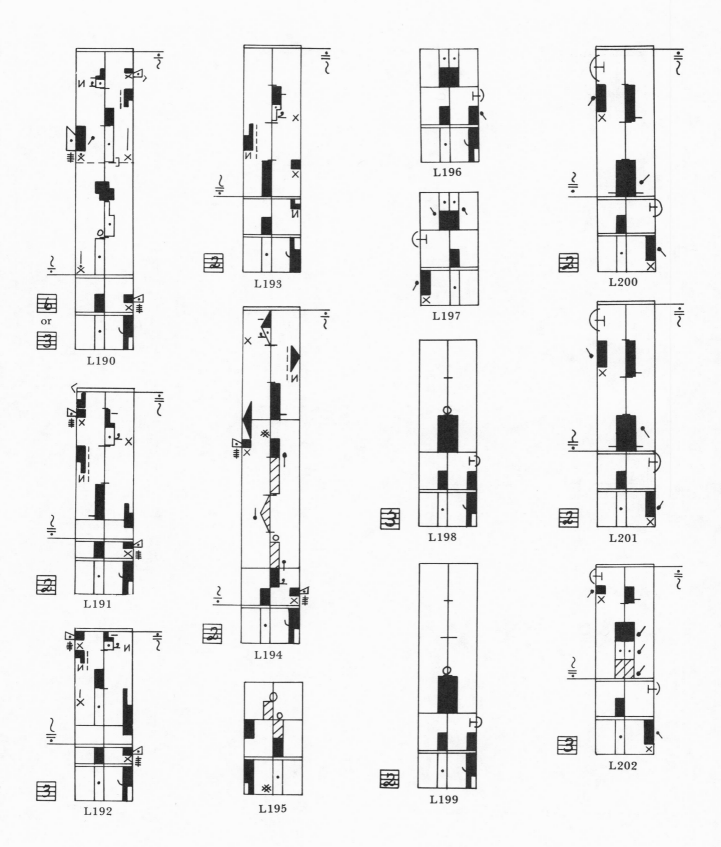

L190

L191

L192

L193

L194

L195

L196

L197

L198

L199

L200

L201

L202

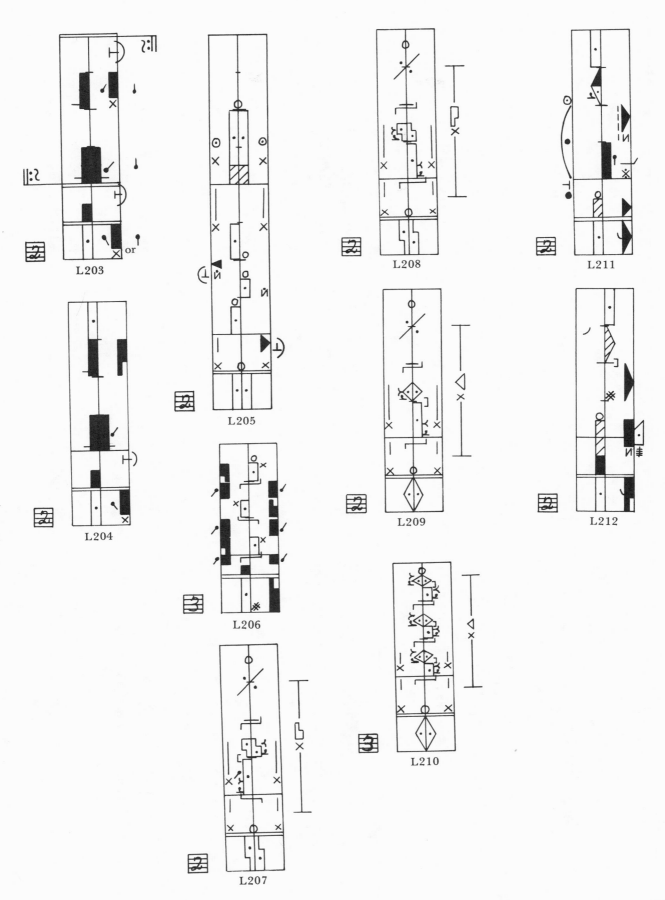

L203

L204

L205

L206

L207

L208

L209

L210

L211

L212

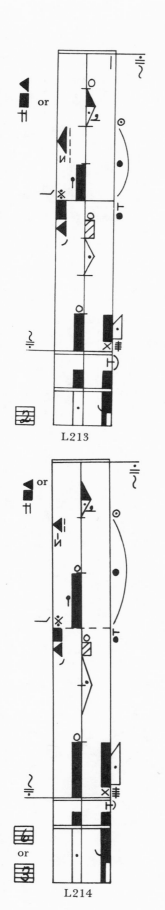

L213

L214

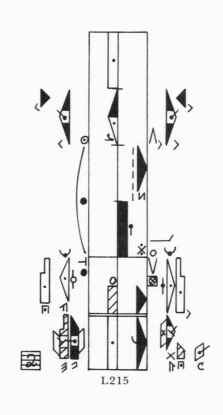

L215

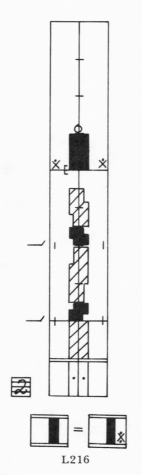

L216

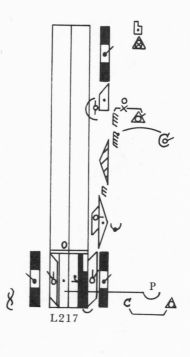

L217

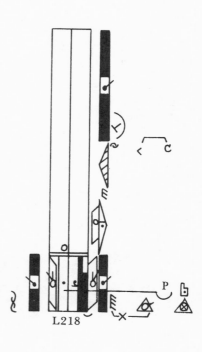

L218

P = Person(s) being honored

Labanotation Examples

Bows before Dancing

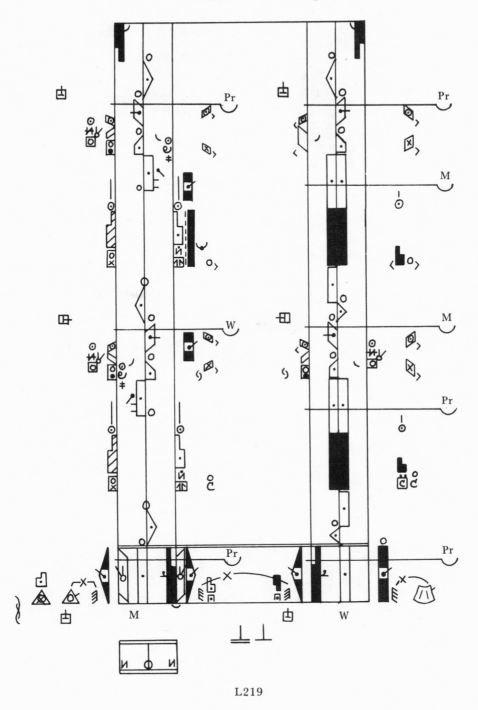

L219

Pr = Presence

APPENDIX TWO
Exercises

The purpose of these exercises is to develop muscular strength, balance, control, and familiarity with the situations most frequently encountered in the step-units. They should be practised each day so that when Chapter Nine, the step-units, is reached, the student will be prepared. The exercises will also be applicable in the study of chorégraphie from p.110 onward. Time taken now to study the exercises and the style of motion they are designed to develop (as analyzed in the Survey of the Components) will ultimately save time and preclude irremediable errors. Students should read the Survey of the Components daily in conjunction with the exercises.

Style   All exercises begin in the first position of the feet. Execute all the exercises with the torso and the head held as shown in the Survey of the Components. The upright position of the spine should be maintained throughout. The arms should be placed as described on p. 136, and the legs rotated outward to forty-five degrees or less if the turnout has yet to be developed. NEVER allow the feet to turn outward more than the knees. To do so will delay technical progress and may cause an injury. The arms, hands, shoulders, and neck—and the expression—should remain relaxed. Unless otherwise indicated, practice the exercises to a sarabande at approximately MM $\frac{3}{4}$ ♩ = 66. All the motions should be very sustained.

EXERCISE I

For bending and straightening the knees.

Meas.	(1)	1	Bend both
		2	knees
		3	slowly.

Without arching the lower spine, keep the heels pressed to the floor; push the knees outward from the hip so that they are over the toes.

	(2)	1	Straighten both
		2	knees
		3	slowly.

Be careful to maintain this outward rotation of the legs when beginning the rise by pushing the knees outward.

EXERCISE II

For rising onto [demi] pointe.

Meas.	(1)		As above (bend)
	(2)		As above (straighten)
	(3)	1	Lift the heels
		2	from the floor rising
		3	onto [demi] pointe.
	(4)	1	Slowly lower the
		2	heels, keeping
		3	the legs braced.

EXERCISE III

To develop strength and flexibility in the insteps. (Mainly for springing.)

Meas.	(1)		As above (bend)
	(2)		As above (straighten)
	(3)	1	Rise as high as
		2	possible on
		3	the toes.
	(4)	1	Lower the heels
		2	halfway to
		3	the floor then
		and	rise up a little in preparation for going downward.
	(5	1	down
		and	rise
		2	down
		and	rise
		3	down
		and	rise.

Without quite lowering the heels to the floor or rising so high that the ankle joint is "locked," bounce up and down using the insteps with flexibility. Keep the legs braced.

	(6)		As above measure.
	(7)	1	Lower
		2	the
		3	heels
	(8)	1	slowly
		2	to the
		3	floor.

EXERCISE IV

To increase the depth of bend.

Meas.	(1)		As above (bend)
	(2)	1	Push down
		2	push down
		3	push down.

Keep the heels on the ground, push downward in the bend without strain, using body weight as much as possible. Straighten the knees as LITTLE between each push downward.

	(3)	As in
	(4)	Exercise I
		meas. (2).

EXERCISE V

For bending the knees, only one leg bearing weight.

Meas. (1)   As above (bend)

(2) 1 Release one foot from the floor as in Pl. 1 p. 74.

2 Hold

3 "

(3) 1 "   While holding this position

2 "   make sure that the leg free

3 "   of weight does not rotate outward more than the supporting leg.

(4) 1 Replace the foot on the floor BOTH KNEES REMAINING BENT.

2 Straighten the

3 knees.

EXERCISE VI

For balance in general and the Position of Equilibrium in particular. (See p. 70.) When sufficient strength has been established, Ex. II can be repeated at this point in daily practice with the following variation:

Meas. (5) 1 Transfer the weight Keep the hip line level.

2 to one foot releasing Tighten the muscles of the

3 the other as shown pelvic girdle and lift the

    on p. 70 upper torso (not the shoul-

(6) 1 Hold ders). Do not tilt or lean.

2 " Pull down the backs of the

3 " legs, for brace and balance.

(7) 1 Transfer back

2 to both feet

3 and

(8) 1 lower the

2 heels

3 slowly.

EXERCISE VII

For springing. Perform to a $\frac{6}{4}$ gigue at approximately MM $\text{\textquotedblright} = 78$ (No faster).

Meas. (1) ♩. Land Bend and spring, rising into

etc. ♩. Land the air off and onto both

Spring into the feet in 1st pos., the insteps

air to land on extended when in the air as

these beats. described on p. 71.

The landing must be controlled through the insteps (prepared in Ex. III), the heels only touching the floor afterward. When sufficient strength has been established to maintain an easy, resilient, soft spring, the heels should not QUITE touch the floor. Remember that the object is NOT to jump as high as possible. Springs should be evenly timed upward and downward.

EXERCISE VIII

For walking on [demi]pointe.

Practice without music to one slow beat for each step.

Begin in 4th pos. on [demi]pointe. The legs are braced and will remain so throughout the exercise.

Walk forward, the leg moving CONTINUOUSLY between each transference of weight. Step as slowly as possible. The insteps should feel flexible, the legs braced. (It is easy to reverse this situation.) The position of equilibrium will be reached and passed in the middle of each step.

Make sure the knee of the stepping leg never relaxes. It is most likely to do so at the moment it is freed of weight. (Check when passing through the pos. of eq.) This exercise is very important. There is almost nothing worse, stylistically and aesthetically, than a dancer walking on [demi]pointe with soggy knees.

Repeat this exercise walking backward, taking care not to lean backward. ALWAYS have the weight very SLIGHTLY forward.

IMPORTANT POINTS

Keep the legs braced (check in the mirror) the insteps flexible;
pull down the backs of the legs toward the floor when on [demi]pointe;
keep the weight forward,
tighten the muscles of the pelvic girdle,
relax the shoulders and expression,
push the heel of the stepping leg forward to maintain the turnout.

MUSIC FOR THE EXERCISES AND LATER STUDY OF THE STEP-UNITS

The exercises require a sarabande and gigue made up of eight-measure strains to which must later be added a bourrée, gavotte, menuet, and passepied for the study of the step-units.

After a time, students should select other pieces of the same types to avoid monotony, and to develop musical adaptability.

The tempi listed on p. 266 serve as a guide to an area of tempo for each type. Slower tempi will be necessary when learning the step-units, especially those beginning with a demi-coupé.

Further studies.

Students who wish to enlarge their repertoire after completing their studies of the present text should turn to the first published collection of ballroom dances, *Recueil de dances composées par M. Pécour*, Feuillet, Paris, 1700. This collection is available in hardcover facsimile from Broude Bros., bound with Feuillet's *Chorégraphie*, or in paperback from Dance Horizons.

The doctoral dissertation by Anne Witherell, listed in the Bibliography, contains a detailed analysis of the nine dances and their music in the collection. The first dance, "La Bourée d'Achille," is one of the simplest danses à deux, while the second, "La Mariée," is one of the most intricate and lively.

APPENDIX THREE
Chronology of Political Events

1638   Birth of Louis XIV.

1643   Death of Louis XIII. His wife, Anne of Austria, places government of France in the hands of Cardinal Mazarin.

1646-   The future Charles II of England lives in Paris with
1648   his mother Henrietta Maria.

1648   The Fronde established as Parlement in Paris.

1649   - Charles I of England beheaded.
      - Cromwell governs England (named Lord Protector, 1653).
      -Charles II begins years of political struggle, and exile in Europe.

1650   The disturbances of the Fronde cause Mazarin to flee Paris.

1653   Dissipation of the Fronde; Mazarin returns.

1654   Coronation of Louis XIV; Mazarin continues to govern France.

1658   Death of Cromwell.

1660   - Charles II restored to English throne.
      - Louis XIV marries Marie-Thérèse of Spain.

1661   - Death of Mazarin; Louis XIV assumes government of France.
      - Colbert becomes chief power in the King's administration.
      - Birth of a son to Louis and Marie-Thérèse.
      - Louis's brother, the Duc d'Orléans, marries Henrietta Anne, sister of Charles II.

ca. 1661   Work on the Palace of Versailles begins.

1662   Charles II marries Princess Catherine of Braganza.

1666   Death of Anne of Austria.

1667   French armies invade Spanish Netherlands in the War of Devolution. The first of a series of wars which continue with little respite throughout Louis's reign.

1670   Death of Henrietta, Duchesse d'Orléans.

1671   Marriage of Duc d'Orléans to Elizabeth-Charlotte (Liselotte) Princess Palatine of Bavaria.

1672-   Franco-Dutch War during which William of Orange
1678   given power in the Netherlands. Louis eventually emerges with profits but many powerful enemies.

1681   Louis achieves annexation of Strasbourg by political means.

1683   Death of Marie-Thérèse. Louis begins close association with, and perhaps secretly marries, Mme. de Maintenon.

1684   Annexation of Luxembourg by the French following a siege. The tide begins to turn against Louis.

1685	Death of Charles II; succession of James II.
1686	League of Augsburg founded against France.
1688	England, under James II, beset by political and religious problems. At the invitation of a group of Protestants, William of Orange, James II's brother-in-law, invades England to aid their cause. James II flees to France. Accession of William to the English throne. William thus secures the strength of England to help check the overgrowth of French power in Europe, a matter of concern to many European leaders.
1689	The War of the League of Augsburg, or the War of the Grand Alliance, or the Nine Years War. A war fought against France by Holland, England, and other allies.
1690	Spain joins the war against France.
1691	Death of Louvois, Louis's most able general.
1697	- The war concludes with the treaty of Ryswick which deprives France of certain territories. Louis retains Strasbourg but relinquishes Lorraine.
	- Marriage of Louis's grandson, the Duc de Bourgogne to Marie-Adélaide, Princess of Savoy. The future parents of Louis XV.
1700	Death of Charles II of Spain. Louis achieves the inheritance for his grandson Philip, Duc d'Anjou.
1701	Death of Louis's brother, the Duc d'Orléans.
1702-	The War of the Spanish Succession.
1713	- Death of William of Orange, succeeded by Anne, daughter of James II.
1709	An extraordinarily severe winter. People die daily from cold and hunger.
1710	Birth of future Louis XV to the Duc and Duchesse de Bourgogne.
1711	Death of Louis XIV's only legitimate son.
1712	- Death of the Duc and Duchesse de Bourgogne.
	- Death of Louis's great grandson, the Duc de Bretagne.
	- Beginning of peace negotiations.
1713	Peace comes with the Treaty of Utrecht. The French Prince retains the Spanish crown, but France is forced to make more territorial concessions. France's finances at a low ebb.
1714	Death of Queen Anne succeeded by George I.
1715	Death of Louis XIV.

Chronology of Political Events

Bibliography

SELECTED FRENCH AND ITALIAN BOOKS, 1581-1700

	Authors	*Choreographers*	
1581	Caroso, Fabritio.	Caroso and others.	*Il ballarino.* Venice: F. Ziletti, 1581. R. (reprint), New York: Broude Bros., 1967.
1589	Arbeau, Thoinot. [Pseudonym for Jehan Tabourot]	Anon.	*Orchesography.* Langres: Jehan des Prez, 1589. -----Trans. Mary Stewart Evans and reprinted with corrections, a new introduction and notes by Julia Sutton, and representative steps and dances in Labanotation by Mireille Backer: New York: Dover, 1967. (See also the discussion of Arbeau's illustrations by Belinda Quirey in *May I have the Pleasure?* pp. 5-7. London: British Broadcasting Company, 1976.)
1600	Caroso.	Caroso and others.	*Nobiltà di dame.* Venice: il Muschio, 1600. [1605] R., Bologna: Forni, 1970.
1602	Negri, Cesare.	Negri and others.	*Le gratie d'amore.* Milan: Pacifico Ponti & Gio. Battista Piccaglia, 1602. R., Bologna: Forni, 1969.
1604			-----Reprinted with new title page as *Nuove inventioni di balli.* Milan: Girolamo Bordone, 1604. R., New York: Broude Bros., 1969.
1623	Lauze, F[rançois] de.	Anon.	*Apologie de la Danse.* 1623. R., Geneva: Minkoff Reprint, 1977. -----Trans. Joan Wildebloode. London: Frederick Muller Ltd., 1952.
1651	Playford, John. [Publisher]	Anon.	*The Dancing Master.* London: John Playford, 1651. [The first of many books of this title published by John Playford. The books contain English country dances and their music popular at court and in fashionable society. Publications of this type continued well into the eighteenth century.]
1682	Menestrier, Claude François.		*Des ballets anciens et modernes selon les règles du théâtre.* Paris: R. Guignard, 1682. R., Geneva: Minkoff Reprint, 1972.
1688 mss.	Lorin, André.	Anon.	*Livre de contredance du Roi.* English country dances selected by Lorin and presented by him to Louis XIV in two mss. For some of the dances Lorin uses a system of notation he devised for this purpose. Mss. Bibliothèque Nationale, Paris.

FRENCH BOOKS, 1700-1725

	Authors and Notators	*Choreographers*	
			(Spelling and use of accents from title pages.)
1700	Feuillet, Raoul Auger.		*Chorégraphie*, ou l'art de décrire la dance, par caractères, figures et signes dèmonstratifs. Paris: l'auteur, 1700. Bound with:
1700	Feuillet.	Feuillet.	*Recueil de dances composées par M. Feuillet.*
1700	Feuillet.	Pécour, Louis.	*Recueil de dances composées par M. Pécour.* Further editions: 1701 (augmented), 1709, 1713 (with a preface by Dezais.)

1700	Feuillet.	Pécour.	*Le Passepied nouveau.* Dance de la composition de Monsieur Pecour. Paris: l'auteur, 1700.
1700	Feuillet.	Pécour.	*La Pavanne des saisons.* Dance nouvelle de la composition de Mons.R Pecour. Paris: l'auteur, 1700.
1701	Feuillet.	Pécour.	*Aimable vainqueur.* Dance nouvelle. . .de la composition de Monsieur Pecour. Paris: l'auteur, 1701.
1702	Feuillet.	Pécour.	*P.er Recüeil de danses de bal pour l'année 1703* de la composition, de M. Pecour. Paris: l'auteur, 1702.
1702	Feuillet.	Pécour.	*L'Allemande.* Dance nouvelle de la composition de Mons.R Pecour. Paris: l'auteur, 1702.
1703	Feuillet.	Pécour.	*II.me Recüeil de danses de bal pour l'année 1704* de la composition de Mr Pecour. Paris: l'auteur, 1703.
1703	Feuillet.	Feuillet.	*La Madalena.* Danse nouvelle. . .par Monsieur Feüillet. Paris: l'auteur, 1703.
1704	Feuillet.	Pécour.	*Recueil de dances* contenant un tres grand nombres, des meillieures entrées de ballet de Mr. Pecour, tant pour homme que pour femmes, dont la plus grande partie ont été dancées à l'Opera. Recüeillies et mises au jour par Mr Feüillet, Me de dance. Paris: Feüillet, 1704.
1704	Feuillet.	Pécour.	*III.me Recüeil de danses de bal pour l'année 1705* de la composition de Mr Pecour. Paris: l'auteur, 1704.
1705	Feuillet.	Feuillet.	*IIII.E Recüeil de dances de bal pour l'année 1706* par M.R Feüillet. . .Paris: l'auteur, 1705.
1706	Feuillet.	Pécour, Feuillet.	*V.me Recüeil de danses de bal pour l'année 1707.* Paris: l'auteur, 1706.
1706	Feuillet.	Various.	*Recüeil de contredanses.* Paris: l'auteur, 1706.
1707	Feuillet.	Pécour, Feuillet.	*VI.me Recüeil de danses et de contredanses pour l'année 1708.* Paris: l'auteur, 1707.
1709	Feuillet.	Pécour, Feuillet.	*VII.e Recüeil de danses pour l'année 1709.* Paris: l'auteur, 1709.
1709	Feuillet.	Pécour, Feuillet.	*VIII.me Recüeil de danses pour l'année 1710.* Paris: l'auteur, 1709.
1709	Feuillet, Dezais.	Pécour, Feuillet.	*IX. Recueil de danses pour l'année 1711.* Paris: Dezais, 1709.
1712	Gaudrau.	Pécour.	*Nouveau recüeil de dance de bal et celle de ballet. . .de la composition de M.r Pecour.* Paris: l'auteur, 1712.
1712	Dezais.	Balon, Dezais.	*X. Recüeil de danses pour l'année 1712.* Paris: l'auteur, 1712.
1712	Dezais.	Various.	*Recueil de nouvelles contredanses.* Paris: l'auteur, 1712.
1713	Dezais.	Balon, Dezais.	*XI.E Recüeil de danses pour l'année 1713.* Paris: l'auteur, 1713.

[1714] ms.	Dezais.	Balon, Dezais.	*XII.ᴱ Recüeil de danses pour l'année 1714.* Paris: l'auteur. Ms. Bibliothèque de l'Opéra, Paris.
[1715]	Dezais.	Balon, Dezais.	*XIII Recüeil de danses pour l'année 1715.* Paris: l'auteur.
[1716]	Dezais.	Balon, Dezais.	*XIIIIᵉ Recüeil de danses pour l'année 1716.* Paris: l'auteur.
[1717]	Dezais.	Balon, Dezais.	*XV. Recüeil de danses pour l'année 1717.* Paris: l'auteur.
[1717]	Gaudrau.	Pécour.	*Danses nouvelles presentées au roy par M.ʳ Pecour maitre a danser de feue Madame La Dauphine. . .*
[1718] ms.	Dezais.	Balon, Dezais.	*XVI. Recueil de danses pour l'année 1718.* Ms. Bibliothèque de l'Opéra, Paris.
[1719] ms.	Dezais.	Pécour.	*XVII Recueil de dances pour l'année 1719* de la composition de M.ʳ Pecour. Paris: l'auteur. Ms. Bibliothèque de l'Opéra, Paris.
[1719]	Dezais.	Balon.	*XVII. Recüeil de dances pour l'année 1719* de la composition de M.ʳ Balon. Paris: l'auteur.
[1720]	Dezais.	Balon.	*XVIII. Recueil de dances pour l'année 1720* de la composition de M.ʳ Balon. Paris: l'auteur.
[1720]	Dezais.	Pécour.	*IIII Recüeil de dances nouvelles pour l'année 1720* de la composition de M.ʳ Pecour.
[1722]	Dezais.	Balon, Pécour.	*XXᴱ ET VIᴱ Recueil de dances pour l'année, 1722.* Paris: Dezais.
1723	Bonnet, Jaques.		*Histoire generale de la danse.* Paris: Chez d'Houry fils, 1723. R., Genèva: Slatkine Reprints, 1969.
1725	Sol, C.		*Méthode tres facile* et sort necessaire pour montrer. . .la manière de bien danser. La Haye: the author, 1725.
1725	Rameau, P[ierre]		*Le Maître à danser* qui enseigne la maniere de faire tous les differens pas de la danse dans toutes regularité de l'art, et de conduire les bras à chaque pas. Enrichi de figures en taille-douce, servant de démonstration pour tous les differens mouvements. . .Paris: J. Villette, 1725. Further editions: 1726, 1734, 1748.
1725	Rameau.		*Abbregé de la nouvelle methode* dans l'art d'ecrire toutes sortes de danses de ville. Paris: J. Villette, 1725.
		Pécour.	The second part of this book contains a selection of ballroom dances by Pécour.

FRENCH UNDATED MANUSCRIPTS

Location	*Notators*	*Choreographers*	
Paris opéra Rés. 841(2)		Pécour.	*Le canary de madame la dauphine par M.ʳ pécour.*
Rés. 817		Feuillet, Pécour, Ballon, Dupont.	Predominantly a collection of theatrical solos for men and women. The largest number of dances are solos for men by Feuillet.

Rés. 934		Pécour, Feuillet, Beaufort, Dezais.	A collection of ballroom dances containing many of Pécour's popular published compositions.
Rés. C2454		Pécour and Anon.	An approximate copy of Feuillet's *Chorégraphie* followed by a collection of notated dances.
Paris: Bibliothèque Nationale 14.884		Pécour, Feuillet, Balon, Bauchand, Favier.	A large collection of ballroom and theatrical dances, the majority of which exist in printed collections.
N.Y.P.L. Dance Collection *MGWM-Res.	Sarron [or Savron]	Leveque.	*L'Obice. Compose par Monsieur Leveque L'Aine mise en corographie par Monsieur Antoine Sarron* [or *Savron*].

ENGLISH BOOKS, 1700-1735

	Authors and Notators	Choreographers	
1706	Weaver, John.		*Orchesography* or the art of dancing, by characters and demonstrative figures. . .Being an exact and just translation from the French of Monsieur Feuillet by John Weaver. London: H. Meere for the author, 1706.
1706	Weaver.		*A Small treatise of time and cadence in dancing*, reduc'd to an easy and exact method. Shewing how steps, and their movements, agree with the notes, and division of notes, in each measure. London: H. Meere, 1706.
1706	Weaver.	Isaac.	*A Collection of Ball Dances Perform'd at Court.* London: the author, 1706.
1706	Siris, P.	Isaac. Pécour.	*The Art of Dancing.* London: 1706. A paraphrase of Feuillet's *Chorégraphie*, with dances by Isaac and Pécour.
[1707]	de la Garde.	Isaac.	*The Princess* by Mr Isaak.
1707	Weaver.	Isaac.	*The Union*. . .Performed at Court on Her Majesties Birthday Febr. 6th 1707.
1708	Siris.	Siris.	*La Camilla*: Dance nouvelle sur un air Italien de L'opera du meme nom par Signor Bononcini. London: l'auteur, 1708.
1708	de la Garde.	Isaac.	*The Salterella*. Mr Isaac's new dance for Her Majestys Birthday. London: J. Walsh. 1708.
[1709]		Siris.	*The Brawl of Audenarde*. Mr Siris' new Dance.
1709	de la Garde.	Isaac.	*The Royal Portuguez*. Mr Isaac's new dance made for Her Majesty's brithday. London: J. Walsh and P. Randall, 1709.

1710	de la Garde.	Isaac.	*The Royall Gailliarde.* M.ʳ Isaac's new dance for Her Majesty's birthday. London: J. Walsh and P. Randall, 1710.
1710	Essex, John.	Various.	*For the Further Improvement of Dancing.* A translation of Feuillet's Recueil de contredanses. 1706. London: J. Walsh and P. Randall, 1710. [The dances in the two collections are not always identical.] Second edition, enlarged, 1715.
1711	Pemberton, [E.]	Various English masters and Isaac, L'Abbée, Pécour.	*An Essay for the Improvement of Dancing.* London: J. Walsh, 1711. [A collection of figured minuets for ladies, the number of participants ranging from three to twelve, composed by respected English masters. The book concludes with three solo dances by Isaac, L'Abbé and Pécour.]
1711	de la Garde.	Isaac.	*The Rigadoon Royal.* M.ʳ Isaac's new dance for Her Majesty's Birthday. London: J. Walsh, 1711.
1712	Isaac?	Isaac.	*The Royal Ann.* M.ʳ Isaac's new dance for Her Majesty's birthday. London: J. Walsh, 1712.
1713	Pemberton.	Isaac.	*The Pastorall.* M.ʳ Isaac's New Dance made for Her Majestys Birthday. London: J. Walsh, 1713.
[1713]		Isaac.	*The Northumberland.*
1714		Siris.	*The Siciliana,* Mr Siris' new Dance For the Year 1714.
1714	Pemberton.	Isaac.	*The Godolphin.* M.ʳ Isaac's new dance made for Her Majesty's birthday. London: J. Walsh, 1714.
1715	Pemberton.	Isaac.	*The Friendship.* M.ʳ Isaac's new dance for the year 1715. London: J. Walsh.
[1716]	[Pemberton.]	Isaac.	*The Morris.*
[17—]		Isaac.	*The Marlborough,* a New Dance Composed by Mr. Isaac. Performed at Court on Her Majesties Birthday Feb. 6 17—. London: J. Walsh.
17—		Isaac.	*The Gloucester,* a New Dance Composed by Mʳ Isaac. Performed at court on Her Majesties Birthday Feb. 6 17—. London: J. Walsh.
17—		Isaac.	*The Royall,* a New Dance Composed by Mʳ Isaac. Performed at Court on Her Majesties Birthday Feb. 6 17—. London: J. Walsh.
1715	Pemberton.	L'Abbée.	*The Princess Royale.* A new dance for His Majestys Birth Day. London: the author [Pemberton], 1715.
1715	Tomlinson, Kellom.	Tomlinson.	*The Passepied Round: O.* A new dance, composed and written into characters in the year 1715. London: the author, 1715, 1720.
[1715]	Essex.	Essex.	*An Essay for the Further Improvement of Dancing.* [Concludes with one dance by Essex.] London: J. Walsh and P. Randall.
1716		L'Abbée.	*The Princess Anna.* M.ʳ L'Abée's new dance for His Majesty's Birth Day. London: J. Walsh, 1716.

1716	Tomlinson.	Tomlinson.	*The Shepherdess.* A new dance, composed and written into characters in the year 1716. London: the author, 1716, 1720.
1717	Pemberton.	L'Abbée.	*The Royal George.* A New Dance composed by M.ʳ L'Abee For the Year 1717. London: the author, 1717.
1717	Tomlinson.	Tomlinson.	*The Submission.* A new ball dance compos'd and written into characters and figures in the year 1717. London: the author, 1717, 1720.
1718	Pemberton.	L'Abbée.	*The Princess Amelia.* A New Dance For His Majesties birthday. London: the author, 1718.
1718	Tomlinson.	Tomlinson.	*The Prince Eugene.* A new dance composed and written in characters in the year 1718. London: the author, 1718.
1719	Pemberton.	L'Abbée.	*The Princess Anne's Chacone.* A New Dance for his Majesty's Birth Day composed by M.ʳ L'Abee. London: the author, 1719.
1719	Tomlinson.	Tomlinson.	*The Address.* A New Rigadoon composed for the year 1719. London: the author, 1719, 1720.
1720	Tomlinson.	Tomlinson.	*The Gavot.* A New dance for the year 1720. London: the author, 1720.
1720	Tomlinson.	Tomlinson.	*Six Dances.* A Collection of all the Yearly Dances, publish'd by him from the Year 1715 to the present Year. London: the author, 1720.
[1720] ms.	Roussau.	Roussau, D'anjeville, Balon, Pécour.	*A collection of new ball and stage dances* compos'd by several masters. Ms. Edinburgh University Library.
1721		Marcelle.	*The Primrose* by Mʳ Marcelle, 1721.
1721	Pemberton.	L'Abbée.	*Prince William.* A New Dance For His Majesty's Birthday. London: the author, 1721.
1721	Tomlinson.	Tomlinson.	*The Passacaille Diana.* London: 1721. Tomlinson claims this publication in his Preface to *The Art of Dancing,* 1735.
[1722]	Weaver.	Isaac, Pécour.	*Orchesography.* [See 1700] The second edition. Three notated dances are added.
1723	Pemberton.	L'Abbée.	*The New Rigadon.* Compos'd by M.ʳ L'Abbee for the Year 1723.
1724	Pemberton.	L'Abbée.	*The Canary.* A New Dance for the Year 1724 by M.ʳ L'Abbé. London: the author, 1724.
1725	Pemberton.	L'Abbée.	*Prince Frederick.* A new Dance for the Year 1725 by Mʳ L'Abbé. London: the author, 1725.
1727	Pemberton.	L'Abbée.	*The Prince of Wales.* A new Dance for the Year 1727 by Mʳ L'Abbé. London: the author, 1727.
1728	Pemberton.	L'Abbée.	*Queen Caroline.* A new dance for Her Majesties Birthday, 1728. London: the author, 1728.
1728	Essex, John.		*The Dancing Master;* or the art of dancing explained. . .done from the French of M. Rameau. London: J. Brotherton, 1728. A second edition of 1731 saw two issues.

1731	Pemberton.	L'Abbée.	*The Prince of Wales's Saraband.* A New Dance for Her Majesty's Birthday, 1731. London: the author, 1731.
1733	Pemberton.	L'Abbée.	*The Prince of Orange.* A New Dance For the Year 1733. London: the author, 1733.
17—	Pemberton.	Caverley.	*Mr. Caverley's Slow Minuet.* A New Dance for a Girl. The Tune Composed by Mr Firbank. London: The Author.
	Pemberton	Pemberton	*La Cybelline.* A New Dance for a Girl. London: The author.
17—	Roussau.	Roussau.	*A Chacoon for a Harlequin.* Roussau. London: the author.
17—	Roussau.	L'Abbée.	*A new collection of dances* containing a great number of the best ball and stage dances composed by Monsieur L'Abbé. . . . London: the author.
1735	Tomlinson.		*The art of dancing* explained by reading and figures; whereby the manner of performing the steps is made easy by a new and familiar method: being the original work, first designed in the year 1724, and now published by Kellom Tomlinson, dancing master. . . . London: the author, 1735.

SELECTED GERMAN BOOKS, 1700-1718.

	Authors and Notators	*Choreographers*	
1705	I.H.P.	Pécour. Anon.	*I.H.P. Maître de Danse oder Tantz-Meister.* Gluckstadt and Leipzig: Gotthilff Lehmann. Johann Friederich Schwendimann, 1705. [Contains some dances with the floor tracks drawn according to the system of *Chorégraphie,* but with the steps given verbally.]
1711	Bonin, Louis.		*Die Neuste Art zur Galanten und Theatralischen Tantz-Kunst.* . . . Frankfurt und Leipzig: J.C. Lochner, 1711. R., München: Heimeran Verlag.
1713	Behren (Behr), Samuel Rudolph.		*L'Art de bien danser oder: Die Kunst wohl zu Tanzen.* I. La methode d'informer dans la Belle-Danse. II. La methode d'informer dans la Danse-Haute. III. La methode d'informer dans la Comique & III. Grotesque. Leipzig: Martin Fulde, 1713. R., München: Heimeran Verlag, 1977.
1716	Lambranzi, Gregorio. (Engravings by Johann Georg Poschner)		*Neue und Curieuse Theatralische Tantz-Schul.* Nürnberg: Johann Jacob Wolrab, 1716. R., with a German commentary by Kurt Petermann, trans. into English by Michael Talbot. Leipzig: Peters, 1975.

			-----Trans. Derra de Moroda, *New and Curious School of Theatrical Dancing*. London: C.W. Beaumont, 1928. R., New York: Dance Horizons, 1966.
(1715) (1972)			-----*New and Curious School of Theatrical Dancing*. A facsimile of a ms, dated 1715, containing the original drawings made for the 1716 publication (not all are identical). With introduction and notes by F. Derra de Moroda. New York: Dance Horizons, 1972.
1717	Taubert, Gottfried.	Pécour, Feuillet.	*Rechtschaffener Tantzmeister, oder gründliche Erklärung der Frantzösischen Tantz-Kunst bestehend aus drey Büchern*. . . . Leipzig: Friedrich Lanckischens Erben, 1717. R., München: Heimeran Verlag. 2 vols. [This work consists of 1176 pages and is divided into three parts, the second of which is concerned with the noble style of dance and dance notation.]
[1718]	Dubreil.	Dubreil.	*La Hessoise Darmstat*. Danse figurée a deux pour le bal & contredance sous la même nom composées & ecrite en choregraphie. . .Par le sieur Dubreil. Munich: 1718.

SELECTED DIRECTORIES AND BIBLIOGRAPHIES

Directories

Benton, Rita.

Directory of Music Research Libraries. Iowa City: University of Iowa, 1967-

Christout, Marie-Françoise and Denis Bablet, (editors).

Bibliothèques et musées des arts du spectacle dans le monde. Paris: Centre Nationale de la Recherche Scientifique, 1960.

Bibliographies

RILM abstracts of music literature. New York: International RILM Center, 1967-

R.I.S.M. *Repertoire internationale des sources musicales*. (International Inventory of Musical Sources). München: G. Henle, 1960-

The following parts of this continuing series are bibliographies which include relevant music scores (the listings are incomplete):

Schlager, Karl-Heinz.
Einzeldrucke vor 1800. 1971-

Lesure, François.
Recueils Imprimés XVIe-XVIIe Siecles. 1960.

Lesure, François.
Recueils Imprimés XVIIIe Siecles. 1964.

The following is a bibliography of books about music and dance published before 1800:

Lesure, François.
Ecrits Concernant la Musique. 1971.

Adkins, Cecil and Alis Dickinson, (editors).
International index of dissertations and musicological works in progress. Philadelphia: American Musicological Society, International Musicological Society, 1977.

Little, Meredith (Ellis), Christena Schlundt, and Judith Schwartz.	*An Annotated Bibliography of Primary Source Literature for the Study of French Court Dance and Dance Music during the Reigns of Louis XIV, XV, and XVI.* To be published by Joseph Boonin (Hackensack, N.J.) in the series called *Music Indexes and Bibliographies* under the general editorship of George Hill. Part I. Meredith Ellis Little. A bibliography of notated choreographies with musical incipits. Part II. Christena Schlundt. Writings about dance and dance notation. Part III. Judith Schwartz. Writings pertaining to dance music.

MODERN WRITINGS ON SEVENTEENTH- AND EIGHTEENTH-CENTURY DANCE

(Only writings *specifically* concerned with this period are given.)

Baron, John H.	"Les Fées des Forests de S. Germain ballet de cour, 1625," *Dance Perspectives 62*, (New York), Summer 1975.
Christout, Marie-Françoise.	*Le ballet de cour de Louis XIV, 1643-1672.* Paris: Editions A. et J. Picard et Cie, 1967. "The Court Ballet in France: 1615-1641," *Dance Perspectives 20,* (New York), 1964.
Cohen, Selma Jeanne.	"I. Josias Priest, II. John Weaver, III. Hester Santlow." In *Famed for Dance: Essays on the Theory and Practice of Theatrical Dancing in England.* New York: New York Public Library, 1960.
Derra de Moroda, Friderica.	"Chorégraphie. The dance notation of the eighteenth century: Beauchamp or Feuillet?" *The Book Collector* (London), Winter 1967. "The Dance Notation of the 18th Century: Lorin-Beauchamp-Feuillet." International Federation for Theatre Research Symposium. Copenhagen, September 1971. "The Ballet Masters Before, at the Time of, and After J.G. Noverre," *Chigiana* (Florence), vol. 29-30 (n.s.no. 9-10), 1972/73.
Fletcher, Ifan Kyrle.	"Ballet in England 1660-1740." In *Famed for Dance: Essays on the Theory and Practice of Theatrical Dancing in England.* New York: New York Public Library, 1960. "Ballet's First Historian." *[Menestrier, 1630-1705]* "Ballet's First Historian." [Menestrier, 1630-1705] *The Dancing Times* (London), October 1961.
Gerbes, Angelica Renate.	"Gottfried Taubert on Social and Theatrical Dance of the Early Eighteenth Century." (Unpublished Ph.D. dissertation, The Ohio State University, 1972.)

Guilcher, Jean Michel.

La contredanse et les renouvellements de la danse française. Paris: Mouton, 1969.

Hilton, Wendy.

"A Dance for Kings: The 17th-Century French Courante," *Early Music* (London), April 1977.

Kunzle, Régine.

"The Illustrious Unknown Choreographer, Pierre Beauchamps," *Dance Scope* (New York), vol. 8 no. 2 and vol. 9 no. 1, 1974/75.

"Jean Loret: A Pioneer of 17th-Century Criticism," *Dance Scope* (New York), vol. 10 no. 2, 1976.

"In Search of L'Acadèmie Royale de Danse," *York Dance Review* (York University, Canada) No. 7, Spring 1978.

Little, Meredith (Ellis).

"Dance under Louis XIV and XV," *Early Music* (London), October 1975.

Martin, Jennifer Kaye Lowe.

"The English Dancing Master, 1660-1728: His Role at Court, in Society and on the Public Stage." (Unpublished Ph.D. dissertation, University of Michigan, 1977.)

McGowan, Margaret.

L'art de ballet du cour en France, 1581-1643. Paris: Centre Nationale de la Recherche Scientifique, 1963.

Quirey, Belinda.

"Minuet—the Beginning of the End," *The Ballroom Dancing Times* (London), May 1961.

Richardson, Philip J.S.

"The Beauchamp Mystery: Some Fresh Light on an Old Problem," *The Dancing Times* (London), March 1947 and April 1947.

Sasportas, José.

"Feasts and Folias: The Dance in Portugal," *Dance Perspectives 42* (New York), Summer 1970.

Skeaping, Mary.

"Ballet Under the Three Crowns," *Dance Perspectives 32* (New York), Winter 1967.

Taubert, Karl Heinz.

"Das Menuett." *Das Tanzarchiv,* (Köln), 1978.

Van Cleef, Joy.

"Rural Felicity: Social Dance in 18th-Century Connecticut," *Dance Perspectives 65* (New York), Spring 1976.

Winter, Marian Hannah.

The Pre-Romantic Ballet. London: Pitman and Sons, Ltd., 1974; New York: *Dance Horizons,* 1974.

Witherell, Anne Louise.

"Louis Pécour's 1700 Recueil de Danses." (Unpublished Ph.D. dissertation, Stanford University, forthcoming.)

Wood, Melusine.

Advanced Historical Dances. London: Imperial Society of Teachers of Dancing, Inc., 1960. [An analysis of the minuet, and some steps and dances of the eighteenth century.]

Wynne, Shirley S.

"The Charms of Complaisance: the Dance in England in the Early 18th Century." (Unpublished Ph.D. dissertation, the Ohio State University, 1967.)

"Reconstruction of a Dance from 1700." In *Dance History Research.* New York: Committee on Research in Dance (C.O.R.D.), 1970.

"The Minuet." In *Institute of Court Dances of the Renaissance and Baroque Periods*. New York: Committee on Research in Dance (C.O. R.D.), 1972.

"Complaisance: An Eighteenth-Century Cool," *Dance Scope* (New York), vol. 5 no. 1, 1970.

SELECTED MODERN BOOKS ON BAROQUE MUSIC

A significant continuing series is: *La vie musicale en France sous les rois Bourbons*.
Paris: Editions A. et J. Picard et Cie.
1re série.-Etudes. 1954-
2e série.-Recherches sur la musique classique française. 1960-

The most relevant *Etudes* in the first series are included in the following list.

Anthony, James R. *French Baroque Music*. New York: W.W. Norton & Company, Inc., 1964. Second edition revised, 1978.

Barthelemy, Maurice. *André Campra: sa vie et son oeuvre (1660-1744)*. Paris: Editions A. et J. Picard et Cie, 1957.

Bénoit, Marcelle. *Versailles et les musiciens du Roi*. Etude institutionnelle et sociale (1661-1733). Paris: Editions A. et J. Picard et Cie, 1971.
Musique de cour. Chapelle, Chambre, Ecuirie (1661-1733). Paris: Editions A. et J. Picard et Cie, 1971.

Borrel, Eugène. *Jean-Baptiste Lully*. Paris: La Colombe, 1949.

Boyden, David. *The History of Violin Playing from Its Origins to 1761*. London, New York: Oxford University Press, [1975, c1965].

Brockpähler, Renate. *Handbuch zur Geschichte der Barockoper in Deutschland*. Die Schaubühne, edited by Carl Niessen. Vol. LXII. Emsdetten, Westfalia: Verlag Lechte, 1964).

Bukofzer, Manfred E. *Music in the Baroque Era*. New York: W.W. Norton & Company, Inc., 1947.

Collins, Michael. "The Performance of Coloration, Sesquialtera and Hemiola (1450-1750)." (Unpublished Ph.D. dissertation, Stanford University, 1963.)

Dean, Winton. *Handel's Dramatic Oratorios and Masques*. London, New York: Oxford University Press, 1959.

Deutsch, Otto Erich. *Handel: A Documentary Bibliography*. London: Adam and Charles Black, 1955.

Donington, Robert. *The Interpretation of Early Music*. London: Faber & Faber, 1963. Second edition, New York: St. Martin's Press, 1965.

	The Instruments of Music. [Third edition revised and enlarged] London: Metheuen, 1970.
	A Performer's Guide to Baroque Music. New York: Charles Scribner's Sons, 1973.
	String Playing in Baroque Music. [With long-playing record] London: Faber & Faber, 1977.
Ellis (Little), H. Meredith.	"The Dances of J.B. Lully." (Unpublished Ph.D. dissertation, Stanford University, 1967.)
Gerold, Theodore.	*L'art du chant en France au XVIIe siècle*. Strasbourg; Librairie Istra, 1921; New York: Columbia University Press, 1921. R., Geneva: Minkoff Reprint, 1971.
Girdlestone, Cuthbert.	*Jean Philippe Rameau*. London: Cassell, 1957.
Isherwood, Robert M.	*Music in the Service of the King: France in the Seventeenth Century*. Ithaca: Cornell University Press, 1973.
Lazarevich, Gordana.	*Music in the Preclassic and Classic Era*. (Schirmer's History of Music. Part IV. New York: Macmillan, 1978).
Lesure, Françoise.	*Music and Art in Society*. University Park and London: The Pennsylvania State University Press, 1968.
Lewis, Anthony and Nigel Fortune (editors).	*Opera and Church Music, 1630-1750*. (New Oxford History of Music. Vol. 5. London, New York: Oxford University Press, 1975).
Manifold, John.	*The Music in English Drama from Shakespeare to Purcell*. London: Rockliff, 1956.
Massip, Catherine.	*La vie des musiciens de Paris au temps de Mazarin 1643-1661*. Paris: Editions A. et J. Picard et Cie, 1976.
Masson, Paul Marie.	*L'opéra de Rameau*. Paris: H. Laurens, 1930.
Mather, Betty Bang.	*The Interpretation of Early Music from 1675-1775 for Woodwind and Other Performers*. New York: McGinnis and Marx Music Publishers, 1973.
Mellers, Wilfred Howard.	*François Couperin and the French Classical Tradition*. London: Dobson, 1950.
Palisca, Claude V.	*Baroque Music*. Englewood Cliffs, New Jersey: Prentice Hall, 1968.
Prunières, Henry.	*Lully*. Paris: H. Laurens, 1909.
Salmen, Walter.	*Haus-und Kammermusik; privates Musizieren im gesellschaftlichen Wandel zwischen 1600 und 1900*. (*Musikgeschichte in Bildern*, herausgegeben von Heinrich Bessler und Werner Bachmann. Bd: IV Lfrg. 3. Leipzig: Deutscher Verlag für Musik Leipzig, 1969.)
Schwab, Heinrich W.	*Konzert Öffentliche Musikdarbietung vom 17. bis 19. Jahrhundert*. (*Musikgeschichte in Bildern*, herausgegeben von Heinrich Bessler und Werner Bachmann. Bd: IV Lfrg. 2. Leipzig: Deutscher Verlag für Musik Leipzig, 1969).

Vinquist, Mary and Neil Zaslaw (editors).	*Performance Practice: A Bibliography*. A guide to the extensive literature [both primary and secondary sources] on the proper performance of music of past centuries. New York: W.W. Norton and Company, Inc., 1971.
Wolff, Hellmuth Christian.	*Oper. Szene und Darstellung von 1600 bis 1900. (Musikgeschichte in Bildern,* herausgegeben von Heinrich Bessler und Werner Bachmann. Bd. IV: Lfrg. 1. Leipzig: Deutscher Verlag für Musik Leipzig).
Yates, Frances A.	*The French Academies of the Sixteenth Century.* London: Warburg Institute, 1947.
Zimmerman, Franklin B.	*Henry Purcell 1659-1695. His Life and Times.* London: Macmillan, 1967; New York: St. Martin's Press, 1967.

SELECTED BOOKS ON FASHION AND DEPORTMENT

Boehn, Max von.	*Modes and Manners.* Translated by Joan Joshua. Philadelphia: J.B. Lippincott, Co., 1932 (1936). Vols. III & IV.
Corson, Richard.	*Fashions in Hair: The First 5000 Years.* New York: Hastings House, 1965.
Ewing, Elizabeth.	*Underwear: A History.* New York: Theatre Arts Books, 1972.
Green, Ruth M.	*The Wearing of Costume.* London: Sir Isaac Pitman and Sons, Ltd., 1969.
Laver, James.	*Costume of the Western World.* New York: Harper, 1951.
Squire, Geoffrey.	*Dress, Art and Society 1560-1970.* London: Studio Vista, 1974; *Dress and Society 1560-1970.* New York: The Viking Press, 1974.
Thornton, Peter.	*Baroque and Rococo Silk.* London: Faber and Faber Limited, 1965.
Wildebloode, Joan and Peter Brinson.	*The Polite World.* London: Oxford University Press, 1965.
Wilson, Eunice.	*A History of Shoe Fashion.* London: Pitman Publishing; New York: Theatre Arts Books, 1974.

Pattern Books

Arnold, Janet.	*Patterns of Fashion: Englishwomen's Dresses and Their Construction.* London: Wace, 1964-66, 2 vols. (v. 1—c.1660-1860; v. 2—c. 1860-1940)
Waugh, Norah.	*Corsets and Crinolines.* New York: Theatre Arts Books, 1970. *The Cut of Women's Clothes 1600-1930.* London: Faber and Faber Limited, 1968; New York: Theatre Arts Books, 1968. *The Cut of Men's Clothes 1600-1900.* London: Faber and Faber Limited, 1964; New York: Theatre Arts Books, 1964.

SCENERY, COSTUMES, AND THEATER ARCHITECTURE

Beaumont, Cyril. | *Five Centuries of Ballet Design.* New York: Studio Publications, 1935.

Bjurström, Per. | *Giacomo Torelli and Baroque Stage Design.* Stockholm: Alquist & Winksell, 1962. First edition, Stockholm National Museum, 1961.

Lesure, François. | *L'opéra classique Francaise XVIIe et XVIIIe siècles.* Genève: Editions Minkoff, 1972.

Mullin, Donald C. | *The Development of the Playhouse.* A survey of theater architecture from the Renaissance to the present. Berkeley and Los Angeles: University of California Press, 1970.

Reade, Brian. | *Ballet Designs and Illustrations, 1581-1940: a catalogue raisonné.* London: H.M.S.O. for Victoria and Albert Museum, 1967.

SELECTED BOOKS ON DRAMA

Chevalley, Sylvie. | *Molière en son temps, 1622-1673.* Paris, Genève: Minkoff, 1973.

Gros, Etienne. | *Philippe Quinault.* Paris: Champion, 1926.

Lewis, D.B. Wyndham. | *Molière, the Comic Mask.* London: Eyre & Spottiswoode, 1953.

Nicoll, Allardyce. | *The World of Harlequin: A Critical Study of the Commedia dell'Arte.* Cambridge at the University Press, 1963.

Saintonge, Paul Frederic and Robert Wilson Christ. | *Fifty Years of Molière Studies. A Bibliography 1892-1941.* Baltimore: The Johns Hopkins University Press, 1942.

Silin, Charles I. | *Benserade and His Ballets de Cour.* Baltimore: The Johns Hopkins University Press, 1940.

Stratman, Carl Josef, Spencer, David and Mary Elizabeth Devine. | *Restoration and Eighteenth Century Theatre Research: a bibliographical guide, 1900-1968.* Carbondale: Southern Illinois University Press, 1971.

SELECTED BOOKS ON FRENCH ART AND ARCHITECTURE

Bjurström, Per. | *French Drawings. Sixteenth and Seventeenth Centuries.* Stockholm: Nationalmuseum. Liberfölag, 1976.

Blunt, Antony, Sir. | *Art and Architecture in France, 1500-1700.* Hamondsworth, Middlesex, Baltimore: Penguin Books, 1957.

Fox, Helen. | *André de la Notre: Garden Architect to Kings.* New York: Crown Publishers, 1962.

Marie, Alfred. | *Jardins Français Classiques des XVIIE & XVIIIE Siècles.* Paris: Editions Vincent, Freal & Cie, 1949.

Thuillier, Jaques and
Albert Chatelet.

La Peintre française de Foquet à Poisson.
-----Trans. Stuart Gilbert, *French Painting from
Foquet to Poisson.* Geneva: Skira, 1963. Distributed in U.S. by World Publishing Company,
Cleveland.
La peinture française de Le Nain à Fragonard.
-----Trans. James Emmons, *French Painting from
Le Nain to Fragonard.* Geneva: Skira, c.1964.

SELECTED BOOKS ON LOUIS XIV AND FRANCE

Louis XIV, King of France,
1638-1715.

Memoirs for the Instruction of the Dauphin. Introduction, translation and notes by Paul Sonnino. New York: Free Press, 1970.

Carré, Henri.

The Early Life of Louis XIV (1638-1661).
-----Trans. from the French by Dorothy Bolton.
Great Britain: Hutchinson & Co. (Publishers)
Ltd., 1951.

Church, William Farr,
editor.

*The Impact of Absolutism in France; national
experience under Richelieu, Mazarin, and Louis
XIV.* Edited by William Farr Church. New
York: Wiley, 1969.

Erlanger, Philippe.

Louis XIV au jour de jour. Paris: La table ronde,
1968.
-----Trans. Stephen Cox, *Louis XIV.* London:
Weidenfelt and Nicholson, 1970.

Hibbert, Christopher
and the Editors of the
Newsweek Book Division.

Versailles. France Under the Bourbons. New
York: *Newsweek*, 1972.

Levron, Jacques.

*La vie quotidienne à la cour de Versailles aux
XVIIe et XVIIIe siecles.* -----Trans. Claire Elaine
Engel, *Daily Life at Versailles in the Seventeenth
and Eighteenth Centuries.* New York: Macmillan, 1968.

Lewis, W.H.

Louis XIV, an informal portrait. London: A.
Deutsch, 1959; New York: Harcourt, Brace,
1959.
The Splendid Century. Some aspects of French
life in the reign of Louis XIV. London: Eyre &
Spottiswoode, 1953; New York: William Sloane,
1954; William Morrow, 1971.

INDEX

BACKGROUND OF COURT AND THEATER

DANCE

Actions and steps (definitions, technique and notation), Arms, Body, Feet, Hands, Head, Legs (action of the joints), Shoulder Area, Space, Spatial Figures, Steps.

pas glissé (sliding), 75, 164-165; in: glissade, 182; pas coupé, 176-178; temps de courante, 201-206; pas marché (walking), 73; 164-165; in: pas coupé, 176-178; pas de bourrée, 183-189; pas de menuet, 191-195

pas sauté (springing), 121, *see also* springing steps

pas tombé (falling), 74-75, 117; in pas tombé (step-unit), 232-235

relationship of: in units to beats, 150-152; first in a unit with a "movement," 156-158

step in chorégraphie, 100

steps terminating in foot positions, 106-107

symbols along the tract, 102-104

pas simple with a "movement," 164-174, 228

demi-cabriole, 228

demi-coupé (half coupé), 164-173; execution of: author's notes, 170; Essex, 166-167; exercises for, 171, 173; in: glissade, 182; pas balancé, 198-199; pas coupé, 176-182; pas de bourrée, 183-189; pas de menuet, 191-195; rise in, 168, 172,; time and arm motions, 169, 171; with leg gestures, 173

demi-coupé échappé: *see* demi-jeté

demi-jeté (half bound), 164; execution of, 174; in: coupé à deux mouvements, 180-182; pas de bourrée, 183; pas de bourrée double, quatre pas, or vite, 189; pas de menuet à deux mouvements à la bohémienne, 195; à trois mouvements, 194-195; temps de courante and demi-jeté, 208

jeté (bound), 164; execution of, 173, 228; in: pas de bourrée, 183; pas de bourrée double, quatre pas, or vite, 189; contretemps ballonné or à deux mouvements, 219-220; pas tombé, 232-235

jeté chassé, 228

jeté échappé: *see* demi-jeté

jeté sans sauté: *see* demi-coupé

springing steps, 121-127

one foot to the other (jeté, bound), notation of, 122, *see also* pas simple with a "movement"

one foot to two feet, notation of, 122; in: pas assemblé, 221-222; pas de gaillarde, 233-235; pas de sissonne, 223-225

one foot to the same foot (hop), notation of, 123-124; in contretemps, 212-220

two feet to one foot, notation of, 124-125; in: pas de rigaudon, 226-227; pas de sissonne, 223-225

two feet to two feet, notation of, 125-127; in: pas de rigaudon, 226-227; pas échappé, 237

step-pattern, 73
step-sequence, 73, 161
step-unit, 73, 83

chassé, 163-164, 230

contretemps, 163-164, 212; contretemps: ballonné or à deux mouvements, 219-220; de chaconne or ouvert, 214; de côté, 214; de gavotte, 212-213; de menuet, 216-217, 301; ouvert: *see* de chaconne; exercise for contretemps: ballonné or à deux mouvements, 248-249; de gavotte, 215, 229, 247-249, 251; de menuet, 217, 242; in the gavotte, 244, 246

glissade, 4n, 163-164, 182

grouping of, for study in Chapter Nine, 175

jeté, 163-164, 228, *see also* pas simple with a "movement"

jeté chassé, 163-164, 228; exercise for, 229

pas assemblé, 163-164, 221-222; exercise for, 251; in the gavotte, 244, 246

pas balancé, 163-164, 198-199; exercises for, 206, 210, 218; in the menuet, 294, 299

pas composé (compound step), 72-73, 104, 105

pas coupé, 163-164, 176-178, 264; exercises for, 180, 205-206; exercises, in the gavotte, 244, 246; exercises including, 210, 227; pas coupé: à deux mouvements, 108-182; avec ronde (tour) de jambe, 178-179; battu, 178-179; sans poser le corps, 179; simple and soutenu, 176-178, *see also* glissade

pas de bourrée, 163-164, 183, 185; exercises for, 186, 206; exercises for pas de bourrée: double, de côté, and emboëté, 190, 229; turning, 200; exercises, in the gavotte, 244, 246; exercises including, 215, 225, 227, 229, 247, 249; pas de bourrée: de côté, 187; derrière, dessous et dessus, dessus, dessus et dessous, 185; double à deux mouvements, quatre pas, or vite, 185, 189; emboëté, 187; fleuret, 184; ouvert, 188

pas de courante, 163

pas de gaillarde, 163-164; exercise for, 236; Rameau, 232-235; Tomlinson, 232-233

pas de menuet, 163-164, 169, 171, 191; exercises for 193, 208, 217-218, 242; pas de menuet: à deux mouvements, 191-193; à deux mouvements à la bohémienne, 195; à un seul mouvement, 195; à trois mouvements, 194-195; rhythm in the menuet and passepied, 191, 294; with hemiola, 239-240

pas de rigaudon, 163-164, 226-227; exercise for, 227

pas de sissone, 163-164, 223-225; exercises for, 225, 229, 249

pas échappé, 163-164, 237

pas tombé, 163-164, 232-235; exercises for, 236, 253

pirouette, 163-164, 209-210; exercises for, 210, 227; with a spring, 211

pointing; *see* temps (pointing)

relationship of: single steps in units to beats, 150-152; units to the musical measure, 83; notation of, 92; number of units to measure in: the different meters, 155; specific dance types, 154; relationship methods of: the author, 159-160; Feuillet, Rameau, and Tomlinson, 158; table of, 163

saillies: *see* pas échappé

table of step-units in Rameau's original spelling, 164

temps, 73, 105

temps (pointing), 163-164, 207

temps de courante, 163-164, 201-205, 264
exercises for, 205-206, 210, 225, 253
in the menuet, 294, 298-299, 301; exercise for, 208
with a demi-jeté, 208, 264

ETIQUETTE

Clothing
clothing, 69
coat, disposition of the hands when standing, 69, 273
fan, carrying, 67, 277-278; management of, 270
gloves, wearing of, 283
handkerchief, affectations with, 269
hat, description of, 274; how to hold, 274-275; remove and replace, 274-275; use in: honours before dancing, 283-285; the menuet, 295, 297, 301, 303-304, 306; wear, 274
muff, carrying, 272
petticoat: *see* skirt
shoes, height of heel, 69

skirt, holding, 68-69, 279, 284, 295, 303-304, 306; width of, 69

waistcoat, disposition of the hand when standing, 273

Honours

honours, 269-271, 276; backward, 279, 281; backward, in honours before dancing, 284-285, 295; forward, 277, 281; passing, 278, 281; some occasions for, 280-281; when presenting as object, 276

honours before: dancing, 284-285; the menuet, 295

Persons

person honoured, 276

the Presence, 85, 87, 262, 284-285

spectators, 87, 282, 286-288

Procedure

arrival of Princesse de Savoie at Versailles, 12-13

confrontation between Louis XIV and Madame, 270-271

procedure at: an appartement, 16; balls, 11-15, 19, 286-288; masked balls, 17-18

Sitting

etiquette of, at balls, 283, 286-288

positions, 280, 282

Standing

carriage and postures for, 67-69, 273

etiquette of, at balls, 286-288

Walking

carriage and manner of, 272

MUSIC

Anacrusis, *see* Upbeat

Barline, 68, 156-158; in dances with a false cadence, 250-254

Beating time, 262-263

Beats, 83

beats and note values, 150

downbeat, 153; relationship to rise, 153, 156-158, in a demi-coupé, 165, 169; to arm motions, table, 160

upbeat, 153; relationship to bend, 153, 156-158, 165, 169; in gavotte, 243, 262; to arm motions, table, 160; table of upbeats, 263

Cadence, 82-83, 258; *see also* Rhythm

fausse cadence, false cadence, 83, 244, 250-253

vrai cadence, true cadence, 83

Cross-rhythm, 75; *see also* fausse cadence

Downbeat, *see* Beats

Flats, 93

Form, 81

binary, 81

rondeau, 81

French violin clef, 93

Ground bass, 81

Hemiola, 239-242

Measure of dance, notation of, 92; *see also* Relationships

Measure of music, notation of, 92; *see also* Relationships

Meter, *see* Rhythm: Metric rhythm or time

Metronome, 171, 265-266

Music room, 286

Music staff, 92-93

Musicians, 238, 261-263, 282

Note values and beats, 150

Note values and rests, 150

Relationships of music and dance, 83; in chorégraphie, 92

in a false cadence, 83, 149; in a true cadence, 83, 149

beats: beats and single steps in units, 150-152; table, 155

upbeat and downbeat to a "movement," 156-158

musical measures: to number of specific step-units per measure (table), 163

to step units in general in specific dance types (table), 154.

to specific meters (table), 155

relationship methods: measures, units, beats, and actions

author, 159-160

Feuillet, Rameau, and Tomlinson, 158

see also Rhythm

Rests, music, 150; chorégraphie, 153; conflict with "movements" 153

Rhythm or cadence, 82-83 (Cadence, *see also* Cadence.)

cadence or temporal rhythm, 82-83, 149, 153, 258, 261-266

metric rhythm or time, 82-83, 149-151

common time, 154-155, 158-159

[Compound] duple-time, 154-155, 247-249, 250-255, 263-266

duple-time, 149-155, 158-160; with each step-unit in Chap. Nine, 263-266

triple–time, 149-155, 158-160; with each step-unit in Chap. Nine, 263-266

quadruple-time, 149, 154-155, 256-259, 263

Rhythmic values (metric) of step-units in dance types: Allemande, Bourrée, Chaconne, Passacaille, Rigaudon, Sarabande, *see* each step-unit in Chapter Nine

Canarie, 254-255

Entrée grave, 258-259

Forlane, 225, 247-249

Gavotte, 243-246

Gigue, 229, 247-249

Gigue lente, *see* Loure

Jig, *see* Gigue

Loure, 233, 256-257

Menuet, pas de menuet, 191, 194; contretemps of, 216-218, 294; with hemiola, 239-242

Passepied, pas de menuet, 191, 194; contretemps of, 216-218; with hemiola, 239-242

Sharps, 92

Speed, *see* Tempo

Strain, 81, 247; notation of, 92; remarkable places in, 82-83, 293; in *Gigue de Roland*, 248; in the menuet, 293-294

Tempo, 83, 262-266

Temps, 161 *fn*; *otherwise see* Rhythm: Metric rhythm or time

Time signatures, 154-155, 159-160

Upbeats, *see* Beats